A Christmas Wish for the Shipyard Girls

Nancy Revell

arrow books

5 7 9 10 8 6

Arrow Books
20 Vauxhall Bridge Road
London SW1V 2SA

Arrow Books is part of the Penguin Random House group
of companies whose addresses can be found at
global.penguinrandomhouse.com.

Penguin
Random House
UK

First published in Great Britain by Arrow Books in 2020

www.penguin.co.uk

A CIP catalogue record for this book is available from
the British Library.

ISBN 9781787464278

by ....

Printed a .... f S.p.A.

Wish for the Shipyard Girls

Nancy Revell is the author of the Shipyard Girls series, which is set in the north-east of England during World War Two.

She is a former journalist who worked for all the national newspapers, providing them with hard-hitting news stories and in-depth features. Nancy also wrote amazing and inspirational true life stories for just about every woman's magazine in the country.

When she first started writing the Shipyard Girls series, Nancy relocated back to her hometown of Sunderland, Tyne and Wear, along with her husband, Paul, and their English bull mastiff, Rosie. They now live just a short walk away from the beautiful award-winning beaches of Roker and Seaburn, within a mile of where the books are set.

The subject is particularly close to Nancy's heart as she comes from a long line of shipbuilders, who were well known in the area.

Why YOU love Nancy Revell

'How wonderful to read about everyday women, young, middle-aged, married or single all coming to work in a man's world. The pride and courage they all showed in taking over from the men who had gone to war. A debt of gratitude is very much owed'

'It's a gripping, heartbreaking and poignant storyline. I couldn't put it down and yet didn't want it to end'

'This series of books just get better and better; a fantastic group of girls who could be any one of us if we were alive in the war. Could only give 5 STARS but worth many more'

'What a brilliant read – the story is so good it keeps you wanting more ... I fell in love with the girls; their stories, laughter, tears and so much more'

'I absolutely loved this book. I come from Sunderland and knew every street, cafe, road and dock'

'This is a book that lets the reader know the way our ancestors behaved during the two world wars. With strength, honour and downright bravery ... I for one salute them all and give thanks to the author Nancy Revell, for letting us as readers know mostly as it was'

'A brilliant five-star read yet again for me'

'Yet another fabulous tale from this author. Her descriptions of the events, the locations, the people and their emotions are all brilliant'

'Another amazing book in the series. What a page turner this turned out to be. Lots of surprises right up to the end'

'What a wonderful writer Nancy Revell is, she never fails to make me laugh, cry and have me totally gripped!'

'I love this series of books and this one certainly did not disappoint. The lives of the shipyard girls give you an insight into the extent of the contribution women made to the war effort during World War Two'

What the reviewers are saying ...

'Well-drawn, believable characters combined with a storyline to keep
you turning the page'
Woman

'The author is one to watch'
Sun

'A riveting read is just what this is in more ways than one'
Northern Echo

'Researched within an inch of its life; the novel is enjoyably
entertaining. A perfect way to spend hours, wrapped up in the
characters' lives'
Frost

'We're huge fans of Nancy's Shipyard Girls saga, and this is as
emotional and gripping as the rest'
Take a Break

'Stirring and heartfelt storytelling'
Peterborough Evening Telegraph

'Emotional and gripping'
My Weekly

'[Nancy Revell] creates loveable characters and gives them storylines
that are guaranteed to tug on even the toughest of heartstrings ...
Each new book is better than the last. I can't wait for the next
instalment of the story'
Ginger Book Geek

'Nancy Revell's strong, vibrant, courageous, vulnerable, generous
and warm-hearted shipyard girls have become firm favourites with
saga readers everywhere'
Bookish Jottings

'With each book I just love this series more and more'
Shaz's Book Blog

To my literary agent Diana Beaumont,
for making my wish come true.

Thank you x

Acknowledgements

A heartfelt thank you to publishing director Emily Griffin and the whole of 'Team Nancy' at Arrow who have worked so hard to make the Shipyard Girls series a *Sunday Times* bestseller.

Thank you also to all the lovely staff at Fulwell Post Office, postmaster John Wilson, Liz Skelton, Richard Jewitt and Olivia Blyth, who have supported the Shipyard Girls from the off, to the wonderful booksellers at Waterstones in Sunderland, the Sunderland Antiquarian Society, especially Linda King, Norm Kirtlan and Philip Curtis, researcher Meg Hartford, Jackie Caffrey, of Nostalgic Memories of Sunderland in Writing, Beverley Ann Hopper, of The Book Lovers, journalist Katy Wheeler at the *Sunderland Echo*, Simon Grundy and all the team at Sun FM, and Lisa Shaw and her fantastic producer Jane Downs at BBC Newcastle.

A huge thank you to artist Rosanne Robertson, Suzanne Brown, Kathleen Tuddenham, Megan Blacklock, Hilary Clavering, of Soroptimist International Sunderland, Kevin Johnson, Principal Landscape Architect at Sunderland City Council, and Louise Bradford, owner and director of Creo Communications, for all your continued determination and enthusiasm to make the commemoration to the real shipyard women a reality. To Ian Mole for bringing the series to life with his Shipyard Girls Walking Tour.

And, of course, to my mum Audrey, dad Syd, hubby Paul, and my 'little' girl, Rosie.

Thank you, all.

'It seems to me we can never give up longing and wishing while we are thoroughly alive. There are certain things we feel to be beautiful and good, and we must hunger after them.'

George Eliot (Mary Ann Evans), *The Mill on the Floss*

Prologue

Sunday 16 May 1943

'Sorry to bother you, Claire.' Dr Parker stood on the door-step of Dr Eris's little cottage in the West Wing of the town's notorious lunatic asylum. It was almost two in the afternoon, although most people's body clocks had been thrown out of sync by a particularly heavy air raid during the early hours of the morning.

'You're not bothering me at all, John, not at all. Come in. Come in.' Dr Eris opened the door wide. 'It seems like it was just two minutes ago that we were saying goodnight to each other.' The pair had been out for a drink the previous evening, which had ended with John walking Claire back to her hospital accommodation and saying a chaste farewell.

'It does indeed.' Dr Parker followed Dr Eris down the hallway. 'Although the intervening time has been some-what eventful.'

'Very true. They're saying it's been the worst bombing we've had to date.' Dr Eris led the way into the kitchen. 'Sit yourself down. Let me make a quick cup of tea. It can be in place of the one you turned down last night.'

Dr Parker felt himself redden. 'I hope you weren't offended. I didn't want the hospital grapevine to go into meltdown. I think the very fact we simply went out for

1

a drink together will have sent the gossipmongers into a feeding frenzy.'

Dr Eris chuckled as she put the kettle on and placed two cups and saucers and a little jug of milk on the small kitchen table. 'That's the downside of working in a hospital that's in the middle of nowhere – the entertainment tends to be generated in-house. You can't sneeze here without just about every member of staff, and probably all the patients too, knowing about it.'

Dr Eris poured boiling water into the teapot and gave it a feisty stir. *She* had actually been the one to get the gossip going by casually dropping into conversations with her colleagues that she and the eligible Dr Parker were going out for a drink and it was most definitely not for the purpose of talking shop. She'd also made a point of informing Denise and Genevieve, the receptionists at the Ryhope and the asylum, where she was going, and with whom – *just in case there was an emergency, of course.*

'So, tell me, to what do I owe this pleasure?' Dr Eris put the pot on the table and sat down.

'I'm afraid I need to pick your brains about a patient who came in last night,' Dr Parker said.

Dr Eris tried to hide her disappointment; she'd hoped the visit was a social one.

'Tell me more,' she said.

'One old chap suffered a nasty bash on his head – fell over on his way to the shelter. He's quite elderly and a bit unsteady on his feet. He's been patched up, but he still seems very confused and I'm wondering whether his memory loss and lack of clarity are due to a possible concussion – or if it's dementia.

Dr Eris poured their tea and added milk.

'I can certainly take a look at him and give you my opinion,' she said, a smile playing on her lips.

Dr Parker narrowed his eyes. 'What is it you're *not* saying?'

Dr Eris crossed her legs and leant forward a little, her teacup in her hands. 'I was just thinking that much as I'm sure you value my thoughts on the matter, it might be more enlightening if you got the office to track down his next of kin and find out if he seemed confused *before* the bombs dropped.'

'Dear me –' Dr Parker combed his hair back with his fingers '– I think it might be me with dementia. In fact, now that I'm thinking about it, I'm sure one of the nurses took a call from his son saying he'd be visiting later. I'll speak to him then. You must think I'm thick.'

'I think you're anything but, John. But I do think you've been working round the clock lately. You need a decent night's shut-eye. The effects of sleep deprivation, especially over the long term, can mirror those of dementia, you know?'

Dr Parker let out a bark of laughter. 'Thanks for the reassurance.' He took a sip of his tea. 'So, tell me, how was last night for you?'

'At the pub or during the air raid?' Dr Eris asked, deadpan.

Dr Parker laughed out loud again. 'I meant the air raid, but I have to say that I personally had a thoroughly enjoyable evening at the Albion.'

Dr Eris smiled. 'Me too.'

As they drank their tea, they both exchanged stories about the aftermath of the bombing. Dr Eris's time had been spent checking and medicating those inmates who had become distressed by the disruption, while until the early hours Dr Parker had been in the Isolation Hospital in the West Wing, which had been converted into a makeshift ward for the injured. All the staff had done their bit, and most had gone to bed when they'd normally be getting up.

3

Having finished his tea, Dr Parker pushed back his chair and stood up.

'Well, I'd best be getting off.' He glanced at his watch. 'Rounds to do.' He looked at Dr Eris. 'And thank you for the belated tea.'

'You're more than welcome,' Dr Eris said, standing up and putting the teacups in the sink. 'And I'll pop in to see your confused elderly gentleman. You've got me curious.'

'Thank you,' Dr Parker said. As he made to go, he suddenly felt a little awkward. It would have been the ideal opportunity to ask Claire out on another date. So why was he hesitating?

'Let me see you out,' Claire said, turning and walking down the hallway.

As she opened the front door, she had to stop herself from slamming it shut again. Helen was walking down the pathway to the Isolation Hospital. Worse still, she'd spotted her and was raising her arm to wave hello.

Dr Eris turned around to face Dr Parker.

'You know,' she said, 'it wasn't just the tea you passed up on last night.'

Dr Parker furrowed his brow in a question as Dr Eris stepped forward, put her arms around his neck and gently pulled him towards her.

Chapter One

Helen and Bel sat on the wooden bench to the left of the entrance to the asylum. The perfectly manicured lawns of the hospital grounds lay stretched out in front of them. A little earlier, the two women had literally bumped into each other in the corridors after they had ended up there following that night's air raid.

Bel had gone to the asylum with her ma, Pearl Hardwick, to visit her ma's friend and boss, Bill Lawson, licensee of the Tatham Arms. The town's hospitals being full to bursting, he'd been taken there after being nearly buried alive when a bomb had landed on the pub he had gone to for a lock-in.

Helen, on the other hand, had gone to the asylum searching for Dr Parker, having felt compelled to tell him her true feelings. She knew she had missed her chance, though, by a matter of seconds, when she saw him kissing his colleague, Dr Eris.

While Pearl had gone off to visit Bill in one of the wards given over to those injured in the air raid, Bel had taken a distressed Helen outside to talk about why she was so upset – an unusual state for Helen, who was not known for any kind of display of emotion.

After chatting for a while, they had fallen into a comfortable silence, their faces turned heavenward, allowing themselves to bask momentarily in the solace of the afternoon sun. The beauty of their surroundings and balmy tranquillity of this most idyllic of spring days afforded a comfort of sorts.

Opening her eyes, Bel turned her head slightly. Helen still looked stunning, despite the smudged mascara and slight puffiness around her eyes. 'Just because you saw him coming out of Dr Eris's accommodation doesn't mean he spent the night there, you know.'

Helen gave Bel a sideways glance. Within the space of a few days, Bel had gone from being simply one of her staff to a family member. A blood relative. Her aunty. Her mother's sister. *Her grandfather's illegitimate daughter.*

'Oh, Bel, that's nice of you to say, but if you'd seen the way they kissed ...' Helen's voice trailed off.

'It mightn't have been what it looked like,' Bel argued. 'Dr Parker might have just popped in there for a cuppa. The kiss could have been innocent.' She glanced down at her watch. 'Anyway, it's a bit late for two people to be *getting up*.'

'This is *exactly* the time they would be getting up.' Helen felt the hurt in her heart as she spoke. 'Whenever there's an air raid, John – and all the rest of the doctors and nurses – work through the night, making sure any casualties are tended to, treated, operated on ...' She stared back up at the sky and closed her eyes. 'I feel such a fool.' She shook her head, annoyed at herself. 'To think that John would want me.'

Bel looked at Helen in surprise. 'I don't see why that would be such a foolish thing to think. I can't see any man *not* wanting you.'

'I don't mean *want* as in simply to desire.' Helen sighed heavily. 'I mean *want* as in want me as his sweetheart. His fiancée.' She turned her face away from the sun and looked at Bel. 'As the woman he wants to spend the rest of his life with.'

It was only then that Bel understood not just that Helen was in love with Dr Parker, but how strong and deep her love for him was. This wasn't simply about some other woman snaring the man she wanted for herself, but Helen losing the man she was desperate to be with – for ever. And Bel knew better than most that love like that rarely came along twice. She had been one of the lucky ones.

'Well, I don't think you should give up until you know the whole story. All the facts. You don't know for certain he stayed over at her place. It might have looked like a kiss between two lovers, but that could have just been your imagination.'

'Mmm,' Helen mused. 'I'm not convinced.' She gave Bel a sad smile. 'But I think you're right in that I do need to make sure I haven't got the wrong end of the stick.' She sighed again. Her thoughts fell back to the last traumatic twenty-four hours – the shocking bombshell about her grandfather, followed by the worst air raid thus far. The pervasiveness of all the death and destruction meted out to the town had driven her determination to tell John that she loved him. That she didn't just want to be his friend, but his lover – his lifelong soulmate.

'Oh, there you are!'

Helen and Bel turned round simultaneously.

An attractive, smartly dressed woman in a brown tailored skirt suit, her shiny, tawny-coloured hair twisted up into a French knot, was walking down the stone steps of the asylum. She had her eyes trained on Helen and a wide smile on her face.

'Oh no,' Helen whispered under her breath.

Bel stared at the tall, slim woman now striding purposefully towards them. She reminded her a little of Katharine Hepburn. Amazing cheekbones, flawless skin with just a dusting of freckles.

Helen stood up and Bel followed suit.

'*Helen*, I'm so glad I caught you before you left.' Dr Eris glanced at Bel and smiled before returning her attention to Helen. 'That *was* you I saw in the West Wing, wasn't it?'

Helen hesitated for a moment. She thought about denying it but realised there was no point.

'Yes, your eyes weren't playing tricks. That was indeed me,' Helen said, trying her hardest to sound upbeat and hoping to God it wasn't obvious that she'd been crying.

'Ah, that's good. Not going mad then.' Claire grimaced a little. 'I worry sometimes about making the crossover.' She cocked her head towards the Gothic, red-brick frontage of the asylum. 'They say it's never a good idea to live and work in a hospital of this kind. One might get confused. Doctor or patient? Patient or doctor?' She laughed lightly. 'I didn't see your friend with you, though?' She looked at Bel.

'No, no, you didn't.' Helen didn't elaborate, but instead turned to Bel. 'Bel, this is Claire – or rather, *Dr Eris*.' Helen pulled her mouth into a mock grimace. 'That is, providing she doesn't "make the crossover".'

Dr Eris laughed and stretched out her arm. 'Pleased to meet you, Bel.'

Bel returned the handshake and gave a polite smile.

'I wonder,' Dr Eris said, focusing her attention back on Helen, 'if I could perhaps have a quick word with you?'

'Of course, fire ahead,' Helen said, showing that the 'quick word' would have to be said in front of Bel.

Dr Eris hesitated before carrying on. 'I just wanted to say ...' her eyes flicked to Bel before she fixed her gaze on Helen '... that, obviously, as you will have guessed from seeing John and me just now –'

Helen felt her heart race.

'– in a rather amorous embrace –'

No room for doubt now.

'– that as we are clearly more than simply colleagues, and because I know John and you are close friends, that just because we are "together" as such, well, this doesn't

8

mean you two can't continue to be friends.' Another smile. 'I'm not one of these women who demand their beaux don't fraternise with any other person of the opposite sex.'

Helen continued to stand and listen. She had a feeling Dr Eris hadn't quite finished what she had come here to say.

She was right.

'But you'll have to forgive him if he isn't able to see you as much as he has been.' Dr Eris gave a self-satisfied smile. 'You know what it's like at the start? You just want to be with each other every minute of every day, don't you?'

Helen laughed a little too loudly. 'I do indeed, Claire. I do indeed.' She looked into Dr Eris's hazel eyes. 'I guess the real teller is when you still want to be with each other every minute of every day once the shine's worn off.'

There was a moment's awkward silence.

'Anyway,' Dr Eris said, 'when I saw you back there, you seemed in rather a rush. Was there something you wanted? I'm guessing it was John you were looking for?' She forced a smile.

Helen gave an equally false smile. 'Yes, it was, but it's not important. It can wait.'

Dr Eris glanced down at her watch. 'Oh my goodness, where does the time go?'

She looked directly at Bel.

'Well, lovely to meet you.' Dr Eris smiled.

Bel thought she had the most perfect teeth she'd ever seen.

'And,' Dr Eris turned to Helen, 'I'm glad we've managed to have this little chat ... Anyway, best get a shimmy on. *Minds to mend* and all that.'

And with that Dr Eris turned and quickly walked back to the main entrance, hurried up the stone steps and disappeared through the wooden swing doors.

Helen looked at Bel. 'Well, I guess that answers that question.'

Bel opened her mouth to offer words of reassurance, but none came out. If there had been any doubt that Helen might have misread the scene, it had been wiped clean away.

'I think that is called staking your claim,' Helen said.

Bel nodded but didn't say anything. She didn't know Helen well enough to offer her any words of comfort, not that she could think of any even if she had. Poor Helen. She looked bereft.

'Are you going to be all right?'

'Yes, of course,' Helen said as convincingly as possible. 'Best get back to work. *Denewood* took a battering last night.' The dry cargo vessel was the yard's most recent launch.

'Really?' Bel was shocked. She'd heard that J.L. Thompson & Sons had been hit during last night's air raid, but not any details. 'Badly?' She knew everyone would be gutted. The whole yard had worked flat out to get *Denewood* down the ways on time.

'She was taking in water this morning, but they've managed to keep her afloat.' Helen straightened her shoulders. 'Honestly, here's me moaning on about some bloke and the whole town's been bombed to smithereens.'

'That might be,' Bel said, 'but Dr Parker isn't just "some bloke", is he?'

'No,' Helen acquiesced, 'but he's going to have to be from now on.'

They were quiet for a moment.

Helen looked at Bel and was again hit by the family resemblance: her mother and Bel had the same blonde hair and blue eyes, the same nose and lips.

'Gosh, you must think I'm so incredibly shallow. I haven't even mentioned the ...' Helen stopped. 'The ... God,

I can't even think of a word to describe the abominable thing my grandfather did.' Helen's shoulders suddenly drooped as she thought of how her grandfather, the revered Mr Charles Havelock, had raped Pearl, then a fifteen-year-old scullery maid – and how that heinous act of violence had led to Pearl becoming pregnant with Bel.

'I'm so sorry, Bel. I still don't know what to say. I don't think it's really sunk in, to be honest.'

'Don't worry about that now,' Bel said. 'A conversation for another time?'

'Yes, definitely,' Helen agreed. 'Yesterday and today have been tumultuous, to say the least.' She looked over at her grandfather's black Jaguar. 'Are you sure I can't give you and your mother a lift home?'

'No, honestly, we'll be fine. Knowing my ma, she'll want some hair of the dog.' Bel rolled her eyes. 'She had a few too many last night. She mentioned nipping into the village afterwards, which means an hour in the Railway Inn before we get on the train.'

Helen felt a sudden jolt of sadness. The Railway Inn had been her and John's favourite meeting place.

'Oh.' Helen let out a bitter laugh. 'Tell her to have one for me.'

Bel's laughter was just as bitter.

'I will. Not that she'll need any encouragement.'

Chapter Two

'Oh, I didn't realise Miss Girling had any visitors.'

Pearl swivelled round on her chair to see a rather rotund nurse blocking the doorway, hands on hips, strands of curly ginger hair escaping her cap.

Pearl was confused, even more than she had already been.

Miss Girling? Who the bloody hell is she talking about? Pearl felt like kicking herself. Why oh why had she got so bladdered last night? Had the bootleg whisky she'd been necking back made her doolally? She shouldn't be here! She should be with Bill, having a laugh about him ending up in the local loony bin and telling him it served him right for going off for a lock-in.

'Miss *who*?' Pearl asked, her voice croaky. She felt the need for a cigarette.

This was all Isabelle's fault. She'd never have ended up here – never have got lost – if Isabelle had come with her.

The nurse narrowed her eyes. 'Well, you're obviously neither friend nor family if you don't know the name of the woman yer sat here yammering away to.' She bustled over to Henrietta, who was sitting, perched like a little bird, on the stool next to the mahogany dressing table, her back to the three-way mirror, her hands clasped together on her lap.

'You all right there, pet?' The nurse towered over her diminutive charge.

'This is my Little Match Girl. *Den Lille Pige med Svovlstikkerne!*' Henrietta explained.

12

Pearl felt herself stiffen. 'Little Match Girl' had been her nickname. Given to her by Henrietta. Mrs Henrietta Havelock. So why was this daft mare calling her *Miss Girling*?

'Course she's your Little Match Girl, pet.'

Pearl was speechless; she couldn't believe anyone had the audacity to call the mistress 'pet'. She watched in disbelief as the nurse gave Henrietta a patronising smile before swinging her girth round to face the scrawny, middle-aged, mutton-dressed-as-lamb intruder.

Glowering down at Pearl, the nurse jerked her head towards the door.

'Hop it!'

Pearl stood up, but as she did so Henrietta leant forward and grabbed hold of her arm.

'You'll come back, won't you?' she pleaded, her face upturned, her eyes desperate.

'Come on then, chop-chop!' The nurse was making no attempt to hide her ire at finding a stranger in her patient's room. Taking hold of Pearl's arm, she gripped it tightly and forced her towards the open doorway.

'You'll come back, won't you, Little Match Girl?' Henrietta's high-pitched, sing-song voice followed Pearl as she left the room.

Once they were out in the corridor, the nurse looked Pearl up and down. 'Yer've not pilfered owt, have yer?'

Pearl didn't give her a mouthful as she would normally have done; she was barely aware of the busybody nurse uttering accusations. Instead, her attention was fixed solely on Henrietta, whose pupils were so large, her eyes looked almost black.

'Cat got your tongue?' The nurse took Pearl's handbag and looked inside. It was empty save for a packet of cigarettes, a lighter and a small leather purse.

Pearl continued to stare at Henrietta, spellbound.

'Blimey, yer smell like a brewery.' The nurse pushed the bag back at Pearl and pointed down the corridor.

'Walk to the end and turn right. Then follow the signs to reception. And don't let me see hide nor hair of you again.'

Pearl took one last look at Henrietta, her former employer, still sitting with her back to the dressing table, still staring at her 'Little Match Girl'. Her eyes still imploring her to return.

As Pearl staggered down the corridor, her mind seemed to have got stuck back in time. She was a young girl again, her only clothes the rags on her back, her few possessions stuffed into a cloth bag, knocking on the doors of the big houses. Desperate for a job. Desperate for a roof over her head and food in her belly. There had been many times since then she'd wished she *had* been turned away – that she had gone to the park across the road, put her head down and died of cold and hunger. Just like the real Little Match Girl. But she hadn't. A Russian-doll woman with garish make-up, outlandish hair and wearing clothes that looked from another era, had waved her in, given her a job and, a few months later, brought her to the attention of the master of the house – her husband, Mr Charles Havelock.

As Dr Eris walked down the corridor, she had to allow herself a self-satisfied smile. After a rather disappointing end to the evening last night, with John politely refusing her offer to come in for a cup of tea and giving her a rather brotherly kiss on the cheek, the tables had been well and truly turned. She felt herself blush as she recalled their earlier kiss. It had been rather wonderful – and long enough for Helen to have seen it. Long enough for her to have turned back and returned to where she'd come from. For good, hopefully.

14

After starting at the asylum in the New Year, Dr Eris had spent the past few months getting to know Dr Parker, chatting to him, making him laugh – making him feel at ease with her. She knew John liked her and found her attractive, but she suspected that Helen might be a potential spanner in the works – that his feelings for his 'friend' were not purely platonic.

When she'd finally met Helen in the canteen the other day, her heart had sunk. The woman was a stunner. Glossy black hair, hourglass figure – and the most amazing emerald eyes. A fool would know that John, or any other red-blooded male for that matter, would want to be much more than just friends. But what had perturbed her most was that it was obvious Helen was mad about him. Thank goodness John clearly had no idea. She just had to make sure that didn't change. After the meeting in the canteen, she knew the clock was ticking. She had competition. Serious competition. She had to act fast before John wised up and realised what was on offer or worse still, before Helen decided to make the first move. Which was why, when she had seen John yesterday afternoon and he'd told her his scheduled surgery had been put back, she'd taken a gamble and suggested they go for a drink in the Albion.

'Watch where yer gannin!'

Turning the corner towards the East Wing, Dr Eris suddenly came face to face with a rather bedraggled-looking woman with badly dyed blonde hair who was wearing clothes that were more suited to someone half her age.

'So sorry, I didn't see you there,' Dr Eris said, moving to the side.

'How do I gerra out of here?' the woman asked, scrabbling around in her handbag.

'Just keep going straight down this corridor, turn left and you'll end up at reception.'

The woman huffed and walked off.

Dr Eris watched as she stopped and lit up a cigarette before disappearing round the corner in a cloud of grey smoke. She wondered whether she should go after the strange woman and check she wasn't a patient but decided against it. The chances were that she was a visitor. They were always getting lost, which was no surprise; the place really was like a maze. If she'd got it wrong and the woman was an inmate, then Genevieve would know; she'd worked here long enough, and although she was getting on, her mind was still as sharp as a pin. She'd call the orderlies and they'd bring the woman back.

As she continued on her way, her mind snapped back to John. And, moreover, their kiss. When she'd opened her front door and seen Helen – or rather, seen the determined look on her face, combined with the fact that she was done up to the nines – well, it didn't take a degree in psychology to know she had come for John.

Helen's unexpected appearance at the asylum made sense after last night's bombing. She'd seen similar impulsive behaviour after air raids. All those thoughts of life and death followed by a sudden compulsion to live for the day.

Some might say her own behaviour had been motivated by such side effects of war, but, of course, it hadn't. Her actions this afternoon had been driven by one thing, and one thing alone: her fear that John might be snatched from right under her nose.

'Ah, Nurse Pattinson,' Dr Eris said, walking into the room of one of her more challenging patients. 'How's Miss Girling doing today?'

'She's been letting strangers into her room,' the nurse said as she smoothed down the divan on the bed. She loved the feel of embroidered silk. 'Some tramp of a townie,' she said, taking the pillows and fluffing them up. 'Reckon she'd either got lost or was looking at what she could pilfer.'

'I think I just bumped into her,' Dr Eris said, pulling up the chair Pearl had just vacated. She took hold of Henrietta's hand and felt her pulse.

'Dear me, Miss Girling. Feels like you've had a quick sprint around the grounds.'

Henrietta looked at the young doctor sitting opposite her, then down at her hands, which were soft and cold. They were milky white. The colour of an opal ...

'Pearl!' Her eyes widened in glee. She had been trying and trying to bring the name to the forefront of her mind, but it felt as though it had got stuck in treacle.

'Who's Pearl?' Dr Eris asked as she let go of Henrietta's hand and tipped her head slightly back. She pulled out a small, pen-shaped torch from the top pocket of her jacket and shone it briefly into both eyes.

'The Little Match Girl.' Henrietta blinked but kept her face still.

Dr Eris got up and unhooked the chart at the bottom of Henrietta's bed. She looked across at Nurse Pattinson, who arched an eyebrow.

'Pearl from *The Scarlet Letter*,' Henrietta explained.

'By Nathaniel Hawthorne?' Dr Eris looked up.

Henrietta nodded.

'Miss Girling, you are quite an anomaly, aren't you? And certainly the most well-read patient I've ever had.'

Henrietta smiled at the compliment.

'Nurse Pattinson, I'm making some alterations to Miss Girling's medication.' She started writing on Henrietta's chart.

'I want to try and bring her dosage down, which means I need you to keep an extra-close eye on her. If you see any changes, good or bad, I'd like you to report them to me, please.'

Dr Eris smiled her thanks; she knew who really ran the asylum, and it wasn't the doctors. Nurse Pattinson had been there nearly her entire working life and she ruled with an iron rod. Dr Eris had met nurses like her before and made the mistake of getting on their bad side.

Walking back to her office further down the corridor, Dr Eris opened the door and went straight over to the battered wooden filing cabinet that looked as old as the building itself. She pulled out the top drawer and rifled through the alphabet.

'Here we are,' she mumbled to herself, heaving out the two-inch-thick file. 'Miss Henrietta Girling.' She plonked the case file on her desk and sat down in her chair.

Rereading the medical notes that spanned more than two decades, Dr Eris started to jot down her observations, but all the while her mind kept skipping back to John. They were going out on a date this evening. A proper date! After their kiss, he'd asked if he could take her out for dinner.

Dr Eris made a mental note to be spontaneous more often.

It had certainly paid dividends for her today.

Chapter Three

'Isabelle!'

Bel and Helen turned round to see Pearl stomping down the steps of the main entrance.

Helen had been about to walk over to the car but stopped.

'Talk of the devil,' Bel said.

'She looks as white as a sheet. Or is she always like that?' Helen spoke out of the side of her mouth. She'd met Pearl a few times before but always in the pub, and invariably through a haze of cigarette smoke.

'She's never exactly the picture of health,' Bel said distractedly, watching her ma make her way over to them. 'God, I hope it's not Bill.'

'The landlord from the Tatham?' Helen asked, thinking of the rather portly but jovial proprietor of Bel's local.

Bel nodded. 'He was brought here last night. He was in the Welcome Tavern on Barrack Street when it got hit.'

'I'm so sorry. I was so wrapped up in my own drama, I didn't even ask why you were here,' Helen said. 'Why was Bill at the Welcome?'

'Lock-in,' Bel explained. 'Getting plastered because Ma got slaughtered and went off with Ronald, our neighbour.'

'Bloody Nora, I thought I'd never get out of there!' Pearl said as she reached them.

'You all right, Ma?' Bel asked, scrutinising her mother. She was puffing away on a fag as though her life depended on it.

'Is Bill all right?' Bel crossed her fingers. They'd been led to believe that those with relatively minor injuries had been brought here – the more serious having been taken to the town's Royal.

Pearl looked at Bel as though she was talking gobbledygook.

'Bill?'

'Yes, Ma. *Bill*. You know, the man we've been looking for all day? Your friend? The one you've been worried sick about?' They had been searching for Bill all over town; had gone to the bomb site where they'd feared he might well have died, then to the Monkwearmouth Hospital over on the north side of the river, before being told he'd been taken to the asylum.

'Aye … course … Bill,' Pearl muttered, shaking her head and taking another drag. 'I got bloody lost. I've not seen him.'

Bel was relieved that her mother's slightly bizarre behaviour was not down to Bill's demise, but at the same time she was also a little worried as to why she seemed so dazed and confused.

'Ma, are you all right? You look like you've seen a ghost.'

'I *have*!' Pearl spluttered.

Bel and Helen exchanged worried looks. Pearl's hands were shaking – in fact, her whole body was trembling.

'Perhaps I should get you both home?' Helen asked, concerned.

'I think that might be a good idea …' Bel nodded. 'Ma, why don't we go back with Helen?'

Pearl stared at the glossy black Jaguar she knew belonged to Charles Havelock – Helen's grandfather. 'Wild horses won't get me in that thing!'

Bel looked at Helen. 'You get yourself off. We'll be all right. Probably do us good to have a walk.'

'If you're sure?' Helen looked at Bel and then at Pearl.

Bel nodded.

Helen headed over to the car and got in. Taking a deep breath, she turned the ignition. She was still very much a novice behind the wheel, but she managed to pull away with just the slightest of judders.

As she drove towards the main gates, she looked in her rear-view mirror at Bel and Pearl.

And she thought she had drawn the short straw when it came to mothers.

'So come on, Ma, tell me what's happened. You went off to find Bill in a relatively normal state, and you've come back here a gibbering wreck. If you don't start making sense, I'll be forced to take you back inside and get them to check you out.'

'Over my dead body!' She watched for a moment as the Jaguar made its way down the driveway, before walking over to the bench by the entrance. Seeing the brass plaque dedicated to *Mr Charles Havelock, philanthropist and entrepreneur*, Pearl's lip curled in disgust.

'Is there no escaping that man?' she spat out before turning her back on it and plonking herself down. She looked up at her daughter. 'Will yer gan 'n make sure Bill's all reet? Or at least leave a message with the auld cow on the front desk – ask her to tell Bill I came to see him 'n that I hope he's out of here soon.'

Bel was observing her mother. Was it fear she could see on her face? She wasn't sure. But whatever it was, it was obvious that nothing was going to make her go back inside.

'All right, Ma. I'll do as you ask, but I want you to reassure me that when I come back you'll still be sat there – and that you'll tell me what on earth is going on?'

'Aye, I will … promise,' Pearl said, lighting up another cigarette from the one she was smoking. Her hands were still shaking.

Forty minutes later, Pearl's hands had stopped shaking, mainly due to the double whisky she was drinking, coupled with having put a good distance between herself and the asylum.

'So, Bill's definitely all reet?' Pearl asked for the umpteenth time.

'Yes, Ma, he's fine. Like I said, he's got a big gash on his head and quite a few cuts and bruises, but other than that, he's fine. Lucky to be alive. And he knows it. He was sat up in his bed looking full of the joys.'

'So why are they keeping him in?' Pearl took a sip of her whisky. 'If he's all reet, you'd think they'd want shot of him.'

'He said it was to "err on the side of caution", with it being a head injury. It did look like he'd taken quite a whack.'

'Ha! That'll teach him. Going to a lock-in at the Welcome, of all places.'

'That's exactly what he said you would say.' Bel gave her ma a probing look. 'I suppose you two must have got to know each other quite well – working day in, day out behind that bar. How long have you been there now? Must be coming up to a couple of years?'

'Not far off,' Pearl said.

'Well, Bill obviously trusts you.' Bel started rummaging round in her pocket. 'Because he's given me the keys to the Tatham and asked you to open up and be "acting landlord" for the evening. He said Geraldine will be able to help out. That she's always up for a shift.'

'Always up for a bit of dosh 'n some free drinks, more like,' Pearl huffed.

Bel laughed. 'Talk about the pot calling the kettle black.'

Pearl took the keys and put them in her handbag.

'Bill also seemed even more chipper when he'd heard you'd gone looking for him, although he was a little puzzled as to why you wouldn't come in and see him, especially after coming all this way.'

'Aye, well, he'll have to wonder, won't he.' Pearl took another drink of her whisky.

'So,' Bel asked, 'what happened after you left me and Helen?'

'I got bloody lost, that's what,' Pearl said, taking another gulp. 'It was like being in one of them nightmares where yer just turning around corners 'n hitting brick walls.'

'So, where did you end up?' Bel asked.

'I heard this voice. Followed it to a room.'

'And?'

'It was like a proper room, in a proper house. A posh house 'n all.'

'In what way?'

Pearl took another drag. 'The way it was decorated. The furniture.'

Bel was watching her ma intently.

'There was this red Chinese cabinet. I recognised it. And there was a woman with her back to me, sitting at a dressing table. I thought she was talking to someone else in the room, but there was no one there. She was just sat there, talking to her own reflection.'

Bel could feel the hairs on the back of her neck start to tingle.

'Then she turned around. Realised someone else was in the room.'

Pearl stubbed out her cigarette.

'And that's when I saw who it was. When I realised why everything felt so familiar.'

'Who was it?' Bel asked.

Pearl looked at her daughter.

'It was the mistress ... *Mistress Henrietta*.'

'Really?' Bel said. 'I just presumed she was dead when you told me about her that day.' *That unforgettable day when they had stood outside the Havelock house, when her ma had told her it was there she had worked as a maid, there she had been raped, and there where Bel had been conceived.*

'Aye, I did 'n all,' Pearl said, sparking up another cigarette. 'Just presumed she'd met her Maker.

'Are you sure it was Henrietta?' Bel asked.

'Oh, aye.' Pearl let out a burst of dark laughter followed by a hacking cough. 'You dinnit get many like her.' She took a drink of whisky. 'The thing is ...' she gave an involuntary shiver '... she looked the same – same red hair all piled up high.' Pearl lifted her arms and waggled her hands about. As she did so, ash fell from her cigarette, just missing her own hair. 'All raggedly-taggedly. Same big skirt. Yer knar, the ones with tiny waists 'n the hoops inside them. Face thick with make-up, red cheeks 'n lips, blue all round her eyes.' She sucked on her cigarette and more ash dropped to the floor. 'It was like I'd been dragged back in time.'

Bel realised why her ma looked like she'd seen a ghost. She *had* seen a ghost. A ghost from her past. And one, she guessed, her ma had no desire to be reacquainted with.

'You must have got a real shock?' Bel asked.

'I did, Isabelle, I did that,' she said, her face deathly serious. 'What I dinnit understand, though –' Pearl finished off her drink '– was that the nurse that come in 'n chased us out called her by a different name.'

'Really?'

'She called her "Miss" for starters.' Pearl looked down at her empty glass. 'And what was it she called her? ... Something "Girl" ... That's it – she called her *Miss Girling*.'

'Well, that *is* strange,' Bel agreed. 'Very strange. Very mysterious.'

'Course, if yer mate Helen hadn't turned up, whining on about some bloke, you'd have been with me, I wouldn't have got lost 'n I wouldn't have seen Henrietta. All I'd be suffering from now would be a hangover from hell – not traumatised after having a sit-down with the walking dead.'

At the mention of Helen, it suddenly occurred to Bel that Henrietta was not just her ma's former employee – the wife of the man who had raped her – she was also Miriam's mother and, therefore, Helen's grandmother. Did *they* know she was here?

Bel watched as Pearl picked up her empty glass and knew there'd be no arguing. They were staying for another whether she liked it or not.

'So, Ma, tell me a bit more about Henrietta – when you worked for her.' Bel looked across at her mother, who was now almost back to her normal self.

Pearl lit another cigarette. 'She must have been in her mid-thirties – up 'n down like a bloody yo-yo, she was. I'd never met anyone like her. Still haven't. She lived off steak 'n caviar 'n a load of pills 'n potions, all necked down with her "special Russian water" – that's vodka to you 'n me. She called Eddy the butler "Heathcliff", and Agatha, the housekeeper, "Maid Marion".'

'Characters from books?' Bel asked, intrigued.

'Aye, that's right. I never knew which books, but apparently there was a "Pearl" in some book she'd read, so I was lucky 'n got to keep my own name.'

Pearl took a drag.

'Most of the time she either had her nose in a book or else she'd be flying round the house, full of energy 'n ideas

25

about this 'n that. She'd go on huge spending sprees in town 'n then there'd be delivery after delivery arriving at the house.'

'And what was she like with Mr Havelock?' Bel kept her voice low; she didn't want anyone in the pub overhearing their conversation.

'Yer never really saw the two o' them together. I only worked there for about seven months 'n most of the time he was abroad. He only came back during the holidays.'

Pearl took a sip of her drink.

'The only time I can recall seeing the pair of them together was when he came back for Christmas 'n Henrietta lined us all up 'n introduced us to him as her "household cavalry". I can still see him now –' Pearl shuddered involuntarily '– standing in his jodhpurs 'n his leather riding boots. I'd been told he liked to give his filly a good thrashing round Backhouse Park when he came back after a spell away.' Pearl took another drag on her cigarette. 'When we'd been dismissed, I went to see Jonny, the young stable lad. He was giving the horse a washdown. I asked why the water was red. Stupid I was then. Young and stupid.'

'He'd whipped the horse so badly it was bleeding?' Bel asked, shocked.

'Aye,' Pearl said, taking a drink of whisky. 'Given it a thrashing in the true sense of the word.'

Bel heard the bitterness in her ma's tone.

'Henrietta must have been quite young when she had Miriam and – what was the other daughter called?'

'Margaret,' Pearl said, looking at the pub's stained-glass window as she recalled the past. 'Miriam and Margaret. Stuck-up little madams they were.'

'They must have been about the same age as you when you worked there?' Bel said.

'Aye, they were. I was a bit younger – looked a bit like them both 'n all. Fair hair. Blue eyes. I was pretty back then, believe it or not. I thought that might have been why Henrietta took me in.'

'Because you reminded her of her daughters, and she felt sorry for you?'

'Aye, that's what I thought,' Pearl said, although as time had gone by, she wasn't quite so sure.

'So, you didn't see much of them?' Bel asked.

'They'd been sent to a "finishing school", whatever that's meant to be,' Pearl said, trying to shake the pull of the past.

'I think that's where young girls go to learn how to be ladies,' Bel said.

Pearl laughed and then started coughing.

'Well, from what I've heard about that Miriam, they didn't do a very good job, did they?'

This time they both laughed and Pearl stubbed out her cigarette.

Bel knew her time as inquisitor was up.

'I think we'll keep this to ourselves for now, eh?' Pearl said, standing.

'You mean you don't want me to tell Helen, with her being a Havelock?' Bel said.

'Aye, that's exactly what I mean.'

Chapter Four

Driving back from Ryhope, Helen allowed herself to wallow in self-pity for a short while. Pulling over in a lay-by near Hendon beach, she looked out to sea, viewing it through a blur of tears, mourning the loss of what could have been. Getting back into the car, she checked herself in the mirror, rubbed the smudges of mascara from under her eyes and applied a fresh layer of her trademark Victory Red lipstick. She had to face the fact that 'happy ever after' just wasn't for her. She should have learnt that she was destined to be on her own after Tommy had chosen Polly, after the debacle of Theodore, after losing her baby ... And now, she had lost John. Not that he had ever been hers to lose.

Pulling back onto the main road, Helen was over the north side of the Wear within five minutes. After parking her car by the Admiral pub, she walked across to the huge metal gates that heralded the entrance to Thompson's.

'Afternoon, Miss Crawford!' The young lad who was manning the timekeeper's cabin shouted down from the counter, tipping his oversized flat cap as he'd seen his elders do.

Carrying on into the yard, Helen was hit by the glare of sunshine reflecting off the hull of a half-built ship that was slowly being brought to life at the far end of the yard. She shielded her eyes and squinted at this urban jungle, this mass of concrete and steel. Looking over at the cathedral-sized doors of the platers' shed, which were open, she saw a crane trundling out, a huge metal sheet dangling from its pinched beak.

'*Helen!*'

She was unable to see the person who had called her name, but she recognised the voice. Moving out of the blinding sunlight, she saw Rosie waving over at her. Her welder's helmet had been pushed right back so that she looked like some modern-day Janus. She was giving Mickey, the little teaboy, some coppers in exchange for a steaming hot can of tea. Behind her was Martha, the group's 'gentle giant'. She was raising her hand and offering a gap-toothed smile in greeting.

As little Mickey trundled off with his jangling pole, Helen saw that Dorothy and Angie were sitting next to Martha on a stack of wooden pallets. They, too, were waving, signalling for her to come over. To their left, she saw Gloria chatting to Jimmy, the head riveter.

'What are your lot doing here?' Helen walked over to Rosie, who was taking a sip of her tea.

'Probably the same as you,' Rosie laughed. 'Getting *Denewood* back on her feet.'

Helen smiled. 'Well, it's certainly going to put us back on schedule if you can. I came in this morning with Harold, but we didn't expect to get much done, other than make sure she'd been plugged up properly so that we didn't find her bedded down on the bottom of the Wear tomorrow.'

'Jimmy and I've had a good look. There's quite a bit shrapnel damage. And it seems her hull's been used for target practice, judging by the number of bullet holes we've chalked around, but they're no bigger than eight inches, so it shouldn't be too hard to get her patched up. With any luck she could be good to go by the end of next week.'

'That'll be brilliant if you can.' Helen looked over at Rosie's squad.

'Hi, Helen!' Dorothy and Angie chorused.

Martha offered her a ginger biscuit, which Helen refused with a smile and a shake of her head.

'You all right?' Gloria asked. She had become like a replacement mother to Helen this past year and, like most mothers, could sense when there was something amiss.

'Yes, yes,' Helen said. She gave a smile that she hoped looked convincing.

She looked at the women in their oil-stained overalls.

'Thank you for coming in today.'

'Well, we're not gonna let Jerry get the better of us, are we?' Angie declared, pushing strands of strawberry-blonde hair back into the confines of her headscarf.

'And when we heard *Denewood* had been damaged, we were livid, weren't we, Ange?' Dorothy looked at her friend, who nodded, her face solemn.

'I don't think Martha's mam was too chuffed, though, was she?' Angie looked back at her workmate.

Seeing the question on Helen's face, Martha explained, 'She reckoned I broke a promise.'

'The promise being?' Helen asked. She knew Martha's ARP work and her job at the yard caused her parents untold worry.

'Mam said I could go and help with looking for survivors, if I was careful and didn't do anything daft.'

'Like walk into a collapsing building,' Angie hooted.

Everyone looked at Helen. She and Martha had done just that when they'd rescued Gloria and her little girl, Hope, during the Tatham Street bombing last October.

'Mam said I could go, but that I had to take the next day off work.'

'Which Martha readily agreed to as she wasn't meant to be working anyway,' Dorothy said, tying her dark brown hair up into a ponytail.

'So, when we tipped up on the doorstep –' Angie pulled a face '– Mrs Perkins was not exactly chuffed.'

'I told Mam I couldn't stay at home, knowing my squad were going in. Especially when they said what had happened to *Denewood*,' Martha said.

'Well, you must tell your mam and dad how much it's appreciated,' Helen said.

'We'll tell them,' Angie chirped up. 'Mrs Perkins invited me 'n Dor back for a roast after work. Said we'd need it to keep our strength up.'

'I'm guessing Polly's all right?' Helen looked at Gloria, knowing she would have seen her when she went to drop Hope off at the Elliots'.

'Oh, yes, she's fine. She said she couldn't just sit at home while us lot were at work, so she's gone to get us some sandwiches from Vera's.'

'Along with Charlie,' Rosie said, rolling her eyes. 'God forbid she misses out on anything.'

In truth, Rosie was glad Charlotte was with Polly after yesterday's drama at the parade.

Still, at least her little sister now 'knew' everything.

Well, *just about* everything.

There were still a couple of things she had yet to tell her.

Polly and Charlotte were walking along High Street East, which, despite a huge clear-up operation, was still looking very much like a war zone. There was rubble strewn about the road, causing the army trucks, fire engines and ambulances to drive slowly. Shattered glass glinted in the sunlight, and there was a trickling rivulet where a water main had burst.

Charlotte had lain awake until the early hours, going over and over everything she had learnt the day before. Every shocking detail – from how her older sister Rosie had ended up selling her body in order to buy Charlotte a future, to the truth about Rosie's so-called welding accident, which had left her with a smattering of small scars across her face.

Rosie had warned her fellow welder Polly, who was temporarily working as a timekeeper until after she'd had the baby, that her sister might well quiz her about what she had found out. And she'd been right. It hadn't taken fourteen-year-old Charlotte long before she had managed to steer the conversation round to when the squad of women welders had turned up on the night her uncle had nearly killed Rosie.

'Were you scared?' Charlotte asked

'Mmm, I think I was more shocked then scared,' Polly said, wishing she could walk faster, but her bump had now ballooned to a size that meant she had to accept her mobility was compromised.

'Rosie said you all just appeared through the darkness like her knights in shining armour,' Charlotte said.

'Well, that's a nice thing to say.' Polly thought back to the evening when they had found Raymond forcing Rosie's head over a live weld. 'Although, to be honest, I don't think we really did a lot. I think your uncle thought we were quite laughable. It was only when Martha suddenly stomped over to him and gave him a shove that we got Rosie away and he ended up tripping over a welding rod and falling into the Wear.'

'Never to resurface!' Charlotte declared triumphantly.

Polly looked at Charlotte. 'But you know, Charlie, none of us wanted him to end up dead, tangled up at the bottom of the river.' She was, of course, lying through her teeth.

'I know. That's what Rosie said,' Charlotte said, forcing herself to slow down. They were nearly at the café and she had a load more questions she wanted to ask. 'I was thinking last night ...' she continued, looking at Polly's long, wavy chestnut hair. Her own hair was a similar colour, though it would take a while for her to grow it as long.

'Mmm?' Polly braced herself.

'It wasn't just Rosie you all saved that night, but me too. If you hadn't saved my sister, he'd have come for me as well.'

Polly felt a shiver go down her spine.

'I don't believe in what ifs. Now, have you still got the list?' Polly asked, relieved to be almost at Vera's. Heaven only knew how Rosie coped with the constant barrage of questions. She'd looked shattered earlier and the relief on her face when Polly had agreed to take Charlie had spoken volumes.

Charlotte dug into her coat pocket.

'Ta-dah!' she declared, waving the list in the air.

'Polly! Charlie!' Hannah hurried over to them as soon as she heard the little bell over the café door tinkle and saw who it was.

'*Pojd' sem!* Come in! Come in!' Hannah, a Jewish refugee from Prague, often broke into her native Czech when she was happy, excited, shocked or upset. Today she was overjoyed to see that those she knew and loved had survived the latest air raid unscathed.

Polly and Charlotte manoeuvred themselves around the tables, most of which were empty, though judging by the crumb-strewn plates and pots of cold tea, the café had been busy.

'Well, this is a surprise!' Hannah wrapped her skinny arms around Charlotte and hugged her, before turning to Polly, taking her hands and squeezing them.

'Your baby is forcing me to keep you at arm's length,' she laughed. 'How are you feeling?'

'Fit as a fiddle,' Polly said, waving over to Vera and Hannah's aunty Rina, who were both busy behind the counter. 'Well, perhaps not quite as fit as I was ...' she looked down at the maternity dress she'd had to buy as none of her old clothes fitted her '... but I'm fine. I *feel* fine.' Polly forced a reassuring smile on her face. She knew how lucky she was to have so many people around her who loved and cared for her, but since she'd nearly miscarried back in March, she felt as though she spent most of her time convincing people that she and her baby were in tip-top health. Even her letters to Tommy these days were mostly about how well she was feeling and reassuring him how easy she was taking it, cooped up in the timekeeper's cabin – and that she was *definitely not* welding.

'You got Olly working here now?' Polly joked as she spotted Hannah's boyfriend coming out of the kitchen.

'Only on his days off,' Hannah chuckled, looking over at Olly, who had taken off his black-rimmed spectacles and was giving them a clean.

'Ah, you've come to give us a helping hand!' Vera exclaimed, rolling up her sleeves.

Charlotte shot Polly a worried look.

'Just fling yer coat over there, pet.' Vera nodded over to the side of the café where there was already a small pile of coats. Seeing the last customers leave, she shuffled over to drop the latch and turn the sign to 'Closed'.

'Just this lot to clear and wash up,' she said, tipping her head towards the tables with the dirty dishes.

'Well ... I'm afraid ...' Charlotte stuttered.

Vera let out a throaty laugh as she bustled back to the main counter.

'She's having you on,' Rina said, walking over to Charlotte and giving her a kiss on both cheeks. She lowered her voice. 'My boss has a strange sense of humour.'

'Ha! "My boss" my foot!' Vera said. She might be old but there was nothing wrong with her hearing. 'I may well be the one paying the wages, but there's only one boss here – and she's stood right there. All five foot ten of her.'

Charlotte chuckled. Vera and Rina were like some odd comedy duo – one short and fat, the other tall and slim. One with a strong north-east accent, the other pure BBC, despite her Czechoslovakian roots.

Vera turned her attention to Polly. She noticed she was twisting her wedding and engagement bands around on her finger – beautiful rings that had once belonged to Arthur's wife, Flo. *God rest their souls.* Arthur, a former dock diver and Tommy's grandfather, had died on Boxing Day, just hours after seeing his grandson married. Vera knew the old man and Polly had become close and that she missed him terribly.

'I'm not gonna ask yer how yer are, pet,' Vera said, ''cos I'm guessing yer sick to death of folk asking. And I'm not gonna ask how Tommy is because I know he's fine too. I can feel it in my waters. Next time yer write to him, tell him there's a bacon butty going spare, so he best sort Jerry out 'n get back here pronto!'

Vera laughed, as did Polly. They both knew that the one thing Tommy missed more than anything – apart from Polly, of course – was Vera's bacon baps. Well, it was a toss-up between that and his mother-in-law's stew and dumplings.

'We've come for some sandwiches for the workers,' Polly said. 'Charlotte and I said we'd go and get them provisions.'

'They're working today?' Aunty Rina asked as she started to clear the tables.

'*Denewood* got damaged,' Polly explained.

'They've gone to patch her up?' Olly asked. He and Hannah had both worked on the ship's plans.

Polly nodded.

'Well, good for them,' Rina said, bustling back behind the counter and starting to slice up a loaf of bread. 'If they don't do it, no one else will – or can. And then we really will be in dire straits.' She walked back into the kitchen, shouting over her shoulder, 'I'm afraid there's not a lot of choice. It'll have to be whatever we've got left.'

Charlotte pushed the list back into her pocket.

'We opened up early,' Olly explained. 'Rina said those doing the clear-up after the bombing would need a "decent cup of tea and some sustenance".'

'Feels like we've had half the east end in here,' Vera said, padding into the kitchen to help Rina.

The two women might be like chalk and cheese, Polly thought, but they worked together like a well-oiled machine.

Five minutes later, Vera was putting the sandwiches into a paper bag and giving them to Charlotte to carry.

'There yer are. They're on the house. And don't even try to argue,' Vera said, looking over her shoulder, 'or else you'll have the wrath of Rina to contend with.'

Chapter Five

When Helen opened the main door to the admin office, she could hear her phone ringing.

Who would be calling the office on a Sunday?

She felt a rush of joy that it might be John, followed by a hefty punch to the gut as her mind caught up with the present state of play.

As she strode across her office to reach the phone, a terrible feeling of depression hit home with the realisation that she had lost the only man she had ever truly loved.

She hesitated for a second. What would she do if it *was* John? How should she react? Should she congratulate him on finding himself a girlfriend? Or pretend she didn't know?

'Oh, for God's sake!' Helen spoke her frustration aloud.

Taking a deep breath, she picked up the receiver.

'Good afternoon, Thompson and Sons Shipbuilders. Miss Crawford speaking.' There was only the slightest tremor to her voice.

'Ah, hello there ...'

It wasn't John. Helen didn't know if she was relieved or gutted.

'So sorry to bother you.' The voice at the other end of the phone sounded very well-to-do. 'I'm trying to get hold of one of your workers,' the man continued. 'I've tried ringing the home number and there's no one answering. And to be honest, I'm becoming a little fraught ... I know there was a bad air raid last night and I ...' There was the sound of a heavy sigh down the phone. 'I thought there might be the slightest chance that the young lady I'm calling about might be at work. I know it's a long shot – it being Sunday and all.'

Helen could hear the concern in the man's voice. There'd been over seventy killed last night and hundreds injured. There was nothing to say that any of her staff weren't among the dead or injured.

'I'm so sorry. I'm just looking at the office now and there's not a soul about.'

'Oh, she doesn't work in the office.' The voice perked up. 'She works in the yard. She's a welder.'

'Oh, what's her name?' Now Helen was curious. She doubted it was Rosie's husband, Peter. Gloria had said his work was very hush-hush and didn't allow for any kind of communication.

'Miss Angela Boulter,' the man said.

'Ah, Quentin!' A picture of a rather short, bookish-looking chap with a mop of strawberry-blond hair sprang to mind. 'Apologies, but I don't know your full name.'

'Foxton-Clarke. But please, just call me Quentin.'

'Quentin, it's Helen here, Helen Crawford.'

The two had met very briefly at Polly and Tommy's wedding on Christmas Day, as well as the night Polly had nearly lost her baby. Gloria had told her that Quentin, who was Angie and Dorothy's neighbour, was giving Angie lessons on 'how to be posh', which Helen thought was the most bizarre form of courtship she'd ever come across – not that Angie would admit that they were actually dating.

'Don't worry. Angie's here. She's absolutely fine. I've just been chatting to her squad. They came in to see what they could do after the raid. The yard took a hit last night. Or rather, one of our ships did.'

Helen heard Quentin exhale heavily.

'Good. Good. That's a relief. I was starting to think the worst.'

Helen could hear voices in the background and wondered what kind of work Quentin did. Angie had told everyone he was a 'pen-pusher', but having met him – and with a name like Quentin Foxton-Clarke – she thought that Quentin might have played down his job description.

'Sorry to be a total pain,' he said, 'but would it be possible for me to have a quick word with her, please?'

'Yes, yes, of course. It'll take me a few minutes to go down there and fetch her. Are you all right to hold?'

'Yes, yes, this is much appreciated. Thank you so much.'

Helen put down the receiver and hurried out of the office, jumping when Winston the marmalade-coloured tomcat shot past her as soon as she opened the doors to the main entrance. Hurrying across the yard, she managed to catch the women just as they were heading across the makeshift wooden gangplank that led from the yard onto *Denewood*'s deck.

'Angie!' she called out.

Everyone turned round and stared at Helen.

'You're wanted on the phone.' Helen skirted a mound of huge chains coiled up like a nest of snakes. 'It's Quentin.'

There was an immediate eruption of jeers and jibing. Angie scowled at the women as she pushed past Dorothy and headed over to Helen.

'Send lover boy our best wishes,' Dorothy heckled as they hurried across the yard.

'Honestly, he's just a mate, yer knar!' Angie huffed as they stopped to let a crane trundle past on its way to the platers' shed.

'Well, he sounded like a very worried "mate",' Helen said, giving Angie a sidelong look and seeing that she had gone bright red.

When they reached the office, Angie hesitated.

'Go on in,' Helen cajoled. 'I'll let you have some privacy. Come and get me when you're finished. And just shoo the cat off the chair,' she added, seeing that Winston had taken her place while she'd been gone and was now looking at them both with big green eyes. 'Honestly, as if his basket isn't good enough.'

'Thank goodness you're all right,' Quentin said as soon as he heard Angie's voice. 'I've been trying to get through to Mrs Kwiatkowski for hours and she's not picking up.' Mrs Kwiatkowski lived in the ground floor flat, above Quentin's basement flat and below Dorothy and Angie's on the first floor.

'She went to church today 'n then she was gannin to her club,' Angie said, holding the receiver a little away from herself, not trusting it. She had only used a phone a few times in her entire life.

'I thought her club was in Low Street, next to Fenwick's Brewery – or should I say what *used to* be Fenwick's Brewery? By the sounds of it, it's now just a mound of bricks.'

'It is – they've gone to Vera's café up on High Street East.' Angie paused. 'Anyway, how did yer knar the brewery had been hit? I thought yer were in London?'

'I am,' Quentin said, 'but we got news of it earlier down the wires.'

Angie was quiet. She would have liked to ask what 'down the wires' meant and why it was he was working today. She thought he was a clerical worker, like Bel, and would, therefore, be exempt from working Sundays.

'So, you're all OK? Dorothy all right?' Quentin asked.

'Aye, Dor's fine. Mind you, it was like trying to raise the dead last night. I swear she would have slept through the whole raid. I had to practically shake her awake.'

She heard Quentin chuckling.

'Oh, 'n thanks fer leaving us the ginger nuts 'n the bottle of pop.'

'Did you feel safe under the Morrison shelter?' Quentin had got an indoor shelter, which was basically a steel table, delivered to his flat. He'd removed one side of the wire mesh and reinforced the top of the table with an extra layer of steel, then tied four gas masks to each leg, adding blankets, quilts and cushions for extra comfort.

'It was that cosy, we had to practically drag Mrs Kwiatkowski out!' Angie laughed. 'Me 'n Dor said it was like being a bairn again – yer knar, when yer make a den.'

Quentin said he did, although he didn't add that he himself had never been allowed to indulge in such childish behaviour as a boy.

'And Mrs Kwiatkowski was singing yer praises, saying yer were "very kind and thoughtful" and that yer'd make someone a good husband.' Angie hooted down the phone. 'I said yer'll have to gan out more if yer want to find yerself a wife.'

Quentin was quiet and Angie heard voices in the background.

'Sounds busy there?'

'It is, but I'm back up the week after next. Just for a couple of days. I thought you might like to have a trip to the museum. I could tell you about some of the oil paintings in there. Introduce you to a few old masters. And then we can go to the Palatine, seeing as the Continental no longer exists.'

Quentin had been going on about taking Angie to the Continental Hotel on the corner of St Thomas' Street for a posh meal since February, but it seemed as though there had been one obstacle after another preventing them making it there, and then in March it had been bombed.

'It's a bit posh,' Angie said little nervously.

'No more than the Continental once was.'

'All right then, yer on,' Angie said, before quickly adding, 'as long as it's not on a Saturday. Dor will go berserk if I dinnit gan to the Ritz with her.'

Chapter Six

Dr Eris smiled as she walked through the entrance to the Ryhope Emergency Hospital. She had put on a pair of cream-coloured slacks and a silk blouse that she kept for special occasions. It was mild enough to go without a coat. Besides, it would also be an excuse for John to give her his coat later on, or better still, for him to put his arm around her to keep her warm while they walked home.

Dr Parker was standing a few yards away from the main reception desk. He had got there earlier than the time he had agreed upon to meet with Dr Eris in the hope of being able to use the phone. As it was, Denise the receptionist was having a lengthy conversation, and from the snippets he had picked up, it was a social call rather than hospital business. Still, he felt it would have been rude to pull rank and ask her to ring off so that he could use the phone for a call that was also personal.

Seeing Dr Eris approach, Dr Parker walked over and gave her a kiss on both cheeks.

'You look lovely,' he said.

Dr Eris put her hands in her pockets and tilted her head slightly.

'Thank you, John. It's nice to have an excuse to wear something other than my work suit.'

Dr Parker glanced over at Denise, who was still chatting away and didn't look anywhere near winding up her conversation.

'I was just going to call Helen, make sure she's all right after the air raid last night. I'm sure it's totally unnecessary to worry, but she normally rings here after we've had a raid and as far as I know she's not left any messages.'

'Oh, she's fine,' Dr Eris said with a smile. 'I bumped into her earlier on.'

'Really? I wonder what she was doing there?' Dr Parker said.

'She was with a young woman – Bel, I think her name was.' Dr Eris knew not to volunteer too much information. If John wanted to think that Helen had come to the asylum for reasons other than to see him, then so be it.

'Oh, yes, Bel, she's her ...' Dr Parker hesitated, thinking of the recent revelation that Bel was Helen's aunt, which was strange as they were about the same age.

'Friend? Work colleague?' Dr Eris said.

'Yes, both, I believe.'

Dr Parker looked at his watch. It was gone six o'clock; she would probably have left work by now. Still, he could possibly catch her at home.

He looked at Dr Eris.

What was he thinking? This attractive and intelligent woman was standing here, waiting to go out with him for the evening, and he was obsessing over Helen – who might also be attractive and intelligent, but she had no interest in going out with him other than as mere friends. *When was he going to give up hoping that Helen might be in love with him?*

'Well then,' Dr Parker said, putting out his arm, 'shall we go?'

As he did so, Denise finally ended her conversation and hung up.

'Oh, Gloria, I feel such a fool,' Helen said. 'I even found myself waiting for his call at work after everyone had gone. We always speak after an air raid. I was sure he'd call. I waited until way after six. The place was practically deserted. Just me and Winston. How sad is that. Me and just the cat for company.'

Gloria bristled as she poured their tea. The ginger moggy always reminded her of the night she and Hope had nearly died, and of her old friend Mrs Crabtree, who would still be in the land of the living if she hadn't gone looking for that damned cat.

'I suppose,' Gloria said, handing Helen her tea, 'if this Dr Eris woman told him she'd seen you, he would have known you were all right.'

'I suppose,' Helen agreed, looking at Hope, who was pushing her bobbed black hair behind her ears as she sat on the rug and played with her dollies. 'And I also suppose I'm going to have to get used to the fact that John will be spending time with his new sweetheart. And not me.'

Gloria nestled back in her chair with her cup of tea balanced on her bosom; she had half an eye on Hope. 'What I don't understand is that in the space of twenty-four hours yer went from having yer mind made up to just keeping Dr Parker as a friend to suddenly deciding to declare yer feelings to him.'

Helen sighed heavily. 'I know. I don't know if it was lying awake, thinking too much during that bloody air raid, or—'

'Or what yer found out about yer grandda?' Gloria volunteered. She too had thought a lot last night after Helen had come over and told her that her grandfather had raped Pearl and fathered Bel. She kept thinking how one vile, violent act could have such far-reaching repercussions, not just back then, but now, more than a quarter of a century later.

'I think on some level it might have,' Helen conceded. She let out a bitter laugh. 'I'm sure Dr Eris would have something to say on the matter. She'd probably say that having the rug pulled out from under my feet left me feeling unstable and grasping for the nearest lifeboat. Either that or the air raid left me feeling I had to grab life – or rather, John – and make the most of what little time might be left.'

Gloria took a sip of her tea.

'I think yer missed your vocation.'

Helen let out rather an exasperated laugh.

'I think I missed the boat. That's for sure.'

Seeing Hope push herself up from the floor, having abandoned her toys, Helen reached out and lifted her little sister onto her lap.

'Which, I have to add,' she said, putting her arms round Hope, who was now curling up and sucking her thumb, 'is probably a blessing in disguise.'

'Why do you say that?' Gloria put her cup and saucer on the coffee table.

'Well, it would have been a bit embarrassing, wouldn't it? I can just imagine the scene now. "Oh, I'm awfully sorry, Helen. You seem to have misread the situation."' Helen deepened her voice. Gloria thought she did a good impression of Dr Parker – posh but not plum in the mouth. '"But I'm afraid a woman who no longer has her virtue – and who got herself pregnant into the bargain – would not be someone I'd want to court."'

Helen exhaled heavily.

'Let's face it, Gloria, any man in his right mind wouldn't want someone else's cast-off. Men in John's position want the first prize, not sloppy seconds. Or as my darling mother would say, they don't want someone who's *sullied*.'

'I think yer right in that a lot of men might think like that, but I'd be really surprised if that's what Dr Parker believes.' Gloria was quiet for a moment. 'I don't know what to say, Helen, but I still think it's a shame yer didn't get to speak to him about how yer felt.'

'Well, I'm glad I didn't,' Helen said, her tone definite. 'I don't think I can stand any more humiliation in my life.'

Neither of them mentioned Theo by name, but they were both thinking of the man who had lied and manipulated his way into Helen's life, then left her pregnant after running back to his also pregnant wife and their children.

'I think it's this little one's bedtime,' Gloria said. 'If yer read her a story, I'll make us a fresh brew.'

Ten minutes later, Helen was back on the sofa, sipping a cup of hot tea.

'I'm guessing you rang Dad this morning before you came into work.'

'Yes,' Gloria said, looking at Helen. 'I phoned him before dropping off Hope. I thought, if she can't see her daddy, she might as well hear his voice at the very least.'

'And how did it go?'

'Well, I said "Daddy" a lot 'n pointed at the phone, then I got Jack to speak 'n put the receiver to her ear.'

'Do you think it meant anything to her?' Helen asked. She had no idea if a toddler, just shy of two years old, could make any sense of the fact that her daddy, whom she had only ever seen when she was a very small baby, was the voice coming out of what she probably perceived to be a toy.

'It's doubtful,' Gloria sighed, 'but I think it meant the world to Jack. And it did to me. I know it sounds stupid, but it felt like the three of us were together for the first time in ...' Gloria thought for a moment '... one year, four months – and nine days.'

'Oh, Gloria, I *do* feel it for you,' Helen said.

Gloria waved it away. 'I can't complain – compared to others I'm lucky. First off, I got a letter from Gordon and

Bobby the other day, secondly, I've not been bombed out of my home, and thirdly, I can speak regularly with the man I love, who might be stuck up in Scotland for what feels like eternity, but at least he's not on the front line risking life 'n limb. Look at poor Polly. I think I'd go doolally if I was in her shoes, knowing the man she married at Christmas is back swimming round in foreign seas, pulling explosives off the bottoms of boats.'

Helen nodded.

'And as for Rosie,' Gloria continued, 'I don't think she has any idea whether Peter is alive or dead.'

They both drank their tea.

'But it still feels unnecessary,' Helen said. 'Dad being banished to the Clyde.'

She thought Gloria looked tired, which wasn't surprising as she had now done a seven-day shift, been up half the night in a cold, damp Anderson shelter, no doubt trying to keep Hope calm, all the while hearing bombs being dropped round their ears.

'Going to war is necessary,' Helen said, 'but Dad having to work in the Lithgows yard rather than one here – and being banned from coming home – is totally unnecessary. Keeping him from his daughter is unnecessary.' She pursed her lips. 'It's not good, a child growing up without her father. It's not fair on Hope. She's the innocent in all of this.'

'Well,' Gloria said, 'there's nothing we can do about that. Your mother's still got a hold over us.'

They were quiet for a moment, thinking of the day, as Gloria had just said, *one year, four months and nine days ago*, when Miriam had summoned Gloria to the house while Jack was there and told them she knew of their affair and, worse still, about their illegitimate child. Helen had eavesdropped as her mother had blackmailed Jack and Gloria,

48

relaying to them various secrets belonging to the women welders that, should they ever be revealed, would not only ruin their lives, but might also put them in grave danger.

There had been nothing Gloria or Jack could do but agree to Miriam's terms: Jack would leave that afternoon, going by train to Scotland to work in one of the shipyards on the Clyde – never to come back.

Gloria had ended up confiding in Rosie, telling her about Dorothy's mum's bigamy, Angela's mam's bit on the side, and Martha's monster of a mother, hung for poisoning her own children. It had helped to confide in someone she could trust, but they had both agreed there was nothing they could do. They were powerless. Jack's exile to the Clyde was non-negotiable.

'But, you know,' Helen perked up, 'Rosie's squad aren't the only ones with skeletons in their cupboards, are they?'

'Yer thinking about your grandda?'

Helen nodded.

'Do yer think Miriam knows?'

'I don't know, but I intend to find out.'

Chapter Seven

Tuesday 18 May

'What's that?' Gloria asked.

'It's a leaflet Jerry dropped during the raid,' Angie said.

Gloria took the leaflet and started to read.

'Where did you get it from?' Martha asked, looking over Gloria's shoulder.

'Marie-Anne brought it in this morning. She wants it back, mind yer – said she had to pay a penny for it. The money's gannin to the Red Cross. She showed it to Bel, who showed it to Polly, who gave it to me 'n Dor,' explained Angie.

Marie-Anne was Helen's secretary and Bel's immediate boss, and her curly auburn hair, sea-blue eyes, fair, freckled face and lilting accent left no one in doubt of her Irish ancestry.

'Apparently she said there were loads of these leaflets showered all over the town,' Dorothy said. 'I'm surprised we didn't see any.'

'That's 'cos all we've been seeing the past couple of days is molten metal – that's all I see, even when I close my eyes.'

'Talking of eyesight,' Rosie butted in, 'have you been changing your protective lenses when you should?'

'Mmm, I think so,' Angie said.

'The days just seem to be merging into one another,' Dorothy added.

'Well, no need to take any unnecessary risks – we'll all have a walk over to the stores later. I don't want anyone

50

getting arc eye, and not just because it's horrendous, but because I can't have any of you off ill. Not with us being a man down.' Losing Polly had taken its toll, but Rosie was still holding off taking on another worker as it would mean training them, which, in turn, would mean they'd be *two* workers down.

'"Why the British government says nothing about shipping losses."' Gloria read out the headline of the leaflet. '"To be told the truth about the state of the battle of the seas would shake the belief in British naval supremacy and ultimate victory ..." Blimey, you want to see all the ships it says they've sunk over the past two years.' Gloria looked up to see that a tired-looking Hannah and an equally jaded-looking Olly had turned up. She moved her chair to make room for the pair to join them.

'Yer all dinnit believe that load of codswallop, do yer?' Everyone turned round to see Muriel, the head dinner lady, standing with a cloth in her hand. 'It's what they call *propaganda*,' she said with the utmost authority. '*Nazi propaganda*, to make us all disheartened and demoralised –'n by the looks on all yer ugly mugs, they've succeeded.'

For once, Rosie was glad Muriel had been earwigging on their conversation.

'So it's not true?' Martha said.

'Nah, like I said, load of claptrap. They're dumping leaflets like this all over the country according to my Brian.' The women knew of, but had never met, Muriel's put-upon husband. 'He says the fact they're having to resort to dropping a load of leaflets full of lies on us means our boys have got them running scared.' She looked at Gloria. They both had sons at sea.

Catching the look, Dorothy agreed. 'Yes, I can believe that. Makes sense. Desperate measures.' She wasn't so sure, though. The U-boats had been a huge thorn in the Allies' backside. And the women themselves knew more than most the pressure they were under to keep replacing the ships being sunk. 'Come on then, let's read some proper news, not made-up stories courtesy of Herr Hitler.'

The women started rooting around in their bags, pulling out a variety of newspapers they had brought for their 'current affairs classes'.

'So,' Dorothy continued, spreading out a copy of the *Daily Mail*, 'I couldn't see much about anything happening in the Atlantic or the Mediterranean.'

She looked up to see Polly arriving.

'Just in time, Pol. Pull up a chair ... No, pull up two!' She laughed at her own joke. Everyone else tutted.

'I'm not *that* big,' Polly said in mock outrage; the truth was, the bigger she got the happier she felt. She wouldn't admit to anyone how much her near miscarriage had shaken her up, but the whole terrifying drama had left her needing to know that her baby was growing. She just wished she could skip forward to when the baby was due in mid-September.

'I believe the main news of the day,' Angie perked up, her copy of the *Daily Telegraph* taking up half the table, 'is this "bouncing bomb" raid.'

'One of the lads in the office said it's been hailed as one of the most daring and ingenious missions carried out by the Allies so far,' Polly said, getting her sandwiches out and unwrapping them.

'Bloody Nora,' Angie laughed. 'Talk about doorstep sarnies. I could have done with one of them to help me do some overhead welds this morning.'

Everyone chuckled. Angie was probably the shortest out of all the women and always struggled with any kind of vertical welds.

'Ma's insisting on making my packed lunch,' Polly said, holding the sandwich in her hands and sighing. 'She says the least she can do is make sure me and the bab are well nourished.'

'I think they might beat Martha's mam's whoppers,' Gloria chuckled, biting into her own moderate-sized cheese and onion sandwich.

'So, Pol,' Dorothy piped up as they ate their lunch and drank their tea, 'what were you doing up in the office?'

'Ah,' Polly said, looking a little shamefaced.

'Yeah, and why were yer not in the timekeeper's cabin this morning when we were all clocking on?'

'Well, the thing is—' Polly started to say.

'Yer've not gone over to the other side, have yer?' Angie blurted out.

'It's not a case of them 'n us, yer know?' Gloria quickly rose to Polly's defence. She, of course, knew about Polly's defection, having spoken to her this morning while dropping off Hope.

'So, have you?' Martha asked, shocked. 'Have you gone to work in the office?'

Polly nodded and took a big bite out of her sandwich. As she did so, Bel and Marie-Anne walked into the canteen and came to sit by her.

'Judging by the looks on all yer faces,' Marie-Anne said, 'Polly's told yer. She's one of us now. Isn't she, Bel?'

Bel smiled. 'She is indeed.'

'But you said you'd never go and work in the offices, Pol?' Martha said, genuinely perplexed.

'I know I did,' Polly said, swallowing hard. 'But to be honest, I thought I might go mad cooped up in that little cabin all day. And there's this new lad who is much more suited to it than me. And, well, when Helen offered me a job as a clerical assistant—'

'A clerical assistant!' Angie had half risen out of her chair.

'Honestly, you lot make it sound like she's committed a crime,' Rosie laughed. She, of course, knew about the move. Helen had informed her, although it hadn't been Helen who had offered her the job, but Polly who had asked for one.

'I'll be back welding after the baby's born,' Polly said, nervously moving the sandwich round in her hand. She had known she'd be in for a verbal battering.

'I reckon being pregnant has made yer gan funny in the head,' Angie said.

Polly burst out laughing. 'Well, I'd agree with that, Angie. That and the war.'

'Well, I'm over the moon,' Bel said. 'It means I get to work with my sister-in-law – and, moreover, Agnes and I won't have to listen to how *boring* it is to work as a timekeeper any more.' Agnes was Bel's mother-in-law, although the two were as close as mother and daughter.

'We didn't think it was *that* bad,' Martha said.

'It was.' Polly nodded. 'Very. I think I did well to stand it for nearly two whole months.'

'Sounds like you didn't really have a choice,' Martha said. 'That is, if you want to stay working here.'

'Exactly,' Polly said with a big exhalation of air, 'finally someone understands. I'm banned from working in the yard. So, it was really the lesser of two evils.' She glanced at Marie-Anne and Bel. 'No offence.'

'Mmm, I still think yer a turncoat,' Angie said.

'Talking about being a turncoat!' Dorothy glared at her friend. 'You always said you'd never go out with anyone who was upper class, and Quentin's practically aristocracy.'

'I'm not gannin out with Quentin,' Angie snapped.

'So, where are you "gannin" next week?' Dorothy asked, looking around at the women's faces and raising her eyebrows.

'The museum,' Angie said.

'And then where's Quentin taking you?' Dorothy asked, again raising her eyebrows.

'The Palatine Hotel.'

They all chuckled.

'I rest my case,' Dorothy said, winking across at Polly.

'Glor, I know you get sick of us asking,' Dorothy said as they all made their way back over to *Denewood*, 'but do you really think Jack's not going to be able to come back any time soon?'

Gloria glanced across at Rosie.

'And why do yer always look at Rosie whenever we ask about Jack?' Angie asked.

'Because she's the boss,' Gloria said, before quickly changing the subject. 'When yer seeing Toby next then, Dor?'

Dorothy had met her boyfriend Toby, a recruiter for the Special Operations Executive, on Christmas Eve, when he'd turned up at Lily's bordello to give Rosie a letter from Peter. He'd mistaken Dorothy for one of the 'girls', which had caused much hilarity and had led to Dorothy inviting him to Polly and Tommy's wedding.

'I'm seeing him next week!' Dorothy clapped her hands together in excitement. 'He's got a forty-eight-hour pass. Why do you ask?' she said, suddenly puzzled.

'Only because you've not mentioned him for – oh,' Gloria looked at an imaginary watch on her wrist, 'must be at least half an hour.'

Angie laughed out loud.

'Yer wanna live with her!' she said, rolling her eyes to the heavens. 'It's Toby this. Toby that. Toby the other.'

As they made their way onto the upper deck and the klaxon sounded out, preventing any more chatter, it occurred to Dorothy that every time she quizzed her about Jack, Gloria subtly changed the subject. She'd have a chat about it with Angie later. They'd thought that something was up for a while now – something didn't add up about Jack being in Scotland, or the fact that he never came back for a home visit. The army got leave to see their loved ones, so it was a mystery why a yard manager wouldn't get a few days off now and again to see his family.

Dorothy glanced across at Gloria and Rosie. She was sure there was something they weren't telling them, and it was about time she and Angie found out what it was.

Chapter Eight

Helen came out of her office, buttoning up her tailored suit jacket. It was olive green and the perfect mix of feminine and professional.

'Bel,' she said, putting her boxed-up gas mask over her shoulder and her arm through her expensive Schiaparelli handbag, 'can I borrow you for a few hours? I have to go to the launch at Pickersgill's to do some hobnobbing. Harold's orders.' She widened her eyes. They all knew Harold hated leaving the confines of his office and that Helen was more or less doing his job as well as her own.

'Yes, of course,' Bel said, pulling a letter she had just finished typing out of her Remington and putting it on top of a pile to her left. She shot a look at Marie-Anne. This would normally be her job. She was, after all, Helen's personal assistant and second in command.

'And Marie-Anne,' Helen added, 'would you mind holding the fort while we're gone? It might be a good idea if you take command of my office. It'll save you running in every time the phone rings, plus I've got a load of invoices I need checking and filing away.'

Marie-Anne's pale, freckled face lit up. Never in all the years she had worked at Thompson's had she known anyone to be allowed to 'take command' of the manager's office – even when it was Jack's office, and he was the most laid-back, unassuming boss she'd ever known, unlike his daughter.

'Yes, of course, no problem,' Marie-Anne said, collecting her handbag from the side of her desk and standing up.

'If there's an emergency,' Helen said, 'just call Mr Royce's secretary and she can get a message to us.'

Marie-Anne nodded. She knew Dahlia, whose family had come over from Sweden after the First War. If her name didn't give her origins away, then her long blonde hair and ice-blue eyes did.

Bel looked across at Polly, who was standing with her back to them, rifling through one of the large grey metal filing cabinets. She looked like a fish out of water. She turned around just in time for Bel to catch her eye and give her a quick wave.

Returning the gesture, Polly heard a few mutterings from a couple of the clerical staff next to her. It was obvious by the whispered snippets she caught that the boss didn't normally take anyone anywhere, let alone to a launch.

Polly thought that they would have been even more surprised if they knew it was the case of a niece asking her aunt to accompany her on an afternoon out.

As soon as Helen and Bel had left, Marie-Anne straightened her skirt, pulled her shoulders back and clapped her hands.

'If anyone needs me, they'll find me in the manager's office,' she announced, trying unsuccessfully to suppress her look of elation.

Two dozen faces glanced up from whatever it was they were doing but no one said anything. Instead, they watched as their acting commander-in-chief sashayed her way over to her new, albeit temporary, abode.

Walking into the office, Marie-Anne decided that she might just have to ring Dahlia, regardless of any emergency, and drop it into the conversation exactly where she was calling from. She'd be green with envy. There was no way in a million years old man Royce would let her take his place when he had to go out on an afternoon jaunt.

Seeing Winston the yard cat sitting on Helen's chair, Marie-Anne started clapping her hands for the second time. This time with aggression. 'Shoo! Yer flea-ridden moggie!'

Winston gave her a lingering look before nonchalantly arching his back in a stretch, jumping from the chair to the floor and padding over to his basket.

Brushing hair from the leather upholstery, Marie-Anne lowered herself into the swivel chair. Surveying her new terrain, she felt like the bee's knees. She was going to have this office spick and span and super organised by the time Helen came back, so determined was she that this would not be the last time she was asked to take charge. Reaching over to empty Helen's ashtray, she nearly jumped out of her skin when the phone rang.

'Good afternoon, J.L. Thompson and Sons Shipbuilders. You're through to Miss Crawford's office, how can I help?' Marie-Anne put on her very best telephone voice.

'Ah, hello there . . . is that Marie-Anne?'

'It is indeed.' Marie-Anne relaxed, recognising the voice at the other end of the line. 'And would I be right in saying this is Dr Parker?'

'You would,' Dr Parker said. He could hear the smile in Marie-Anne's voice, as well as the return of the Irish brogue. He let out a short chuckle. 'You sounded different there. Thought Miss Crawford might have got herself a new secretary.'

'Oh, no,' Marie-Anne was quick to correct him, 'I'm not going anywhere. I'm in charge of the office for the next few hours.'

'Ah, I take it that means Miss Crawford is not there?'

'You've just this minute missed her, Dr Parker. She's gone to the launch of SS *Chiswick* at Pickersgill's.' Marie-Anne hesitated. 'Along with Mrs Elliot.' Marie-Anne wasn't sure why she added this bit of information as she was certain it was of no interest to Dr Parker.

'Oh,' Dr Parker said. Helen's meeting with Bel and Pearl must have gone well. He thought it was something Helen would have wanted to share with him. 'I'm guessing that means she'll be gone a good few hours.'

'I would have thought so,' Marie-Anne said. 'All that chit-chat and rubbing of shoulders to be done.'

'Well, can you tell her I called when she gets back, please?'

'Of course,' Marie-Anne said. 'I'm writing a memo as we speak. I shall make sure she gets it and rings you back at her earliest convenience.'

'You'll have to prise Marie-Anne off your chair when you get back, you do realise?' Bel said.

Helen laughed. 'I know.'

'The look on her face,' Bel chuckled. 'It was as though world domination was just within her grasp.'

Neither of them said it but they both knew that Marie-Anne had been given free rein as a trade-off for Helen taking Bel to the launch. Something she had never previously done with any of her staff.

As they walked past the timekeeper's cabin, the young lad tipped his cap. 'Afternoon, Miss Crawford ... Mrs Elliot.'

'So, he's the young boy who's taken over Polly's position permanently?'

'He is,' Helen said as she rifled round in her handbag.

'He looks awfully young,' Bel said, her eyes drawn to a gleaming green sports car that had been parked near the Admiral pub.

'He *is* awfully young,' Helen said, 'thirteen going on fourteen. His father didn't want him to follow the family tradition and end up spending most of his life down the mines and the rest of it coughing them up, so he asked his mate Jimmy, the head riveter, if he could get him a job here. We started him on weekends, and now, thanks to Polly's low boredom threshold, he's got a full-time job.'

Bel suddenly realised that *this* was the real reason for Polly's move to the 'other side'. She'd suspected her sister-in-law wasn't being entirely honest with her.

'If I was his ma, I'd be counting my blessings,' Bel said. 'There's no way I'd want a son of mine working down the mines. If it was a toss-up between the shipyards and the mines, I'd choose the yards any day.'

Helen smiled. Bel, she'd realised, was naturally maternal towards all children, not just her own.

'Wow!' Bel exclaimed as Helen stopped in front of the sports car, pulled out a set of keys from her handbag and jangled them in the air. 'This isn't yours, is it?'

'It is,' Helen said. 'I managed to convince the powers that be that as yard manager I really needed my own transport, and that I was willing to provide said transport and double up as my own chauffeur in return for them applying for a fuel allowance, which, of course, they did, and got.'

Helen opened her door. 'I think they agreed it was a more than fair deal.' She looked across at Bel, who was still staring at it in disbelief. 'Hop in!'

'What made you want to learn to drive?' Bel asked as she opened the passenger door.

Helen laughed. 'Bunny-hopping the St John's ambulance with Polly and Dr Parker in the back all the way to the Royal. Afterwards, I realised I'd spent my whole life letting other people drive me around and it was time I took the controls myself.' Helen sat in the driver's seat, swinging her legs in afterwards. Bel copied, feeling the leather seats and the varnished walnut dashboard.

'She's gorgeous, isn't she?' Helen said, putting the key into the ignition. 'And so much easier to drive than Grandfather's old Jag.'

At the mention of Mr Havelock, the mood changed.

'God, I never thought the mere mention of the old man would bring with it such *horrible* feelings.' Helen looked across at Bel. 'Heavens knows what it must make you feel like.'

When Bel didn't answer, Helen turned the ignition and fired up the engine. It was louder than Bel had anticipated, but not so loud as to prevent conversation. They drove up the embankment.

'Is that why you've asked me to accompany you to the launch?' Bel asked. 'So we can have the chat we talked about that day at the asylum?'

Helen let out a bitter laugh.

'*Asylum*. That's another word that makes me feel terrible, although for different reasons.'

Turning left onto Dame Dorothy Street, Helen slowed down to let a bus pull out.

'Yes, you're right. I did ask you to come with me so we could have a chat. You don't mind, do you?'

'Far from it,' Bel joked. 'An afternoon off work and a drive in a car I've only ever seen pictured in magazines.' As they turned right and drove through Monkwearmouth, an area known locally as the Barbary Coast, she looked at Helen. 'Seriously, though, I don't mind. I think now that you know, we need to be able to discuss it. It's good that we can. And it'll be easier just the two of us, without Ma.'

Helen nodded, keeping her eyes on the road. 'I still find it beyond bizarre that you're my aunty.'

'Likewise,' Bel said. 'Makes me feel ancient.'

'Which you're not.' Helen gave Bel a sideways glance. She was a very pretty woman and always immaculately presented. She knew most of the comptometer operators were sweet on Bel, and if she wasn't married, there'd be a scrabble to ask her out.

'The thing is,' Helen said, 'I've thought and thought about it this past week since I found out, but I'll be damned if I know what to do, to be honest.' She touched the brakes as a child stepped off the kerb only to be yanked back by her scolding mother. 'I don't know whether to confront my grandfather about everything – what he did to your ma ... about you ... I really just *don't know*.' This was the first time she had been able to speak her thoughts to another person. She would have given anything to have chatted through her concerns and confusion with John, but he still hadn't called. He was clearly all-consumed with Claire.

'I'm of the same mind,' Bel said. 'I've spent an endless amount of time wondering what to do – if anything. Should I let sleeping dogs lie? I know that's what Ma and Joe would prefer, even if they won't come out and say it.'

As they drove along the high road that overlooked the Wear, Bel looked out of the passenger window. Viewed from this perspective, you could see the snaking bends of the river, its waters crowded with a mass of ships, colliers, cargo vessels and tugs.

'But it's not just about me or Ma, is it?' Bel said. 'There's other people to consider.' She looked at Helen. 'Like your grandma, Henrietta?'

'Oh, Grandmama died years ago,' Helen said. 'When I was very small.'

Bel thought either Helen was a very good liar or she genuinely believed her grandmother was dead.

'She must have been quite young when she passed. What did she die of?' Bel asked, trying not to sound like she was probing.

'I have no idea,' Helen said. 'Funnily enough, you're not the first person to ask me that of late.' She thought of Georgina Pickering, the private eye she had employed to find out about Bel's parentage, whom she and John had nicknamed 'Miss Marple'. She, too, had asked about Helen's grandmother.

They drove in silence for a while.

'Well,' Bel said, 'if neither of us is sure what to do, let's wait until we are. I hardly think he'll want to know – and I'm not entirely sure I want him to know.' Bel gave a long sigh. 'And even if we confronted him, my feelings are he'd just deny it. There's no proof. It'd be Ma's word against his. And let's face it – who are people going to believe? The great Mr Havelock, the people's saviour, the man with money who gives to those in need – or my ma, a barmaid with barely two pennies to rub together, who's had two children out of wedlock, one of whom is coloured. He'd probably just say Ma was after his money.'

'Which is an interesting point,' Helen said. 'I wonder how the law would stand if it was *proven* that you're family.' Helen's mind went to the report she had locked away in her office, compiled by her Miss Marple; it made for compelling reading. Whether or not the contents of that report would stand up in a court of law, though, was another matter.

As they approached the rather magnificent wrought-iron gates to W. Pickersgill & Sons, Helen asked, 'When did you find out – about Grandfather?'

'Well, like you, I got a little obsessed with discovering the truth. I'd always known Ma was lying when she said my da was dead, but when Maisie burst into our lives and there was all this talk about who *her* father was, it got me thinking.'

Helen knew that Pearl had given up Maisie for adoption just hours after giving birth to her in a Salvation Army hospital for unmarried mothers in London. Twenty-eight years later, Maisie, who was of mixed race, had tracked Pearl down, causing quite a stir when she'd declared herself at Bel and Joe's wedding a year and a half ago.

'Ma seemed happy to tell Maisie all about her da, a stoker from the West Indies, but she wouldn't tell me about *my* father. It took me a while, but I managed to wear her down in the end.'

Helen looked surprised. She couldn't imagine anyone wearing Pearl down. The woman was like granite. Which told Helen that Bel was a lot stronger – and harder – than she appeared on the surface.

'She ended up taking me to your grandfather's house – well, not to the house as such, but we walked along Glen Path and stood on the other side of the road.' She felt a sudden well of emotion as she recalled that day. 'That was back in June last year.'

'And you've known all this time?' Helen asked, suddenly realising that it was not long afterwards that Bel had applied for a job at the yard.

Bel nodded as one of the shipyard workers standing by the entrance waved them through. Another flat-capped man pointed to the parking area. They both saw Mr Havelock's black Jaguar at the same time.

'Oh, dear. I didn't think he'd be here today. I heard he was at Doxford's on Tuesday to see the launch of *Avonmoor*.' Before Helen had agreed to come here today in place of Harold, she had got Marie-Anne to find out if her grandfather had attended the earlier launch. 'He never does two launches in a week.' Helen felt herself panic. This had taken her by surprise.

She looked at Bel, who looked equally stricken.

'If Grandfather's here, it goes without saying Mother will be here too.' Helen started fishing around in her handbag for her Pall Malls and lighter.

'You don't have to come up to the launch,' she said, opening the passenger door and then lighting her cigarette. 'If you want to go and see Dahlia and have a cup of tea with her, I can meet you back here afterwards?'

Bel thought for a moment. Part of her desperately wanted to run all the way back home to Joe and Agnes. They would wrap her up in love and tell her she never had to go anywhere near the man who was her father if she didn't want to.

But she knew she couldn't.

It was time to face her fears.

'No, I'm coming,' she said.

Chapter Nine

'And God bless all those who sail in her!'

The sound of cheers and horns was deafening as SS *Chiswick* slowly and with a certain majesty ploughed her way into the river. As always, the sound of jubilation dropped a little while the tugs did what they had been designed to do and coerced the newly-born around so as to avoid the other side of the riverbank, manoeuvring her with just the right amount of pull to keep her on an even keel.

Bel had not seen the launch as she had been keeping an eye on Mr Havelock and Miriam. She had forced herself to look at them, albeit surreptitiously; it was as though by acquainting herself with their every nuance, it might diminish their power and therefore lessen her own anxieties.

As SS *Chiswick* reached the fitting-out quay, the spectators turned to go home and the shipyard workers made their slow return to the adjacent basin, where there stood another half-built vessel that would soon follow *Chiswick* down the ways.

Bel thought that she and Helen might have escaped having to chat to Mr Havelock and Miriam. When they'd arrived, Helen had waved over to them, but the pair had been surrounded by the town's dignitaries and big-wigs, all demanding their attention. Then the proceedings had begun, speeches were made, a bottle of champagne smashed, and the ship birthed. But just as they were turning to make their way out of the main VIP area, she heard Miriam call out.

'Helen, darling, how lovely to see you!'

They both turned round to see Miriam and Mr Havelock just a few feet away.

'I had to check it was you, I see you so little these days,' Miriam said, leaving Mr Havelock in conversation with the mayor.

'Hello, Mother, I didn't think you'd be here.' Helen made a point of looking down at her watch. 'Shouldn't you be at the Grand? Honestly, they'll be sending out a search party for you if you don't get your skates on.'

Miriam let out a tinkle of laughter that was more becoming to a young girl than a middle-aged woman.

'My daughter has a very wicked sense of humour,' Miriam said, squinting as she scrutinised Bel. 'I recognise you, my dear, from Christmas Day. The welder's wedding.' She thought for a moment. 'Elliot, that's it, Mrs Elliot, isn't it?'

Miriam threw her daughter a triumphant look before returning her attention to Bel.

'My daughter likes to claim age is causing my memory to fast deteriorate, so I like to prove her wrong whenever I get the chance.' She offered her hand. 'Nice to meet you again, Mrs Elliot.'

Bel shook hands and forced a smile.

'Helen, good to see you!'

Miriam moved aside to give her father centre stage. Charles Havelock was wearing a black three-piece suit, starched white shirt and a red tie.

'Haven't seen you for a while, my dear,' he said, looking Helen up and down. 'Where've you been? No, don't tell me! I know.' He stabbed the ground with the end of his ebony walking stick. 'You've been working flat out at that yard of yours.' He patted the back of his slicked-back grey hair. 'Well, I certainly hope Mr Thompson appreciates you devoting your life to that place?' Someone he knew caught his eye and he waved to them. 'Anyway, what's this about you learning to drive? Eddy told me you borrowed the car the other day. Good for you, my dear. Good for you!'

It was clear to Bel that Mr Havelock had no interest in hearing the answer to any of his questions.

'I'm guessing you're here in lieu of Harold?' he said.

Suddenly he did a double take as his attention was caught by Bel.

'And who, may I ask, is this?'

'This, Grandfather, is Mrs Isabelle Elliot. She's my secretary. We've got a meeting with Mr Royce in a few minutes, so we best be making tracks.'

'Hold your horses, Helen. Where have your manners gone?' He put his hand out. Bel noticed he was wearing a gold Masonic ring.

'Pleased to meet you, Mrs Elliot.'

Bel hesitated for a fraction of a moment.

'Don't worry, I won't bite.' Mr Havelock laughed. 'Much as some might claim.'

Bel forced herself to shake hands.

As though realising her reluctance, Mr Havelock held on to Bel's hand, squeezing it tight and clamping his other hand on top of it. She resisted the urge to yank it away.

'We've not met before, have we?' His watery pale blue eyes narrowed. Bel felt as though he could see right through her.

'Mrs Elliot was at Arthur Watts's funeral,' Helen butted in, 'with her little girl Lucille, and her husband Joe. He was in his regimental uniform.'

'Yes, yes, Seventh Armoured Division. Desert Rat. Bad leg. Shrapnel injury. I remember him. And, of course, his wife.' He kept staring at Bel. 'Never one to forget a pretty face.' He finally let go of Bel's hand.

'Mr Havelock! Mrs Crawford!'

They all turned to see the photographer from the *Sunderland Echo* standing with his camera held to his chest. He had lined up a row of suited men wearing either bowler hats or flat caps. A space had been left in the middle.

'Duty calls,' Mr Havelock said, giving Bel one last, curious look.

And with that Mr Havelock and Miriam turned and were gone. Much to Bel and Helen's relief.

'Let's go before we get hooked in as well,' Helen said, knowing that as soon as the photographer realised there was a third-generation Havelock in his midst, she'd be coerced into posing and playing happy families.

'You all right?' Helen said as they walked across the yard.

'Yes,' Bel said, her voice croaky as she realised she hadn't spoken a word during the whole interaction. 'Do you really have a meeting with Mr Royce?' She desperately wanted to get as far away as possible from Helen's family – from *her* family. She felt trapped.

'I'm afraid so,' Helen said. 'I'll make it as quick as I can – although I have to warn you, the old man does go on.'

'Miss Crawford! Lovely to meet you at long last!'

Helen and Bel had just been shown into the manager's office by Dahlia, whom Helen thought seemed very chirpy and rosy-cheeked. On seeing the man who was presently greeting them, she realised why. He was the epitome of tall, dark and drop-dead gorgeous.

'I'm sorry,' Helen said, 'but we've got a meeting with Mr Royce today.'

'I know, but I'm afraid you've got me instead. My father has had a minor stroke, so I'm the stand-in.' Mr Royce's son stood up straight, walked round the desk and put his hand out. 'Matthew Royce, but please, call me Matthew. I have an aversion to formalities.'

'Well, I'm afraid I *don't* have an aversion to formalities,' Helen said, shaking his hand. 'So, please, call me Miss Crawford. And –' she turned to Bel '– this is Mrs Elliot, my secretary.'

Half an hour later, they were walking back to the car. Bel was thinking lots and saying nothing.

'I know what you're thinking,' Helen said, looking across the yard and comparing it to Thompson's. It was smaller and therefore, in her eyes, not as impressive.

'What's that?' Bel said. She was also looking around the yard, although her reason for doing so was to check that Mr Havelock and Miriam were nowhere to be seen.

'You were thinking,' Helen said, 'that I was a little hard on Mr Matthew Royce and his *aversion to formalities*.'

Bel smiled and nodded.

'The thing is,' Helen said, 'he would *never* have said that to my father – or grandfather, or any other yard manager, for that matter. So why should we be any different? Just because we're women?'

By now they had reached the car.

Helen started fishing about in her handbag for her keys.

'And if Mr Royce thinks me rude, then I say, tough. I'm not in this business to be liked.'

Matthew Royce was standing at the window of his office looking out over the yard. He had both hands in his pockets and a big smile on his face as he watched Miss Crawford and her secretary walk over to a rather snazzy little green sports car. His eyes widened on seeing Miss Crawford walk to the driver's side, then pull out a set of keys from her handbag.

He continued to watch with growing fascination as she very elegantly lowered her very shapely behind into the driver's seat and swung a pair of equally shapely legs into the footwell.

'Dahlia …' he called out, keeping his eyes glued to the car as it slowly made its way out of the main gates.

'Yes, Matthew?' Dahlia stood, lipstick freshly applied, at the door to his office.

'You know what's-her-name … the Irish girl from Thompson's?'

'Marie-Anne?'

'That's the one. You two get on, don't you?'

'Yes, we do. She was just on the phone earlier.'

'Well, wheedle out of her a list of all Miss Crawford's up-and-coming engagements … There's a good girl.'

Chapter Ten

A few minutes after Helen had walked back into her office and bent down to give a surly-looking Winston a stroke, she saw a note on her desk informing her that John had called. Feeling her heart leap with joy, she reprimanded herself.

How sad it was to have only just realised that the excitement she had always felt on seeing John – or even just speaking with him – was not normal when someone was simply a friend. God, she could beat herself with a stick to pay penitence for her total stupidity. Why hadn't she realised that she'd had those feelings because she was in love with him?

She picked up the phone and dialled a number she knew by heart.

'Good afternoon, the Ryhope Emergency Hospital.'

'Afternoon, Denise, how are you?'

Helen listened but didn't hear a word.

'That's good to hear. Can you put me through to Dr Parker, please?'

There were a few moments of dead air before there was a click and Denise was back.

'Sorry, Miss Crawford, but there's no answer. Shall I tell him you called?'

'Yes, please, Denise. Tell him to call me when he gets the chance.'

Helen hung up. The ball was in his court now. She didn't want to be one of those women who didn't know that two's company and three's a crowd.

*

A few minutes after taking the call, Denise spotted Dr Eris walking through the main entrance.

'Hello, Denise, how are you today?' Dr Eris asked.

'I'm good, Dr Eris. Thank you.' She hesitated, not wanting to seem overfamiliar. 'I don't suppose you're going to see Dr Parker by any chance?'

'As it happens, I am. Did you want to pass on a message?'

'You must be a mind-reader as well as a mind-mender,' Denise joked.

Dr Eris laughed. 'If only!'

'Can you tell him that Miss Crawford called, please? She said for him to call whenever it's convenient.'

'Leave it with me, Denise.'

'Here! Catch!' One of the workers had grabbed his mate's flat cap and was tossing it across to another worker. As he did so, he bumped into Polly, causing her to stagger a little and grab hold of the ferry's railing.

'Watch it!' Bel bellowed at the men. 'There's a pregnant woman here yer just about to push into the Wear!'

'Sorry, pet. We didn't realise,' the man said, looking down at Polly's bump.

'I'm fine, honestly,' Polly said, self-consciously pulling her cardigan tighter. Taking Bel by the arm, she manoeuvred her so that they were looking towards the mouth of the river. Bel's explosion of temper had shocked her far more than the shove itself. As had the way Bel had spoken. She'd sounded just like her ma. Not that she'd dare say so, otherwise she might well end up in the Wear after all.

'Are you all right?' Polly asked.

'I'm fine,' Bel said, 'it just really annoys me when buffoons like that are messing about with no consideration for anyone else around them.'

Polly glanced at her sister-in-law – her face was full of fight. She squeezed her arm.

'Come on, Bel, tell me. What's up?' she asked. 'We've known each other since we were bairns. It's not often I see you angry, but when I do there's always a reason – and it's not because of someone having a lark around.'

Bel was quiet for a moment.

'Lucille's almost the same age as we were when we first met ...' she said.

'It seems a long time ago now, doesn't it?' Polly said.

'It does and it doesn't.' Bel looked down at the dark, murky water slapping against the side of the paddler steamer. 'Sometimes it feels just like yesterday.'

'You were sat on your doorstep, crying your eyes out ...' Polly said.

'...'cos Ma had gone off with some spiv,' Bel finished her sentence.

The two women moved to the front of the ferry as it reached the south docks. Polly blushed as the men who had been playing piggy in the middle with the flat cap now splayed out their arms to stop others from pushing through, allowing Polly and Bel to get off first.

'Thank you,' Polly said. She glanced at Bel, who forced a smile.

As they made their way up to High Street East, they walked in silence until they turned left into Norfolk Street.

'It must have been a bit strange for you, going to a launch with Helen this afternoon?' Polly asked tentatively.

Bel ignored the question, instead looking to her left at the Norfolk House pub. It was beginning to fill up with workers who had finished their shift.

'Ma loved that pub,' Bel said. There was no nostalgia in her voice, just hardness.

Polly didn't say anything. She knew the pub had been one of Pearl's haunts as they had gone looking for her there the evening she'd gone on a bender after Maisie's revelation at Bel's wedding.

'I loved that pub because every time Ma went there, she'd go off with some bloke round the back and then afterwards we'd go and get some fish 'n chips.'

Polly could hear the mix of emotions in Bel's voice and asked, 'What happened today?'

Bel looked at her with ice-cold eyes.

'I met him – at the launch.'

Polly didn't have to ask who. Bel had confided in her about who her real father was the night of the air raid. She'd been shocked that Bel had kept it from her for so long, but not as shocked as she had been to learn who Bel's real father was and, moreover, what he'd done. She kept thinking about how it must have felt – to have a baby spawned by rape growing in your belly.

'And did you talk to him?' Polly asked.

'He doesn't really talk to people,' Bel said. 'He talks *at* them.'

They waited to cross the Borough Road, which was busy with trams and men on bikes heading home for their tea.

'He shook my hand,' Bel said, her voice a monotone.

Polly glanced at Bel as they crossed the road.

'And?' she asked.

'And I felt like a coward,' Bel said as they started walking down Tatham Street.

'I don't understand,' Polly said. 'Why would you feel like a coward? You're probably the least cowardly person I know.'

'I felt like Judas. Like I was betraying Ma.'

Polly looked at Bel. Her blue eyes were now shining with tears.

'I should have spat in his face, not shook his hand.'

As they stopped outside their house, Polly could see a return of the anger from earlier.

'Do you want to go somewhere to chat?' Polly asked.

'No, I'm fine, honestly,' Bel said, taking a deep breath and squeezing Polly's hand. 'You need to get your feet up and look after that baby.'

They walked through the open doorway and Bel gave Polly a knowing look.

'And then you can tell us all about your exciting day in the office. And why it is that office work is *so* much more interesting than being a timekeeper.'

Having popped in to see John, who was on the night shift, Dr Eris was making her way back to the asylum. She knew she was taking a bit of a risk by not passing on Helen's message, but she had covered herself. She had purposely gone to check on one of the recently arrived soldiers who had suffered shrapnel injuries but was also exhibiting signs of shell shock – or rather 'post-concussion syndrome', as the government had told them to refer to it. If John found out that she'd been given the message, she could simply claim it had slipped her mind. After all, a traumatised soldier took precedence over something as trivial as passing on a note that a friend had called. *It was hardly the end of the world, was it?*

'Good old Albert,' Agnes muttered as she took some carrots and potatoes, still caked in mud, and put them in the sink.

'He brought you the spoils of his allotment?' Bel asked.

Agnes nodded.

'I've asked him round for some tea tomorrow,' Agnes said.

77

'And I bet you he said, "Aggie, pet, yer dinnit need to feed me just 'cos I brought yer a few manky tats."'

Agnes laughed. 'More or less word-perfect.'

'I think he misses Arthur,' Bel said.

'I think yer right. And he wouldn't be the only one.' Agnes dried her hands on her pinny. She looked at Bel, who was patting Pup, who, in turn, was giving Bel doleful eyes in the hope of a treat.

'So, tell me, Bel, what is it yer want to talk about?' Agnes said as she topped up the pot of tea and gave it a stir. The Irish in her voice was strong, showing she was tired.

'What makes you think there's something I want to talk to you about?' Bel said as she fetched the milk jug.

Agnes sighed.

'Bel, I've known yer since you were knee-high. Yer like one of my own. I can read yer like a book.' She started pouring the tea into cups. 'Which is more than I can say for Pol.' She added milk and pushed Bel's cup and saucer across the table. 'I had no idea she had an ulterior motive for wanting to do office work. I stupidly thought being pregnant had changed her – got her hankering after a job "normal" women do.'

Bel let out a burst of laughter.

'Don't let Polly's squad hear you say that. Or any of the other women working the yards, for that matter. They'll have your guts for garters.'

'Ah, yer know what I mean,' Agnes said.

'Well, they're braver women than me, that's for sure,' Bel said. 'There's no way I'd want to do what they're doing. Hard graft. Dirty work. Dangerous. Out in all weathers.'

'Oh, I think you'd be brave enough 'n could stand the hard graft, 'n the cold – but not the dirt,' Agnes said with a smile.

Bel laughed.

'So, come on,' Agnes said. 'Spit it out. You've had that look on yer face since the moment yer stepped through the door 'n yer did that thing yer always do when yer trying to hide something.'

'Which is?' Bel asked.

'Make everyone else the focus of attention.' Agnes poured tea into her saucer and blew on it to cool it down. 'I'm guessing it must be important if yer've stayed down here with me on one of the rare nights Joe's not out doing his Home Guard duty.'

'I know. I think Major Black and his unit see more of my husband than I do.'

Agnes smiled. She knew her daughter-in-law didn't really mind; if anything, they were both grateful that the Major had signed Joe up shortly after he'd been medically discharged.

Bel looked at her mother-in-law. She looked tired, and for the first time Bel noticed that her hair was now more grey than brown.

'I don't know what I'd have done if you hadn't taken me in and looked after me,' Bel said, her voice a little shaky.

Agnes put her saucer down and gave Bel a look she couldn't quite read. It was as though she was going to tell her something but then decided against it.

'Is this about yer not falling?'

'No,' Bel said wearily. 'I'm actually tired of thinking about not getting pregnant, never mind talking about it.'

Agnes had stopped telling Bel to just 'give it time'. Her daughter-in-law had given birth to Lucille exactly nine months after marrying Agnes's other son, Teddy, who had been killed in North Africa at the start of the war. It was now a year and a half since Bel had tied the knot with Teddy's twin, Joe, and still nothing. Something wasn't right.

'So, if it's not that, what is it?' Agnes asked.

Bel took a deep breath and finally told Agnes what she had told Polly on the night of the air raid. Unlike Polly, though, Agnes was not so much shocked by what had happened to Bel's ma, but rather by who had done it. She also realised with a heavy heart that Bel had been stewing on this for a long time. Almost a year, which was not good. Not good at all.

'When I saw him today,' Bel said, 'I just felt so angry. I kept looking at him acting like butter wouldn't melt, being the centre of attention, having everyone fawning over him. I felt like pushing them all away and screaming at them, telling them what he's really like.'

Agnes rested her hand on Bel's. She knew there were no words she could say to assuage her fury. She could only listen.

'And then I felt so angry with myself for being one of those people. For just standing there, letting him chat away. *For shaking his hand.*'

'It must have been difficult for you at Arthur's funeral as well.'

Bel let out a bark of mirthless laughter.

'I just kept looking at them in the church – him and Miriam – and thinking, "That's my father. That's my sister" – well, half-sister.'

'Which makes Helen your niece,' Agnes said. 'That must be strange too. What with you two working together?'

'It is and it isn't,' Bel said, her anger ebbing. 'I get on with her, which helps.'

'And does she know?'

Bel nodded.

Agnes thought of Helen's impromptu visit the day before the air raid. They'd all thought she'd come to see Polly, but she hadn't; it was Bel she'd wanted.

'Last week. When she came here. She knew?'

'She'd guessed,' Bel said. 'She thought it had been some kind of affair, but Ma put her right.'

Agnes sat back. 'Must have been a blow. To find out that about your own grandfather.'

Bel nodded. 'I think she's been avoiding him. Today – at the launch – was the first time she'd seen him since then. We both couldn't get away quick enough.'

Agnes let out a long sigh.

'Dear me, this is a turn-up for the books.'

She looked at Bel.

'And how are you feeling now?'

'Angry,' Bel said. 'Angry and hurt. It hurts me to think of my ma being so young, just *fifteen years old*, and going through what she had to go through. Then she nearly died having me – *and then couldn't have any more*. He ruined her life. And nearly mine too. Would have if it hadn't been for you – and Pol.'

Bel looked at Agnes.

'I feel like I've spent my whole life being angry at Ma, but I understand now – you know – why she was the way she was.'

Bel slumped in her chair, exhaustion beginning to replace the anger.

'But most of all I'm angry that man's gone through his entire life totally unpunished for what he's done. And I keep feeling so frustrated because I want to do something about it, but I don't know what.'

After finishing her shift at the pub, Pearl walked over the whitewashed front doorstep and straight into the hallway. Agnes tended to leave her door open, especially in the warm weather, but today it was because of the haddock stew she'd cooked and the live crabs she'd boiled up after a trip to the quayside. Leaning against the wall, Pearl took off her shoes and rubbed her feet. It had been a busy night and she'd not even had her usual ten-minute fag break.

'*So, come on. Spit it out.*'

It was Agnes.

Pearl continued to listen.

And Bel.

Pearl didn't move. It wasn't in her nature to eavesdrop, but there was something about her daughter's tone of voice that sounded serious. Leaning forward and straining to catch everything Bel was saying, her heart sank. *That bloody man.* It was bad enough he'd tainted her life; now he was contaminating *her daughter's*.

When it sounded as if the conversation was coming to a natural end, Pearl quietly put her shoes back on; as she did so, thoughts of Henrietta sprang to mind. Not that thoughts of Charles's wife were ever far from her mind these days, not since they'd been reacquainted at the asylum.

Pearl gave the front door a good push, making it sound as though she had just come in.

'Eee, I dinnit knar,' she said, clomping down the hallway, 'any Tom, Dick or Harry can just come waltzing in here.'

Pearl walked through the kitchen doorway.

'And I think they'd waltz straight back out as soon as they got a whiff of the place,' Agnes batted back.

'Aye, yer right there.' Pearl acted surprised on seeing Bel. 'Eee, yer up late. What's up?'

'Nothing, Ma,' Bel said, getting up and giving Tramp and Pup a quick pat on the head each. They were curled up by the range. 'See you in the morning.'

'Aye,' Pearl said, heading towards the back door. 'See yer in the morning.'

She looked at Agnes, who was taking off her pinny.

'Last one of the day,' she said, poking in her handbag and pulling out her cigarettes.

'Night, Pearl,' Agnes said as she walked out the kitchen and padded up the stairs to her room.

Opening the back door, Pearl felt one of the dogs brush past her and trot out into the backyard.

For the next few minutes while she smoked her fag, Pearl kept hearing her daughter's words loop round in her head.

I want to do something about it, but I don't know what.

Agnes might have practically brought her daughter up, but Isabelle was still her flesh and blood and she knew that girl better than anyone. Better even than Agnes did. And what she'd heard this evening did not bode well. It wasn't just Bel's deep-seated anger and long-held resentments that were causing Pearl concern – but more what was bubbling underneath.

Bel wanted – *needed* – retribution.

And worse still, Pearl knew Bel would not rest until she'd got it.

Chapter Eleven

Sunday 23 May

'Before we all start this morning,' Rosie said to Gloria, Martha, Dorothy and Angie, who were all sitting on a large stack of wooden pallets within a stone's throw of the edge of the river, 'I want to say thank you for really pushing yourselves that extra mile this week. *Denewood*'s nearly there. I reckon we can get her finished today, which means tomorrow they can start getting her ready for her sea trials.'

'So, she's only a week behind schedule?' Martha asked, taking out a packet of biscuits from her holdall.

'If that – they've managed to do quite a bit of the fitting out while we've been patching her up,' Rosie said, topping up her tin cup from her tea flask.

'Well, it's good to know the long hours have been worth it,' Angie said, yawning.

'And thanks for coming in today. I know how much you enjoy your Sunday lie-in,' Rosie said. 'Especially after a night at the Ritz.'

Rosie, Gloria and Martha looked at Dorothy and Angie, who still looked half-asleep.

'I know this is the fourteenth day on the run you've had without a day off, so next week you've got the whole week-end off – boss's orders,' Rosie said, shaking her head when Martha offered her a biscuit.

'Brilliant,' Dorothy said, smiling at Martha and taking two biscuits, then handing one to Angie. 'That means we can go out on Friday night as well, doesn't it, Ange?'

Angie didn't look so sure. 'I think that might be when Quentin's coming up. I said any night but Saturday.' She took her biscuit from Dorothy and bit into it.

'I'm sure Dorothy won't mind,' Gloria said, declining Martha's offering and patting her belly; she'd struggled to get her waistline back after having Hope. *'Will you?'* Gloria glared at her workmate.

'Looks like I don't have a choice,' Dorothy said in a surly voice.

'So,' Rosie said, taking one last sip of tea and throwing the remnants onto the concrete, 'we've just got the very top part of the hull to finish off today, which means scaffolding work and vertical welds.'

Angie groaned through a mouth full of oatmeal biscuit.

'But not overhead,' Rosie reassured, picking up her haversack.

'Thank goodness for that,' Dorothy said. 'We're going to have arms like Popeye if we keep on like this.'

They all looked at Martha.

'Not that there's anything wrong with having arms like Popeye,' Dorothy added, nudging her.

'Come on, then, let's get this done,' Rosie said, putting the top back on her flask.

As they trooped over to the dry basin, Rosie waved up at the admin office window.

Gloria looked up to see Charlotte smiling down at them and waving back. 'I would have thought she'd have been enjoying a lie-in and having the house to herself?'

Rosie sighed. 'No such luck. In her words, "that's what boarding school does to you."'

'What?' Angie asked. 'Makes you *not* wanna have a lie-in?'

They all navigated round a haphazardly stacked pile of sheet metal.

'I think it's more that it's a hard habit to break,' Rosie said.

Angie guffawed. 'What? Getting up at the crack of dawn?'

'It's a different life,' Dorothy tried to explain. 'Going to boarding school.'

Angie resolved to quiz Quentin about *his* boarding school.

They stepped over a load of metal girders that had been laid out on the ground.

'And I'm guessing because she was always with other people from dawn to dusk, she's finding it hard to be on her own,' Dorothy said. As a child she had often dreamed of going off to boarding school so she wouldn't be on her own so much.

'I think that could be part of the reason,' Rosie said.

'Is she all right?' Gloria asked. All the women now knew that Charlie had recently found out the truth about Rosie's 'other life'.

'I think so. She seems OK. She's not been down or upset or angry, quite the reverse. But she doesn't seem to want to be on her own at all. And I mean *at all*.'

'Hence her being here on a Sunday morning?' Gloria said, waving over to Jimmy, the head riveter, who was heading over to the platers' shed.

'Exactly,' Rosie said. 'I said she could come with me today if she stayed up in the office and did her homework – I even tried to put her off by saying that there was a good chance Helen would be in and that if she needed her to do any chores, she had to oblige – but even that didn't work.'

'And what about her little friend Marjorie?'

'Thank goodness, she's planning on going to see her next week, but she doesn't want to stay over.'

'She probably just needs time to adjust,' Gloria said as they reached the dry basin.

'I hope so,' said Rosie.

Five hours later, they all downed tools.

'We've done it!' Dorothy declared.

'We certainly have. Well done, everyone,' Rosie said, looking at her workmates' dirt-smeared faces. Everyone looked shattered.

'I'm guessing everyone's heading home – and then staying home?' Rosie asked, looking over to see Charlotte appearing through the double doors at the bottom of the admin block.

Everyone mumbled that was exactly what they were going to do.

'You too?' Martha asked.

'No such luck,' said Rosie, with forced laughter.

Everyone looked round to follow her gaze.

'Charlie has repeated several times over that it's been a *whole week* since she saw Lily, so we're popping in for a little while.'

'*Entrez! Entrez!*' Lily waved Charlotte and Rosie across the threshold of the West Lawn bordello in Ashbrooke.

'*Ma chère,*' she exclaimed, putting her heavily jewelled hands on Charlotte's shoulders and planting a kiss on both cheeks. 'It has been one whole week since I have seen my favourite fourteen-going-on-fifteen-year-old.'

Rosie sighed, knowing when it came to Lily and Charlotte, she was fighting a losing battle. She might as well be done with it now and capitulate, saving herself some time and energy. The madam of a bordello, though, would not have been her first choice as a substitute mother for her little sister.

'Go straight into the kitchen, Charlotte,' Lily said, opening her fan with the flick of a wrist. 'If you ask nicely, I'm sure Vivian will make you one of her special *chocolats chauds*.' She started fanning herself. 'Just thinking about it has me breaking out into a hot sweat.'

'*Délicieux! Et merci!*' Charlotte spoke French like a native.

'I'm going to take that child to *gai Paris* one day when this wretched war is over,' Lily promised, more to herself than to Rosie.

Hurrying down the hallway, Charlotte disappeared into the kitchen.

Rosie could hear Vivian's American drawl welcoming her – her impersonation of Mae West now pretty perfect – then Maisie's southern accent commenting on how Charlotte's hair could do with a good cut and didn't she fancy having a bob.

'How long have we got?' Rosie asked.

'Until seven,' Lily sighed dramatically. 'Then the pumpkin turns into a carriage and the first clients arrive. Or is it the other way round?' She waved her hand dismissively. 'Anyway, tell me, how's she been?'

Rosie pulled a face.

'Clingy.'

This past week, Rosie had not been to the bordello, which she now part-owned, due to Charlotte sticking to her like a limpet and her not having the heart to abandon her sister at home on her own.

'Mmm,' Lily said. 'Not surprising, all things considered. Could be worse.' It had been Lily who had told Charlotte about Rosie's former life as a call girl and the vile actions of her uncle Raymond.

She looked at Rosie.

'You look tired, my dear. Not often I see you with dark circles,' she said, before turning and walking down the hallway.

'So, *ma petite* ...' Lily bustled into the kitchen and took a seat at the head of the table. 'We want to hear all about you and what you've been up to.'

Before Charlotte had time to answer, they heard the front door clash shut and the sound of a walking stick striking the parquet flooring.

'George, *mon amour*!' Lily looked at Charlotte and winked. 'Come and join us. We're slumming it in the kitchen.'

George appeared, looking dapper, as always, in a grey three-piece suit and tie.

'Ah, Charlotte, lovely to see you.' He took off his trilby and smiled at their guest.

'Sit down, darling.' Lily pulled out the chair next to her and patted the cushioned seat. 'Charlotte was just going to regale us with what's been happening this week.'

'Nothing. Just school,' Charlotte said as Vivian put a steaming hot chocolate down in front of her. *'Merci beaucoup,'* she said to Vivian, who was wearing a cream-coloured dress with a plunging neckline that left little to the imagination.

'De rien.' Vivian somehow always seemed to make any French words she spoke sound American.

'No after-school clubs? Hockey matches?' Lily asked.

'We played a tournament yesterday,' Charlotte said.

'And?' Lily asked.

'We were runners-up,' Charlotte said.

'Charlie!' Kate came bustling into the kitchen. She was holding a dress over her arm as though she were a maître d'. As always, Kate looked chic but comfortable, her trade-mark black stylish rather than sombre. An onlooker would never have guessed she had spent years begging and living rough before her old friend Rosie had spotted her in a shop doorway and taken her to Lily's, where she had been given a bed, clean clothing – and, most importantly, a sewing machine.

'How are you?' She went over to Charlotte and gave her a kiss on both cheeks.

She looked at the blue dress Rosie's younger sister was wearing – and which she had worn every time Kate had seen her since she had made it for her.

'Pop into the boutique when you get a chance and I'll see if I can rustle up a summer dress for you,' she said.

'My, my, Charlie,' Vivian said, putting her hands on her hips and widening her eyes, 'consider yourself honoured. Most of us have to wait in line for Coco Chanel here to work her magic.' She looked at Kate and raised a perfectly arched eyebrow. 'Unless your name's Alfie, of course, and then you just go straight to the front of the queue.' Alfie was the former timekeeper at Thompson's who had recently got a job in admin. It was obvious to just about everyone but Kate that he was sweet on her, and that he called upon her seamstress's skills as an excuse to spend time with her.

'Alfie gets pushed to the front of the queue because his tend to be just quick tailoring jobs,' Kate defended.

Vivian and Maisie looked at each other. They had joked on more than one occasion that Alfie purposely ripped his clothes so as to have an excuse to see Kate.

'Never mind *Alfie*,' Vivian cooed as she inspected the dress draped across Kate's slender arm. 'This looks *fabulous*. I do believe it's been worth the wait.'

'Why don't you try it on?' Kate said, handing over the dress.

Vivian gently took the garment as though it were a sleeping child she did not want to wake.

'I'll come and give you a hand,' Maisie said, putting her cup of tea down.

George went to put on a record of the Glenn Miller Orchestra playing *Rhapsody in Blue*, a choice met with relief by Lily, who had been complaining about George's new affinity for what she called 'screeching jazz', and a few minutes later Vivian and Maisie were back – with the bordello's very own Mae West giving an impromptu fashion show in her new dress.

For the next hour Charlotte revelled in the chatter and laughter filling the kitchen and in the company of those she now felt were family. A rather unusual – some might say dysfunctional – family, but a loving and caring one all the same. Lily had become a surrogate mother of sorts, replacing the one Charlotte had lost when she was just eight, while George had become a quiet but concerned fatherly figure. Maisie and Vivian were akin to two eccentric aunties who just wanted to have fun and would happily lead Charlie astray if Rosie was not on guard.

Kate was definitely the 'middle sister', having known Charlotte as a small child when she'd lived in the same village. By an uncanny coincidence, she and Charlotte had been orphaned at the same age, albeit years apart. But whereas Charlotte had been sent to a posh all-girls' boarding school in Yorkshire, Kate had been taken to live with the nuns who ran the Nazareth House children's home – a place that was far more ungodly than any house of ill repute.

Later on that evening, after Rosie and Charlotte were long gone and the bordello was bustling with activity, Maisie popped her head round the kitchen door.

'Sorry,' she said, seeing that Lily and Kate were poring over bridal magazines spread out on the table. 'I'll come back later.'

'No, no, *ma chère*, come in. I can sense Kate is getting tetchy because she's been parted from her beloved Singer for at least an hour.' Lily looked at Kate. 'She always starts shuffling round on her chair and I know my time's up.'

Kate tutted but didn't deny the accusation; instead, she gathered up her magazines and made quick her exit, ducking under Maisie's arm as she held the door open.

'Good job I've got plenty of time before the big day,' Lily said.

'You still set on a New Year's Eve wedding?' Maisie asked as she shut the door.

'I am,' Lily said, getting up and retrieving a bottle of Rémy from the armoire. 'Although which New Year's Eve that might be, I'm not so sure.' She winked at Maisie and poured out two brandies.

'I'm guessing whatever you want to tell me is confidential?' Lily asked, waving her arm at the chair adjacent to hers.

'It is,' Maisie said, 'and it's a tricky one.'

She sat down at the table, crossed her legs and put her slender, manicured hands around her glass.

'Can you remember a while ago when I was worried about a client?'

'That he might be Bel's father?'

'That's right,' Maisie said.

'And it all sorted itself out – it wasn't him?' Lily said.

'That's right. It did. Thank God.'

Lily took a sip of her brandy.

'The thing is …' Maisie paused, re-crossing her slim, stockinged legs.

'Go on,' Lily said, reaching for her Gauloises.

'Night, Geraldine … Night, Pearl!'

Bill was standing at the doorway to the Tatham, his attention momentarily drawn away from his two barmaids by a striking full moon, its beauty visible thanks to a perfectly clear night sky.

'Aye, night night, Bill,' Pearl shouted out as she crossed the road. 'Mind the lops don't bite!'

Geraldine swung her gas mask over her shoulder and looked at Bill, whose attention was now back on Pearl. He was laughing. He'd been in good spirits since last week's air raid; some might say it was because he'd dodged death, but Geraldine thought it had more to do with how well he'd been getting on with Pearl. *God only knew what he saw in her.*

'See yer tomorrow, Bill,' she said, gazing up at the star-speckled sky. She felt a shiver go down her back. The sky was clear. Just like the night of the last air raid. Clearer, in fact, for tonight the moon was full and bright, as though rebelling against the blackout.

Chapter Twelve

When the air raid alarm sounded out at exactly 2.49 a.m., Charlotte woke with a start.

She had gone to bed thinking about whether there was an afterlife and if her parents knew all that had happened after they had died, and if there was, did that mean her uncle Raymond was there too? She hoped not and that instead he would be stuck in purgatory – it seemed the least he could expect as punishment for everything he had done.

'You know the drill!'

She heard Rosie's voice through the wall and forced herself out of her warm bed and into her siren suit.

A few minutes later, she and Rosie were making their bleary-eyed way into Mr and Mrs Jenkins' Anderson shelter in the back garden next door.

The Elliot household, as well as Beryl and her daughters, Iris and Audrey, had made it round the corner to the air raid shelter in Tavistock Place in record speed.

'You feeling all right?' Agnes asked Polly, who was wrapping a blanket around herself and Lucille. The little girl had snuggled up and had her head on her aunty's bump.

Polly nodded, brushing her niece's blonde hair away from her forehead.

'We're fine,' she said, smiling. 'All three of us.'

Reassured, Agnes sat back and started chatting to Beryl.

Polly looked across at Pearl, who was curled up with her coat wrapped around her, gently snoring; the woman could sleep through anything.

Next to her was Bel, who had her head on Joe's shoulder. Her eyes were closed. Seeing her brother and her sister-in-law together, their arms wrapped around one another, Polly felt the slightest twinge of envy.

What she wouldn't give for Tommy to be here with her now.

She closed her eyes and let her mind's eye conjure up a picture of the man she loved. She saw Tommy as she had that first time, when he was being hauled out of the river after a dive. Her heart still hammered remembering how the linesmen had removed his huge twelve-bolt copper helmet and she'd seen him. It really had been love at first sight. She pictured Tommy standing at the altar, looking so handsome in his Royal Navy uniform, his eyes glued to her as she walked down the aisle. Recalling that day, and their 'back to front honeymoon' at the Major's flat, made her feel almost giddy with happiness. She just wished she could stay in that moment – at least until the air raid ended.

But the tremors from the bombs that had just started to drop on the town wouldn't let her and instead her thoughts moved on to her near miscarriage, and the awful feeling she still couldn't shake of what it would feel like if she lost her baby – as well as Tommy. It was now five months since Tommy had left for Gibraltar. Five months of yanking mines off the hulls of enemy ships.

Everyone thought she was being so stoic about Tommy going back to Gibraltar, but when she had been faced with losing his baby – coupled with the very real chance that she might also lose Tommy – she'd known she wouldn't be able to carry on.

That feeling was still fresh and had persevered despite Dr Billingham's reassurances that she and her baby were 'doing just fine'.

Her bravery was conditional, and in her mind that wasn't being brave at all.

'So, Mother, did you have a good time at the launch?'

'Which one?' Miriam said, pulling the quilt she had brought from her room more tightly around her shoulders.

'The *Chiswick*,' Helen said.

'Was that Doxford's or Pickersgill's?' Miriam asked. 'They all blur into one after a while.'

'Pickersgill's,' Helen said, taking a sip of her water and putting it back on the little side table next to her chair.

'Ah, yes, I did, thank you very much.' Miriam eyed her daughter as she lit another candle. 'There was a little drinks do afterwards. It would seem Mr Royce's son is nothing like his dear papa.'

'Why?' Helen asked. 'Because he wants to drink and schmooze and socialise rather than roll up his sleeves and do a decent day's work?'

'Well, darling, being a workaholic has done Mr Royce senior no favours. No favours at all.'

'Because he's had a minor stroke?' Helen asked.

Miriam let out a scathing laugh. 'Darling, I don't know what you've heard, but the stroke was far from minor. The old man's finished. Apparently, he's paralysed down one side and talking like a drunk.'

Helen was riled by her mother's total lack of compassion. She liked Mr Royce. He was a fair, straight-up man. He would never have partied while his employees worked. Even after a launch.

'I think your grandfather was rather disappointed that you and your little friend didn't stay and partake of the festivities,' Miriam said, opening the door of the cabinet next to the single bed she was sitting on.

'Mrs Elliot is not a "little friend", Mother – she was there in her capacity as my secretary.'

'I thought that Irish girl was your secretary?' Miriam said, pulling out a half-bottle of Gordon's.

'They both are,' Helen said, watching her mother. There hadn't been the slightest hint that she thought Bel was anything but a friend and co-worker. It cemented her belief that her mother had no idea the woman she had been chatting to earlier on in the week was her sister.

'Oh, who's getting all la-di-da. *Two* secretaries.' Miriam poured a slosh of gin into a glass tumbler she had retrieved from the cabinet.

'And your grandfather wasn't the only one disappointed by your no-show after the launch.' She took a sip of neat gin and grimaced. 'Mr Royce Junior was also decidedly down in the mouth you didn't grace us with your presence.'

Now it was Helen's turn to ignore her mother. She started looking around for a blanket. Finding one, she shook it out and wrapped it around her shoulders.

'I told him that you were all work and no play, and that was why you were still single and hadn't been snapped up.' Miriam paused. 'However, I might have let it slip that you were being hotly pursued by a highly regarded and very eligible surgeon from one of the county's top hospitals.'

Helen's head snapped up and she looked at her mother.

'That really annoys me!' Helen spat out the words and glared at her mother through the semi-darkness. 'You have no right talking to complete strangers about me like that. And John is not "pursuing" me. Like I've told you a million times already – *we're just friends.*'

'Darling, don't be getting all irate at me—'

They heard an explosion and Miriam took a large sip of her gin. 'God, I'm going to have to remember to bring some tonic down here next time ... So, where was I? That's it ... You see, Helen, sometimes you have to listen to your old mama. I know you think I can be scheming –'

Miriam ignored Helen's forced laughter.

'– but, you see, you have to play your cards right,' she lectured, 'and sometimes in this world you have to be a little manipulative to get what you want. Much as I know how fond you are of dear Dr Parker, there's not a cat in hell's chance of bagging him for a husband. I'd bet my inheritance that John likes you – more than likes you – and definitely finds you attractive – that goes without saying – but he will never marry you. I know it hurts to hear this, but he knows too much about you – and quite simply, he won't want used goods. It's just the way men are. Men of a certain standing, anyway.'

Helen took a deep breath to stop herself from going over to her mother and shaking the living daylights out of her.

'But Mr Royce Junior, on the other hand,' Miriam continued, 'doesn't know anything about you. Just all the good stuff. And even if he were to know, he's a widower, and widowers are known for preferring a woman who might have been round the block once – or even twice. Providing they've been discreet, of course.'

Helen looked at her mother.

'Quite finished?'

Miriam took a quick sip of her drink. 'So, I told him he'd better stake his claim before the good doctor.'

Helen let out a gasp of exasperation.

'Well, you seem to have it all worked out, don't you, Mother dearest. There's only one problem – I'm not remotely interested in either Mr Royce or getting married, so I'm afraid you're wasting your time and your breath.'

'Give it another year,' Miriam said with complete confidence. 'You're no spring chicken and you'll be even less of a one this time next year.'

'We'll see,' Helen said, equally confident.

There was another explosion and they were quiet for a moment.

'On a completely different topic,' Helen said, 'now that we're both down here and being so honest and open with each other, I think it would be the perfect opportunity to talk about the elephant in the room.'

Miriam looked round the small, dark basement.

'What elephant?' she laughed. 'I don't see any elephant.'

They both jerked automatically on hearing another explosion.

'Although it sounds like there's a few stomping round out there.' Miriam looked up at the basement ceiling.

'The elephant being Father,' Helen said. 'And the fact that it is now totally ridiculous that you won't allow him to come back here.' Helen thought of Gloria and Hope. If her father was back home, he'd be with them now, making sure they were both safe. 'I really think you have made your point – that you have made everyone suffer enough.'

'*Pfft!*' Miriam almost choked on her gin. 'Suffer enough? *They're* not suffering. Your father's doing what he loves – only over the border – and I hardly think his bit on the side and his bastard are suffering. They've got a cosy little flat. She's got a job which, by all accounts, is a decent wage, especially as she's only got two mouths to feed. *And* she's got shot of that husband of hers, although I think she was foolish to divorce him. Chances are he'll die out there in the Arctic and if he does, she will have missed out on a nice payout.'

'God, Mother, have you not a shred of humanity in you?'

'I have humanity for those who deserve it,' she said.

There was another muffled explosion.

Helen took a deep breath.

'It's wrong to keep a father from his daughter, and I don't just mean Hope – I'm talking about myself. I don't think you've ever once considered what it's been like for me not having Dad here.'

Miriam tutted. 'Oh, you're a big girl now, Helen. I'm sure you'll survive.'

Her comments were followed by the sound of another bomb hitting the town.

They were quiet for a while.

'The point is, Mother,' Helen said, deciding to change track. She hadn't really believed a call on her mother's empathy would work; she should have known, you can't play on something that doesn't exist. 'Even if you don't care about anyone's suffering other than your own, I still believe you need to allow Father to come back home – while you can still control the situation.'

Miriam sat up. 'What do you mean, "control the situation"?'

'What I mean, Mother, is that the time might come when Angie's mam leaves her husband and takes up with her young chap, and when Dorothy's mother comes clean about her bigamy and works out some kind of a deal with the town's magistrates. She's got money – and "standing". I can't see her being hauled in front of the courts, or worse still, put in jail. And as for Martha, well, I'm getting to know her a little more of late, and I don't think she would really give two hoots who knows what about the woman who gave birth to her.' Helen was pleased with the plausibility of her argument. She was even convincing herself. 'Use your head, Mother. People are going to start to wonder and ask why it is that Father is in Scotland while his family and workplace are here.' Helen stared at her mother through the flickering darkness. 'I'm sure you could come to some arrangement with Dad whereby he keeps his relationship with Gloria under wraps for a while. Do it gradually so it doesn't cause a stir.'

Miriam looked at her daughter and smiled.

'Oh Helen, you really have no idea, do you?'

Helen saw the coldness in her mother's eyes – and something else that she couldn't quite decipher.

'This isn't just about making your father suffer, or that woman and her brat. Or because I don't want the scandal or the humiliation. This is about *me*,' she said. '*I* don't want him in this town, never mind in his house, or working down the road. I'd banish him to the Outer Hebrides if I could, never mind just Glasgow. This is about *me*,' Miriam repeated.

'*I don't want to ever set eyes on your father ever again as long as I'm still drawing breath*,' she hissed.

And that's when Helen realised what she had seen in her mother's cold blue eyes.

Hurt.

And it was a hurt that cut deep.

'The Germans couldn't have wished for a better night for it,' Dr Eris said, looking at the full moon. She was standing with Dr Parker, staring at the glowing skies blanketing Sunderland town. The teardrops of orange flares would have seemed almost pretty as they sailed down onto the town like a snow flurry, had they not been followed by Hitler's harbingers of death. There had been countless explosions and from where they were standing it looked as though the whole town was on fire.

'I know,' Dr Parker said, not attempting to disguise his anger.

Dr Eris took his hand and squeezed it. They had talked quite a lot during the past week about the war and John had confessed to her that he felt frustrated that the Ministry of War had turned down his repeated requests to use his skills on the front line. She knew the ire she was hearing was partly caused by that, but also by the feeling of powerlessness that came hand in hand with every air raid.

'Don't be bitter,' she said. 'You're saving lives here. And what's more, you're giving these men the hope of a future.' Dr Eris had heard what a brilliant surgeon John was – how he had saved both lives and limbs, and that he was spending every spare minute he had researching advancements in prosthetics.

'Do you know how many casualties are expected?' Dr Eris asked.

'No, we were just told to be on standby. We're full to the brim, so I've given instructions to bring them here so they won't have to worry about numbers.'

'Dr Eris!'

They both turned to see one of the nurses at the main entrance.

'Coming, Nurse Howden!' Dr Eris shouted back.

She gently took hold of the lapels of Dr Parker's white coat and kissed him on the lips. 'Pop in for a cup of tea when you've patched everyone up, and don't worry about the gossips. Let them have their fun.' She looked into the distance at the sanguine skyline. 'God only knows, we have to take it when we can.'

Dr Parker nodded. He looked over at Nurse Howden, whose body language spoke her impatience.

'You better go. I'll see you later.'

Looking back towards the town, Dr Parker's thoughts naturally went to Helen.

Providing she was in her basement, she'd be all right. And at this time of the morning she wouldn't be anywhere else. Would she?

All of a sudden, he felt a stab of jealousy that seemed to come out of nowhere.

Perhaps that was why she hadn't called him back. Too busy with someone else?

He immediately reprimanded himself.

How could he be jealous when he had just started seeing Claire?

Noticing a vehicle's headlights swing round off the main road and start up the long drive to the hospital's entrance, Dr Parker flashed his torch to show them the way.

When would he get it through his thick skull that he and Helen were simply friends?

Chapter Thirteen

The raid in the early hours of Monday morning lasted just under one hour and twenty minutes. The Heinkel bombers had first dropped flares, which, aided by an unusually bright full moon, had laid the town bare. They hit homes and factories, shops and shipyards, leaving scars that would remain on the landscape of the town for many years to come, and on the souls of those living there for ever.

As soon as the all-clear sounded out, Martha was out of the front door. Mr and Mrs Perkins knew it was pointless trying to stop her. Wild horses wouldn't prevent her from doing what she could to save lives. Seeing a fire engine heading down Villette Road, Martha followed it. In its wake came an ambulance, followed by an army truck that pulled over, its passenger door swinging open, signalling Martha to climb in.

Passing a huge crater that looked at least thirty feet deep, the driver told Martha that was where a 1,000-kilo bomb had dropped, but amazingly no one had been hurt.

A few minutes later the convoy arrived at the far end of Lodge Terrace, where a surface air raid shelter had once stood. Before the bombs had dropped, the communal shelter had been a substantial brick and concrete structure built to hold around forty people. Twenty-eight minutes after the sirens had sounded out and families had ensconced themselves inside, a 250-kilo bomb had hit. The walls had shattered, and the shelter had canted over to an angle of about fifteen degrees. Two women and a mother and her children had managed to scramble out and raise the alarm, but the rest of the men, women and children remained trapped inside.

Martha, along with firefighters and other wardens, worked frantically to free those trapped, digging by the light of a nearby fire started by incendiaries. They lifted and heaved blocks of stone with their bare hands before some tools were scavenged from a garage down the road and used to aid their attempts at rescuing those inside.

Shortly after Angie and Dorothy had got Mrs Kwiatkowski back to her flat, her phone rang.

'You get it, Angela.' She pointed a shaky finger at the black Bakelite. 'I've a feeling it'll be for you.'

'Hello?' Angie said, looking across at Dorothy, who was making a pot of tea.

'*Quentin!*'

Dorothy and Mrs Kwiatkowski looked at each other and smiled.

'Yes, yes, we're all fine,' said Angie. 'We've just got back to Mrs Kwiatkowski's. Dor's making us a brew.'

She listened.

'No, our street's not been hit.'

Another pause.

'No, don't worry, we'll stay indoors.' She looked over at Dorothy and rolled her eyes.

'Anyway, what yer deeing up at this time?' She glanced up at Mrs Kwiatkowski's kitchen clock. 'It's quarter-past four in the morning, yer knar?'

She listened intently.

'Oh, I see, all right then, see yer next week.'

She put the phone down just as Dorothy was putting a cup of tea into Mrs Kwiatkowski's hands.

'How's lover boy?' Dorothy asked.

'I wish yer would stop calling him that, Dor, it's starting to really get on my wick.' She glowered at Dorothy who was adding a heaped spoon of sugar into Mrs Kwiatkowski's tea.

'He wanted to know if we were *all* OK.' She cocked her head over at Mrs Kwiatkowski, whose hands were still shaking slightly.

'Mmm,' Dorothy said, taking the old woman her cup.

'Thank you, my dear,' Mrs Kwiatkowski said. 'That boy works too hard,' she suddenly declared, before taking a sip of her tea.

'How did he know about the raid?' Dorothy asked, putting the tea cosy on the kettle and the milk back into the little refrigerator.

'Said he was working late,' Angie said, picking up both of their gas masks, 'and that it came "down the wires".'

Dorothy gave another 'Mmm,' before bobbing down next to their elderly neighbour. 'We'll come and check on you in about half an hour, all right?'

'Be careful. The pair of you!' Mrs Kwiatkowski raised her voice.

'We will,' Angie reassured.

'Won't be long,' Dorothy said, as they hurried out the flat.

Five minutes after heading back up to their own flat, they'd changed into their work overalls and were clomping across the cobbles to check that Gloria's flat was still standing, and then along to Tatham Street, which, they were relieved to see, had also escaped the bombs. Walking into the town centre, Dorothy made a joke that it was a good job the museum hadn't been hit as Angie would still get to meet the 'old masters', but her attempt at humour fell on deaf ears.

As they turned the corner into Fawcett Street, they saw that a bomb had been dropped into the empty shell of the already blitzed Binns – once the town's most exclusive store. Dorothy looked at where she had once worked as a sales assistant in the china department. The world they now inhabited couldn't be any more different.

Stopping an exhausted-looking fire warden heading towards Holmeside, Dorothy asked which streets had been hit. Feeling reassured that the rest of those they knew and loved were all right, they headed back home, where they found Mrs Kwiatkowski fast asleep in her chair, still clutching her cup of tea.

Relieved the air raid was over, everyone hurried back to Tatham Street, all apart from Pearl, who idled behind, making the excuse that she wanted to have a fag and get some fresh air, which Bel told her was a complete contradiction in terms.

As she watched her daughter walk on ahead with Agnes on one side and Joe carrying Lucille on the other, Pearl once again thought about the conversation she had overheard the other night between her daughter and Agnes – and, again, about her recent discovery that Henrietta was not only still alive, but incarcerated in the local nuthouse.

She wondered, not for the first time, about Henrietta's real reason for giving her a job when it had been made clear by Eddy the butler that none were available. He'd made a point of telling Henrietta that they had just replaced the last girl who had got herself in the family way and already had more staff than they needed. Had it simply been because a pitiful-looking Pearl had reminded Henrietta of her own daughters, or her beloved Hans Christian Andersen character – or was it something more sinister? Had Henrietta known about everything that had happened to her after stepping over the polished-brass threshold of the house on Glen Path? Or had she been oblivious to it all?

*

'Careful there, Mr Havelock.' Eddy took the old man's arm and helped him up the last few steps out of the cellar and into the main kitchen.

'I'm fine!' Mr Havelock grumbled. 'You're my butler, not my damned nurse!'

Eddy had to bite his tongue. He was just about anything the master wanted him to be at any given moment in time.

'Do you want a hot drink?' Agatha asked as they all finally made it out of the cellar and into the kitchen. They all stood, taking a moment to get their breath back.

Mr Havelock ignored the housekeeper and shuffled out of the kitchen, shouting over his shoulder, 'I'll have a brandy, Eddy. In the office. Quick as you like.'

He was angry that he felt so tired and his body so stiff after being cramped up for the past hour and a half. Dropping down into the leather seat of his chair, he leant forward and snatched up the phone. Dialling a number that he knew off pat, he cleared his voice and waited, hoping that no one would answer. He cursed under his breath when he heard the click of the phone being picked up. The place was still standing.

'Good morning, this is the Sunderland Borough Asylum, how can I help you?' The elderly voice sounded tired but still completely professional.

'Ah, Genevieve? Is that you?' The old man pressed the receiver to his ear; lately even his damned hearing seemed to be failing him.

'It is ... Is this Mr Havelock?'

'It *is*, Genevieve,' Mr Havelock barked down the phone. 'So glad to hear you're all right and have survived this damnable raid. I'm praying that the asylum is still in one piece?' There was still a shred of hope that part of the place might have taken a hit.

He listened, clenching his hand in frustration.

'Good, good. As long as everyone's all right?'

Hearing Eddy knock lightly on the office door, he bellowed across the room, 'Come in!'

He returned his attention to the handset. 'My apologies, Genevieve. What were you just saying?'

He listened, pointing to the spot on his desk where he wanted Eddy to put his large glass of brandy.

'What? The colliery got hit?' Mr Havelock again shouted down the phone.

He looked up at Eddy, who was waiting to be dismissed. Mr Havelock shooed him away as one might dismiss a tiresome child.

'Any casualties?' Another bark.

He listened.

'Just the one? Still – one too many.' He uttered the words expected in such a situation.

'Well, Genevieve, call me when you get his name and I'll make sure the poor chap's family can give him a decent burial.'

Mr Havelock listened as the old receptionist said what she knew would be expected in the light of such generosity, before hanging up.

Sipping on his brandy, Mr Havelock looked down at his desk. Seeing the small business card embossed with the words *The Ashbrooke Gentlemen's Club*, he allowed himself a smile. He had heard extremely positive feedback about the place. As most of his friends were either six foot under or incapable, with Dr Billingham in tow he wouldn't have to patronise the place on his own.

At least there was something to look forward to, even if Jerry couldn't manage to drop a bomb on the one place that, if obliterated, would relieve him of a burden that had been dragging at his heels for what felt like an eternity.

Chapter Fourteen

'I could just go to Lily's for breakfast and then go to school from there,' Charlotte argued as they were walking up Tunstall Vale. They were passing the turn into West Lawn.

'No, not without giving Lily notice. That's not fair. Or good manners,' she said.

'I don't think Lily would mind,' Charlotte persevered.

Rosie sighed as they crossed the road and continued along the Cloisters. She doubted very much whether Lily would either.

Turning left onto Stockton Road, Rosie wondered how best to deal with Charlotte's insecurity. This morning when she had begged to come to work with her, she hadn't had the heart to make her stay at home, even though it made no logical sense for her to trail all the way to Thompson's, only to troop all the way back half an hour later.

They both slowed their pace on seeing a huge mound of plaster, bricks and timber where there had once been a row of half a dozen houses in a smart residential area known as George's Square. Standing next to a huge crater that must have been almost a hundred feet wide, there was a young woman taking photographs. She had her camera pointed at a tree near to the bomb site. A woman's blouse and other clothing from one of the bombed houses had been blown high into the air and were hanging, fluttering forlornly in the breeze, from the branches.

'Georgina?' Rosie grabbed Charlotte's arm, checked for traffic and hurried across the road.

Turning round and seeing who was calling her name, Georgina's face broke into a sad smile.

'Rosie ... Charlie!'

She walked over to them, pushing her boxed-up gas mask and slinging her camera over her shoulder.

She hugged them both.

'Isn't it awful?' She looked over at the mound of rubble and the remaining shells of houses that were still standing. These were the homes that Rosie had passed most days when she had lived in a bedsit further down the road in Cowan Terrace.

'It is,' Rosie agreed.

'Six dead,' Georgina said, tears in her eyes. 'More than a dozen injured.'

'Charlie, this is my old friend I told you about?'

'The one who knew Mam?' Charlotte looked at her sister and then at Georgina.

'That's right,' Georgina said with a smile. 'Our mams used to meet for coffee. She used to mention you. Said you were a right terror.'

Charlotte laughed. 'Are you a photographer?' she asked, looking down at the small camera that was hanging from a strap round her neck.

Georgina held up her little Brownie

'No, no, I guess it's more of a hobby. It might seem a little morbid, but I just felt that I had to capture the dreadfulness of all this death and destruction. I don't know why.'

'So that we'll never forget,' Charlotte said.

Georgina looked at Rosie's little sister and gave her the saddest of smiles.

'Perhaps that's it, Charlie. Perhaps that's why.'

They all stared for a moment at the smouldering ruins. A young woman and her son were picking through bricks and mortar. A plume of smoke from one of the fires that had sprung up from the ruins and which firefighters had yet to extinguish billowed around them.

'One of the wardens I was talking to said it was bad all over,' Georgina said, glancing across at Rosie.

'I know. My neighbour's husband was just coming back when we were leaving. He said there'd been three communal shelters hit.'

'Three?' Georgina asked, shocked.

Rosie nodded solemnly. 'Bromarsh, Bonnersfield and Lodge Terrace. Sounds like quite a few didn't make it out.' She looked at her watch. 'We'd better get off.'

'You taking Charlie to work?' Georgina asked.

'Just until school starts,' Rosie said.

'That seems a bit of a haul,' Georgina said. 'You'll be turning around and coming back as soon as you make it there.'

Neither Rosie nor Charlotte said anything.

'Why don't you stay with me, Charlie, until it's time to go? You can take a few photos if you like?'

Charlotte's eyes lit up.

'Can I?'

Rosie looked at Georgina. 'Are you sure? You not got any books to balance or accounts to audit?'

Georgina felt her cheeks flush and hoped it wasn't noticeable. She had lied about what she did for a living. She'd had no choice. There was no way Rosie, or any of her squad, could know what kind of work she really did.

'No,' Georgina said, shaking her head, 'bookkeeping jobs are pretty scant at the moment.' She looked at Charlotte and smiled. 'Anyway, it'll be nice to have some company.'

Rosie mouthed 'Thank you', making sure her sister couldn't see, before asking, 'Why don't you come round to ours for some tea? I should be back by half six.'

'She can come earlier,' Charlotte suggested. 'Can't she?' She gave Rosie a pleading look. 'I'll be there. We could go and get some fish and chips for when you get back?'

Rosie looked at Georgina.

'Sounds like a perfect plan,' Georgina agreed. 'I can meet you after school if you want, Charlie? Help you with any homework?'

'Yes, please!' Charlotte was over the moon.

As was Rosie.

Gloria had the receiver jammed between her shoulder and her ear. Hope had her legs wrapped around her mammy's waist and her hands clasped around her neck. Her head kept bobbing forwards as she lapsed back into the land of Nod. Gloria tried to turn away from the impatient glares, but it was hard to move. There was barely room to breathe. The telephone box, she thought, had been appropriately named.

'Yes, Jack, we're both fine,' Gloria reassured. She looked through the glass panel, her vision marred by the criss-cross of anti-blast tape. The queue was getting longer. Everyone was wanting to do exactly what she was doing now and, by the looks of it, feeling the same – tired and impatient.

'Yes, it was a bad one, but nothing's going to happen to me 'n yer little girl. We were out the door 'n into that shelter faster than a bolt of lightning.' Gloria tried to sound jovial but didn't succeed. She was shattered. She had been up half the night with the air raid, and on top of that Hope had developed a cough that had kept her up for the rest of it.

'I'll see if I can get her to say hello.'

Gloria jigged Hope round so that she was on her hip.

'Say hello to Daddy, sweetheart.' Gloria held the speaker up to her daughter and nodded encouragingly.

113

'Dadda,' Hope said, her face creasing up with laughter as though this was some game, but the laughing soon turned into a coughing fit.

Gloria put the receiver back to her ear.

'Yes, she's fine, Jack. Just a bit of a cold. It's going around at the moment.'

Hope continued to cough.

Gloria caught sight of a man in the queue raising his wrist and prodding his finger at his watch.

'I'd better go. Just wanted you to know we're all right.'

The pips went just as Jack was telling them both how much he loved them.

Forty minutes later, having dropped Hope off at the Elliots' and been crushed on the ferry across the Wear, Gloria stood with Rosie, Dorothy, Angie and Polly, looking at SS *Denewood*. Or rather, what they could still see of *Denewood*. Her top deck and funnel were visible, but most of her hull was submerged.

'I think I'd feel like crying if I wasn't so angry,' Dorothy said.

'You 'n me both,' Gloria agreed.

'They'll be able to refloat her,' Rosie said.

'Aye, but it's not just gonna be bullet holes we'll be welding this time, will it?' Angie said.

'Helen said a parachute mine landed on her,' Polly added. She had dropped off her bag in the office before going to see her old squad.

'Hi everyone!'

They looked behind to see Hannah and Olly approaching.

'Martha's not coming in today,' Hannah told Rosie.

'She all right?' Gloria asked. Everyone was staring at Hannah.

'Yes ... she's fine,' she replied.

'Martha's been up all night,' Olly said, pushing back his fair hair. 'Mrs Perkins told us she'll be back tomorrow, but she needs to rest today. She's been at Lodge Terrace until the early hours of the morning.'

They were all quiet, having heard the heartbreaking news about those who had died.

'We'll gan 'n see her after work,' Angie said, looking at Dorothy, who nodded.

'We'll come too,' said Hannah. 'Come and get us before you leave.'

'I heard there was damage to the drawing office?' Rosie asked.

Olly nodded.

'And the platers' shed,' Hannah added.

Polly sighed. 'Looks like half the yard's taken a bashing.'

They all looked back at *Denewood*.

'The *Chinese Prince* has also taken a hit,' Rosie said.

Everyone groaned.

'All our hard work, just wiped out in the space of a bleedin' hour!' Angie's voice was full of fury.

'No, it hasn't been,' Rosie said, looking along the row of forlorn faces. 'It's just a temporary setback. Like Polly says, they'll be able to refloat *Denewood*, and *Chinese Prince* will probably just need a bit of a patch-up here and there. She's still *on* the river, not *under* it. The damage can't be that bad.'

She inspected her squad.

'We're just going to carry on doing what we do, all right?'

The women looked at Rosie as though she was their commander, which, in a way, she was.

'All right,' they all agreed, albeit rather wearily.

'Terry's just told me the last count at Lodge Terrace was thirteen dead, and at least ten badly hurt,' Marie-Anne said as she sat down at her desk and fed paper into her typewriter.

Bel shook her head.

'There aren't words,' she said.

'Well, I think it's a disgrace,' Marie-Anne said, clearly able to find the words. 'My dad's always saying he can never understand why they didn't build *all* of the communal shelters underground.' She started typing away on her Remington. '"Disaster waiting to happen", he's always said. And now that disaster has happened.'

Bel shot Marie-Anne a look and fed into her own typewriter sheets of both plain and carbon paper.

'They would have been better staying at home,' Marie-Anne added.

Bel started to type, but stopped. She gave Marie-Anne a black look.

'Well, what about the three people killed in the Bromarsh shelter – and the family of five who didn't make it out of the one in Bonnersfield? They were both below ground,' she said testily before starting to bash away on her typewriter.

After a pause she stopped typing and stood up. 'Do you want a cuppa?'

Marie-Anne nodded.

Bel turned to walk away but stopped and turned back to look at Marie-Anne.

'The thing is, Marie-Anne, it's all right you and your dad spouting off about whether it was a good idea to build shelters above ground, but that's not the point. It's Jerry's fault – no one else's.'

Bel turned on her heel and stomped over to the little kitchenette.

Marie-Anne hoped no one else was there – the mood Bel was in she'd pick a fight with a feather. They were all upset about the bombings, but she felt Bel's bad mood wasn't just about the air raid. If she had to take a bet, she'd say it had to do with her monthlies – and the fact she was still getting them. She'd married Joe a year and a half ago and her stomach was still as flat as a pancake.

When Harold told Helen that two bombs and a load of firepots had landed in Ryhope Colliery, she breathed a sigh of relief that both the asylum and the hospital had escaped unscathed. She was saddened to hear a sixty-year-old fire watcher had been killed, but knew that if the hospitals were unharmed then John would be too.

It still didn't stop her from wanting to call him. She was just about to pick up the phone – John, she argued, was still her friend, after all – when it rang.

'Miss Crawford? Miss Helen Crawford?'

'Yes, this is Miss Crawford speaking, although if you had let me answer the phone properly in the first place, you wouldn't have had to ask.'

Her ill humour was met by a hoot of laughter down the phone.

'Ah, Miss Crawford! Lovely to hear your dulcet tones. It's Matthew Royce speaking.'

'Ah, Mr Royce. How can I help you?'

'Well, there's been a bit of a shout-out to all the local businessmen and –' he added quickly '– businesswomen to attend this evening's variety performance at the Empire Theatre. The old gal got a bit of a battering last night but not enough to keep her down. Or rather, to keep the curtain down. The manager has just rung to ask if I can give him a hand in getting bums on seats – show Jerry we won't be beaten. Send out a clear message, you know – the show must go on and all of that.'

There was a moment's silence before Helen spoke.
'Time?'
'Seven for pre-show drinks. Seven thirty curtains up.'
Helen hung up, leaving Matthew listening to the disconnect tone, a smile on his face.

Chapter Fifteen

For the rest of the week Rosie's squad and just about every other man and woman in the town's nine shipyards worked until they dropped, their hearts growing heavier as the number of those killed in the bombing climbed. The final count told of eighty-three dead, with a hundred and nine injured.

Hearing about the children who had been killed – and the sight of several small coffins being transported to church in the traditional black horse-drawn carriages – caused even the most hardened of hearts to break. But if Hitler thought he could beat into submission the people who lived and worked in the biggest shipbuilding town in the world, he was wrong. If anything, the deaths of the innocents simply made the townsfolk's determination stronger still, their resolution that they would not be beaten even greater. The whole town pulled together, helping in whatever way they could. Workers toiled round the clock to reconnect electricity and gas supplies, as well as repair damaged sewers and water supplies. As three and a half thousand people had been made homeless, rest centres were set up to give them temporary shelter at least; mobile canteens and a dozen emergency feeding centres were also put into operation.

A number of schools, churches, chapels, theatres, cinemas, shops and businesses were closed until repair work could be carried out.

Two mortuaries were opened to deal with the dead.

Shipbuilders in the south docks worked flat out to repair the two ships that had been hit, and workers at the North Eastern Marine Engineering plant repaired the Hudson and Hendon docks.

As Rosie had forecast, the *Chinese Prince* hadn't been too badly damaged. When they had done what they could, they moved on to help with *Denewood*. Riveters, platers and welders worked together to get her back on her feet and ready for her sea trials. It freed up the other welders to work on *Caxton*, a screw steamer that had mercifully escaped with barely a scratch and was scheduled to be launched the following week.

In Tatham Street, Agnes and Beryl were taking in even more children for those mothers who needed, and wanted, to do overtime. The two adjoining houses were bursting at the seams. Agnes surprised everyone who knew her by getting her husband Harry's First War Military Medal out of her bedside cabinet and putting it on display on the mantelpiece, next to the framed photograph of Teddy in his Desert Rat uniform. She even let the children who turned her house into bedlam between the hours of eight and five hold it and rub it in their hands.

Meanwhile, Joe and his Home Guard unit were working round the clock to help any which way they could; Vera and Rina were filling up workers' flasks for free to show their support; Mr and Mrs Perkins invited Dorothy and Angie back for a meal every day, knowing they wouldn't have the energy to cook themselves anything decent when they got in from the ten-hour shifts they were pulling; and Kate had hung a notice in the window of the Maison Nouvelle telling those in need of clothing to come and see her. She put all her paid-for orders on hold, so that those who had been bombed out could at least clothe themselves and their children. As demand outstripped her supply, she asked her more affluent customers to donate any unwanted items. Helen dropped off two boxes of clothes, as well as suits and shirts her father had left behind, plus a few of her mother's skirts and blouses that she knew Miriam wouldn't miss.

Despite the madness of work and the long hours, Helen still found herself thinking of John. A few times she picked up the phone to call him but stopped herself.

'If he wanted to speak to me, or see me, he'd call,' she told Bel. 'It's obvious he's too busy with Claire to spare me the time.'

'And *work* – he'll be busy with *work*,' Bel countered. Everyone knew all the hospitals were run off their feet.

'No,' Helen waved away Bel's argument, 'it's like the good Dr Eris said that awful afternoon outside the asylum: "You know what it's like at the start, you just want to be with each other every minute of every day". Those who are *just friends* have to take a back seat.'

'But it's like you said,' Bel reminded Helen, 'that's only until the "shine's worn off".'

'Ha!' Helen laughed bitterly. 'I only said that to be a cow. Make her paranoid.'

'You're not going to fight for him then?' Bel asked.

Helen shook her head. 'No, it'd be a fight I could never win.'

Bel looked at Helen. She was surprised how defeatist she was being. When Helen had wanted Tommy, she'd gone all out to get him. Talk about dirty tricks. Helen had thrown the lot into the pot to get Tommy. Lies, manipulation – she'd even spread false rumours that Polly had gone off with some plater. Bel was only just getting to know Helen, but still, she thought, she had changed a lot these past few years. *Mind you, hadn't they all?*

'Well, I wouldn't give up,' Bel said. 'Not if you love him, which I think you do?'

Helen sighed.

'I wish I didn't. No one tells you how much love can hurt.'

The women tried to keep up their 'lessons' in current affairs, although it was generally only Polly who remembered to buy a national newspaper, usually the *Daily Mirror* as it had always been Arthur's favourite. Marie-Anne brought in the *Sunderland Echo* to keep abreast of events closer to home and had been particularly excited to see a photograph of Helen with Mr Royce Jnr at the Empire on Monday evening; she'd immediately rung Dahlia, who used the conversation as an opportunity to quiz Marie-Anne about Miss Crawford's commitments over the next few weeks.

They weren't the only ones to see the photo and the article. Dr Eris had also seen it and made sure that a copy of the paper, open at the pertinent page, found its way into the staffroom over at the Ryhope.

Mr Havelock and Miriam were also taking up column inches – much to Bel's annoyance. Both impeccably dressed, they were pictured handing over a cheque to the children's hospital in town, which had been damaged in the recent raids.

When Polly read out an article reporting that the government was now allowing church bells to be rung for any purpose, the women's reaction was lukewarm. The bells had initially been silenced so that they could act as an alarm should the country be invaded. Everyone should have been joyful – the government clearly no longer feared a German invasion. But the news didn't bring quite the reaction that it might have done as, with the number of funerals taking place across the borough, the bells seemed more like death knells.

Quentin had to cancel his trip back up north due to 'work commitments'.

Dorothy imparted the news with a comically sad face and theatrical eye-rolling in Angie's direction.

'Honestly, Dor, it's not as if I'm pining to see him or owt!' Angie snapped.

'I never suggested you were,' Dorothy said, 'but it's funny you thought it.'

Angie chucked her crusts at her best friend by way of a reply.

Hannah had been noticeably subdued after this latest air raid, and when a concerned Rosie asked if she had heard any news about her parents in the Auschwitz concentration camp, she shook her head, but explained that her aunty Rina had heard that a man called Josef Mengele was being transferred there as a medical officer.

'Isn't it a good sign that they've appointed someone in charge of those who aren't well?' Martha asked.

Hannah had given Martha the most melancholic of smiles and related to the women with tears in her eyes that Dr Mengele was not a good man. Before the war he had published academic papers on those born with genetic abnormalities and he had an unhealthy interest in dwarfs and twins.

'I don't think he's a doctor of healing – more of experimentation,' Hannah said.

They were deathly quiet. All of them trying to comprehend this level of evil.

'Says here the miners are being asked to increase coal output,' Angie said, breaking the silence and staring down at the *Daily Telegraph*. 'Tell that to my dad 'n his marrers. They hardly see daylight as it is.'

Polly looked at the article Angie was reading.

'"If the gap between production and consumption is not closed, the war could go against us,"' she read out.

'That's all we need to hear,' Martha said, her broad shoulders slouching a little. She had been working overtime with Jimmy and the riveters.

'If we don't build enough ships, we're doomed ... If we can't mine enough coal, we're doomed,' Dorothy moaned.

'It'll be the same for them,' Rosie said. 'I'm sure they've not got a limitless supply of ships and coal either.'

'Exactly,' Gloria said, trying to lift the mood, even though she herself felt exhausted. Hope's cough was still bad.

Rosie's own worries about Peter seemed to be weighing on her more heavily than normal. It had been almost six months since she had received her last communication from him – a letter brought to her by Toby on Christmas Eve. Toby, who had recruited Peter, had become her one tenuous connection with her husband. Every time Dorothy saw him, she half hoped for, half dreaded hearing any news. She kept telling herself that no news was good news, but that argument was wearing thin.

Not that she had too much time to dwell on it, what with the demands of work and, even more so, of Charlie, who was hanging on to Rosie and Lily as though they were life rafts. Lily had said to let her be as clingy as she needed to be – the phase would pass.

One of the main problems was that Charlotte seemed overly anxious about spending the time between Rosie leaving for work and the start of school on her own. Rosie had a word with Lily and asked, since the bordello didn't open up shop until after midday and the school was just a few minutes' walk away, if it would be possible for Charlotte to go to Lily's for breakfast.

'A perfect solution,' Lily declared.

'It will mean, though,' Rosie eyed Lily, 'that Charlotte turns up on your doorstep at around *seven*,' Rosie stressed, 'when I leave to go to work.'

'I know *exactly* what time you start work,' Lily said. 'Don't you think I'm capable of getting up so early?'

Rosie couldn't help but laugh.

'Lily, in all the time we have been acquainted, I've never once known you to get out of bed before midday.'

Lily waved her words away with a heavily jewelled hand and marched off in search of an alarm clock.

Needless to say, when Rosie told Charlotte of the arrangement, she was ecstatic.

The following morning, her little sister stood outside the front door, yelling at her that if she didn't get a move on, Rosie would be late for work, and what kind of an example was that to set her squad?

Chapter Sixteen

Friday 28 May

'John, what are you doing here?' Helen felt her heart start pounding.

'Sorry for just turning up like this . . .' Dr Parker stood still in the doorway. Seeing Helen always took his breath away.

'No, no, it's lovely to see you.' Helen ushered him in with a wave of her hand. 'Sit down. Marie-Anne's just brought in a tea tray.'

Watching as Dr Parker made his way over to the chair, pushing a stray lock of blond hair away from his eyes, Helen wished she could anaesthetise herself to the attraction she felt for him.

Pouring out two cups of tea, she forced herself to be calm.

'I had a consultation at Monkwearmouth Hospital,' Dr Parker said. 'And as I was on this side of the river, I thought I'd take a chance and see if you were free.'

'Well, you couldn't have timed it better.' Helen handed Dr Parker his cup and saucer, hoping he wouldn't see the slight tremor in her hands.

She sat down just as the klaxon sounded out.

'Two minutes,' she said, bobbing back up, smoothing down her dress and hurrying out.

Dr Parker watched as Helen walked into the main office. She had on a simple but perfectly fitted dark green dress. She looked ravishing, as always.

'Before you dash off,' she addressed her staff, 'I just wanted to say thank you for all your hard work. I know you've given it your all this week, during a very difficult time, but you'll be pleased to know, it's paid off – we're almost back on schedule.'

There were a few random claps and joyful exclamations from the staff. Helen spotted Polly's smiling face near the back of the office. They hadn't had time to have their usual catch-up this week, but she looked well. Very well.

'So, as promised,' Helen looked round the room, 'you've all got the whole weekend off and I'll see you back here Monday morning, rested and refreshed.'

Not needing further encouragement, everyone started to pack up and leave. Helen went over to have a quick word with Marie-Anne and Bel, before turning and walking back into her office.

'Is that Polly I see loitering by a filing cabinet in the corner, looking like a duck out of water?' Dr Parker asked as Helen sat back down behind her desk and took a sip of her tea.

She laughed.

'It is. Although she has made me promise, cross my heart and hope to die, that I will let her go back to welding after the baby's born.'

'And do you think she'll want to? Once she's had the baby?' Dr Parker looked at Helen. Any kind of baby talk, he knew, was still painful for her; not that she would ever admit it.

Helen took a cigarette from her packet of Pall Malls. 'I'm really not sure. I don't think I'd be inclined to lay a bet either way.'

Dr Parker put his teacup on Helen's desk. 'I feel there's so much to catch up on.' He suddenly felt nervous about what he had to say, which was ridiculous.

'I know,' Helen said, 'it's amazing how much can happen in just a couple of weeks.'

And how much I've missed you.

'So, how have you been?' she asked, lighting up a cigarette.

'Well, like you, by the sounds of it, the hospital's had a rather hectic couple of weeks – what with these damned air raids. The Royal is really struggling to cope, even though the Ryhope's taken in quite a few of the injured. And the Monkwearmouth is just about full to the brim now,' he said, taking a sip of tea.

They chatted for a little while about the bombings. Dr Parker told Helen about his patients and Helen told him about the injured *Denewood* and how they had managed to save her twice over.

'Looks like we've both been patching up the war wounded,' Dr Parker said with a smile.

'And has there been anything else keeping you particularly busy?' Helen narrowed her eyes and gave Dr Parker a quizzical smile.

'Well, as a matter of fact,' Dr Parker said, 'there is.'

Did she know?

'I've started to see Claire. Dr Eris,' he said. 'Well, we've been out on a few dates – that's all. Nothing serious.'

Why was he playing it down? It wasn't as if Helen would give two jots either way. Would she?

'I have to say, I think it's about time.' Helen forced her voice to sound light and jocular. 'You've been single for as long as we've known each other.'

Dr Parker forced a smile.

If only you knew why.

'And I think you and Claire make a very compatible couple,' Helen said, surprised at how convincing she sounded.

'Yes, yes, I guess we do.' *Helen was clearly happy for him. As any friend would be.* 'But I don't want you to feel that we can't keep the friendship we have.' He looked at Helen, who was getting up from her desk and picking up her handbag and gas mask.

'Of course not,' Helen said, another convincing smile. 'As long as Claire doesn't mind?' She was now taking her summer coat off the hatstand.

'No, no, not at all. She's made a point of saying it's important for us to remain friends.'

Helen bit her tongue. *And if you believe that, you'd believe anything.*

Dr Parker stood up. 'Are we going somewhere?'

'Yes,' Helen said. 'I think this calls for a celebration, don't you?'

As they walked out of the front gates, Helen gave Dr Parker a sidelong glance.

'Actually, I now also have a significant other in my life.'

Dr Parker looked at Helen, desperately trying to keep at bay the raging green-eyed monster that had just jumped out.

'Really?'

His mind went to the newspaper article he had read – and, moreover, the photograph printed alongside it.

'It wouldn't, perchance, be the gentleman you were pictured with in the *Echo* the other day?'

Helen laughed. This time it was genuine.

'Matthew Royce?' Helen chuckled again. 'Not in a million years. That man's a charmer and a chancer. The kind that only loves one person. Himself.'

'I'm guessing it was some kind of work engagement?' Dr Parker asked, trying to sound casual, unaware that they had come to halt by a rather snazzy-looking green sports car.

'Morale booster,' Helen said, distractedly. 'There were loads of shipyard bigwigs there. The press always uses pictures of relatively young, preferably good-looking people over a load of balding old men with bellies bigger than Polly's.'

Dr Parker was suddenly aware that Helen was looking at him, her eyes wide, and then she stared down at the car in front of them.

'This is it!' she said, excitedly.

'I'm confused,' Dr Parker said. His mind was still stewing over the picture in the paper – Helen and this 'charmer' Matthew weren't just young and good-looking, they could have passed as a glamorous Hollywood couple.

'This,' Helen said, putting her arm out to show off the polished bonnet, 'is *my* significant other.'

Dr Parker let out a bark of laughter. He hoped it hadn't sounded as desperately relieved as he felt.

'It's yours?' he asked.

'It certainly is,' Helen said, rummaging in her bag and pulling out a set of keys.

She dangled them in the air.

'Fancy a spin?'

'Do I even need to answer?' Dr Parker chuckled.

Helen got in, leant over and opened the passenger door.

Climbing into the front seat, Dr Parker felt aware of how close he was to Helen. He could smell her perfume and the size of the interior was forcing their shoulders to touch.

'I know it's rather an extravagance, but,' Helen looked at Dr Parker and gave him a sombre face, 'it's needed for work.'

Dr Parker looked equally deadpan.

'Of course it is.'

Neither spoke as Helen drove up the embankment, turning right and driving along Dame Dorothy Street and Harbour View before turning left along Roker Terrace. Feeling a little reckless, she decided to keep going and drive all the way up the coast road past Whitburn village to Souter Lighthouse and then back again. A few times when she changed gear her hand brushed John's leg. Both of them pretended not to notice.

Pulling up on Side Cliff Road, outside Helen's house, Dr Parker turned to look at her. 'Well, I can honestly say that your driving is one hundred per cent improved.'

'I don't think it could have been any worse,' Helen laughed.

'A walk to the Roker Hotel?' Dr Parker suggested, climbing out of the car.

As they crossed the road and started to walk down Roker Park Road, Helen automatically linked her arm through John's, before quickly pulling away.

'Sorry,' she said.

Dr Parker looked at her, his brow furrowed.

'It doesn't seem right,' Helen explained.

'What do you mean?' he asked, although he knew exactly what she meant.

'Well, as you are now a "taken" man –' she gave a nervous laugh '– I don't think it's appropriate that I ... that I *manhandle* you so.'

They walked through the main gates of the park and continued in silence for a little while, passing the model boating lake before coming out of the park and strolling down Ravine Terrace.

'So, tell me,' Dr Parker asked, as they turned right along Roker Terrace, 'what's been happening in your life these past few weeks? How are all your shipyard women?'

131

'They're all good. Well, as good as can be expected, all things considered. Gloria says Hannah's worried about the situation over in Poland.'

Dr Parker nodded grimly. 'I'm not surprised. She's right to be.' One of his colleagues who was Jewish had told him that the Warsaw Ghetto uprising that had started five weeks previously had ended with thousands of Jews being killed, and tens of thousands being sent to concentration camps.

'And how's Hope?' he asked, wanting to talk about life, not death.

'She's got an awful cough. But other than that – and the fact she hasn't had a cuddle from her father for nearly a year and a half now – she's fine.'

Dr Parker could sense that Helen's chagrin about her father's banishment was getting worse. He wished he could have put his arm around her and given her a squeeze, as he would have done before.

'Talking about families,' Dr Parker said, 'the last time we saw each other you were set to have a chat with Bel and Pearl?'

'Oh,' Helen groaned. 'I'll tell you once we're sat down and I've a vodka and tonic in my hand.'

'That bad?' Dr Parker said as they reached the main entrance to the Roker Hotel.

He pulled open the front door and they were hit with a blast of smoky warm air and the smell of spilled beer.

A quarter of an hour later, Helen had brought Dr Parker up to date.

'It was as you thought all along, wasn't it?' Helen said, taking a sip of her drink. 'But were too polite to say.'

Dr Parker nodded dolefully.

It was true. He had thought it was unlikely that Pearl and Mr Havelock had had an affair – and that what had happened had been far from consensual. Just as he'd also wondered if Mr Havelock had gone for young girls who looked like his daughters.

'And how are you coping with all this?' he asked.

Seeing Helen reach for another cigarette, he wanted to put his hand on hers and stop her – to hold her hand and give her the comfort she was seeking.

'Honestly,' Helen said, pulling out a cigarette, 'you've clearly been spending too much time with Dr Eris.' She forced a smile, silently cursing herself for bringing the conversation back to Claire.

'No, seriously!' Dr Parker asked again.

'Oh, I'm fine,' Helen said. 'The shock is slowly sinking in. And funnily enough, Bel and I seem to have forged a friendship out of it all.'

'I did wonder,' John said, taking a sip of his bitter, 'when Marie-Anne told me you had taken Bel to a launch at Pickersgill's ...'

It was on the tip of Helen's tongue to ask why he hadn't returned her call, but she didn't. Instead, she told him how she and Bel had chatted properly for the first time about her grandfather, and how Bel and Mr Havelock had met for the first time at the launch.

'How do you think Bel feels about all of this? Do you think she wants to do anything about it?' Dr Parker asked.

Helen shook her head. 'Doubtful. Like Bel says, who's going to believe Pearl's word over my grandfather's? I mean the man's practically hero-worshipped in these parts.' She paused. 'I, on the other hand, would love to do something.'

Dr Parker smiled. 'Why doesn't that surprise me.'

'But I couldn't,' Helen said. 'If anything is said or done, it's going to have to be Bel's decision. And she's said that, for now, we should just keep what we know to ourselves.'

'And what would you do if you could?'

Helen looked at Dr Parker.

'I'd use it to get Dad back,' she said, her words spoken without hesitation.

'Really?' Dr Parker said. Helen had clearly given this some thought.

'I'd use it to cancel out the bartering chips Mother has over Gloria and Father.'

Dr Parker knew about the women's secrets and how they were being used to keep Jack on the Clyde.

'So that your father and Gloria can finally be together.' Dr Parker smiled. 'Underneath that hard, no-nonsense exterior, you really are a romantic at heart.'

Helen laughed out loud.

'I'm afraid I might be more shrewd than sentimental. The reason I'd use Bel's paternity against my mother and my grandfather would be so that Hope could finally have a father in her life. That's what's really important. To have a mum *and* a dad in her life.'

Dr Parker thought how lucky Hope was to have a big sister like Helen, a sister who was not only fiercely loyal, but was there for her, watching out for her, come what may.

For the next hour they sat and chatted, their bodies touching occasionally, and enjoyed the time they were sharing, the friendship, their closeness.

When it came to saying goodbye, Dr Parker bound for the Monkwearmouth Hospital, Helen for home, there was a moment's awkwardness before they both gave each other a chaste kiss goodnight.

Walking back, Helen was hit by an awful feeling of emptiness. It felt wrong for John to be going off in one direction and her in another. It had been such a relief to speak to him about her grandfather – to talk about the unspeakable to someone she trusted implicitly, who she knew cared for her, and most of all, who understood. John had been there from the start. From her first niggles about who it was that Bel reminded her of, to the moment she had realised that Bel was the spit of her own mother after seeing them together at Polly's wedding. He'd been there when she had employed Georgina, and he had been a support when her 'Miss Marple' had relayed her findings, which she had typed up in a detailed report on two sheets of paper so that the truth was there in black and white.

She thought about the night they had been out for a drink and she had agreed he could walk her home. She had been on the verge of telling him how she felt then, only for the air raid sirens to start wailing, forcing her to run home and John to head off to the Royal.

Not long afterwards she had arranged for them to go for a meal at the café on the seafront, after which she had been determined to show John exactly how she felt – but Polly's near miscarriage had put paid to that.

The gods were clearly against their coupling. John might love her as a friend, he might well want to bed her, but he didn't want her as his sweetheart, as the woman with whom he would walk down the aisle.

It was why she could not do as Bel suggested and fight for him. And if Bel knew about her past, she would understand, would probably tell her she was doing the right thing. She should walk away with her dignity intact. There was no getting away from it – Helen was damaged goods and men of John's standing, as her mother kept saying, didn't have to go raking about in the bargain bucket – not when they could afford something brand new.

As she reached her front door and got out her keys, she realised that she had been fighting her feelings for John for a long time. By admitting the truth to herself, she had unwittingly let the genie out of the bottle and in doing so she had got to know what true love felt like.

As she kicked off her shoes and hung up her coat, she felt the cold of the terracotta tiles on the soles of her feet. She knew that she had no choice but to push the genie back into its bottle and move on. She could not – would not – spend her life hankering after something she couldn't have. It would be a life wasted. And this war had taught her one thing: life really was precious.

Chapter Seventeen

Monday 31 May

On Monday morning there was a noticeable energy in the office. The two days of enforced rest and recreation had worked wonders. As had the fact that everyone had been able to continue to enjoy undisturbed sleep; the air raid sirens had, thankfully, remained dormant for the past fortnight.

When Helen saw Polly come back into the office at midday as everyone else was leaving for the canteen, she waved her in. Polly mouthed 'Two minutes' before having a quick word with Bel and handing her a copy of the *Daily Mirror*. Dumping her handbag and gas mask by her station towards the far end of the office, she manoeuvred her considerable girth around desks and tables and into Helen's office.

'Sit down,' said Helen. 'You look like you need it.'

Polly plonked herself in the chair and looked at Helen. Both women burst out laughing.

'Don't!' Polly said. 'Otherwise I'll have to go to the toilet. Again.'

Her comments only made both women laugh even more.

'I'm sorry,' said Helen, getting up and pouring them both a cup of tea, 'it's just that sometimes you look so ... so ... well, so comical.'

'I know,' Polly said, wiping her eyes and taking the proffered tea. 'I feel like Billy Bunter. Heavens knows what I'm going to be like in a few months.'

Helen sat down at her desk. 'I think it's because you've always been so slim. It's so strange to see you … well, expand so.'

'That's a nice way of putting it,' Polly said, taking a sip of her tea. 'At least I'm giving everyone a bit of a laugh, so there's some good come of it all.'

'So, come on,' said Helen, 'tell me what the *wonderful* Dr Billingham had to say today?'

Polly knew Helen didn't share her feelings about Dr Billingham, even though she had employed his services on her behalf.

'Dr Billingham's not that bad, you know. He comes across as a bit arrogant and hard-nosed, but I think it's all a bit of a charade.'

'Mmm,' Helen said, unconvinced. He hadn't been particularly sympathetic when she'd had her miscarriage. Not that she'd cared; she hadn't cared about anything at that point in time.

'He's good at his job, which is the main thing,' Helen said, sitting back. 'Anyway, go on, I'm all ears.'

'Well, we spent most of the time talking about his daughter, Mary.' Polly smiled. 'He thinks the world of her.'

'Is this the one who's in the Wrens?' Helen asked.

'That's right. He's just got the one,' Polly said. 'I think he misses her. And I think it's a case of when he sees me, he thinks of her, which makes him talk about her.'

Helen took a sip of tea.

'But apart from that,' Polly said, seeing that Helen was waiting for an answer to her original question, 'everything's going to plan. I'm apparently in tip-top health. As is the baby. Although he did admit today that I am slightly larger than average at this stage.'

'He doesn't think it's twins then – even though they run in the family?' Helen asked.

'No, he had a good listen and can still only hear the one heartbeat, so he says he's fairly confident that there's just the one baby in there.' Polly put her hand on her bump and smiled. 'Although Ma's convinced I'm carrying "double the trouble", as she puts it.'

Helen smiled. 'And let me guess, Bel's hoping your mum's right?'

'Yes,' Polly said, 'you've got Bel down to a T. The more babies the better.'

Polly took another sip of her tea.

'I wish Bel was pregnant,' she said suddenly, her voice sad, 'and that *she* was expecting "double the trouble".'

The following day heralded the start of June and with it a change in the tide of war.

There was a visible spring in the steps of those heading to the town's shipyards, the Wearmouth Collicry and all the other factories and industries working flat out to do their bit for victory. Reports had come through that Germany was withdrawing its remaining U-boats from the North Atlantic as so many were being sunk by Allied forces – the heavy losses said to be due to the new anti-sub tactics.

Naturally, during the lunch break, it was the main conversation amongst all of the yard's workers, the name of Admiral Karl Dönitz, who had ordered the withdrawal, peppering all their conversations.

'At last!' Martha proclaimed.

The women were sitting by the quayside as the weather, like everyone's mood, was sunny.

'I knar.' Angie was leaning against her workmate's solid mass. 'At long bloody last.'

They'd all admitted to feeling wrung out.

Dorothy was sitting cross-legged on one of the wooden pallets. 'It says here that they reckon forty-one U-boats were lost last month alone, compared with thirty-four of our own ships.'

They all looked at Gloria, who had a look of relief on her face.

'I might get my boys back home yet.'

'The *Mirror*'s calling it "Black May",' Polly said. She was now spending every break with the women. She missed her work and her squad, though not half as much as she missed Tommy.

The following day there was lots of cheering and joviality at the launch of *Caxton* at Thompson's and *Wrenwood* at Austin's, but the day after the newspapers were full of the news that *Gone with the Wind* star Leslie Howard had been killed when the passenger plane he was on was shot down over the Bay of Biscay. He had been flying from Lisbon to Bristol. All seventeen people aboard had perished.

'I know it sounds stupid, but I feel like I knew him,' Dorothy said.

The rest of the women murmured their agreement. Dorothy had, after all, dragged them to see him in just about every film he'd ever been in.

Pickersgill's had a luncheon to mark Matthew Royce taking over from his father, who had recovered enough to attend the event, if not to return to the helm. Helen went, along with all the other shipyard managers, partly because she had to, but also because she wanted to say her farewells to the old man in person. She'd always had a soft spot for him even though he had a tendency to talk the hind legs off a donkey.

Despite the launches and the sunshine that heralded the start of summer, after two of the worst air raids to date the townsfolk were still living on tenterhooks. The RAF were getting their revenge with a blanket bombing of Wuppertal, but the women, hearing of the thousands of civilians killed in the air raid and the ensuing firestorms created by the mass of incendiary devices, were left with a bad taste in their mouths. The Germans might be the enemy, but they were just ordinary folk – men, women and children – who, like so many Brits, had died simply because they lived in an area dense with industry.

The start of the month might well have brought the sun out, but the hot weather made for sweaty work.

'Don't forget to keep yourselves covered!' was Rosie's new mantra.

On hearing her, the women's hands would automatically go to their neck scarves to make sure they were in place; they did not want to risk getting caught out. They'd all been branded at least once since they had started as welders and they didn't want to have any more scars.

When the klaxon went for lunch, the first thing they all did was unbutton their overalls and head for their spot by the quayside to catch the sea breeze.

At the end of the week they all listened as Polly read a news report telling them that a French general called Henri Giraud had been made commander-in-chief of the Free French Forces. Although Rosie was not able to talk about what Peter was doing in the war – or where he was – the women all knew French was his second language, and as Dor said, 'It doesn't take a genius to work out where they've sent him.'

'Free France and its Fighting French Forces – I won't even attempt to say it in French ...' Polly had Angie's *Daily Telegraph* spread out on one of the pallets '... have appointed General Henry – I don't know how to pronounce his surname. Anyway, he's been made top dog, by the looks of it.'

'So,' Martha said, 'they support the Resistance in France?'

'That's right,' Dorothy said. 'The Free France movement set itself up in London back in the summer of 1940 – it became what's known as a government-in-exile, led by Charles de Gaulle.'

They all looked at Rosie, who had gone quiet.

'He's gonna be all right,' Gloria said, leaning over and squeezing her hand.

'I know, I know,' Rosie lied. She let out a laugh that sounded more like a sob. 'I just wish he'd get himself back home so he can give me a hand with Charlie.'

They all chuckled.

'Is she still arguing her case for going to Lily's with you on an evening?' asked Bel.

'Oh, yes,' Rosie nodded solemnly. 'She most certainly is.'

'And are you going to give in?' Bel asked. Maisie had told her how Charlotte was determined to make Lily's her second home and how she'd often come down for breakfast to find Lily puffing on a Gauloise and Charlotte munching on a slice of toast, both chatting away, sometimes in French.

'I'm holding fast. It's helped that Georgina's been an absolute star and has been more or less babysitting Charlotte on an evening.'

'Don't let Charlie hear you say that,' Gloria chipped in. 'She'll go berserk.'

Rosie laughed. 'I know. *Keeping her company* might be a more acceptable way of describing it. Anyway, they've been to the library and Georgina's helping her with her homework, not that I think Charlotte really needs help.' Rosie took a sip of her tea. 'But the thing is, Georgina won't always be able to be there. She works for starters, and her father's health is precarious. Sounds like she has to look after him quite a lot.'

'Well, I think we should have another group trip to the flicks – keep Charlotte company and invite Georgina as well so we can meet her properly,' Dorothy said.

'Sounds like a perfect plan,' Rosie agreed. 'I'll tell Georgina.'

'But not this weekend,' Dorothy said, deathly serious. Not waiting for the women to ask why, she continued, 'Because a certain someone – name beginning with Q – has finally been given leave.' She let out a long sigh. 'Although, he could only get a pass for Saturday, which, as you all know, is sacred.'

Everyone looked at Angie, who let out an equally long sigh.

'So, as I'm sure yer'll all guess, I now owe Dorothy *big time*,' she informed the women, her eyes going to the skies.

Chapter Eighteen

Saturday 5 June

'Wow! You look stunning!' The words were out of Quentin's mouth before he could haul them back in.

Angie felt herself blush. 'Yer only think that 'cos yer normally only see us in a pair of scruffy overalls.'

They walked down the stone steps belonging to the flats.

'This is the dress you wore for Polly Elliot's wedding, isn't it?'

Angie laughed. Quentin had a habit of calling people by their full name, though his friends by their surname, which made no sense at all.

'It is – but she's Polly Watts now,' Angie said, feeling a little self-conscious walking down the street in her canary-yellow dress. She wished she hadn't been bullied into wearing it by Dorothy. It felt a little over the top.

'And how's Polly these days?' Quentin asked.

Angie let out a loud laugh as they reached the end of Foyle Street and turned right towards the museum.

'*Blooming* – in all senses.' Angie stretched her hand out in front of her to show Quentin just how *blooming* Polly was.

'Her mam thinks she's expecting twins, but the doctor told her she isn't.'

Quentin smiled. 'But I'll bet Mrs Elliot's not convinced.'

'Aye, that's Agnes fer yer. Polly reckons she's got the gift of foresight – her being part Irish 'n all – but she's hoping 'n praying her mam's got it wrong this time. There's no way she wants two in one go.'

'Why?' Quentin asked.

'Because!' Angie gasped dramatically, looking at Quentin as though he was round the bend. 'Twins are a nightmare. Hard work. Polly knows they might look cute, but she saw what her brothers were like. She said they used to run her mam ragged.'

As they crossed the road, Quentin took Angie's arm and was pleased she let him. Normally, she'd tell him she wasn't some 'auld grannie' and shrug him off.

'Pol wants more children, just not all in one go,' Angie said, a little distracted by Quentin's touch.

'And you? Do you want children?' Quentin asked. They were now walking up to the very grand entrance of the Sunderland Museum and Winter Gardens.

'Suppose so,' Angie said. 'But I'm not gonna have a load like my mam.'

Quentin looked at Angie's face light up as she spotted Wallace, the town's famous stuffed lion. They both walked over. Angie stroked it as though it was a pet dog. Quentin copied her.

'It feels rough,' he said. This was the first museum piece he had ever dared touch, having been brought up to believe any kind of displayed artifact was sacrosanct.

As they wandered around the ground floor of the museum, Quentin pointed out paintings that were particularly revered or important, or which depicted significant events in history.

'They're all so big, aren't they?' Angie said, rubbing her neck, which felt stiff from the overhead welds she'd been doing all week.

'Come and sit down here.' Quentin gestured to a broad leather bench in the middle of the room. They both walked over and sat down.

'They've been put here for people who have been on their feet working all day,' he said, deadpan.

'Really?' Angie said, before her face crumpled and she batted Quentin on the leg. 'Eee, yer had me going there.'

'You're meant to sit here and look for a long time at the paintings,' Quentin said, giving Angie a sidelong glance. She had the most perfect skin. 'And you have to wear a look on your face as though you are having the deepest and most meaningful of thoughts.'

Angie looked at Quentin and smiled. She loved his take on life, and how he'd gently make fun of those who took themselves too seriously.

They both sat for a few minutes while other visitors walked past, talking in muted tones. Both put very 'deep and meaningful' expressions on their faces, while all the time feeling the closeness of their bodies. Quentin fought the urge to take hold of Angie's hand. In the end, when he thought he might lose the battle and embarrass himself as well as Angie, he stood up.

'Well, I don't know about you, but I'm starving.'

'Me too,' said Angie. 'I could eat a horse.'

Quentin laughed. 'Come on, then. I'm not sure they'll have anything equine on the menu, but we can ask.'

'That'll be all, thank you,' Quentin said, handing his menu back to the waiter.

'Eee, it really is very posh in here, isn't it?' Angie looked down at the silver cutlery and felt relieved for those evenings in Mrs Kwiatkowski's kitchen, laughing and drinking tea while they pored over a guide to etiquette and good manners.

'It is,' Quentin said. 'But I'm just keeping my side of the bargain.'

Angie looked at him.

'Yer knar yer dinnit have to do that any more? Give me lessons 'n all that?'

Quentin smiled at the memory of Angie turning up at his door late on Christmas Eve and telling him he could accompany her to the wedding the next day, providing he gave her 'lessons in being posh'. He'd felt as though he had been gifted a lifetime's worth of Christmas wishes all in one hit.

'I know I don't *have* to,' Quentin said, 'but I *want* to.' He looked at Angie. 'As long as you still want me to?'

Just then the waiter appeared and poured a small amount of wine into Quentin's glass. Angie watched in fascination as Quentin gave it a quick swirl, inspected it for a moment, then smelled it before finally tasting it. He smiled at the waiter, who then proceeded to pour them each a glass.

Having read a guide to ordering wine in a restaurant, Angie did not need to ask why this little bit of theatre had been played out – why the waiter held the bottle in front of Quentin so that he could see the label, or the reason for offering him the cork.

'Yer knar,' Angie said, waiting until the waiter was out of earshot before she spoke, 'before I knew what all that malarkey was about, I would have thought it a bit barmy.'

Quentin looked at the young woman opposite him. *Did she have any idea how totally in love with her he was?*

'And you don't still think it's all a bit barmy?' he asked.

Angie took a sip of her wine and her eyes widened. 'Cor, this is *nice*.' She took another sip and put it down. 'It's hard not to just neck it in one go.'

Quentin smiled.

147

'So, you're going to see your parents and your siblings tomorrow?' he asked. He knew Angie and Dorothy went to see their families every Sunday. It was their trade-off for being allowed to live independently.

Angie nodded.

They were both quiet as the waiter brought them their starter of mushroom soup.

'They must look forward to seeing you?' Quentin probed.

'Mmm,' Angie said. 'I think they look forward to me bringing them a bit of dosh and cooking a dinner for them all. Especially since Liz has run off and become a Lumberjill.'

'They must be proud of you?' Quentin said. 'Doing what you're doing? I bet you there's not that many women in the country who can weld. And not only that, but who work in the shipbuilding industry.'

'If they are, they've never said so,' Angie said. 'I think they think it's a bit odd. Yer knar, being a woman 'n working in the yards.'

'Even though your mother works in the ropery?'

'I suppose that's true. But women have always worked in the ropery – 'n the shipyards have always just taken on men. Until now.'

For the next few minutes, Angie concentrated on consuming her soup in the way she had learnt, which was the opposite of how she had been doing it all her life. When she'd finished, she relaxed and looked at Quentin.

'Yer parents must be proud of what *you* do?' she asked.

'Well, if they are, they've never said so.' Quentin smiled.

'I'm not daft, yer knar,' Angie continued. 'I know yer more than a pen-pusher. Mrs Kwiatkowski was telling me that yer've got a really important job. She said yer used to work for local government, but yer got a promotion 'n that's why yer now work at Whitehall for the War Office.'

Quentin smiled but didn't say anything. He was glad Angie hadn't asked him outright what he did. He would hate to have to tell her he wasn't able to divulge that information – and for her to think he didn't trust her enough to tell her.

They both thanked the waiter when he came and took the bowls away.

'What are they like – your mother and father?' Quentin asked.

'They're all reet,' Angie said.

'Do you think they're happy?'

'What? With each other?'

They were both quiet as the waiter came and replen ished their wine glasses.

'Nah,' Angie said, dropping her voice so no one could hear and looking about the restaurant to make sure she didn't know anyone, which was highly unlikely.

'Mam's got a fancy man.'

'Really?' Quentin was shocked, not by Angie's mam's infidelity, but by Angie's honesty.

'Aye, she's got herself some young bloke lives on St Peter's View.'

Quentin knew the street in Monkwearmouth. It was only a few streets away from her family home.

'That's a bit close for comfort,' Quentin said.

'I knar.' Angie leant forward across the table. 'Dor 'n I saw her with him. They were in the back lane.'

Quentin looked shocked.

'Nah, not like that. I think he lives there. They had a quick cuddle 'n went in the back gate.'

'She's taking a bit of a chance if your father finds out,' Quentin said.

They fell silent as they were served their main course. Angie couldn't remember the last time she'd had beef. And a steak at that.

'That's what I wanna tell her,' Angie said, 'but it's her business. My dad's not a bad man, but I'd be worried what he'd do if he found out. He's a big bloke. He's given me a fair few backhanders. It feels like I've had my block knocked off, but he doesn't think it hurts. Says I need to toughen up.'

Quentin had to look down at his plate to prevent Angie seeing his anger. No wonder her mother was having an affair.

'Do you think your mother's serious about this other bloke? In love, even?'

Angie put her knife and fork down and looked at Quentin.

'Yer knar, I've never once thought about that. But now yer've asked, yer've made me wonder.'

They both ate for a little while – enjoying this rare luxury.

'What about *yer* mam 'n dad?' Angie asked as she cut a piece of beef. She popped it in her mouth and savoured it.

'Very different to yours, but also not too dissimilar.'

Angie put her hand to her mouth to stop herself laughing. She swallowed.

'Eee, Quentin, yer do make me laugh. Sometimes you speak in riddles. What does *different but not too dissimilar* mean?'

'You're right, I do, don't I?' He cut his steak. 'I think what I'm saying is that our parents are probably poles apart, but not so much our mothers.'

'Really?' Angie said, her eyes widening in surprise. She dropped her voice. 'Yer mean, she's having it off with someone else as well?'

Quentin nodded.

'But,' he said, keeping his voice low, 'I think my mother might be a tad more discreet than yours – and unlike your father, I think mine might know exactly what's going on.'

'Eee, well I never,' Angie said. 'I guess we're not that different after all.'

Quentin smiled and raised his glass.

'I'll drink to that.'

The pair chinked glasses.

Angie thought this was the best night she'd ever had. Even better than the ones she'd had with Dor at the Ritz. Not that she'd tell her that, of course.

When Angie let herself into the flat, she was relieved that Dorothy was still out with Marie-Anne. She wanted to be alone with her own thoughts for a while, before the inevitable barrage of questions. Going into the kitchen, she poured herself a glass of water and sat down. The wine and the food this evening had been out of this world. Going out with Quentin had felt as though she had stepped into one of the films she and Dorothy went to see at the flicks – and she'd only just stepped back out. Her head was a swirl of thoughts and feelings, most of which made her feel incredibly happy, but also extremely confused.

Downstairs in the basement flat, Quentin sat down at the kitchen table with its reinforced steel top. He hoped it wouldn't be needed for much longer. The outcome of the war was still uncertain, but it was going in the right direction. The German Army had been defeated in North Africa, the Americans had the Japanese on the back foot, and now their troops were being prepped to take Italy.

As he sipped his cup of tea, thoughts of war were overtaken by ones of love.

He thought about the first time he had clapped eyes on Angie. It must have been six months ago – a few weeks before Christmas. He had to chuckle to himself. It had hardly been the most romantic first encounter, with Angie storming down the road, cheeks flushed, a face like thunder, demanding to know what he was doing trying the main door to the flats and looking as though she was about to lynch him.

He'd explained that he had mislaid his keys and Angie had backed down, telling him, rather gruffly, that she'd thought he was trying to 'rob the place'.

He didn't know what he had fallen for the most – her fierce but beautiful face, flushed with fury, or her bravery in confronting a potential burglar. He had laughed later that evening when he and Mrs Kwiatkowski were enjoying a cup of tea, having been formally introduced to Angie and Dorothy. They had both agreed they would have felt sorry for anyone who *had* been trying to break into the flat.

It had been a case of love at first sight for him. He hadn't even tried to fight it; hadn't wanted to. He'd tried to chat to Angie whenever he had the chance, which was infrequent as most of the time he was in London. But when she had come knocking on his door on Christmas Eve dressed in her stunning citron-coloured dress that showed off her lovely curves, he had felt like whooping with joy. Of course, he knew that he had only been asked – or rather, Angie had only been coerced into asking him – because Dorothy had found herself a date for the wedding and she needed Angie to have one too. He didn't know to whom he was most indebted – Toby for sweeping Dorothy off her feet, or Dorothy for forcing Angie to ask him to the ball.

And they really had had a ball. After a little awkwardness at the start, and a fairly unsuccessful attempt to teach Angie how to waltz, they'd got on like a house on fire and had a rather magical Christmas Day. Certainly, the best one he'd ever had.

Since then he'd managed to see Angie every time he'd been back up north, either when he had leave, or when he had work assignments. At first it hadn't mattered that most of their 'lessons in being posh' were conducted in Mrs Kwiatkowski's kitchen, as he had simply revelled in every moment he was in Angie's company, but lately he had become quite desperate to spend time with her on his own, and when she had agreed to go out for a meal, he'd felt like sprinting all the way from London to Sunderland.

It was obvious that Dorothy and Mrs Kwiatkowski knew how he felt.

Angie, on the other hand, seemed totally oblivious.

He hoped after this evening she might have an idea – even if it was just an inkling – of how he felt towards her.

It pained him that, at this moment, Angie was just twenty feet away from him. Or rather, above him. How he wished he could be with her now, holding her, kissing her. He had never felt this kind of yearning for a woman before. He just had to work out how she felt about him, and for that he needed to be able to see more of her – something that, at the moment, was just not possible. He had to go back to London early tomorrow, and he had no idea when he was going to be able to come back again.

'You're just going to have to be patient,' he said, looking up to the ceiling with longing. 'All good things come to those who wait.'

He sighed.

'I bloody well hope so.'

Chapter Nineteen

Monday 7 June

By the time the klaxon sounded out the end of the lunch break on Monday, all the women welders, as well as Polly, Bel, Marie-Anne, Hannah and Olly, had been privy to a blow-by-blow account of Angie's date on Saturday night. It wasn't Angie, however, who had regaled them all with every minute detail of the evening, down to what vegetables they had been given with their meal – but Dorothy.

And the reason Dorothy knew every cough and spit of Angie's evening at the museum and then at the Palatine was down to her having spent the best part of Sunday grilling Angie about every aspect of her 'date', which Angie kept repeating was not a 'date'.

Dorothy had been exasperated by Angie's lack of observation regarding much of the evening. She had gasped in disbelief when Angie was unable to tell her if any VIPs had been dining there; when she could tell her next to nothing about the decor, and hadn't known the name of the wine they had drunk. ('It was in French!' said Angie.) And when Angie admitted they had consumed the whole bottle, Dorothy had screeched so loudly that Mrs Kwiatkowski had stuck her head out of her front door and shouted up the stairs to ask if they were both all right.

Angie had eventually managed to deflect the attention away from herself by saying what a brilliant idea it would be for Toby to take Dorothy to the Palatine when he was here next, then she could see it all for herself. Dorothy had jumped up and down in excitement, before reprimanding herself for not having thought of it first.

Polly had been sitting next to Angie during the lunch-time reenactment of Angie's date-which-wasn't-a date and could see that her former workmate seemed unusually quiet and a little withdrawn. She asked her if she was all right, but Angie had said she was just tired.

Polly then made her chuckle by saying that she would be exhausted all the time if she shared a flat with Dorothy.

Later that week they all had a trip to the flicks to see Deanna Durbin in *The Amazing Mrs Holliday* at the Regal and everyone met Georgina for the first time. As Rosie knew would be the case, everyone loved her and the next day they all agreed that she was now officially part of their gang.

Georgina was also overjoyed to be welcomed into the fold. She just hoped that they never found out about her private-eye work, and especially that she had dug up dirt on all of them. She mightn't know why Helen's mother had employed her to do what she'd done, but she was pretty certain it was not for any kind of altruistic reason. And Georgina certainly wouldn't want her new friends knowing she'd been tasked by Helen to find out about Bel's bloodline, even if she was sure that Helen – unlike Miriam – didn't want to use the report Georgina had given her to hurt anyone. She didn't think so, anyway.

The following day, during their lunch break, Dorothy read out with pride an article in the *Echo* about the young girl who'd had to have her hands amputated and whom Polly had secretly gifted some of Tommy's gratuity pay when she had thought he was dead.

'"It is now three years since she and her mother and father had been sheltering in the family's brick surface shelter,"' Dorothy read, '"when a Heinkel crashed into their home, trapping them in their shelter, killing her mother and injuring the then fifteen-year-old newly appointed post-office girl probationer with dreams of becoming a telephonist."' She looked up at the women, who were all listening avidly. '"When both her hands had to be amputated, she never thought she'd fulfil that dream. Today the eighteen-year-old started work as a telephonist at Telephone House with her new artificial limbs."'

Dorothy looked up. There was not a single dry eye.

For Dorothy the weekend couldn't come quickly enough as she was desperate to speak to Toby and tell him that he would be taking her to the Palatine next time he got leave. When she did, he laughed and said he'd better start saving up.

Gloria had also been ringing Jack on a daily basis as he had been threatening to jump on a train after hearing that Helen had got the doctor to take a look at Hope. Gloria managed to keep him from crossing the border by reminding him that three families would be thrown into chaos if he did, and could he live with his conscience?

'Hope's going to be fine,' she reassured him.

There was silence down the phone.

'Honestly,' she reiterated. 'The doctor Helen sent round told me what I knew already – that it would work its way out 'n that it's nothing sinister.'

'Mmm.' Jack was still unconvinced.

'Bobby 'n Gordon had the exact same cough when they were Hope's age, 'n they were fine.'

It was hard to know what Jack was thinking – she would have liked to have seen his face as he wasn't the most loquacious of men – but she was hopeful that she had managed to placate him. Still, she rang him every day, just to be certain.

Later on in the month, Bel went to the launch of *Empire Camp* at Short Brothers with Helen, although this time Helen made sure her grandfather and mother would not be in attendance, and Bel found herself being photographed alongside Helen and making it into the *Echo*, much to everyone's excitement. The photographer had wanted to get another shot of Helen and Mr Royce together as he was also at the launch, but Helen had insisted the readers would much prefer to see 'two stunners' staring out at them over their tea, rather than just the one. Matthew had roared with laughter and wandered off, still chuckling to himself.

Bel told Polly about her trips out of the office, and Polly was pleased that Bel and Helen seemed to be getting on so well, but she also felt that their burgeoning friendship was at the expense of her own relationship with her sister-in-law.

Or was it, she wondered in a letter to Tommy, because of her expanding belly?

Tommy had written back that it would be understandable if that was the case, but was there anything else it could be?

Polly wondered if Bel's true paternity was troubling her. She wasn't sure. She just knew something was going on and her sister-in-law wasn't confiding in her like she normally did – like she had done ever since they were small.

Pearl had also noticed a change in Bel. Since overhearing her conversation with Agnes that evening back in May, she had been keeping a close eye on her and she didn't like what she saw.

'She's more moody than normal – 'n quiet,' she told Bill. 'And when Isabelle's quiet, she's thinking, 'n I've gorra nasty feeling I knar exactly what that mind of hers is chewing over.'

And with these thoughts of her daughter's simmering need for retribution came images of Henrietta, her dark eyes imploring her Little Match Girl to come back and visit.

The newspapers the women were reading every day at work seemed to verify that the war was going in their favour. The British 1st Infantry Division took the island of Pantelleria, between Tunisia and Sicily, capturing 11,000 Italian troops, followed shortly afterwards by the neighbouring island of Lampedusa. Five days later, the Allies bombed Sicily and the Italian mainland – showing that an invasion was imminent.

In Germany, the RAF continued their attacks on the Ruhr valley – this time, though, families from the area were evacuated, much to the women's relief.

Later on in the month, American troops under the leadership of General Douglas MacArthur pushed for victory in the Pacific. They were landing troops in islands close to New Guinea, continuing their strategy of 'island hopping', which entailed taking over an island and establishing a military base, from which point they would launch another attack and another takeover of another island.

Closer to home, it was reported that of the 322 soldiers from the town who made up the 125th Anti-Tank Regiment, known to have been in Singapore when it fell into Japanese hands, 204 were POWs.

The mood was lifted when Gloria read out an article about how twenty-two-year-old Mrs Sarah Bambrough of Cleveland Road had given birth to triplets in Sunderland Municipal Hospital. There was, naturally, much shrieking and laughter. Polly did not find the suggestion that she too might have triplets at all amusing, nor Angie's comments that 'yer definitely big enough!'

It was now five weeks since the last air raid and so far, the town's sirens had been resting – but it was something the women would not talk about for fear of jinxing the respite.

Chapter Twenty

The launch of the armed cargo ship *Greenwich* at Doxford's seemed to have attracted the whole town. Getting anywhere near the slipway on the south bank of the Wear was nigh on impossible.

The reason: royalty. Minor royalty. But royalty all the same.

'As this is the first time a member of the royal family is to perform the naming ceremony on an ordinary trader of the Merchant Navy,' Rosie told the women with unusual solemnity, 'we have been given a few hours off to go and watch the launch.'

Rosie braced herself for Dorothy's anticipated histrionics.

She was not wrong to do so, for her words were immediately followed by an ear-splitting scream, which was accompanied by Dorothy raising her arms in the air as though she was a weightlifter raising a barbell and steadfastly holding it aloft. A few heads turned, but most of the platers and riveters they worked alongside had become accustomed to the regularity of Dorothy's shrieks and screams and carried on with their own conversations.

'Cor, how did you manage to wangle that, miss?' Angie asked. She had mostly been successful in her bid to stop calling Rosie 'miss', but it still occasionally slipped out.

'Yeah,' Gloria said. 'I'm intrigued.'

'Me too.' Martha dropped her voice. 'How come we've got to go and others haven't?'

'Get your stuff together and I'll tell you en route.' Rosie looked up at the clock. 'We've only got half an hour to get there, so we best get a shimmy on.'

'Has Hannah been allowed to go too?' Martha asked.

'Of course,' Rosie said.

'Don't tell me she's coming without Olly?' Dorothy asked.

Rosie laughed. 'That's right. It's a women-only jolly.'

Dorothy and Angie looked as though they were going to burst with excitement. They hooked arms and did what could have passed as a synchronised Irish jig all the way to the drawing office.

Rosie, Gloria and Martha followed, big grins on all three faces, all shaking their heads at the comic duo.

'I've got to warn you,' Helen said to Bel, 'my grandfather's going to be there – as well as my darling mother. Neither of them would miss rubbing shoulders with royalty for all the tea in China.'

Bel hesitated. She had turned down the last invite, to the launch of HMS *Bugloss*, a Flower-class corvette at Crown's, knowing Mr Havelock would be there. She'd done so because she couldn't face the way seeing him left her feeling: angry, resentful – and in need of retribution.

'I'd be mad not to go.' She took a deep breath. 'And besides, I can't keep avoiding him for the rest of my life.'

Or his. How she wished he'd drop down dead and out of their lives.

'I can't keep running away from him – like my mam's done her whole life.'

Helen remembered what Georgina had written in her report about Pearl stealing away in the middle of the night after the master had raped her. From what she could gather, she'd not stopped running since, one way or another.

'Well, I think you're being very brave,' Helen said.

'So, come on then, spill the beans,' Angie said to Rosie as they all slipped under one of the ropes that segregated the townsfolk from the shipyard workers. Their uniform of oil-smeared denim overalls meant no one stopped them, although if they had, Rosie had been told to tell them that they had been asked to the occasion by Mr Royce Jnr, who everyone knew was very close to the Doxford family.

'Well,' Rosie said, pointing over to an area near the slipway that didn't look too congested. 'I was talking to Helen and she was saying that the Princess Royal was going to meet and chat briefly with some of the women shipyard workers at the yard.'

'Really?' Dorothy's eyes were out on stalks.

'Shame she couldn't have come to one of our launches,' Gloria said.

They shouldered their way into a gap within spitting distance of the rostrum and the towering bow of the ship waiting patiently on the ways for her christening.

'I'd never have had you down as a royalist, Glor,' Dorothy said, grabbing Angie's arm and pulling her into prime position in front of the barrier that had been put in place to keep the riff-raff away from the royalty.

'And,' Rosie continued, putting her hand on Hannah's back and manoeuvring her into a gap where she would be able to see the proceedings, 'we both agreed that as those women were getting a pat on the back by a princess for working in a shipyard, then we should also give our women shipbuilders a show of appreciation.'

They had seen some of the other women who worked as general labourers at Thompson's jump on a tram before them when they'd been walking along Dame Dorothy Street.

'It's a shame Polly didn't feel up to coming,' Martha said.

'Yeah,' Angie said. 'I mean, she's still one of us, isn't she?'

'I don't blame her for not coming, though,' Martha said.

'I knar, she looks ready to drop, 'n she's still got another two 'n a half months to gan.'

They all heard a few cheers and claps.

They craned their necks and could just see the Princess Royal in the distance. Dressed in her ATS uniform, she looked more like a general about to carry out an inspection of the troops.

As she turned to shake hands with a waiting line of women workers, Dorothy quickly scanned the crowds and did a double take when she spotted a bird's nest of orange hair.

She nudged Angie.

'Oh my God,' she hissed into her ear. 'Look who's here.'

'I can't remember the last time I came to a launch,' Lily said. She was standing next to Maisie. As she looked around, she was pleased they had arrived early and managed to get themselves a good position. They were near to where all the action was going to take place, but not too near. She didn't want to attract too much attention, which was never easy – what with her looks and Maisie's caramel-coloured skin.

'You probably don't *remember*, because you've never been to one before,' Maisie said, feeling a little uncomfortable. She too had never been to a launch, nor anywhere near any of the town's yards, *never mind* practically within touching distance of a ship – a tramp steamer, no less. She had to chuckle to herself – *tramp* steamer.

'No, I have!' Lily suddenly remembered. 'Must have been a good year and a half ago now. At Thompson's. Dear me, how could I forget? It was the first ship launched after Rosie had trained up her women welders.' She got out her fan and snapped it open.

'A first for you, though, my dear.' Lily looked at Maisie. 'Not often, I'm guessing, you can lay claim to that.'

Maisie allowed herself a smile. It wasn't often that she was alone with Lily. And on the rare occasions it was just the two of them, she was sure her boss allowed herself to be a little bit more outrageous. Lily also dropped the faux French, reverting to her natural cockney – probably, Maisie guessed, because they were both Londoners.

'Oh, there she is!' Lily exclaimed.

They both stared, just like everyone else, at Princess Mary, Countess of Harewood.

'Oh dear,' Lily whispered, 'I don't think much of her get-up. I thought she'd have made more of an effort. You'd think she was a man were it not for the skirt.'

Maisie laughed. 'She *has* to wear that. She's commandant of the ATS.'

'Mmm.' Lily didn't sound convinced. 'Now, check out the woman next to her. That dress ... that fascinator ... Now that's what I call class.'

Maisie looked at the slim, blonde-haired woman Lily was 'checking out'. The smile left her face. She looked at the small gaggle of VIPs who were strolling behind the Princess Royal and saw Mr Havelock. She felt herself bristle.

She glanced at Lily.

She too had gone a little sombre and was scrutinising the entourage of men and women following the Princess Royal as she made her way towards the rostrum.

*

'Is that your sister I can see?' Helen whispered to Bel. She'd just spotted Maisie standing next to the eccentric-looking woman with dyed auburn hair and make-up that looked as though it had been put on with a trowel. She'd seen her at Polly and Tommy's wedding as well as Arthur's funeral.

'Yes, it is,' Bel said, surprised. 'She didn't tell me she was coming.'

'Is there a husband about? Children?' Helen asked. As she spoke, she spotted Matthew bobbing his way through the crowds and groaned inwardly.

'Maisie? Married with children?' Bel laughed. 'No. No chance. She's not the marrying kind – nor particularly maternal.'

Helen wanted to find out what Maisie did for a living but thought it a bit rude to ask outright. She'd quizzed Gloria, but she'd said she didn't know much about Maisie.

'You sound very different from one another,' she said.

Damn, Matthew had spotted her and was waving.

She pretended not to see him.

'I think you could say we're chalk and cheese. In looks and personality,' Bel said. She was still looking at her sister, wondering why she was here. She could only think it was at Lily's bidding. But then again, why would Lily want to come to a launch?

'But it sounds as if you get on?' Helen asked.

'Yes, we do, strangely—' Bel stopped short on catching sight of Princess Mary. 'Oh, my goodness, here she is.'

They stared, along with hundreds of others, as the Princess Royal came into view.

'She's in uniform,' Bel said, surprised.

The crowd cheered and waved. The Princess Royal smiled and slowed to chat to a few women shipyard workers who worked as 'humpers', helping the platers haul the huge metal sheets about.

'From what I know,' Helen said, 'she's a bit of royal radical – well, for a woman anyway. Pretty hands-on. Worked as a nurse. Does loads of charity work and – *oh, blast!*'

'What's wrong?' Bel looked at Helen.

'It's bloody Matthew,' she hissed out of the corner of her mouth.

Bel looked around just in time to see Matthew apologising his way through the crowd. He was hard to miss. Bel reckoned he must be at least six foot, and there was no denying he was what Marie-Anne would call 'a bit of dish' with his short dark hair, the few streaks of grey only seeming to add to his attractiveness.

'Blimey!' he said, finally reaching them, his dark eyes on Helen. 'Good job we don't get royalty at every launch – the town would grind to a halt.'

He tipped his fedora at Helen and Bel.

Bel smiled. Helen didn't.

'Hello, Mr Royce,' Bel said.

'Mrs Elliot,' Matthew replied.

'Couldn't have wanted a better day for it, could we?' He looked up at the clear sky and squinted into the sun that had also come out for the day. 'I see your grandfather's graced us with his presence today,' he went on.

He didn't notice the smile drop from Bel's face.

'Only a sudden death – *and that being his own* – would keep Grandpapa away today,' Helen said, not attempting to disguise her disdain.

Matthew laughed.

'Nothing like families, eh?' He looked at Bel. *She always looked as white as a sheet.*

'Ahh, and your mother's here too.' He looked at Helen, who was giving her full attention to the Princess Royal as she made her way to the rostrum.

166

'Looking very glamorous as always,' he added. 'Although taking the spotlight off the princess somewhat, it has to be said.'

'Mr Royce,' Helen said, as she continued looking straight ahead, 'there really is no need for a running commentary. I feel like I'm standing next to a BBC radio correspondent.'

Any more chatter was impossible anyway, as Princess Mary took the bottle of champagne and swung it with gusto at the bow of *Greenwich*. A huge cheer rang out.

Bel tried to focus on the princess, but her gaze kept being drawn to her father. And sister. Half-sister. It suddenly occurred to her that both her sisters were within a stone's throw of each other. She and Maisie might be at opposite ends of the spectrum looks-wise, but Miriam was her double. Just older.

'That was a kind gesture your grandfather made the other day.' Matthew had to speak loudly to be heard. 'Giving that rather substantial cheque to the children's hospital.'

'Well, he can afford to be kind,' Helen said. 'It's easy to give it away when you've lots of it.'

Helen had just spoken Bel's thoughts. She watched Mr Havelock step forward to chat to the princess as the huge chains attached to the *Greenwich* untangled themselves at a rapid rate before becoming taut as the ship was just about to hit the other side of the Wear.

If only people knew. If only the Princess Royal knew. Would she be shaking his hand, giving him the time of day – chatting to him as she was now?

'Still,' Matthew said, persevering with his reverence of Mr Havelock, 'you can't deny your grandfather does an awful lot of good. I'd say a good few of the townsfolk wouldn't be here today if it wasn't for the money he gave to our hospitals – and the asylum.' He looked at Helen, who remained tight-lipped.

'And the money he invests in the shipyards,' he added.

'*Invests* being the optimum word,' Helen said eventually. 'As in he will make money from the shipyards. It's hardly selfless.'

'But the money he gives to the hospitals is,' Matthew countered.

He did not catch the look that passed between the woman he was determined to win over and her secretary. Each knew the other felt the same sense of shame at being related to such evil. An evil that did such a good job of manifesting itself as good.

Gloria was finding it hard to keep her attention on the princess; her eyes automatically strayed back to Miriam.

That woman! God, how she hated her.

Gloria immediately scolded herself. *Stop being so resentful!*

Age – and, even more, her marriage to Vinnie – had taught her that hate and resentment were self-destructive. It was hard, though. Hope being unwell had made her tired, sleep-deprived and irritable. Over the past month work had been unrelenting. It would have helped enormously if Jack had been there as a shoulder to lean on and an ear to moan to, but most of all so that her daughter could have had her dad about too and not just her mam.

There they were again: the demons – hate and resentment – dancing about in her heart, stomping out love and happiness.

Gloria watched as Mr Havelock introduced his daughter to Princess Mary.

She felt a fleeting sense of joy as the Princess Royal gave Miriam all of a few seconds before turning and making her way back to the main building. There was no reason to loiter – *Greenwich* was already being tugged away.

Gloria continued to watch, giving her dancing demons free rein.

Miriam looked more like royalty than the Princess Royal.

Miriam had always led a gilded life, always got what she wanted, regardless of what it took. She'd got Jack. Snatched her sweetheart right off her when she and Jack were about to get engaged – seduced him, lied to him, saying she was pregnant when she wasn't. She'd got him down the aisle, lying again a few months later that she'd had a miscarriage.

Watching Miriam chatting to the mayor, Gloria thought how relaxed she looked, so fresh – so *unworn out*. No wonder! She'd never had to work a day in her life. She'd never even had to cook or clean. She lived the life of Riley.

Gloria eyed her perfectly coiffured hair, and felt her own dry, unruly hair breaking free from her headscarf. She saw Miriam's hand shaking some bigwig's as they tailed the princess. She could see her glossy red nails from here. Gloria glanced down at her own hands. They were dry and chafed – more like an old fishwife's.

But none of that really mattered. What did was the control Miriam had over her and Jack – how she was making their daughter suffer the absence of a father in her life.

An absence that looked set to continue for an awful lot longer.

'Hello, anyone home?' Dorothy's voice interrupted the dance of the demons.

'Eee, Glor, yer look like yer in a trance,' Angie joined in.

'Time to go,' Rosie said, eyeing Gloria and the rest of the women.

'Back to the grind,' Dorothy griped.

'We've just had half the afternoon off, Dor, we can't complain,' said Martha.

They all started to make their way out of the shipyard. They made slow progress as they had no choice but to go at a snail's pace because of the crowds. People were still trying to catch one last glimpse of the princess.

'Shame Jack couldn't have been here today,' Dorothy said, throwing Angie a look. Despite several discussions over the past month, they still hadn't been able to work out why he'd not been back.

'Aye, a real shame,' Angie said. 'He would have been hobnobbing with the princess – then he could have told us what she's really like.'

They all walked through the main gates and along Pallion New Road to the bus stop.

'He's still not been given any time off?' Hannah asked.

Gloria shook her head but didn't say anything.

'I think it's cruel,' Dorothy said. 'Working him like that, not letting him come back home for a visit.'

'Do you think we should ask Helen – see if she can get him back?' Martha asked.

'What a good idea!' Hannah said. 'Why haven't we thought of that before now? Helen can chat to Harold.'

Dorothy looked at Angie.

'We also had an idea,' she said.

'We'll buy yer a ticket to Glasgow,' Angie said.

The pair looked at Rosie.

'And you could get Glor the time off, couldn't you?' Dorothy asked.

'That's sounds like a brilliant idea,' Martha said. 'Especially now we don't seem to be getting any air rai—'

Everyone shouted her down.

'*Dinnit say it, Martha!*' Angie shouted.

Gloria sighed. 'That's kind, but it's too long a journey for Hope.'

Rosie glanced across at Gloria. She looked flushed, tired and worn out. It can't have been easy watching Miriam. If she had been in Gloria's boots, she would have struggled not to clamber over the barrier and throttle Miriam within an inch of her life. Seeing the woman who had been the bane of her life flouncing around hobnobbing and looking like the cat that got the cream was the last thing Gloria needed.

Rosie looked behind at Dorothy and Angie, who seemed to be chatting conspiratorially with Martha and Hannah.

Perhaps the time had come for Gloria to tell the women the truth.

'We're gonna have to tell them, aren't we?' Gloria said.

'You read my mind.' Rosie looked at her friend. 'I don't think we have much choice.'

'It's gonna be hard. Really hard,' Gloria said with a heavy sigh.

'I know, but it sounds like they might take things into their own hands if we don't,' Rosie said, also sounding deflated.

'I know. Did yer hear Hannah?' Gloria said. 'I guarantee she'll be in Helen's office first chance she gets, arguing the case like she's at the Old Bailey.'

They walked on. Rosie checked no one could hear what they were saying.

'All right, let's get everyone together.'

It was on the tip of Gloria's tongue to suggest they also invite Bel, but she stopped herself. Only Helen and Polly knew that Bel was Miriam's sister. And that was a secret only Bel could disclose.

God, so many secrets. So many lies.

'We'll go somewhere we can chat in private,' Rosie said as she waved up at the young timekeeper. 'No chance of being overheard.'

As they waved goodbye to Hannah, who was heading over to the quietness of the office, Rosie looked at Gloria.

'I've just thought of the perfect place.'

'Rushing off without saying goodbye to your dear old grandpapa?' Mr Havelock said, stabbing his walking stick into the ground as he made his way over to Helen and Bel.

'Dear me,' he puffed, finally reaching them, 'seems like the only time I get to see my only grandchild is at a launch.'

'That might be because I'm busy, Grandfather. No time for sitting around chatting and drinking cups of tea. I'm a working woman – there's ships to be built, a war on,' Helen said, forcing a smile.

'Excuse me,' Bel said. 'I'll be back in a minute.'

'Oh, Mrs Elliot,' Mr Havelock said. 'A pleasure to see you again.'

Bel stretched her lips into a line by way of a smile and left.

'I'll meet you back at the car,' Helen called as Bel hurried off.

Mr Havelock stared as Bel made her way through the crowds.

'Why do I get the feeling your secretary doesn't like me?' he asked.

'Don't be ridiculous,' Helen said. 'Old age is making you paranoid.'

Mr Havelock laughed, pulling out his monogrammed handkerchief and wiping his brow.

'Good to see Royce Junior in such good fettle,' he said, then paused and eyed his granddaughter. 'You could do worse, you know.'

Helen looked at her grandfather with what she hoped was a look of disbelief.

'Matchmaker now, are you?'

'It would be a good union,' Mr Havelock continued. 'Two wealthy families joining forces. Especially now your doctor friend seems to be out of the equation. Sounds like he's got himself quite a catch there with some psychologist over at the asylum.' He tapped his head with a long, bony finger. 'What's the name?'

His eyes lit up.

'Eris. That's it. Dr Claire Eris ... Now there's a perfect match. Both doctors. Both their fathers are doctors. Wealthy. Good lineage.'

'Dear me, Grandfather, gossipmonger as well as matchmaker.'

Helen looked down at her watch.

'Gosh, is that the time? I'd better get a move on.' She forced herself to give her grandfather a peck on the cheek and left.

As she walked back to the car, making her way impatiently through the slow swell of spectators heading home, she wondered whether she was the one who was being paranoid. Had her grandfather known his words would hurt?

Mr Havelock watched as Helen hurried away.

His granddaughter had been a bit off with him of late. Not as warm as she used to be. It had started after she'd had her miscarriage. He should have tried to have appeared a little more empathetic. It would have benefited him in the long run.

173

He turned to head back to the gaggle of sycophantic big-wigs all fawning over the Princess Royal. Seeing Miriam loitering about, desperate for another few words with the princess, irked him. Why were both Miriam and Marga-ret total washouts? Completely inept when it came to any-thing to do with business – or work of any kind, for that matter. Why the bloody hell hadn't Henrietta been able to give him a boy? The one thing he had wanted from her – what most other women on the planet seemed able to do – and she couldn't even do that.

Good job he had a granddaughter who wasn't work-shy and was pretty savvy into the bargain. She'd manipulated him into paying Dr Billingham's fees, knowing he wanted to get back in her good books after his insensitivity over her miscarriage. She'd shown herself to be a chip off the old Havelock block. *She* would continue his legacy. Not that he had any intention of popping his clogs any time soon.

'You all right?' Bel asked.

'Yes, just a bit browned off,' Helen said, firing up the engine and slowly driving out of the car park.

'Because?'

'Oh, it's nothing,' Helen waved her hand dismissively, 'just something Grandfather said about John and Dr Eris.' She changed up a gear as they drove out of the gates and turned onto the main road.

'I'm guessing they're still an item?' Bel asked.

'It would seem so,' Helen said, 'and as my dear Grand-father has just reminded me, they make a very suitable match – in all ways.'

They drove in silence while they crossed the Queen Alexandra Bridge over to the north side of the Wear.

'And Matthew?' Bel asked tentatively. 'He seems very keen on you.'

'Keen on marrying money,' Helen said. She knew the Royces weren't as affluent as they liked to make out.

Bel thought for a moment as they drove through Southwick, a suburb on the north bank of the river. She didn't feel it her place to say that, in her opinion, Mr Royce Jnr's keenness wasn't driven by monetary gain. But what did she know? The middle and upper classes were a different breed.

Helen glanced across at Bel. 'I have to say, I think that's a good way to deal with seeing my grandfather.'

'What? Running away?' Bel's laugh was acrid.

'I don't see it as running away,' Helen said. 'I wish *I* could. No, I meant that you choose not to be in his company.'

Bel nodded. She didn't trust herself to say anything more.

'I thought you might have used your escape as an opportunity to go and say hello to your sister?' Helen asked.

'No, I just went to the ladies,' Bel said. Where she had stayed until she had been able to stop herself from shaking with frustration and anger. 'Then I headed back to the car.'

'She obviously got time off work,' Helen probed, her curiosity about Maisie getting the better of her.

'Yes, she must have,' said Bel, not volunteering any more information.

Chapter Twenty-One

Lily sat down at the table by the window in what was becoming her regular haunt – the Holme Café, next door to Kate's boutique on Holmeside.

'Well, that was interesting,' she said, getting out her fan and cooling herself. 'Is it me or is it hot in here?'

'It's you,' Maisie said automatically. 'It's always you.' Lily asked the same question at least once a day without fail.

They both looked up at the skinny blonde waitress. She had a big smile on her face as they were her favourite customers – and also her biggest tippers.

'I need water, *ma chère*,' Lily said dramatically to the young girl. 'I feel like I've been stuck out in the Sahara all day and I have finally reached my oasis.'

The young waitress chuckled. The strange woman with the orange hair and odd accent always brightened up her day.

'And of course,' Lily added, 'a pot of tea for two.' She looked at Maisie, who shook her head. 'No other nourishment for the moment, though.'

The waitress smiled at Maisie – she was the most beautiful coloured woman she had ever seen; actually, the *only* coloured woman she'd ever seen.

'So come on, why did you really want to go to the launch?' Maisie asked.

Lily eyed her protégée but didn't say anything.

'And would I be right in saying that it might be connected to the "tricky" problem I came to discuss with you a little while ago?' Maisie asked. She had not seen as much of Lily as she did normally due to her boss's new routine. As a rule, they'd have a bit of a catch-up at the end of the evening, but since Charlotte had started to come for breakfast, Lily had been in bed by eleven at the latest.

'Your deductions would be correct, my dear,' Lily said.

Maisie got out a slender black Sobranie from its packet and put it in her ebony cigarette-holder. 'So, tell me, what did you do?'

'I thought about it for a while,' said Lily, 'and obviously I discussed the problem with George.'

Maisie nodded. George was not just Lily's lover but her confidant and adviser.

'George, of course,' said Lily, 'totally understood why you didn't want to give the man a membership. Or be anywhere near him, for that matter.'

'This afternoon was near enough for me,' Maisie said, lighting her cigarette.

They both fell silent as the waitress arrived at their table with their tea tray.

'*Merci,*' Lily said, noticing the young girl's frayed cuffs.

When she had gone, Lily continued.

'So, I wrote a letter.'

Maisie blew out smoke, her attention rapt.

'In which I explained that, unfortunately, the club was presently oversubscribed, but to rest assured that I would inform him as soon as a vacancy arose,' Lily said, keeping her voice low.

'And?' Maisie had a bad feeling in her gut. The sensible part of her knew she should have sanctioned his membership, that Bel and her ma need never have known – but she couldn't. Every part of her being had rebelled against the very thought.

'And,' Lily said, putting down her teacup, 'now we wait.'

'So, you've not heard anything?'

'No, but I only sent the letter a few days ago.'

'But you don't think this will be the end of it, do you?' Maisie asked.

'No,' Lily said simply.

'Is that why you wanted to see him today – in the flesh?'

Lily nodded.

'I wanted to get a sense of what we might be up against.'

Maisie tapped her cigarette in the ashtray. She understood. Seeing Mr Havelock today, she had got a good take on him. She had known men like him before – unfortunately. They were men you tried to keep well away from; men you certainly didn't cross unless it was absolutely necessary.

'Port and lemon, please, Bill,' Bel said, looking around the pub.

Bill took a tall narrow glass off one of the shelves, gave it a polish and held it up to the light.

'And don't dare say it's on the house,' said Bel, getting her purse out. ''Cos I know my ma probably guzzles a good part of your profits.'

Bill didn't say anything; he could see there was no arguing with Bel today. He had known Bel for a few years now and it was only very occasionally that he saw her mother in her. Now was one of those occasions.

'Is that my Isabelle I can hear?' Pearl appeared from the snug; she was carrying a load of dirty glasses on a tin beer tray. 'I've just had the auld grannies in there having their weekly grouse.' She used her foot to push the door shut.

'Thanks, Bill.' Bel paid him the money for her drink.

'Yer not givin' her it on the house? Yer stingy auld git,' Pearl said, setting the tray down on the bar.

Bill laughed. 'Enough of the "old".'

'I *told* him I was paying, Ma – seeing as you drink the place dry most nights.'

Pearl whooped with laughter.

'Not every night,' she chuckled, winking at Bill. 'Just every other.'

Pearl pulled up the hatch and went behind the bar. She looked about the pub. 'Yer husband not here? Pol? Yer new mate, Helen?'

Bel narrowed her eyes at her mother.

'No, I just wanted a minute to myself,' she said, taking a sip of her drink.

Just then the main door to the lounge bar opened and Ronald came in.

Bel looked at Bill and pulled a face.

'I'm going to have a sit-down,' she said, walking away and pretending not to see her ma's drinking buddy. She couldn't stand the bloke.

'Yer all right there, Pearl?' Ronald always spoke loudly. As usual, he had his sleeves rolled up, showing off his sinewy arms covered in tattoos.

'Aye, I'm good,' Pearl said, turning around to the optics and pushing a shot of whisky into a glass for herself. 'Yer keeping all right?' She walked towards the hatch.

'Good as gold ... Good as gold,' Ronald said, his eyes on Pearl. 'Yer up for a game of poker later?' He watched as she lifted the hatch and ducked under it to the other side.

Pearl shook her head. Every time she saw him, it reminded her of getting blotto the night of the air raid.

'Not tonight, Ronald. Need to catch up on my beauty sleep.' Her laughter was forced.

179

Walking over to where her daughter was, she scraped out a stool and plonked herself on it, making sure her back was to the bar.

'So, what's up?' she asked Bel. 'Yer look all done up. Yer been somewhere?'

Bel sighed. 'You're probably the only person in town not to know that we had a visit from royalty today.'

Pearl chuckled. 'I dinnit think they could have sent anyone lower down in the pecking order. What is she? Niece twice removed to the King, or summat like that?'

'I think you'll find she's George V's daughter and the great-granddaughter of Queen Victoria.'

'Oh, who's all la-di-da these days. Must be that new mate of yers.'

Bel ignored her mother's jibe.

Pearl pulled out her packet of cigarettes and lit one. It took her a few moments before the light bulb pinged and she understood why Bel was in a bad mood. If there was royalty at some launch, *he'd* be there. Without a doubt.

'So, come on,' Pearl said, blowing out smoke. 'Why yer here?'

'The thing is, Ma, I've been thinking a lot lately—'

'Aye, tell us about it,' Pearl mumbled.

Bel ignored her mother and continued. 'And I remember you said something about there being another maid – a chambermaid – who left just before you got your job there.'

'Mmm ...' Pearl took a drink of her Scotch.

'That she had "got herself in the family way"?'

'Aye.' Pearl puffed on her cigarette, her eyes scrutinising her daughter through the smoke.

'Well, I don't think it would be a massive leap of faith to assume that what happened to you had happened to her?' Bel asked.

Pearl nodded.

Bel gasped at her ma's lack of outrage. 'I'm guessing that means *yes*? That the same happened to that poor girl as happened to you?'

'That's what I *think* happened, but that's not to say that it *actually* happened.'

'Oh, come on, Ma, we're not in a court of law now. It's pretty obvious that man was using young girls for what he wanted and then chucking them away like dirty rags when he was done with them.'

Pearl took a sip of her drink and a long drag on her cigarette.

'Isabelle,' she said through a swirl of grey smoke, 'that's life, that's what men like him do. They always have 'n always will.'

'For as long as they can get away with it,' Bel hissed.

'Aye,' Pearl said, ''n men like him get away with it. Men with money 'n power.'

'But that's just not right, Ma!' Bel leant across the table, trying to keep her voice down, but it was hard. She was angry.

'Aye, 'n as yer well knar, Isabelle, life's not fair. And it's no use getting yer knickers in a knot about it now, 'cos there's nothing you can dee about it. Yer can't change what happened.'

Realising her daughter needed placating, she added, 'And look at the auld man, he's got one foot in the grave – he won't be up to any of that now.'

'Yes, but that's not the point, Ma!' Bel was incredulous. 'He's got away with it his whole life! His *whole* life!' Bel took a deep breath. 'Everyone treats him like he's a saint! You should have seen him today. Chatting to the Princess Royal. God, I felt like grabbing hold of the microphone and telling everyone there exactly what he's like. What he's *done*!'

'Aye, 'n what good would that have done yer?' Pearl snapped. 'Yer'd have humiliated yerself 'n been seen as some madwoman. Would have been carted off to the local loony bin.' Suddenly, an image of Henrietta in her room at the asylum sprang to mind. Lately, she was never far away from her thoughts.

'Yeah, like his wife,' Bel said, as though reading her ma's thoughts, 'your *Mistress Henrietta* – no wonder she went mad, being married to someone like him. Enough to send anyone round the bend.'

Bel bit down on her lip. What her ma had said was true, though. Who would believe her, even if she did tell the world about the real Mr Havelock? She took a large gulp of her port and lemon.

Pearl looked at her daughter. 'It's a bit early fer yer, isn't it?'

Bel let out a loud, joyless laugh. 'Words fail me.'

Pearl glanced over at Bill, who returned her look of concern.

'Why don't you want him to get his comeuppance?' Bel demanded.

Pearl turned her head and lifted her glass at Bill.

'Because, Isabelle,' she said, looking her daughter in the eye, 'it's all water under the bridge now. There's nothing to be achieved. Sometimes it's best to just let well alone.'

'You two ladies all right?'

It was Bill with Pearl's whisky.

'Aye, right as rain,' Pearl said, her tone belying her words. She took the drink from him.

Bill picked up the two empty glasses.

'Same again?' He pointed at Bel's drink.

She shook her head.

'No thanks, Bill,' she said. 'Ma here thinks it's a bit early for me.'

Chapter Twenty-Two

One week later

Wednesday 7 July

'At last, the workers return!' Agnes shouted through from the scullery.

'Sit yerselves down,' she said, coming back into the kitchen and reaching to take the kettle off the hob. 'I'll make us a nice cup of tea.'

'No, you won't, Agnes. I'm going to make us a nice cup of tea,' Bel said, beating her to it and picking up the kettle.

Polly flumped down in the armchair. 'Eee, I never knew doing next to nothing all day could be so exhausting.'

'Did I just hear there was a brew going spare?' Pearl asked as she came bustling in from the backyard, bringing with her a waft of cigarette smoke.

'Shouldn't you be helping Bill open up?' Bel looked at the clock on the mantelpiece above the range.

'Aye, I should,' Pearl said, 'but I wanted a quick word with Agnes first.'

'She'll be after something,' Bel said to Agnes, who had gone back into the scullery and was chopping up bacon rind and tearing up stale bread for the dogs' supper. Tramp and Pup were already waiting in anticipation.

Pearl glanced at her daughter and then at Agnes.

'I *was* wondering if perhaps yer might be able to lend us one of yer dresses.' Pearl shifted uncomfortably. 'Not

183

yer best one – perhaps that faded blue one yer wear occasionally.'

Agnes, Bel and Polly all looked at Pearl with looks of stupefaction on their faces.

'Ma, when have you ever wanted to wear a dress that drops below the knee, never mind anything that Agnes might wear?' Bel shot a look at her mother-in-law. 'No offence.'

'None taken,' Agnes said, still looking at Pearl. 'Although I have to agree with yer daughter, Pearl. I'm a little surprised yer'd want to wear anything of mine.'

"Bout time I started dressing my age,' Pearl said.

The expressions on their faces said they weren't convinced.

'And I might be going out for the day with Bill,' she added.

Now all three faces were a mix of surprised smiles.

'But dinnit yer be getting the wrong idea,' Pearl said. 'It's not what yer think.'

'So, what is it?' Bel asked.

Agnes put down the bowl of food for the dogs and wiped her hands on her apron.

'Just because we practically live on top of each other,' she said, looking at Bel, 'doesn't mean to say we have to know all of each other's business, does it?'

'I couldn't have said that better myself,' said Pearl, giving her daughter a victorious smile as she followed Agnes out of the kitchen.

'Yer boys all right?'

Gloria thought Jack sounded tired. She knew that all the shipyards on the Clyde were also working at full pelt.

'Yes, they both sounded in good spirits,' she said. 'Bobby wrote a full page about how the Short Sunderland had sunk a U-boat just off the west coast of France.' The RAF flying-boat patrol bomber had been developed and constructed by Short's shipyard in the town. 'All quiet there?' she asked.

'Aye,' said Jack, 'not that there's much left to bomb.' Like his hometown, Jack's place of exile was also a prime target for Hitler's Luftwaffe due to it being Britain's main entry point for Allied merchant and military shipping.

'Have you got Hope there?' Jack asked.

Gloria took a deep breath.

'I have. Helen's got her. They're just waiting outside.' Gloria hesitated. 'I wanted to tell yer something first.'

'Oh, aye, sounds ominous.'

Gloria heard a male voice shout out Jack's name.

'I'll be there in a minute!' he shouted back.

'Sorry, Glor, go on,' Jack said.

'We've decided to tell them,' Gloria said, her ear pressed to the phone.

'What? About Miriam? About what she knars?' Jack said, his voice anxious.

'Yes, we've not got much choice,' Gloria said, making a face at Hope, who had her arms and legs wrapped around Helen. 'They know something's amiss. I think they've had their suspicions for a while.'

'Are yer sure? It's going to be hard fer them if they dinnit knar about their mams already. Especially Martha.'

'Well, we're gonna keep shtum about Martha's mam. It should be enough telling them about Angie's and Dorothy's. They're pretty hardy. It'll be a shock, but they'll deal with it.'

'They'll not have a choice,' Jack said.

There was silence. An angry silence.

'Those poor girls,' Jack said. 'They've done nothing wrong. They're working like dogs in that yard 'n now

185

they've been drawn into something that's nowt to do with them.'

He sighed heavily.

'They're taking the brunt for us.'

'Well, like I say, Jack, we've no choice. Hannah went to see Helen the other day to plead your case to come back to the yard. She and Olly had written a list she had compiled with Dor and Angie of the reasons why it was better for everyone if yer came back.'

Gloria allowed herself a sad laugh.

'She'd even divided up the list into two – one for you coming back to Thompson's and the other if you returned to Crown's.'

Jack sighed again, this one long and weary.

'Anyway, Helen's stood here with Hope.' She pushed open the heavy door to the phone box. 'Come and say hello to Daddy, sweetie.' Helen handed her Hope, who made a grab for the phone.

'Daddy!' she said.

Helen shook her head. *Her little sister was going to think the bloody phone was called 'Daddy'.*

186

Chapter Twenty-Three

Tuesday 13 July

'It's all looking good,' Dr Billingham said, sitting himself down behind his desk and making some notes.

Polly breathed a sigh of relief.

'Thank goodness,' she said, smoothing her hand over her bump. 'I'll be glad when this one's out.'

'And you can tell your mother there's still only the one heartbeat.'

Polly smiled.

Dr Billingham turned his attention to the calendar laid out on his desk. His desk, like his appearance, was immaculate. 'Not long now. You're due in the middle of September, so just another eight weeks to go.' He looked up at Polly. 'Trust me, it'll fly by.'

'And you'll take the stitch out before?'

'I will indeed.'

There was a tap on the door and Polly looked round to see Dr Billingham's secretary coming into the room with a tea tray.

'Thank you, Mrs Wilson, just pop it on the table. I'll manage the rest,' Dr Billingham said.

Polly smiled at the secretary as she put down the tray.

'Don't forget, you've got an appointment at half eleven,' Mrs Wilson said, her words clipped.

Dr Billingham nodded solemnly. 'I won't, Mrs Wilson. Mrs Watts will have had enough of me well before then and I will ask her to leave my door open in expectation of my next appointment.'

Mrs Wilson scowled and left the room, closing the door behind her.

'So,' Dr Billingham said, as he poured their tea, 'have you heard from Petty Officer Watts since I saw you last?'

Polly's face lit up as it always did whenever Tommy was mentioned. 'Yes, he's well. Alive. Nagging me to take it easy.'

'Awful news coming from there last week,' Dr Billingham said, getting up and handing Polly her tea.

'The plane crash?' Polly said. She smiled her thanks.

'Something odd going on there. A B-24 crashing into the sea just minutes after take-off ...'

Polly and the women had read about the crash, which had been reported in most of the national newspapers. The plane had been carrying the prime minister of the Polish government-in-exile, General Władysław Sikorski, and like Dr Billingham had just said, there had been no apparent reason why the plane had crashed, killing all those on board apart from the pilot, who'd had a miraculous escape.

'Makes me wonder if there was subterfuge involved,' Dr Billingham mused.

'I think Tommy might have been part of the salvage operation,' Polly confided. Tommy had to be careful with what he wrote in his letters, but he had mentioned that his unit had been involved in the clear-up afterwards.

'He says hello, as usual,' Polly added, taking a sip of her tea, 'and as always thanks you for keeping a good eye on me.'

Dr Billingham dismissed this with a wave of his hand.

'I get paid for it, don't I?'

His comment sent a wave of unease through Polly. Since Bel had told her the secret of her paternity, she had felt uncomfortable that it was Mr Havelock footing the bill.

'And how's Mary? Have you heard any news from her?' Polly had seen the recruitment slogans on posters: *Join the Wrens today and free a man to join the Fleet.*

'She's doing well. Very well. Never better,' Dr Billingham said, reaching for his cigarettes and lighting one. 'Working hard in the capital. Putting that expensive education of hers to good use. Did I tell you she can speak three languages?'

Polly nodded. He had. Several times. It must be lovely, Polly thought, to have a father who doted on you. It was times like this that she missed having a dad.

'So, they've not drafted her to one of the stations on the coast?' Polly asked. Dr Billingham had told her that Mary was going to use her linguistic skills to intercept and translate enemy signals.

'No, not yet. But soon. Very soon. And then she'll be home before we know it. Safe and sound.'

Dr Billingham always said the same thing when he talked about his daughter. It was obvious he was anxious to see her. Polly wasn't sure how often the Wrens were given leave. She'd love to meet her.

There was a rat-a-tat-tat on the door and Mrs Wilson appeared.

'You've a call,' she said. 'Shall I say you'll ring back?'

Polly finished her tea and stood up.

'No, please don't. I've got to get off. Back to the office.' She pulled a face before looking at Mrs Wilson and adding quickly, 'Not that there's anything wrong with working in an office.'

Dr Billingham laughed and waved her off.

'Same time. Two weeks. And do as that husband of yours is telling you. Take it easy.'

Polly would have liked to have told him that she couldn't do anything else. Filing was not exactly hard work. She'd never thought she would say it, but she missed physical hard work: the aching limbs at the end of a day of welding, and the heavy sleep that came with it.

Polly smiled her goodbyes to Mrs Wilson, who reciprocated with a stern nod.

Just as she walked out into the corridor, Polly heard the secretary shout through to Dr Billingham's office.

'It's Mr Havelock. I'm putting him through now.'

Mr Havelock was sitting in his office with the door closed. He didn't want anyone listening in on his conversation. The maid was in today and Agatha seemed to be on the prowl.

He shuffled in his chair, vexed – angry. He'd just come back from a break in Scotland to hear the news that had undone all the rest and relaxation of the past ten days.

Why Eddy hadn't told him before he'd left for his stay with Margaret and Angus, he did not know.

He snorted through his nose, thinking of Eddy's apologies, backed up by Agatha's claims that they hadn't wanted to tell him before he left for fear of spoiling his holiday.

Terrified, more like, that I'd have cancelled the break and stayed put.

'Richard ... Charles.' Mr Havelock did not like to waste time or energy on greetings, unlike Dr Billingham, who always asked him how he was whenever they spoke.

'Actually, I'm not good. Not good at all ...'

Mr Havelock clenched his fists.

God, the man could prattle on.

Impatience got the better of him and he spoke over him.

'There's nothing wrong with me, old chap – it's that damned Gentlemen's Club.'

Another pause.

'Yes, the one I was meant to be getting us both memberships for. Your bonus for looking after the Watts girl.'

Mr Havelock fingered the business card, tapping the corners on the desktop.

'The Ashbrooke Gentlemen's Club.'

Dr Billingham tried to say something along the lines that it really didn't matter, but only got the first few words out.

'That's not the point, Richard!'

Dr Billingham managed to ask why membership had been refused.

'Bloody good question. *Why?*' Spittle hit the receiver. 'It would seem the club is so popular that they have no room for any more members.' He took a sip of whisky. 'Have you ever heard the like!'

Dr Billingham managed to speak quickly and suggested that perhaps they were unaware of who he was.

'That was exactly my initial thought,' Mr Havelock snapped, rotating his glass tumbler, 'so I got Eddy to call and make sure they were in possession of all the facts. I thought the place might be run by foreigners. Perhaps some of these bloody refugees they keep letting into the country.'

If Mr Havelock could have seen Dr Billingham, he would have observed his lips tighten and his cheeks redden.

'Which might well be the case there!' He continued his rant. 'The woman Eddy spoke to sounded French. Of course, he made it quite clear to her who I was and she *seemed* to be well aware of who I was, but she said she was still terribly sorry, "*très désolée*", but they were now totally oversubscribed and would call the moment there was a vacancy – *a vacancy!*' Mr Havelock let out a noise that showed his disgust and disbelief.

Dr Billingham thought about advising him to try to stay calm for the sake of his blood pressure and not to put himself at risk of a stroke, but didn't. Instead, he tried to reassure him that really, it was not a problem, they could go to the Gentlemen's Club on the corner of Mowbray Road. Even though, if he was honest, he had no real interest in going to any kind of Gentlemen's Club. Not that he would say so. Charles wanted him to be his companion, so he would be one – even if it had been wrapped up to look like it was Charles who was doing him the kindness.

As Dr Billingham continued to listen to Charles's diatribe, he felt sorry for this Frenchwoman and her Gentlemen's Club. She clearly hadn't realised that she had just made a huge mistake, for which she would pay – dearly.

Chapter Twenty-Four

The Albion, Ryhope

Monday 19 July

'So, John, *please* tell me what's been happening in your world. In the *real* world.' Dr Eris sighed theatrically and took a sip of her wine. 'I do love my work, but living and working in the same place does not bode well for a healthy mind. I worry I'll become institutionalised.'

'I can't see that ever happening.' Dr Parker smiled and took a quick sup of his beer. 'Although it has to be said, the asylum really is more like a hamlet than a hospital.'

'Ooh, I like that description – *a hamlet*.' She looked at the man she was now officially courting. His mop of blond hair, sparkling brown eyes – that smile. He really was rather perfect – in all ways. '*You* did the sensible thing and took lodgings in the village.'

'Perhaps,' Dr Parker said. 'Not that I'm there much. And not that I had much option. The Ryhope's barely got enough room to accommodate the patients, never mind the staff as well.'

'Perhaps I should also take a room somewhere in the village.' Dr Eris turned as the barmaid brought them their meal.

'It mightn't be a bad idea,' Dr Parker said, smiling his thanks to the young girl, who didn't look old enough to be working in a pub. 'I can ask my landlady if she knows of anywhere suitable?'

'Thanks, John, that'd be nice,' Dr Eris said, although she had no intention of moving anywhere – not unless it was into her new marital home with her new husband.

'So, come on, give me a résumé of what's been happening,' Dr Eris asked, a twinkle in her eye. She congratulated herself on seeing John most days – even if it was just snatching a quick cuppa in the canteen. 'A lot can happen in a couple of days.' *Just as a lot can happen in a couple of months.*

She listened intently as Dr Parker told her about a particularly complex operation he'd had to perform, forcing herself to look ever so slightly tearful when he told her about the difficult conversation he'd had to have with the young man who had just had both legs amputated, as well as the talk he'd had with the poor man's fiancée, who, judging by her reaction, wouldn't be his fiancée for much longer.

'How awful,' Dr Eris said, apparently with the utmost sincerity, though what she was really thinking was *sensible woman*. 'Whatever happened to true love – for better, for worse, in sickness and in health?'

They chatted on, mainly about work, but by the time their puddings arrived, Dr Eris had managed to find out more about John's background and, in particular, his family. Reading between the lines, his mother was a total cow. Claire knew the type. Rich, middle class, well educated, but had never worked in her life. Did well for herself by marrying John's father, also a surgeon, who, unlike his wife, didn't seem to care too much for money or status and spent as little time at home as possible. He would be a breeze to charm; the mother, however, would be more of a challenge. If everything went to plan, 'meeting the parents' would happen soon. She had already briefed *her* mother and father that they would be coming up to visit, possibly next month. They, of course, would love John. Who wouldn't? He was every woman's dream husband – as well as every parent's ideal son-in-law.

The path to married life wasn't totally obstacle-free, though. Helen was still a potential fly in the ointment. Claire had decided the best way forward was to purposely avoid any mention of Helen, but if John brought her up in conversation, she had primed herself to appear interested. She had managed to do so – *heaven knew how* – when he had told her of the evening he'd spent with Helen back in May. Inwardly, she had screamed, although she'd been pretty sure John had no idea how incensed she'd felt, and she'd done a good job of feigning great excitement at hearing how Helen had bought herself a 'smashing green sports car', in which she had taken John for a spin up the coast.

John hadn't mentioned Helen of late, which she took to be a good sign. She hoped that any trace of the shipyard sex siren would soon be scrubbed out of his life, helped along by the arrangement she'd made with Denise that whenever Helen rang, she would tell Claire – not John.

In return, Claire was to set Denise up with one of the eligible young doctors she knew both here and in town. Denise wasn't a bad-looking woman, but she was going to have to get a move on if she didn't want to be left on the shelf. It was something Claire related to. Not that she would ever admit it.

'You haven't mentioned your star patient this evening,' Dr Parker asked as he paid the bill and they both got up to leave.

'I know – doesn't time fly when you're having fun,' Claire said, giving John a slightly mischievous look. The last time he had come back to her accommodation they had lost track of time and John had been forced to sneak out, for fear of being seen.

'I've forgotten her name,' Dr Parker said.

'Miss Girling,' Dr Eris said, touching Dr Parker gently as he held the door open for her.

'That's it, *Miss Girling*,' Dr Parker said, following Claire out into the dark night. 'I don't know why I never seem to remember her name.'

'She's getting along very well,' Dr Eris said. 'Since her medication's been reduced, she's definitely becoming more lucid. And according to Nurse Pattinson, she's sleeping less. But it's a fine balance, and I've got to be careful that she doesn't become hyperactive.'

They walked in comfortable silence for a while.

'Do you still think she's been wrongly diagnosed?' Dr Parker asked.

'I'm not sure,' she mused. She slid her arm around John's waist, and he put his arm around her shoulder and pulled her close. 'Even if she has been wrongly diagnosed, I wonder whether there's much hope for the poor woman. I can't see her ever leaving the asylum permanently. She's been here too long. Now, *there's* someone who *is* institutionalised.'

As they walked the remaining distance back to the asylum, the talk turned to the latest war news – the invasion of Sicily, described as 'the stepping stone to Hitler's back door', and the bombing of Rome, as well as the start of the German withdrawal from Kursk in western Russia.

'Let's not end the evening with talk of war,' Dr Eris said when they reached her front door. She reached up to kiss him. 'Why don't you come in?' She kissed him again, this time more passionately. 'We can talk of frivolous things.'

Dr Parker pulled her to him, feeling himself respond to the closeness of her body.

'In fact,' she said, 'we don't have to talk at all.'

Dr Parker kissed her; he could feel the heat between them.

'I don't know if that would be such a good idea,' he said, pulling back and gently putting his hand to her face and caressing her cheek.

He could see the hurt.

'Not because I don't want to,' he said. 'I just think it mightn't be wise.'

Dr Eris kissed him once more.

'I think you might be right,' she lied.

Closing her front door, Dr Eris cursed herself. She'd been too pushy. And if there was one thing guaranteed to cool a man's ardour, it was appearing too keen – too available.

She was going to have to take her foot off the pedal and slow down.

She needed to make sure she got this right.

If she was to make John her husband, she had to play it right and ensure that nothing she did would rock the boat. She wanted to sail down the aisle as effortlessly as possible – and not get shipwrecked just before she reached the altar. Like before.

She had learnt her lesson the hard way – and she was damned if she was going to make the same mistake twice.

Dr Parker stepped out into the cool night and was glad of the half-mile walk back to his digs. Why had he said that? *It mightn't be wise*?

He had hoped the inference was that he would find it hard to rein in his feelings – to hold back from making love. Which it probably would have been. But what had *really* stopped him was that he knew as soon as he stepped over that particular threshold, there would be no going back.

In his books, making love to a woman was akin to asking her to marry him.

Some might call him old-fashioned, but that was just the way he was.

Coming out of the asylum's main entrance, Dr Parker got out his torch. It was pitch-black. He started down the long pathway.

If it had been Helen standing in the doorway, inviting him in, would he have acted the same way? *Of course he wouldn't have. There wouldn't have been a second's hesitation.*

Dr Parker looked up to the heavens and sighed, exasperated with himself.

For God's sake, man! Please don't go down this road again.

Helen doesn't want you to carry her over the ruddy threshold! Whereas Claire does.

And you like Claire – you find her interesting, funny, desirable. So, what's the problem?

Hearing a vehicle approaching, he moved over to the side of the road. Why couldn't he just leave his love for Helen behind – chuck it under this oncoming car? Was he not letting go because deep down he believed there was a crumb of hope that Helen might see him as more than just a friend?

He let out another heavy sigh of pure exasperation. He was truly delusional.

Chapter Twenty-Five

Friday 23 July

'You look nice.' Agnes had to keep the surprise out of her voice and from her face on seeing Pearl as she bustled into the kitchen.

Pearl stopped and looked down at the faded blue dress that Agnes had loaned her. Agnes had told her she could keep it for as long as she wanted and just to give it back when she had no more use for it.

'I dinnit knar about that,' she huffed. 'Still, it does the job.' She grabbed her handbag and boxed-up gas mask.

Agnes dried her hands on her pinny. 'I've got a really nice shawl that goes with the dress, if yer want? It'll keep the chill off, if it gets a bit nippy.'

Pearl hesitated. 'Aye, go on then.'

Agnes disappeared upstairs and returned with a cream-coloured crocheted shawl.

Pearl looked at it. Normally, she would never have even considered wearing something so old-fashioned and fuddy-duddy, but it was perfect for today.

Agnes draped it over Pearl's shoulders and stood back. There was no denying that Pearl had made a real effort to look smart and respectable. She'd kept her make-up simple and hadn't plastered it on like she normally did, and her hair had been pulled back into a neat bun, only a few dyed-blonde strands managing to break free.

'You and Bill going anywhere special?' Agnes asked as Pearl put her cigarettes and lighter into her handbag.

'Seaham,' Pearl lied.

'Well, have a lovely time,' Agnes said as Pearl walked down the hallway.

Turning around at the last moment, Pearl looked at Agnes.

'Thanks,' she said, 'yer knar, for the lend of yer clothes.'

For the second time that morning, Agnes tried to keep her surprise from showing.

'Yer all set then?' Pearl said to Bill as she reached the entrance to the Tatham.

'I am indeed,' Bill said, tipping his trilby and putting out his arm.

Pearl batted it away. 'We dinnit have to get into character until we're there, yer daft bugger.' She looked over Bill's shoulder and saw that Geraldine was taking chairs off tables. 'Yer sure yer can trust her?'

'I'm sure,' Bill said, turning and giving Geraldine a mock salute. 'We're off now. Patricia will be in at midday to give yer a hand.'

Geraldine's mouth dropped open on seeing Pearl.

Unlike Agnes, she didn't try to hide her astonishment.

As the train pulled out of Sunderland station, Bill felt ever so slightly nervous. A good, exciting nervous. A first-date kind of nervous, which was ridiculous for a man of his age, and even more ridiculous because this wasn't even a date. Much as he would have wanted it to be. No, today's trip had been Pearl's call. *She* had been the one to ask *him* to accompany her on a day out to Ryhope, not Seaham as she had asked him to tell everyone.

Suddenly remembering that he had brought something to aid today's subterfuge, Bill started to fidget around in his pocket.

'What yer looking for?' Pearl asked, touching her bun self-consciously, then smoothing her dress out.

'Here we are,' Bill said, unfolding a white handkerchief to reveal a gleaming gold wedding band. 'If we're going to pretend to be married, then you'd best be wearing a ring.'

Pearl eyed it suspiciously. 'Where did yer get that from?'

Bill laughed. 'I didn't nick it, if that's what yer thinking.'

'So, if yer didn't nick it, where did yer get it from? It's too small to be yers.' Pearl picked up the ring from the folds of the starched white hanky.

'It's the ex-wife's,' Bill said, watching Pearl as she held up the ring and inspected it.

Now it was Pearl's turn to be shocked.

'Yer ex-missus?' she said, staring at Bill. 'I didn't knar yer'd been married.'

Bill laughed, enjoying seeing Pearl's disbelief.

'There's a lot yer don't know about me, Pearl.'

'She's not dead, is she? I'm not wearing owt that's been taken off a corpse.'

Pearl's lack of sensitivity made Bill laugh loudly, causing a few passengers to stop their own conversations and look at the couple sitting opposite each other in the rear of the carriage.

'I didn't have you down as superstitious,' said Bill.

'I'm not,' Pearl said, still pinching the ring between her thumb and index finger. 'It's just bleedin' ghoulish. Wearing something off a dead person.'

Bill chuckled. 'Don't worry, the ex is very much alive and kicking. The ring was tossed back at me with quite some velocity when she walked out. I kept it. Knew it would come in handy one day.'

'Aye, well, it has. Silly mare should have kept it, she'd have got a few bob for it,' Pearl said, sliding it on her wedding-ring finger and holding her hand out to look at it.

'Suits yer,' Bill said with a smile.

'Fares, please,' the conductor boomed as he stepped through the connecting door and into their carriage.

Pearl scrabbled round in her bag and fished out their tickets. The conductor smiled at Pearl and tipped the peak of his cap.

'Thank you, ma'am,' he said, clipping their tickets and handing them back.

'You both have a good day,' he said, nodding at Bill and moving on to the family of four in the seats further down the second-class carriage.

Pearl leant forward and whispered, 'So, this is how yer get treated if yer a respectable married woman?'

Bill looked at her. He wanted to say it might have more to do with the fact that she looked lovely in her blue dress, which showed off her pale blue eyes, and that her hairdo and the lack of heavy make-up highlighted her naturally attractive face. But he didn't.

'So, what's the plan?' he asked instead.

Pearl sat back and took a deep breath.

She wished there was a plan as such, but there wasn't – other than to find out the truth: had Henrietta known about Charles, colluded with him in order to satiate his perverted needs? Underneath that veneer of eccentricity, was Henrietta as rotten to the core as her husband? And why was she now incarcerated – under a false name – in the local asylum when she was meant to be six feet under? Normally, Pearl would have left a situation like this well alone. She had spent her whole life running away from her past – away from everything to do with the Havelocks – but not now.

Not now she could see her daughter's need for retribution growing steadily day by day, week by week.

She needed to find the truth – whatever that might be.

When the train pulled into Ryhope station, Pearl and Bill got off. This time when Bill put out his arm, Pearl took it. A few minutes later, they'd walked to the bus stop just up from the Railway Inn.

'We'll pop in on the way back?' Bill suggested.

Pearl nodded. 'Our reward, eh?'

'Definitely,' Bill said, looking at Pearl and thinking she had the look of a woman on her way to the gallows.

Once they'd got on the bus and sat down, Pearl turned to Bill. 'What if the auld cow in reception recognises me?'

'She won't,' Bill said. 'Remember, the last time she saw yer, you'd been scrabbling about bomb sites looking for me.' Bill felt his chest puff up at the thought of Pearl charging all over town, from one bomb site to the next, trying to find out if he was alive or dead. 'From what Bel told me, you looked like one of the inmates rather than a visitor.' He looked at Pearl, but she wasn't laughing. 'Yer look totally different, Pearl. And yer didn't even talk to the receptionist. Bel said you'd been that rude to the one at Monkwearmouth that she forbade you from doing any of the talking when you got to the asylum.'

This time Pearl did laugh.

'She can be a reet bossyboots that daughter of mine.'

Bill breathed a sigh of relief.

'Anyway,' he said, changing the subject. 'You've not told me how Polly's doing. How far along's she now? I'm guessing the bab's all right?'

'Aye.' Pearl knew Bill was trying to take her mind off what she was about to do. 'She's seven months gone – give or take – and looks every bit of it. Every day I see her I swear she's got bigger. I'm betting it's a boy 'n it's going to be a bruiser.' Pearl was quiet for a moment, suddenly thinking of when she had been expecting Bel. She'd bled on and off and hadn't even realised she'd been with child until it was too late to do anything about it.

'Sounds like she's being well looked after,' Bill said.

'Aye, she's got some posh doctor. Must be costing a fair whack.'

'Who's picking up the tab?' Bill asked, knowing the Elliots, like most families, struggled to make ends meet.

'The Havelock girl's paying for it,' Pearl said. *Why did everything seem to lead back to the bloody Havelocks?*

Seeing their stop, Bill rang the bell and they both got up.

Within minutes of getting off the bus, they were walking through the main gates of the Sunderland Borough Asylum.

Bill took hold of Pearl's hand.

'For appearance's sake,' he explained.

Pearl raised her free hand and looked at her watch.

'We're reet on time fer visiting hours.'

'Remember,' Bill said as they fell in behind another couple who were making their way to the main entrance, 'we're a respectable married couple, come to see your mother's cousin who's not been well for a while. We've visited dozens of times,' he said, slowing down as they walked up the stone steps. 'So there's no need to ask directions or even acknowledge the receptionist.'

Bill let go of Pearl's hand to open the door. As soon as they were in the main foyer, he took hold of it again. They walked on, passing the receptionist, who was answering a call. They took the corridor to the left. Bill kept his fingers crossed that he was right. He'd got to know the layout of the asylum during his short stay after the air raid. From what Pearl had told him, he thought he knew where it was in the hospital she needed to go. He hoped so.

Reaching the end of the corridor, they turned left, then walked down another corridor and went right. Halfway down, Pearl stopped outside a room, the door of which was slightly ajar.

She stood and listened.

She could hear a gentle, bird-like voice singing a song she recognised from many years ago.

'This is it,' Pearl whispered. 'Remember, two loud knocks if yer see the fat ginger nurse. And remember, if anyone asks us, we've got lost.'

Bill nodded and Pearl slipped into the room.

'Henrietta.' Pearl kept her voice low, not wanting to risk anyone in the rooms on either side hearing that there was someone visiting. She knew it unlikely that her old employer received many visitors, if any.

As she walked over to her former mistress, Pearl had to fight to stay in the here and now, but it was hard, made harder still by Henrietta looking exactly the same as she had back then – just older. Her thick make-up showed up the creases in a face that had once been youthful and smooth. Pearl worked out that she must be in her sixties, although she only looked to be in her early fifties.

'Oh!' Henrietta dropped the book she was reading and put both hands to her rouged cheeks. 'My Little Match Girl!' She was obviously overjoyed to see her unexpected guest.

'That's right,' Pearl said, walking over to her so that she wouldn't feel the need to shout. She sat down on the bed, which was next to where Henrietta was sitting, her feet touching the end of Henrietta's long, plum-coloured taffeta skirt. Her waist was still as tiny as Pearl remembered, clearly nipped into place, as it always had been, by a tightly laced corset.

'You came back!' Henrietta exclaimed, a smile illuminating her face.

Pearl winced. Henrietta's sing-song voice could be quite high and seemed to resonate around the room. She put a finger to her lips. 'Shush. I dinnit want anyone to knar I'm here.'

Henrietta mimicked Pearl's actions and put a finger to her own lips.

'Yer said yer wanted me to come back and see yer, remember?' Pearl said.

Henrietta nodded; as she did so, a strand of dyed red hair from her chaotic updo fell across her face and she brushed it away.

'Well, I *can* come 'n see yer,' Pearl explained, 'but only if yer dinnit tell anyone.' She looked at Henrietta. Her eyes were still like saucers, but she could see the brown in them this time.

'Do we have a deal?' Pearl put her hand out for Henrietta to shake.

Henrietta nodded excitedly and took Pearl's proffered hand.

Looking down, she spotted Bill's gold band on Pearl's wedding-ring finger.

'My Little Match Girl got married!' she declared.

Pearl took a deep breath and nodded.

'She did.'

Taking hold of Henrietta's other hand, Pearl forced her to have eye contact.

'Henrietta, I want to talk to yer about the old days? Is that all reet?'

'So, come on, tell me all about it.' Bill put the drinks on the small round table in the corner of the Railway Inn and sat down. He had purposely picked the quietest table so they could talk in private.

'Eee, Bill, I feel exhausted,' Pearl said, taking a sip of her whisky.

'Did you find out what you needed to?' he asked.

'Not really.' Pearl lit up a cigarette and blew out smoke. 'But I didn't expect to, if I'm honest.'

'Does that mean you're gonna have to come back?' he asked.

'Aye, I think so. Might take a few more visits to get to knar what I want.' Pearl looked at Bill to gauge his reaction.

'Well, I'll be happy to be your partner in crime until you do,' Bill said.

Pearl smiled for the first time that day.

'Ah, Bill, that'd be brilliant. It'll help me out no end. And I reckon it'll be easier next time. Not so fraught, if yer knar what I mean?'

'I know exactly what yer mean,' Bill said. He felt like throwing his hat in the air with pure joy.

'So, did you manage to get any sense out of her?' he asked, before taking a mouthful of beer.

'Mmm, a bit. I mean, the woman's barking, but she didn't seem quite as bad as the last time I saw her. Mind you, I dinnit think I was all that reet in the head myself.' Pearl took a sip of her drink. 'The good thing is she's not that gone that she can't remember the past. I got her talking about the other servants that was there when I was, 'n she seemed to remember them all.'

'That's good,' Bill said. He had a glug of his beer. 'Makes you wonder what's wrong with her, doesn't it?'

'Dunno,' Pearl said. 'She was always a few shillings short. But I never thought she was bad enough to end up being carted off by the men in white coats.'

Chapter Twenty-Six

Monday 2 August

'Thanks, Basil,' Rosie said as the old man touched the tip of his tweed flat cap and disappeared out into the yard.

Rosie breathed in the still air, aromatic with the smell of polished wood. *This was not going to be easy.* She turned and faced five serious faces.

Gloria, Dorothy, Angie, Martha and Hannah were sitting in the high, light drawing office, where the ships they worked on began their life. The rows of wooden tables around them were littered with pencil sharpenings, bottles of Indian ink and rolled-up tracing paper. One table had a large drawing weighed down by two heavy round rulers. At the far end of the room there was a rudimentary ship's model, made to scale.

Angie took off her headscarf and started fanning herself with it. The drawing office was always warm and quiet, even when it was cold and noisy outside, but today the sun had been out all day and there had been little wind, making all of the yard's offices warmer and stuffier than normal.

'Eee, this all feels a bit serious,' she said.

'Yeah,' Dorothy agreed, 'like when you've been told to go and see the boss and you know it's not about a rise.' She copied Angie and took off her red checked headscarf, allowing her dark hair to fall onto her shoulders.

Martha, whose short hair didn't necessitate a headscarf, rolled up her sleeves and wobbled a little on the wooden stool that wasn't quite big enough to accommodate her.

'Is everyone who works here as small as you?' She looked at Hannah.

'Mmm,' the group's little bird said. 'Thinking about it, there's no one particularly big. Although there are quite a few tall people.'

'It's *you* that's big, Martha,' Dorothy declared. 'Not them that's small.'

Just then Polly walked through the door. Or rather, waddled. Her sensible flat shoes tapped on the linoleum floor.

Angie laughed loudly.

'Yer've got company now, Martha. 'Ere, Pol, come and sit next to Martha!'

They all settled themselves at the table.

Rosie looked at Gloria, who was also perched on one of the stools, looking equally uncomfortable, although it was not because the hard wooden seat was too small.

'Right, now that we're all here,' Rosie said, 'I guess we better get started.'

'And the lesson today is …' Dorothy spoke in a deep, headmasterly voice.

'Actually, it's not me that's taking the class today—' Rosie said.

'It's *me*,' Gloria interrupted. 'You're all here because of me.'

Polly shuffled around on her stool. 'Is everything all right, Glor?'

'Is it about Jack?' Martha asked.

Gloria smiled at Martha and nodded. 'Yes, yer right, Martha, it's about Jack.' She took a deep breath. 'But it also involves yer all.'

'Eee, Glor, yer've gor us worried now. I've got butterflies in my stomach,' Angie said.

'What – like when you're with Quentin?' Dorothy jibed, shoving Angie a little too robustly and nearly pushing her off the stool.

Angie looked daggers. 'No, Dor, not like when I'm with Quentin. Yer dinnit get butterflies when yer out with a friend, 'cos otherwise they wouldn't be a friend, would they?'

'Methinks you protest too much,' Dorothy said.

Rosie sighed. Sometimes she did feel like she was the teacher and they were her naughty pupils. She looked at Gloria, who gave her a look that said she wanted Rosie to take over.

'A while ago,' Rosie started, 'quite a while ago – can you remember when I went off to Guildford after Peter sent me that telegram?'

'And you came back a married woman,' Hannah piped up.

'That's right. Well, when I left for the day, you might recall that Gloria had to leave for a little while.'

'Aye, I remember. Billy the yard foreman came strutting over, saying yer had to have a word with management,' Angie said.

'Because Rosie had just dilly-dallied off to see her *lover*,' Dorothy added.

'The thing is,' Gloria said, 'it wasn't management who wanted to see me.'

Everyone thought back to that afternoon just a few days into the New Year more than eighteen months ago.

'Who wanted to see you?' Polly asked.

Gloria took a deep breath. 'Miriam – it was Miriam who wanted to see me.'

'*Oh my God!*' Dorothy gasped.

'Because?' Martha said.

'Because she'd found out about you and Jack?' Hannah said, clasping and unclasping her hands. She didn't like the way this was going. She hated anything bad happening to her friends. They were her security blanket.

'Yes, she had,' Gloria said.

'Hang on,' Dorothy said. This was huge and she wanted to know every second of what had happened. *She couldn't believe Gloria hadn't told them all before now.* 'So, what happened after you walked off with Billy? Where was Miriam?'

'At home,' Gloria said. 'Billy told me to go to the main gates. Harold was there.'

'And what did he say?' Martha asked.

'Oh, he just said it was nothing to worry about – that I was needed elsewhere and pointed over at the company car.'

'Blimey, Glor, yer must have been wetting yerself,' Angie said.

Gloria let out a sad laugh. 'I was a bit. Especially when I got in the car and we started driving towards Roker and I guessed where we were going.'

'What? So, you went to her house?' Martha asked, shocked.

'I did,' Gloria said. 'The door was open in expectation of my arrival. Miriam was there to greet me, gin and tonic in hand.'

'Blimey, sounds like something out of the books yer read,' Angie said, turning and looking at Dorothy, wide-eyed.

'It did feel a bit unreal,' Gloria admitted.

'But if she'd found out about you and Jack,' Polly said, 'why didn't she just have it out with Jack? You wouldn't have thought she'd have wanted the *other woman* there as well.'

'That's exactly what Jack said when I walked in 'n he saw me.'

211

'What? He didn't know you were coming?' Hannah asked.

Gloria shook her head.

'What did yer say?' Angie said, thinking of her own mother. *There was no way her dad would be asking her mam's fancy bit round to the house for drinks and a chat.*

'I apologised,' Gloria said, 'for any hurt 'n upset I'd caused.'

Everyone stared in disbelief.

'It was the right thing to do,' Gloria defended herself. 'And Jack apologised about not telling her before. We'd been intending to tell her ...'

'And did she knar about Hope?' Angie said.

'Oh yes, she knew about everything,' Gloria said. 'Actually, I felt relieved that it was all out in the open.'

The women understood. They all knew Gloria hated lying about anything.

'But then it soon became obvious that for Miriam, having everything out in the open was not an option.' Gloria sighed. 'Looking back, I was so naïve. I should have realised she'd have moved heaven 'n earth to save herself the humiliation of everyone knowing that her husband had left her fer another woman.'

'So, how did she manage to silence you?' Hannah asked, her expression deathly serious.

'That's where it gets a bit complicated,' Gloria said, glancing nervously over to Rosie.

'How so?' Polly asked.

'Well,' Rosie took over, 'Miriam had employed a private investigator.'

'A private investigator?' Dorothy's voice was raised.

'Eee, it really *is* like one of Dor's books,' Angie said.

'So, what did this private eye find out?' Martha asked.

'A lot of things that she could use against me,' Gloria said.

'What, to keep yer trap shut?' Angie asked.

Hannah looked puzzled.

'Mouth,' Martha interpreted, 'to keep her mouth shut.' There were still some expressions Hannah struggled with or hadn't heard before.

'So, what did she find out?' Hannah asked.

'Well,' Gloria said, 'she found out that yer aunty Rina was in debt. That she wasn't getting her money back from those she was giving credit to.'

All eyes were on Hannah. It seemed a long time ago since Rina had been a credit draper.

'Miriam threatened to get Hannah sacked,' Rosie chipped in.

'In the hope,' Gloria added bitterly, 'yer would end up penniless 'n in the workhouse.'

'Well, I hope you told her that Aunty Rina and I are made of sterner stuff!' Hannah had gone red. 'And that even if we had ended up in a workhouse, it would have been like a palace compared to where my mama and papa are.' There were tears in Hannah's eyes.

Polly put her arm round her workmate's skinny shoulders and gave her a cuddle.

'The thing is …' Rosie said, her eyes focused on Hannah; she'd never seen her so riled '… it wasn't just you that she'd discovered things about.'

They all looked at Rosie.

'Did she find out about Lily's?' Polly asked the question everyone was thinking.

'No,' Rosie said, 'thank goodness that was something she didn't find out.'

'And she can't have had anything on me?' Polly asked.

'No,' Gloria said, 'but she did threaten to spread a rumour that you were seeing someone 'n that the rumour would find its way over to Gibraltar – that it wouldn't be good for someone working with explosives, and who also had a tendency towards dark moods.'

'What a total cow!' Dorothy exclaimed.

'I could think of worse words,' Angie said.

Polly put a hand on her bump. 'How horrible.' She looked back at Gloria. 'But she can't threaten that now, can she? There's no way in a million years Tommy would ever believe anything like that now.'

She looked down at her bump. 'And definitely not with me like this.' She let out a light laugh. 'I think it would be a physical impossibility.'

Everyone chuckled, enjoying the break in the mood.

'So that leaves me, Ange and Martha,' Dorothy said.

There was an awkward silence.

Neither Gloria nor Rosie could find the right words.

Angie glanced at Dorothy, a worried expression on her face.

'I'm guessing that if this investigator person went snooping around my way, they might've found out summat about my mam?'

Gloria and Rosie nodded.

'That she's having it off with some bloke down the street ...'

Gloria and Rosie nodded again.

Everyone was silent, not knowing what to say.

'We weren't sure if you knew,' Rosie said.

'Well, I've gor eyes in my head,' Angie said. 'And I dinnit think my mam's been that discreet. It's a good job my dad's not the sharpest. Plus, when he's not working, he's clapped out in the chair with a bottle of beer. I doubt he'll ever find out unless someone tells him.'

'But if he did find out, I'm guessing he'd go mad?' Rosie asked.

Angie nodded, her face grim.

Everything fell quiet again. No one wanted to imagine the possible scenario that could ensue if Angie's dad was told of his wife's infidelity.

Rosie waited a short while before addressing Dorothy.

'And she found something out about your mum, too, Dor.'

'Yer mam's not gorra bit on the side 'n all, has she?' Angie asked.

Dorothy shook her head but didn't say anything.

None of the women had ever seen the group's joker so serious.

Gloria and Rosie looked at each other.

This time Gloria spoke.

'Apparently,' she said, 'yer mam didn't divorce yer dad before she married yer stepdad.'

Another taut silence.

'That's right,' Dorothy finally conceded. 'My mother is what the law would call a bigamist.'

Everyone continued to stare at Dorothy.

'And, like I'm sure Miriam was told,' Dorothy stated, 'being married to two blokes is illegal.'

'What? Yer can get done fer it?' Angie was shocked.

'You can,' Dorothy said. 'You can get sent to prison.'

The women were all quiet, digesting everything they had just heard. The irony that it was the two comics of the gang who were hiding such serious secrets was not lost on them.

Rosie flashed Gloria a look.

'So, that's why Jack can't come back,' Rosie said, not looking at Martha. 'If he does, she'll spill the beans and the consequences will not be good.'

'I think you might have forgotten *my* mam,' Martha suddenly piped up.

Now it was Rosie and Gloria's turn to look surprised. Never in a month of Sundays had they expected Martha to know the truth about her parentage.

'What, Mrs Perkins?' Angie said in disbelief. 'I can't imagine yer mam deeing anything wrong.'

Martha smiled. Her mother was pretty much perfect in her workmate's eyes.

'Not that mam,' she said, 'my other mam.'

'What, your biological mother?' Hannah said. They all knew Martha was adopted. It had been obvious from the moment they had met both her parents. Either that or the apple had fallen many miles from the tree.

'Yes,' Martha said.

Gloria and Rosie sat back, shocked but relieved that Martha knew the truth.

As they listened to her tell the women about her 'real mam', a woman who didn't deserve the title of mother, the one who was almost folklore in these parts, they couldn't help but admire Martha even more than they already did.

Afterwards, it was decided they all needed a drink.

Hannah, who had been left in charge of the keys, locked up the drawing office and within five minutes they were all sitting in the Admiral.

'Blimey,' Angie was staring at Martha, 'it's amazing yer here – I mean, that she didn't poison yer as well as the rest of the babs.'

'I think she might have tried,' Martha said, taking a sip of her shandy.

'Really?' Polly said. She had been particularly affected by Martha's revelations. *How could a mother do that to a child?*

Martha nodded solemnly.

'But nothing stops our Martha,' Dorothy said, squeezing one of Martha's muscular arms.

Polly looked at Gloria.

'Does Helen know?' Something told her she did.

Gloria nodded. 'Yes. She was there that day – at the house.'

'What? When you and Jack were there?' Dorothy said, outraged.

'No, not in the same room as us,' Gloria said. 'We didn't know it at the time, but she was earwigging at the door.'

'Was it her that told Miriam about you and Hope?' Dorothy asked.

Gloria nodded. 'She saw Jack when he came to visit me in hospital – that time after Vinnie laid into me in the yard.'

'Blimey, that seems ages ago,' Martha said.

'Before Helen and I became close,' Gloria said, not wanting everyone to apportion blame. It had taken a long time for Helen to win their trust.

'I can't believe you've been keeping this to yourself for so long,' Hannah said. She had always known that Rosie and Gloria were behind her aunty Rina getting a job at the café, but not why they'd done so.

'Me neither,' Angie said.

'Me too,' Dorothy agreed.

'So that was why Jack never came back for Arthur's funeral,' Polly said. It had struck them all as odd. The two men had been very close since Jack was a boy.

'I can't believe we didn't realise there was something up before now,' Polly said.

'*We* thought something was up,' Angie said, nodding over at her best friend.

'But not that you were being *blackmailed*,' Dorothy said, still shocked.

Everyone took a sip of their drinks.

'So, that's it,' Hannah said, her hand around a glass of lemonade. 'Jack has to stay in Scotland for ever and ever.'

'Hopefully not for ever,' Gloria said. 'I'm sure something will happen.'

'Yeh, like a ten-ton weight drops on Miriam,' Angie said.

'Is it all right to tell Bel?' Polly looked round the table.

'Course it is,' everyone agreed. 'She's one of us.'

'Yeah, even though she's in the office,' Angie said.

Polly looked at Martha. 'You sure?'

'Of course. I've got nothing to be ashamed of.' Martha looked at Gloria. 'And I really would be all right if it all came out and everyone knew about my real mam. I've got broad shoulders.'

Angie spluttered on her gin and tonic. 'Eee, yer have too, Martha. Dead broad.'

'No, but honestly, I'd be fine,' Martha reassured them again.

'But it's not just you, is it?' Gloria said. 'It would be awful for yer mam 'n dad. There are some wicked people out there. The kind that like to make other people's lives a misery. Back-stabbers. Gossipmongers.'

'Yes,' Hannah agreed. She knew Mr and Mrs Perkins well. They were a lovely couple, but their shoulders were not as broad as their daughter's. They would not do well with that kind of attention. 'They would be looked at wherever they went. Everyone would treat them differently. People can be very cruel.' Hannah's words hung in the air. Hitler had taught them that the human capacity for cruelty and prejudice seemed to know no bounds.

They were quiet.

Rosie sipped on her brandy. She felt like she needed it.

'I could try and have a word with my mam,' Angie volunteered. 'But I don't think she'd listen to me. And I don't think she'd stop seeing this bloke.' She had been thinking about her mam since her date with Quentin. 'I think she might even be in love with him.'

Dorothy looked at Angie.

'You've never said that before.'

Angie just shrugged her shoulders. *She wished she could tell Quentin all about what had happened.*

'I've had a go at my mother about ...' Dorothy looked around. The pub was starting to fill up, and a load of platers had just plonked themselves on the table next to them. She lowered her voice. 'About you-know-what. But she just gives me short shrift, says no one will find out – that it doesn't matter. She says she hasn't seen my real father for God knows how long and she's not doing anyone any harm.'

'Does your stepfather know?' Polly said. She wished more than anything she could tell Tommy about everything. *God, she missed him.*

'No,' Dorothy said. 'And I think that's what's *really* at the bottom of it all. The fact that Frank doesn't know.'

'Oh dear,' Martha said gravely.

Dorothy looked at Gloria.

'Sorry, Glor. I feel that my blummin' mother is stopping Jack from coming back.'

'Aye, and mine,' Angie chipped in.

'And mine,' Martha added. She had just taken a big mouthful of shandy and now had white froth on her upper lip. Hannah got out a hanky and wiped it off.

'It's no one's fault,' Gloria said. 'If anything, it's my fault fer falling in love.'

'You can't blame falling in love,' Polly defended.

'Nah, there's only one person to blame in all of this,' Angie said.

'Yeah,' Dorothy agreed. 'Helen's vindictive, callous cow of a mother.'

Chapter Twenty-Seven

As it was now the summer holidays, and therefore there was no school to keep Charlotte busy, it had been decided that she should take on two part-time jobs. The mere suggestion might have had other young girls kicking and screaming in outrage, but not Charlotte. She had been over the moon to be splitting her time between waiting tables at Vera's café and helping out at Thompson's. She wasn't sure why, but ever since what she called 'the day of revelations', she hadn't wanted to be alone. She knew it was a pain in the backside for her sister, but she couldn't help it.

Vera and Rina kept her busy and if it was quiet they showed her how to cook and bake cakes. They made it far more interesting than the old bag who taught home economics at school. She was also starting to like Vera; she wasn't as scary or as awful as she had initially thought. On top of which, the old woman liked telling her about Rosie and Peter, and how their courtship had been conducted in her café – even though, she said, neither of them would admit they were courting at the time.

'Ha!' Vera said. 'Yer should have seen the pair o' them. All gooey-eyed, oblivious to anyone 'n anything around them. The number of times I had to stop myself banging their heads together to make them see sense.'

Vera enjoyed being the storyteller and Charlotte listened enrapt; her imagination spiked as the old woman related over tea and a buttered scone how she'd called them 'the copper 'n the woman welder', and how Peter always used to order cake even though neither of them was ever hungry.

'Love does that to you,' Vera said.

Charlotte looked at the old woman with spittle in the corner of her mouth and crumbs on her chin and couldn't begin to envisage Vera being in love.

Peter, Vera told her, would always give her very generous tips and in return she would make sure their favourite table in the corner was always free when they came in every Wednesday.

'That one there?' Charlotte pointed over to the one set slightly apart from the rest.

'Aye, that's the one,' Vera said, slurping her tea and eating her scone.

Hearing of her sister's romance with Peter made Charlotte see Rosie in a different light. She and Peter were romantic lovers – not just boring husband and wife.

'They got there in the end,' Vera mused, before giving Charlotte a stern look. 'He's a good 'un, so you be nice to him when he gets back.'

She stood up and walked off, mumbling, 'That's *if* he comes back.' Which made Charlotte think all the more.

At Thompson's, Charlotte experienced a totally different working life. The offices were hot and stuffy and when she went out to have her lunch with the women welders, she understood why Rosie had always wanted her to have an education. The women would sit in the shade, their neck scarves flung to one side, the arms of their overalls dangling down as they attempted to cool themselves. Often, they were too tired to talk – all apart from Dorothy, of course, who saw silence as sacrilege.

They would often be joined by the 'red-leaders' – the women who painted the hulls of the ships. Charlotte thought that the splattered red paint on their overalls made them look as though they worked in an abattoir, not a shipyard. She decided that it must be the worst job ever. It looked boring and exhausting, and they all had similar dry coughs. It made her glad she was working in the office, the bonus being that she worked closely with Polly, whom she modelled herself on and wanted to be, minus the huge bump. If Polly had her hair in a ponytail, it was guaranteed Charlotte would come into work the next day with her hair in the same style. 'If Polly shaved off all her hair, would you?' Rosie joked one day, seeing Charlotte struggling to put her own thick, wayward curls into a bun. Charlotte, who had also taken to copying Dorothy's dramatic facial expressions, had given her sister a scathing look and rolled her eyes to the bathroom ceiling.

If Lily thought that Charlotte's busy summer holidays might give her a respite from breakfasts at the crack of dawn, she was to be disappointed. Charlotte was still for-saking any kind of a lie-in, and after hurrying Rosie out of the house and off to work, she would head off to West Lawn to enjoy several slices of Marmite on toast with the woman she adored and whose every word she hung on.

Polly and Helen also continued their regular catch-ups over a cuppa during lunch breaks. Helen knew her deter-mination to see Polly give birth to a healthy baby was really about her own slightly irrational belief that it some-how went towards making up for her miscarriage. The irony that Helen's baby would have been almost the same age as the baby growing in Polly's belly did not escape her. She tried to wipe this fact from her mind but couldn't. She had to accept what had happened to her, just as she had to accept that John could never be hers. The loss of her baby and the loss of her love still hurt. She just hoped it would lessen over time.

Polly suspected what had happened to Helen, having overheard Dr Billingham and Dr Parker chatting when she had been going into theatre to have her cervical stitch. She also suspected this was why Helen was so anxious that Polly's pregnancy went to full term. It was why she didn't want her workmates freezing Helen out because of her part in Jack's banishment.

Agnes naturally continued to nag Polly to take it easy, and Polly continued to repeat that if she took it any easier, she'd grind to a halt.

The women's excitement continued to grow along with Polly's pregnancy, with Angie still fascinated by Polly's growing girth. 'My mam's had six bairns 'n she's never been as big as you are now – not even when she was about to drop.'

Gloria, as the eldest of Rosie's squad, was finding the work under the unforgiving summer sun the hardest and was hitting the sack not long after she put Hope to bed, not that she minded. Telling the women the truth about why Jack was stuck up in Scotland, and seeing how grounded they were about their families' secrets, had taken a huge weight off her shoulders. Perhaps that was why she was so tired, as though finally, having the weight lifted, she could rest and recuperate.

Hope was still no nearer to having a father in her life, but, just as Scarlett O'Hara said in Dorothy's favourite film, Gloria resolved to worry about that another day.

And over in Ryhope, Dr Parker continued to see Claire. If they weren't going out on proper dates, he always seemed to bump into her during the day – even though her base was the asylum and his the military emergency hospital. It had been a long time since he had courted and he had forgotten what it felt like to be with a woman, to kiss and caress, although he was always careful not to let himself go too much.

But despite his growing closeness to Claire, he still couldn't get Helen out of his thoughts.

He'd tried, but it was no good.

And to make matters worse, she had now started to make an appearance in his dreams – as though her absence in his everyday life had forced her into his night life.

Chapter Twenty-Eight

Sunday August 15

'... *Happy birthday to you ... Happy birthday, dear LuLu ... Happy birthday to you!*'

Everyone cheered and Joe lifted up an unusually shy-looking Lucille to blow out her candles. There were five of them on the cake and she managed it in one gusty blow.

Everyone cheered again, the sound filling Vera's café and spilling out onto the main road as the hot weather meant the café door had been lodged open. The birthday venue had been Lucille's present from Vera and Rina. They had moved all the tables and chairs to the side for the partygoers to sit and eat their sandwiches, leaving most of the wooden flooring free so that Lucille and all her little friends could run around and play.

'Make a wish,' Bel whispered in her daughter's ear. She caught sight of Hope padding her way towards them – a look of determination on her face.

'And remember,' Bel said, giving her daughter a quick kiss on the cheek, 'you can't tell anyone, otherwise it won't come true.'

In the corner of her eye she saw Dorothy whisk Hope up and away.

Bel and Joe watched as Lucille closed her eyes and scrunched up her pretty little face.

'All done!' she declared.

'That didn't take much thinking about,' Joe joked.

'That's because she always wishes for the same thing,' Bel mumbled.

Joe gave a quizzical look before he guessed.

'Ahh,' he said. 'Of course.'

It was the same thing her mammy wished for every day.

'LuLu ...' Polly had appeared, one hand on her huge bump, the other stretched out to her niece. 'Are you going to help me cut the cake?'

'Yeah!' Lucille yelled as Joe put her back down.

Bel and Joe watched Polly take Lucille's hand and walk around the table that had been used to display the cake. Hannah was there, ready with a stack of plates to dish out slices of the much anticipated chocolate sponge. Lucille teetered on tiptoes to put her small hand over her aunt's and help cut the cake. Hannah stepped in and lifted her up so she could reach. Joe chuckled seeing that Polly was also struggling to reach the cake due to her bump.

'I think my *not-so-little* sister will be glad when she finally has the bab.' Joe glanced at Bel. She was also watching Polly, but seemed in another world. He took her hand and squeezed it. More than anything, he hoped that Lucille's birthday wish was granted. And soon.

'Please, my dear, don't tempt me. I can feel my waist expanding just looking at it,' Lily said, putting her hand up.

'Are you sure,' Charlotte said. 'It's a proper chocolate cake. Not one that looks like one but tastes like cardboard.'

'I should hope it *doesn't* taste like cardboard, the amount it cost to get all the ingredients,' Maisie said, taking one of the plates.

Lily threw Maisie a disapproving look. 'One should never talk about money in public, especially when it concerns a gift. It's very uncouth.'

226

Charlotte bent down and handed a plate to a little boy who was standing waiting patiently by her side.

'Well,' Charlotte said, looking over to Lucille and her friends, who all had identical chocolate-smeared faces, 'I think they would tell you it was worth every penny.'

When Charlotte left to continue handing out the cake, Maisie turned to Lily. 'We haven't had much chance to chat since I got back.'

'I know, my dear,' Lily said, looking over at Rosie, who was chatting away to Gloria and Helen. 'We'll have a proper sit-down tomorrow during the day.'

Maisie had been in London for the past month, checking all was well with La Lumière Bleue in Soho – an annual trip that Lily usually took, but this year she had sent Maisie. She couldn't possibly have left Charlotte.

Maisie watched as Pearl crouched and gave Lucille a quick hug. She stood up and tugged her short skirt down. Seeing Maisie, she nodded over at Bill, making a face as though he was forcing her to go when more than likely it was the other way round; children's parties were not her ma's idea of a good time. Maisie waved her goodbye and watched as Pearl hurried out, fag in hand, still pulling at her skirt.

'I was wondering,' Maisie said, 'whether you heard anything while I was away.'

Lily squinted at Maisie. 'My dear, my short-term memory is now so short I walk into a room and completely forget what I went there for.'

Maisie suppressed a smile. She had seen Lily on a number of occasions walk into the kitchen or reception room, look puzzled and walk out again, only to come back a few minutes later.

'Before I left, you wrote a letter *to a certain someone*,' Maisie said, her voice low, not that it needed to be, though, as the cake had refuelled the children, who were charging about, laughing and shouting. She watched Martha help Angie set up for another game of musical chairs, while Dorothy rounded up the children. They had taken over from a tired-looking Agnes and Beryl, who were now enjoying a well-deserved sit-down and cup of tea.

'A letter to do with the Gentlemen's Club,' she added.

'Ah, yes, of course,' Lily said, her face becoming sombre.

'You'd posted it before the royal launch, which seems ages ago now,' Maisie said.

'It was.' Lily was also keeping her voice low, although the screams of excitement had been replaced by loud music. She looked to see Vera standing by an old gramophone that had been placed on the counter, her hand hovering over the needle. 'And it took longer than I expected to get a response – but just after you'd left, about four weeks ago, I received a call about the matter.'

'What? From *Mr Havelock*?' Maisie asked, aghast.

'Gawd, no. There's no way a man like him would lower himself to making such a call. No way.' Lily put her cup and saucer down and lit up a Gauloise. She looked around for an ashtray. Stepping over to a table of young mothers, one of whom was trying unsuccessfully to get her crying baby to have its bottle, she smiled, requisitioned the metal ashtray, and quickly moved away.

'And?' Maisie was staring at Lily, whose cheeks had suddenly reddened. She guessed her boss was having one of her hot flushes.

'The old man got one of his minions to ring,' Lily said. 'Wanted to know if I *knew who Mr Havelock was*.'

'And?'

'And,' Lily spoke through a plume of smoke, 'I said in my best French accent that I knew *exactly* who he was and that I was *très désolée*, but the club was simply oversubscribed. Of course, I waffled on about fire regulations, how being a new club we had to adhere to the letter of the law and all that.'

'And do you think he was convinced?' Maisie asked.

'Mmm,' Lily said. 'I think the minion might have been, but I'll bet the cost of my wedding that the man himself won't be. No one says no to people like him. Regardless of any kind of rules or regulations. He's above all of that – or rather, he believes himself to be.' She took a deep drag. 'Men like that don't like it when you don't jump up and dance to their tune.' Grey smoke swirled from her mouth as she spoke.

Maisie nodded. It was why she was nervous about the whole situation.

'Men like him thrive off conflict,' Lily mused. 'They love the thrill of the fight, and unfortunately I think we might just have provided him with a battle.' She stubbed out her cigarette.

'And what do you reckon? Do you think there's going to be any ramifications?' Maisie asked, her face betraying her concern.

Lily laughed, but her face was serious. 'Oh, yes, most definitely.'

'You all right?'

Lily and Maisie both jumped.

It was Bel with Lucille by her side, beaming up at her aunty Maisie and the strange woman with hair the same colour as her new birthday dress.

'Yes, yes, of course,' Maisie said, before turning her attention to her excited-looking niece.

'Oh, goodness me!' She made a pantomime look of surprise. 'Is that a medal I see?'

Lucille nodded energetically. It had been Agnes's present to her granddaughter – to wear her granddaddy's medal on her special day.

229

Maisie looked at the plate she was holding; her cake was untouched.

'Is the birthday girl allowed another piece?' she asked Bel.

'Please, please, *please*, Mammy!' Lucille jumped up and down in excitement.

Bel nodded and Maisie handed over the cake. Her conversation with Lily seemed to have killed her appetite.

Chapter Twenty-Nine

'Well, I think it's safe to say that was one very successful birthday party,' Joe said, getting into bed and propping up his walking stick against the bedside cabinet.

'And Kate worked miracles in getting her to wear a dress that wasn't a bigger version of the yellow one she's been wearing for God knows how long,' Bel said. 'She really is a star. She actually stitched little figures into the dress where you couldn't see to make it more enticing.'

'She didn't stay long at the party,' Joe said. He had noticed Kate slip away after about an hour.

'Kate never stays anywhere for long,' Bel said. 'Maisie says she's obsessed with what she does. If she's not making clothes, she's designing them. I suppose that's why she's so good.'

Bel sat on the edge of the bed, her mind wandering off.

'Are you all right?' Joe asked, sitting up. 'I mean *really* all right?'

Bel didn't answer; instead, she took off her dress, put on her nightie and climbed under the covers.

'Talk to me,' Joe said. 'Tell me what's going on in that brain of yours.'

Bel sighed.

'I went to see Dr Murphy on Friday,' she said, giving Joe a sidelong glance. She saw his surprise.

'Really? You didn't tell me you had an appointment.'

'I know. I didn't want any fuss. Didn't want anyone to know. They'd all be asking me why I was going and what was wrong, and I'd have to say …' Bel took a deep, shuddering gulp of air to try and stop the tears that were threatening.

'You'd have to say you were going because of yer not falling,' Joe finished her sentence for her.

Bel nodded. 'Everyone's so excited about Polly being pregnant, I don't want to spoil that.'

'You think yer'd be chucking cold water on everyone's good cheer,' Joe said, looking at her expression, reading her thoughts.

'Exactly,' said Bel, looking down at her hands and turning her gold band around. She must have lost weight as it seemed looser than normal. What she would give to be fat, with swollen hands and ankles. 'And I keep looking at Polly – and feeling so jealous. I hate to even admit it … I know she's not had it easy and she's worried sick about Tommy, not that she'll admit it, but I just keep looking at her and feeling so woebegone that I'm not pregnant as well. I think it hurts all the more because I know what it's like to be pregnant. The feelings you have. That wonderful inner peace. Joyfulness. Sense of great expectation.'

They were both quiet for a little while.

'So, what did Dr Murphy say?' Joe asked, taking hold of Bel's hand.

'Well, he asked me lots of questions about my monthlies and gave me an examination and looked back on my notes from when I was pregnant with Lucille, to see if I'd had any womanly problems since then, which I haven't, but he didn't seem to have an answer. He agreed that it was unusual that I hadn't fallen after this amount of time.'

Joe did the maths in his head. They had been married in November 1941.

'Over a year and a half,' he said.

'Twenty-one months.' Bel smiled sadly. 'Dr Murphy said that normally I would have fallen in that time span, but he said that these are not normal times and that the war was affecting people in all sorts of different ways. He said in my case, it might be that all these air raids and uncertainty are somehow affecting me. Stopping me from getting pregnant.'

'Mmm,' Joe said, 'sounds a bit airy-fairy to me. Especially as you got pregnant with our Teddy so quickly.'

Bel squeezed Joe's hand. Sometimes it still felt strange that she had fallen in love with her husband's brother – his twin brother at that – but that had never been the case for Joe. He felt it was the most natural thing ever.

'What if the problem's with me – not you?' Joe asked.

Bel smiled for the first time and looked with love at the man she had known since he was a boy. 'Oh, Joe, I think you're one of the few men who would even suggest that it might be the man's fault – not that it's anyone's *fault*.'

'But it could be,' Joe said.

'Well, actually, that was something Dr Murphy did mention,' Bel said. 'You know what he's like – not one to mince his words.'

Joe chuckled. Dr Murphy had been their doctor since they were children.

'He said it was extremely unlikely to have anything to do with you because of Teddy,' Bel explained.

Joe frowned in confusion.

'Because of you being twins – *identical twins*. He said that you were, therefore, identical in most ways – including your ability "to sire a child".'

'That sounds like Dr Murphy.' He took a deep breath. 'So, is there anything he can do?' Joe looked at Bel. He dreaded to think of how it would affect Bel if she couldn't have any more children. She had managed to take her mind off it with her work at the yard, even learning short-hand and climbing the career ladder, but he couldn't see that filling the hole that would be left if she wasn't able to have another child.

'I don't think there's anything I can do. Dr Murphy just said that I'd have to keep trying – that I had time on my hands because of my age. And to try not to worry about it.'

'That sounds like positive advice,' Joe said, pulling Bel close.

It was a few minutes before he realised that Bel was crying. He felt her tears on his chest and then came the gentle shuddering. Bel never cried much – hardly at all – so when she did, it seemed the saddest thing ever.

Joe had known Bel nearly all her life. She had been a regular presence in their house from the day Polly had brought her home, dirty and upset, after her ma had up and left with some bloke she'd just met. He had watched her grow up and knew all she had ever wanted was her own family. A big, happy family. To be a mum several times over.

He turned and switched off the light and gave his wife a cuddle.

How he wished he could wave a magic wand and make it happen.

He worried, for he knew if Bel couldn't have any more children, it didn't matter how much he loved her, and how much she loved him and Lucille, she would always carry with her a deep sadness.

Chapter Thirty

When Polly reached Arthur's grave, she went about her usual routine of taking away the old flowers and replacing them with a new bunch she had picked on the way. Even if she could have afforded to, and if she could find a florist that was still open, she knew that he would have preferred the hand-picked wildflowers – and that he wouldn't have reprimanded her for pinching a few from the park.

'Not long now before the bab arrives, Arthur,' she said as she busied herself. 'A couple more weeks. Thank goodness!' She heaved herself up straight and looked down at the grave. 'There,' she said, putting her hand on her huge belly, 'all neat and tidy.'

She then turned her attention to Flo's grave, going through the same routine. Polly had never met Tommy's grandmother, but she felt as though she had a sense of the woman she had been. And she felt a certain closeness to her. She wore her rings, after all.

Polly knew this baby was going to be Tommy's world. With no mam and dad, and now that Arthur had gone to join Flo, she and this lively little being inside of her would be his only family.

'Ohh.' Polly let out a gasp of air. She smiled. He or she was awake and letting her know it. She looked around and spotted a nearby tree stump she could sit on. She walked over and lowered herself down onto it. She just hoped she'd be able to get up again.

It had taken Mr Havelock a while to find someone who could find out what he needed. Mr Havelock had cross-examined Eddy again, and it was clear that, despite the owner's Gallic descent, she was most definitely aware of who he was, and more so, how important he was. Something wasn't right.

The first private investigator he had gone to – a family firm called Pickering & Sons – had shut up shop. The old man, who had been highly recommended by an old acquaintance, was now too infirm. He'd been told the daughter had taken over, but hadn't the stomach for it and was now some sort of photographer.

It had, therefore, taken him longer than he'd first anticipated, but he had finally found a man – a retired detective whom Mr Havelock had known years ago. He'd been as bent as a nine-bob note, so Mr Havelock knew he'd be perfect for the job. No need to worry about him working within the confines of the law, or to have any concerns about him adhering to any kind of ethical code of behaviour.

He knew the ex-plod wasn't the fastest gun in the West, but he had a name for being thorough. Besides, he wasn't in a huge rush. He'd always been a believer in that old English proverb: Slowly, slowly, catchy monkey.

And he was quite sure – the monkey would be caught.

Polly just about managed to get herself up off the tree stump. She had considered waiting for a helping hand, but after a few goes, she'd managed. She went to Albert's, something she often did after visiting Arthur's grave, to have a cup of tea and a chat and then headed home. She was shattered when she got in and went to have a rest on her bed, but instead fell fast asleep. She slept so deeply there could have been another air raid and she wouldn't have woken up. Thankfully, there wasn't one. In fact, there hadn't been any more air raids since the one in May.

When she did wake up, it took her a while to orientate herself. Looking at the clock, she saw it was past eleven. The front door went and she knew it would be Joe, back from his Home Guard duties. She heard the tap of his walking stick in the hallway, followed by the scuffling sound of the two dogs as they scrambled to welcome him, and then the cabinet door was opened, which meant her brother was having a nightcap. Pulling on her dressing gown, trying to stretch it a little as it now barely covered her bump, she padded into the kitchen.

'How was Lucille's first day at school?' Polly asked, yawning. 'I feel awful. I came back, everyone was next door at Beryl's and I just closed my eyes for two minutes ...'

Joe chuckled. 'Well, I think I'd be knackered if I was hauling around a sack of coal day in, day out.'

Polly arched her back as she sat down at the table. 'Don't get me started. I think new mothers are sworn to secrecy about the reality of pregnancy – for fear of extinction.'

Joe laughed. He poured himself a shot and put the bottle back in the cabinet. Polly saw him flinch as he manoeuvred himself back down onto the kitchen chair.

'You all right?'

'It's me that should be asking you that,' he said, stretching his bad leg out in front of him.

Polly knew not to fuss.

'So, come on, tell me all about my niece's first day,' she said instead.

'Oh, well, not surprisingly, LuLu loved it,' Joe replied. 'She did not stop talking from when Bel and I went to pick her up to the moment she flopped into bed. She was very excited. She seems to have made lots of new little friends who, by the sound of it, she has already started to boss around.'

'That'll be Agnes's influence.' Polly laughed.

'Exactly my thoughts,' Joe agreed, taking a sip of his drink. 'And, of course, I think the whole school now knows that she is to have a cousin *very* soon.'

Polly laughed again. 'She keeps asking me when the baby's due and I keep telling her. I reckon she thinks if she keeps asking, the baby will somehow come earlier.'

'God forbid,' Joe said, thinking of his sister's near miscarriage.

They were quiet for a moment.

'Do you feel excited?' Joe asked.

'I do,' said Polly, 'but I don't feel as though I can let myself get too excited until the baby's here and everything's all right.'

Joe nodded. He understood. His sister had had one hell of a scare when her waters had broken early. He also thought Polly wasn't showing her excitement for fear of upsetting Bel.

'The school just the same?' Polly asked.

'Yes, same as when we were all there.'

'Really?' Polly grimaced. 'Don't tell me they've still got the same teachers there?'

'No, I didn't recognise any of the names. Bel asked one of the teachers about the dreaded Miss Flint and was told she's not there any more.'

'Thank the Lord. Although I pity the school that's got her now,' Polly said.

'Aye, I know,' Joe laughed. 'I'm kind of glad they didn't know, though – the mood Bel's in, she'd probably have gone there 'n given her a mouthful.'

Polly looked at Joe.

'I wish she'd get pregnant,' she said.

'Mmm,' said Joe.

'You think there's more to it?'

'I think getting pregnant would help – a lot,' Joe said. 'But I don't think it's just that.'

'Mr Havelock?'

Joe nodded solemnly.

'I wish I could do something to make it better,' said Polly.

'So do I.' Joe let out a sad laugh.

Polly thought of the terrible anger and depression that had hit Bel on hearing that Teddy had been killed. Joe had been the one to pull her through it all. He had unwittingly been the light at the end of the tunnel.

If she and Joe couldn't help her, Polly wondered who could.

Later, when she went back to bed, Polly read Tommy's latest letter for the umpteenth time. When her eyes couldn't stay open any longer, she gave in to slumber, the page falling to the floor as she drifted off, thinking about Tommy, his pale, angular face, his serious hazel eyes as he looked at her when they made love; how afterwards, he would wrap his arms around her and pull her to his chest. As sleep enfolded her, Polly thought she could smell him, felt the slightest bristle of his stubble on her skin – and with it came a contentedness and lightness of being, as though there was no war, no worries, no past, no future – just her and Tommy and their baby.

Chapter Thirty-One

Two days later

Friday 3 September

When Polly got up – or rather rolled herself up and off her bed – she felt better than she had done for the past few days.

Opening the curtains and the blackout blinds, she looked out onto Tatham Street, then down at her belly.

'Not long now,' she said, putting her hand on her bump. 'Only two weeks to go.'

And it can't come fast enough.

'You feeling all right?' Agnes said. She had asked the same question every morning for the past week.

'Fine, Ma, honestly,' Polly said. She had given the same answer every morning for the past week.

Polly poured herself a cup of tea as Agnes ladled porridge into her bowl. She could hear Bel and Joe getting up. Even though they slept in the attic room, you could still hear Joe's stick on the wooden floorboards, and their bedroom door had a creak that no amount of oil seemed to cure.

'Actually,' Polly added, 'I've felt surprisingly well this past day or so. Like I've got a bit more energy.' She laughed. 'Not that that would be hard.'

Agnes looked at her daughter as she stirred a little milk and sugar into her hot oats. 'Yer don't have to work right up to the birth, yer know? No one will think any less of yer if yer pack in today 'n just put yer feet up for the next two weeks.'

'I know they wouldn't, Ma,' Polly said, looking across at the dogs curled up in their basket. 'But unlike Tramp and Pup, I'd go mad if I was just sat around all day.' She blew on a spoonful of porridge. 'And it's not as if working in the office is exactly physically demanding. I'm sat down most of the time – on top of which, I'm sure Helen's told Marie-Anne to give me the easiest, least demanding work possible—'

'*Filing, filing and more filing,*' Agnes butted in, repeating the words she had heard dozens of times since her daughter had given her timekeeper's job over to the little miner's lad. She laughed. 'Wait till yer've had the little 'un, then yer'll be begging to go back to all that lovely filing.'

There was no one there – just the two of them. He watched as she came towards him, her emerald eyes not once leaving him, showing him her love. He felt his lips touch hers as he bent down and kissed her.

He could taste her lips; smell her as he kissed her face and neck.

She loved him.

She loved him as he loved her.

And desired him as much as he desired her.

'*Dr Parker.*' Louder. '*Dr Parker.*'

Dr Parker opened his eyes. Startled. *Where was he?*

'Sorry, Dr Parker, but you're needed on the ward. Bit of an emergency.'

It was one of the junior consultants and he had a look of worry and uncertainty – a constant for those in their first year of practice.

Dr Parker sat up and raked his hair back. He was in the on-call room. Or rather, cupboard. There was just enough room for a single bed and not much else. The junior consultant's face was staring at him from behind the door, which was allowing in enough light for Dr Parker to scrabble around for his shoes. He was still wearing his white doctor's coat and stethoscope. He must have crashed out as soon as his head hit the pillow.

As he followed his colleague down the corridor, he tried to bring the image of Helen with him, to keep the feeling of her lips on his, and the smell of her natural perfume. But it was no good; before he knew it, he was back to reality.

'I'll bet you're glad the schools are back?' Helen asked.

Rosie was sitting in her office. They had just finished discussing what new equipment was required and where Rosie's squad was needed next.

'Mmm, just a bit.' Rosie sighed.

'She's a good worker,' Helen said as she stroked a purring Winston. 'There'll always be a place here for her if she wants a job – temporary or otherwise.'

Rosie looked through the window and saw Polly sitting down at a large desk, sorting out sheets of papers into piles. With her bump pressing against the edge of the desk, she was having to stretch her arms out fully to reach.

'I'll tell her that, she'll be chuffed. Praise from the scary Miss Crawford is praise indeed,' Rosie said.

Helen laughed. 'Her fear of me is all your fault. You told me to be awful to her when she first tipped up here? Remember? *Be a bitch*, I think were my orders.'

Rosie chuckled, remembering the day well, although she doubted Helen had ever taken orders from anyone.

'I'm guessing, though,' Helen said, pulling out her packet of Pall Malls, 'that a job in a Sunderland shipyard is not what you envision for your sister's future?'

'Well, I *would* like her to go to university,' Rosie said.

'In other words, she *is* going to go to university.' Helen took out a cigarette, but didn't light it.

'She seems keen,' Rosie said, 'but I don't think she wants to go far afield – she keeps saying Durham and Newcastle have good reputations.'

'Sorry for interrupting.'

Rosie turned around to see Marie-Anne in the doorway. She was holding aloft a copy of the *Sunderland Echo*.

'You've made the headlines again,' Marie-Anne said, trying her hardest to hold back her excitement, but failing. 'Along with Mr Royce Junior, of course.' She walked over, opened the paper at the appropriate page and laid it out on Helen's desk. 'Dahlia and I think you make a good couple.' Marie-Anne knew she was overstepping the mark but was unable to help herself. She'd just got off the phone with Matthew's secretary and they had both worked themselves up into a frenzy, saying how it would be the wedding of the year.

'I have to agree.' Rosie was leaning forward to get a good look at the photograph of Helen looking very glamorous next to Mr Royce at the launch on Tuesday.

'Goodness, don't you start too, Rosie,' said Helen. She looked across into the office and saw Polly waddling her way towards the exit.

'Marie-Anne, begone!' she said, shooing her away with her hands. 'And check on Polly. That must be the fifth time she's gone to the loo today.'

Marie-Anne turned, stifling her irritation. *The woman was preggers. Everyone knew pregnant women were always going to the bloody bog!*

Helen turned over the page.

'Looks like Georgina's getting her foot in the door with the local rag,' she said, turning the paper round so Rosie could see. 'She's not daft. Looks like she's covered the launch of *Cormea* at Austin's, knowing that the *Echo* photographer would have been at Doxford's.'

'Good photo,' Rosie said, 'not that I know much about these things, but there's something quite striking about it.'

They chatted for a little longer – work talk.

In the corner of her eye, Helen saw Polly come back into the office and Marie-Anne obeying instructions and seeing if she was all right.

'Well, I think that's everything,' Rosie said, standing up. 'I'll leave that order with you.'

'Yes,' Helen said, looking down at the list she had made, 'and we're agreed, we'll definitely get you a trainee if Polly doesn't want to come back after the baby's born.'

As Rosie made her way out, she saw Bel chatting to her sister-in-law. Polly looked pale, and the way she was arching her back, she was clearly in discomfort. Her mind slipped back to Hope's birth here in this very yard. Lightning didn't strike twice, did it? No. Besides, Polly had another fortnight to go – on top of which, she had that stitch to keep the baby in. Mind you, judging by the size of Polly, she doubted a stitch would do much good if the baby did decide to come early.

As Dr Parker headed back to the on-call cupboard room, he looked at his watch.

Only another hour and he was off.

Thank goodness. He'd found it hard to concentrate since he'd had *the* dream.

It was becoming more frequent.

Kicking off his shoes, he flopped down on the bed, lying on his back with his hands clasped on his chest.

Part of him hoped to fall back into Helen's arms, to lose himself in her face, her kisses, but then again he hoped he wouldn't – the pain when he woke and realised that what had felt so real was purely a fantasy was unbearable.

The insanity of it all was that whenever he had 'the dream' he felt guilty when he saw Claire – as though he had been unfaithful to her somehow.

He forced his eyes shut, but he knew it wouldn't do any good. Only a heavy dose of what he'd just given his last patient would get him anywhere near sleep.

After Rosie left, Helen lit her cigarette and looked down at the sepia photograph of her and Matthew in the *Echo*. It had been quite an occasion for various reasons.

She tapped her Pall Mall in the ashtray.

She'd have to have a word with Matthew. She wanted to make sure he'd got the message, and that he didn't think she wasn't just playing hard to get.

She didn't mind having her photo taken with him, or even chatting to him; she quite enjoyed their verbal sparring, but she did not *want* him – or anyone else.

Anyone else apart from John, of course.

But that was out of the question.

A pipe dream.

It could never be a reality.

The whole yard was working hard – their toil made harder still by the fact that the weather was still glorious. Autumn was slow off the mark this year, not that anyone was complaining – even the women admitted they would rather be hot and sweaty than freezing cold or, worse, wet and at the mercy of the mighty north-east wind.

This afternoon, Rosie, Gloria, Martha, Dorothy and Angie were working on the deck of an injured cargo vessel that had been dragged into the slipway over the weekend. They were repairing the ship's funnel where, Rosie had explained to them, in peacetime there'd have been an upper mast, but at the start of the war they'd been removed to evade detection by the enemy. The women had laughed and said they might as well have left the mast up, judging by the number of bullet and shrapnel holes they were now having to patch up.

'Lovely day, isn't it, Dr Parker?'

Dr Parker looked at Mr Sullivan. The old man had both gnarly hands gripped to the large steering wheel, concentrating on his driving.

'Yes, it is – lovely,' Dr Parker agreed, even though all he could see was Helen's face, her eyes, as she leant in to kiss him. It had seemed so real. And now, *unbelievably*, here he was, *acting on a dream! Was he crazy? Did he really believe that the dream might be true?*

'Where yer headed for in town?' Mr Sullivan asked. 'I can drop you off anywhere yer want.'

Dr Parker looked out the window. They were still on the Ryhope Road, but it would only be a few minutes before they were hitting the town centre.

'Drop me off at the Wearmouth Bridge, Mr Sullivan, if you don't mind. That'd be great. I can walk from there.'

'Yer sure? I can take yer right to where yer going? To the door?'

'No, thanks anyway, the bridge'll be fine. The walk will do me good.'

Five minutes later, the old man was indicating and pulling over at the top of Bridge Street.

'You take care, Dr Parker,' he said. He'd known the doctor for a good while now and had never seen him in such a daze.

'Thanks again, Mr Sullivan.' Dr Parker slammed the door. He heard someone beep as the old man drove away.

Taking a deep breath, Dr Parker hurried down Bridge Street and across the Wearmouth Bridge. Looking down at the river to his right, he could see his destination.

J.L. Thompson & Sons, Shipbuilders.

He looked at his watch. It was nearly five o'clock. Helen would be there. Even if she'd been to a launch elsewhere in the town, she'd be back at her desk now. And if she wasn't, he'd find out where she was and track her down. He had to put an end to this insanity.

By the end of the day he was going to feel either the biggest chump on earth, or the happiest man alive.

Chapter Thirty-Two

Dr Parker's coat flapped open, but he didn't notice. Nor did he feel the warm breeze in the air, or see those he was hurrying past, or hear the squeal of a tram's brakes. His mind was elsewhere. Never before had he experienced such an overpowering urge to act on what he knew was a fabrication of his own mind.

'Watch yerself, mate!'

Dr Parker stopped dead in his tracks.

'Sorry,' he apologised as the man, grumbling, carried on his way.

He'd argued with himself that any self-respecting doctor would know that a dream is simply the subconscious uncovering the wishes that the conscious mind has learnt to repress.

That was Freud's take on it anyway.

That was what Claire believed.

Claire!

What on earth was he doing? Claire was lovely. Intelligent. Funny. Attractive. They got on like a house on fire. He liked her. A lot. She liked him. A lot.

So, why was he striding like a mad man towards another woman? A woman who, until recently, he really did not think loved him. She'd hardly bothered with him much of late, rarely returning his phone calls. He hadn't thought she was remotely interested in him ...

That was – until this dream. This damnable dream that had changed everything. That had caused him to go a little insane.

But this dream didn't feel like wishful thinking. It felt different. As though it was giving him a message. One that said, loud and clear:

Helen loves you.

She wants to be with you.

And he *so* wanted to be with her.

He turned right, down to the yard.

It was time to find out the truth.

The first person Dr Parker saw when he walked into the main office was Helen.

She looked up the moment he stepped through the main doors.

His heart felt as though it really had missed a beat. She looked exactly as she had in his dream. Those green eyes looking straight at him—

But then he heard a familiar sound.

A very real and familiar sound.

Someone was in pain.

He tore his attention away from Helen and looked over to see Polly, hunched over in agony, sitting, or rather perching, on one of the wooden chairs.

'Thank God you're here!' Helen shouted across the office. She was by one of the desks. She banged the handset she was holding back into the cradle.

Dr Parker looked around – taking in the scene for the first time.

Bel was ushering the office workers out, telling them all to grab their bags and gas masks and leave.

'Don't worry about coming back,' she told them, looking across to Helen for confirmation.

'Yes, yes! Go!' Helen agreed, before looking around for her secretary.

'Marie-Anne!' she ordered. 'Go and make sure the young timekeeper – God, I always forget his name ...'

'Davey,' Marie-Anne said.

'Tell Davey to expect the ambulance – make sure the gates are open and the way clear,' Helen commandeered.

Dodging the flow of workers hurrying towards the door, Dr Parker strode over to Polly. He bobbed down in front of her as Marie-Anne rushed past him.

'Tell me what's happening?' he asked, keeping his voice calm.

Polly's face was flushed, and she was scrunched up in agony.

'Pain,' she said, puffing out air. 'Contractions ...' more puffing '... I think.'

'She's gone into labour,' Helen said, walking towards him as Bel herded the last of the workers out of the main office and shut the door.

Dr Parker turned his attention back to Polly.

'Has Dr Billingham taken your stitch out?'

She grabbed Dr Parker's hand and instead of crying out in pain, squeezed it with such strength that it was John who thought he might shout out in agony.

'No, he hasn't!' Polly said, panicked.

'All right. That's all right,' Dr Parker reassured. 'When are you due?'

Polly didn't answer; instead, she sucked in air.

'Oh my God, here's another,' she gasped, before bending over and squeezing his hand again. Dr Parker thought this time his circulation had been cut off.

'She's due in two weeks,' Helen said, her eyes holding John's attention, speaking her fear.

'Is it too early? Is the baby going to be all right?' Polly blurted out as she lifted her head up. Her face was covered in sweat and was blotchy red.

Bel hurried around to Polly's right side and took hold of her other hand.

'Don't worry,' Dr Parker said. 'It's not too early. Your baby's going to be fine. But we do need to get you to the hospital ... and quick.'

He looked back up at Helen, who was wringing her hands, her face white with worry.

'I've called the ambulance,' she said. 'It should be here any minute.'

Just then the doors swung open and Marie-Anne came rushing in.

'Has it arrived?' Helen shouted out.

'Not yet,' Marie-Anne said, her eyes glued on Polly.

'Go and stand by the window!' Helen barked. 'Tell us as soon as you see it.'

'Oh no ...' Polly said, staring down at the floor.

Everyone followed her gaze.

There was a pool of water.

Dr Parker looked around the office and then up at Helen and Bel. 'Can you clear that table over there?' He cocked his head at the large wooden table that was used to sort the mail.

They both hurried across the office.

Helen pushed piles of letters, papers and files off the table with both hands. Bel picked up what she could and put it on a neighbouring desk. They both lifted the table into the middle of the room.

Polly looked at it and then at Helen, Bel and Dr Parker.

'I can't have the baby here!' she said, aghast. 'I've got to go to hospital.'

Her face scrunched up in agony again.

'Dr Billingham ...' was all she managed to say before the iron fist gripped her insides again. The pain was unbearable. She'd never known such agony in her entire life.

'Don't worry,' Dr Parker said. 'We'll get you to the hospital as soon as the ambulance turns up ...' He looked over at a grave-looking Marie-Anne, who shook her head. 'In the meantime, we just need to get you on the table and have a look at what's going on.'

Polly tried to stand but was hit by more pain.

'My back's killing me,' she said, looking at Dr Parker.

'That's normal too,' he said.

'Let's try and get her onto the table.' John glanced at Helen. She caught his look of concern and returned one of her own.

'I'll take this side,' Helen said, as Bel took hold of Polly's right arm. They both tried to heave Polly onto the table, but she was a ton weight.

'Martha?' Helen suggested.

'Good idea,' Bel agreed, letting go of her sister-in-law's hand and hurrying off.

Seeing Bel go, Polly panicked. She desperately wanted to shout for her to come back. But she didn't. She thought of Tommy. She had to be brave.

'The baby's coming!' Bel shouted at the top of her lungs. The sound of her voice seemed to get lost in the hammering of metal and the pneumatic thumping of the rivet guns.

The women saw her before they heard her.

'Oh. My. God,' Dorothy said, pushing up her mask. She nudged Angie, who was concentrating on a vertical weld. Turning and seeing Bel, she tugged hard on Martha's sleeve.

'It's Polly!' Bel shouted as she finally reached them. 'She's gone into labour!'

'What? She's having the baby? Here?' Gloria said.

Bel nodded. She felt as though she had just ripped a few vocal cords.

'Martha ...' She stepped across a welding machine to get to the group's gentle giant. 'They need you up there to help move Pol,' she shouted into her ear.

Martha immediately dumped her rod and mask on the ground with a clatter, and without a second glance she strode off across the yard, breaking into a lumbering jog so she wouldn't have to wait for a crane to pass.

'Can we do anything?' Gloria shouted.

Bel nodded again.

'The ambulance,' she hollered. 'Meet it at the gates – tell the driver where to go.'

Rosie, Dorothy and Angie did exactly as Martha had just done; they downed their tools and masks and made a bee-line across the yard.

Polly watched as Dr Parker spoke a few words to Helen before shaking off his coat and rolling up his sleeves. She saw Helen take the coat and gently squeeze his arm before hurrying off and out of her line of vision.

She heard the door crash open and Martha appeared. Her face was serious. Martha disappeared from view again and then she felt herself being gently lifted onto the table.

She turned her face and saw that Helen had brought Dr Parker a bowl of water and a bar of soap. They were talking quietly. Dr Parker seemed to be reassuring Helen, whose face was tense and angst-ridden. She passed him some paper towels and he dried his hands quickly, chucking them on the floor.

For a split second Polly thought she was in the hospital – before she heard the klaxon sound out.

End of shift.

Dr Parker suddenly came into view.

'I'm going to give you a very quick examination.'

Polly craned her head up and nodded her acquiescence before being hit by another contraction.

Dr Parker looked at Helen, who hurried to her side and took Polly's hand.

'It's all right,' Helen said, trying her hardest to sound reassuring before turning to look at Marie-Anne.

'Can you see anything?' she shouted.

'No, I don't think so.'

'What do you mean, *you don't think so*?' Helen yelled, anger replacing anxiety.

'I can't *see!*' Marie-Anne shouted in return.

The pain ebbed and Polly again craned her neck. Marie-Anne had half her body hanging out the window; one slight push and she'd be gone.

'The entrance's blocked!' she turned back and shouted over at Helen.

'*Bloody hell,*' Helen hissed through clenched teeth.

Polly caught the look of despair Helen threw Dr Parker, who was now back in her line of vision.

'What? The ambulance can't get in?' Polly asked, looking from Helen to Dr Parker.

The doors suddenly banged open.

It was Bel. She hurried over to Polly. 'How're you feeling?'

'Like I'm dying,' Polly spluttered. Another contraction.

'Don't worry,' Bel said in earnest. 'That's totally normal.'

Polly spluttered, laughed, then cried out in agony. It was the first time she had vocalised her pain.

'It'll be worth it,' Bel assured.

Polly caught sight of Dr Parker at the end of the table. He had blood on him.

'Oh, God,' she gasped.

'Remember, the same happened with Gloria ...'

Polly heard Martha's reassuring voice behind her.

'It's fine, Polly. Everything is going exactly as it should. All of this is perfectly normal,' Dr Parker said with the utmost authority.

Polly suddenly exploded into semi-hysterical laughter.

Having her baby on the sorting table in the admin department of Thompson's shipyard was not what she would call 'perfectly normal'.

'I want to go to hospital!' she demanded. 'I want Dr Billingham!' Polly glowered at Dr Parker.

'I don't think this baby's going to wait,' Helen said, throwing Dr Parker another worried look.

'But—' Another contraction stopped Polly from saying any more.

'Are you all right giving me a hand?' Dr Parker asked Helen.

Polly heard Helen's heels clip-clopping on the vinyl flooring before she appeared next to Dr Parker.

'Pol,' Bel said, drawing her attention away from Helen and John, who had started to talk in hushed tones, 'just keep a hold of my hand.'

Polly turned her head to see her sister-in-law.

'And mine.'

She turned her head a hundred and eighty degrees to see Martha, who was now where Helen had been.

She grabbed both their hands as though her life depended on it.

Rosie, Gloria, Dorothy and Angie were halfway across the yard when the klaxon blared out. In total synchronicity, the workforce stopped dead. It had been another hot day. Most had been counting the minutes until the end of the shift. Now it was a race to either the pub or home.

All of a sudden, the women found themselves in a tide of bodies, their progress slowed down as everyone headed for the gates, creating the usual bottleneck at the timekeeper's cabin.

'Move!' Angie bellowed at the top of her lungs. She was at the front of the women's vanguard.

'Fire!' Dorothy screeched. She had heard that if you needed people to move, you had to pretend there was a fire; apparently, people then scattered like rats. She had been falsely informed. A few of the men turned their heads, but seeing it was Dorothy, returned to their chatter.

'Davey!' Rosie shouted over to the young lad, but he couldn't hear. His little face flushed as he grabbed the clocking-off cards that were being waved up at him impatiently.

Finally, they made it to the main gates. Rosie stood on her tiptoes, straining to see if the ambulance was anywhere in sight.

'There it is!' she shouted.

But any joy immediately died when she saw that its progress was even slower than their own.

Ten minutes later, Marie-Anne swung her head round.

'It's here! It's here!' she screamed. 'The ambulance is coming through the gates!'

'Too late,' Dr Parker said. 'The baby's coming.'

As if on cue, Polly suddenly felt an overwhelming urge to push.

After the ambulance finally made it through the throng of workers to the main gates, Rosie jumped into the passenger seat, squashed herself up against the nurse and directed the driver to the outside of the admin building.

'A woman called Polly Watts has gone into labour,' Rosie explained, trying to stay calm and convey as much information as possible in the shortest time possible.

'She's not due for another two weeks and she's had some sort of stitch put in her cervix because she nearly lost the baby when she was about three months gone.'

Rosie looked at the nurse's face; she clearly had no idea what she was talking about. She also looked very worried.

'Luckily, there's a doctor with her,' Rosie said. 'Dr Parker.'

The nurse's face instantly showed relief.

The driver pulled over and Rosie opened the door and jumped out.

The young nurse grabbed her bag and followed.

'This way!'

It was Gloria.

She took the nurse to the entrance, where Dorothy was holding open the door.

As the nurse followed Gloria up the stairs, Dorothy saw Angie coming out of the drawing office with Hannah and Olly.

'Come on! Hurry up!' she shouted across, waving her free hand at them before screeching in excitement at the top of her lungs.

'Polly's having her baby!'

For the next twenty-five minutes, Polly's world became a blur of faces, noises and voices.

The nurse who had arrived with the ambulance looked terrified as she hurried to and fro, carrying towels or bowls of water. Polly was glad that Helen had remained second in command to Dr Parker.

She listened as John told her very matter-of-factly that her baby was in the right position, 'head down and face towards the spine'. The stitch had worked its way loose.

This, he explained, was excellent news and meant the birth shouldn't take long – or be too painful.

Polly wanted to scream that it was already too painful, but the words never made it out of her mouth as another contraction again took away her ability to sound anywhere near coherent.

Bel and Martha stayed exactly where they were. They had no choice. Polly's grip was like a vice.

Polly was vaguely aware of what was happening around her. She caught glimpses of Marie-Anne bobbing in and out of the admin doors, but it was only when she heard Dorothy shriek that she realised the women welders were waiting at the top of the steps outside the entrance to the office.

She tried hard to obey Dr Parker's commands, reiterated by Helen, telling her to push or to stop pushing.

But then Dr Parker gave her the go-ahead for one last almighty effort.

'Do it!' Helen commanded.

The pain was off the Richter scale. There were a few seconds of silence. And then she heard her baby cry. And she, too, started crying.

'It's a boy!' Dr Parker declared.

'You've got a baby boy!' Helen said, her voice choked.

Polly watched through a blur of tears as Dr Parker cut the cord and brought her baby straight to her.

And that's when she fell in love for the second time in her life.

Chapter Thirty-Three

Dorothy and Angie had their faces pressed up against the window of the double doors that led into the office-cum-delivery-ward. Both were giving running commentaries on what they could and could not see. Both were thankful that Dr Parker was obscuring their view so that they didn't have to witness all the blood and gore, as they had at Hope's birth.

Marie-Anne was coming and going, giving updates.

After what felt like an age, she opened the door with tears in her eyes and a big smile on her face and declared:

'It's a boy! And mother and baby are fine.'

Rosie, Gloria, Dorothy, Angie, Hannah and Olly all cheered, then laughed and cried, all breathing the biggest sighs of relief that Polly and the baby were alive and well.

Now in full Irish brogue, Marie-Anne said they'd be allowed to see 'mammy and the bab' in a few minutes, but as Dr Parker wanted them taken to the hospital 'post-haste', they had to be quick.

While they were waiting impatiently to be given the green light, Charlotte came rushing up the stairs and, like Dorothy, jumped for joy on hearing the news.

She was immediately dispatched by Rosie to go and tell Agnes she was now a grandmother to a beautiful baby boy and that she should go to the Royal.

Dr Parker stood back and let the women crowd around Polly and her new baby.

Helen moved out of the way too. She looked at him and smiled. For a moment he was back in his dream. Only this wasn't a dream. This was reality. Her emerald eyes locked on to his own.

'Helen,' he said, his voice barely above a whisper as she moved closer.

She was going to kiss him!

Suddenly, he felt someone bump into him from behind.

'Oh, so sorry, old chap!'

He turned around.

It was Matthew bloody Royce.

Matthew ignored him; he only had eyes for Helen.

'There you are!' He nudged his way past Dr Parker so that he was facing Helen. Dr Parker noticed he was carrying a bunch of flowers. 'Thank God you're all right! I saw the ambulance and naturally thought the worst.'

Dr Parker watched as the man Helen had referred to as 'a charmer and a chancer' kissed her on both cheeks.

Dr Parker now stood looking at Matthew's back. He fought the urge to lamp him one.

'Polly went into labour ...' he heard Helen explain.

'And had the little bugger, by the looks of it!' Matthew let out a huge guffaw. He held the flowers out for Helen. 'These were meant for you, my dear, but I'm guessing it would now be more appropriate to give them to the new mother.'

Helen laughed. 'I'm guessing you would be right.'

She touched Matthew's arm to stop him charging over to Polly with the bouquet.

'Matthew, meet John ... Dr John Parker.'

Matthew spun round, a surprised expression on his face, as though he had just noticed him for the first time.

'Hello, old boy!' Matthew stuck out his hand.

Dr Parker put both blood-smeared hands up in front of him.

'Sorry,' he said, 'I've not had a chance to clean up.'

Matthew glanced down and grimaced.

'Not a problem, old chap. Nice to finally meet you. I've heard so much about you.'

Dr Parker looked at Helen.

'Oh, John, sorry, this is Matthew. Matthew Royce. He's the new manager at Pickersgill's.'

'Ah, yes, of course,' Dr Parker said, as if he didn't know.

'Ha! Didn't expect to find the office had transformed itself into a maternity ward,' Matthew exclaimed.

Dr Parker forced a smile.

'And by the looks of you, my dear Helen,' Matthew said, 'it would appear that you too have been helping the good doctor with bringing life into this world.'

'Well—' Helen started to speak.

'I'd better get Polly to the hospital,' Dr Parker interrupted. 'She might need a little patching up.' He looked over at one of the phones. 'Is it all right to call the hospital, so they can get a message to Dr Billingham?'

'Yes, yes, of course,' Helen said. 'I'll get Polly down to the ambulance.'

If Dr Parker had stayed just a few minutes longer, he would have realised that the reason Matthew had brought flowers for Helen was by way of an apology, for he had made a rather crass attempt at kissing her after the launch at Doxford's the other day.

He hadn't known what had come over him. One minute Helen was standing in his office chatting to him about a new commission from the Ministry of War Transport, and the next he was bending his head to kiss her – and would have succeeded if she hadn't snapped her head away from him just as their lips were about to touch.

Helen had been very forgiving about the whole episode; she had laughed it off, which was a little disconcerting, acting as though it was nothing, which it probably was for her. She must have men falling at her feet every time she stepped out of her front door. Like that Dr Parker. He was clearly still hoping he was in with a chance. Miriam had been right. The look he'd given him when they'd been introduced had said it all.

After his clumsy faux pas, bringing Helen flowers today was his way of redeeming himself. And he did intend to redeem himself. He mightn't have succeeded in his first attempt to woo Helen, but that didn't mean he'd given up. Far from it.

He'd decided that this woman was going to be his wife. It might take time, but he had plenty of that.

Helen looked around, but John had gone.

Damn it. She'd wanted to speak to him. Wanted to celebrate little Arthur's birth, and the fact that Polly had asked her to be his godmother – along with Bel. It wasn't every day you helped bring life into the world. They had just shared something momentous – didn't he want to chat about it and relive the drama of it all over a drink in the Admiral?

She suddenly felt as though she'd just had the wind taken out of her sails.

She hardly saw John at all these days. She'd rung him a couple of times, but he hadn't returned her calls. Too busy with Dr Perfect, no doubt.

'I think we should all go and wet the baby's head!'

Matthew's loud voice broke her out of her reverie.

There was cheer of agreement from the women and a smile from Olly, who had been helping Hannah to clear up the mess and now looked several shades paler than he did normally – and he was pale at the best of times.

'And the drinks are on me,' Matthew added.

Helen looked at them all and smiled.

She wondered why John had dropped by in the first place; probably just popped in for a quick cuppa after a consultation at the Monkwearmouth.

'All right, why not?' she agreed. 'But I must insist that the drinks are *on me*.'

Matthew sighed. He had his work cut out with Helen, there was no doubt about that – but he had a feeling he was going to enjoy every minute of it.

As Dr Parker made his way back to Ryhope on the train, he felt consumed by the biggest and darkest cloud imaginable.

Helen and Matthew were clearly an item. They'd been pictured together just recently; he'd been a fool not to realise. *Of course, they were.* It was a perfect match. They were both managers of shipyards, both from shipbuilding families. *God, they even looked similar* – both dark and strikingly good-looking.

Dr Parker looked out the window. It was just starting to get dark. He closed his eyes in frustration.

How could he have been so stupid? To keep hope alive – all because of a dream? For the rest of the thirty-minute journey, he berated himself. He had a good mind to check himself into the asylum. And thoughts of the mental hospital made him think about Claire. Was he mad? Did he have some kind of death wish for his love life? Claire was lovely – she was ideal for him.

By the time he arrived at Ryhope station, Dr Parker had made up his mind. This really was it. No more ridiculous fantasies about making Helen his, or about Helen wanting him. He'd had enough.

It was time to leave this boyish crush behind and get on with being an adult. A man. A man who had a real relationship with a real woman.

Chapter Thirty-Four

'Congratulations, my dear!' Dr Billingham said as he walked through the door that had been left open by the nurse who had just left. He came over to the bed and peered down at baby Arthur, who was fast asleep, having had a hearty feed.

'You have a perfect little boy there. Perfectly gorgeous and perfectly healthy.' Dr Billingham had given both mother and baby a good checking over after their admittance.

'Your husband is going to be a very proud father – talking of which, do you want my secretary to send a telegram to Petty Officer Watts to tell him the good news?'

Polly's face lit up. She had been thinking of Tommy constantly, wishing he was there, imagining he was there, talking to him in her head, telling him all about their little creation and how perfect he was.

'Oh, yes, please! That would be wonderful! Thank you! Thank you for everything, Dr Billingham.'

'Righty-ho, I'll get on the case,' Dr Billingham said, turning to leave.

'Before you go ...' Polly leant forward and made to hand Arthur over. 'Do you want to hold him – say a proper hello?'

'Why not, eh?' Dr Billingham took the swaddled baby.

Polly looked up at the man who had been there for her these past six months. She watched him staring down at little Arthur and thought she saw a shard of sadness.

'Hopefully your Mary will meet someone soon, get married and give you a lovely little grandson or granddaughter to carry on the Billingham line.'

'Oh, wouldn't that've been nice,' he said, taking a last look and handing Arthur back.

'There's still time,' Polly said, wanting to cheer him up. 'She's still young. Hardly an old maid.'

Dr Billingham put his hands on his hips. Took a deep breath.

'Right, best get that telegram off.' He glanced down at Arthur. 'Try and get some sleep. You'll be needing it!'

And with that he was gone.

Bel was sitting on the side of Polly's bed, holding baby Arthur in her arms. He was wrapped up in a white blanket that Agnes had brought up to the hospital. Tears were running down her face. She cuddled him gently and he reached up to touch her face.

Polly looked at her sister-in-law. Her eyes were wet too. How she wished for the day when their roles at this moment were reversed.

'I'm crying because I'm happy, you know,' Bel said, her words coming out a little choked.

Polly mouthed 'I know.' She was crying again; she hadn't really stopped since Arthur had come into the world.

As they both cried and gazed at the very robust-looking baby boy who was gurgling away to himself and staring up at his aunty Bel with love and awe, Agnes bustled back into the room. She had a cup of tea.

'Ah, thanks, Ma,' Polly said.

'*Pfft!*' She nestled herself down in the armchair by the bed and took a sip. 'I need this after all the stress 'n worry yer've caused yer auld ma today.' She took another sip. 'Yer've added another ten years.' Another sip. She looked at her daughter and her daughter-in-law. Bel always looked such a natural with babies. 'Well, that's one lucky little lad there.'

Bel laughed and stood up.

'One lucky and very *heavy* little lad,' she said, handing Arthur back to Polly. 'No wonder you were so big.' Bel laughed lightly. '*Ten pounds and two ounces*!'

'But, thank goodness, not twins, eh?' Polly said, taking the baby and looking at her ma.

'I was sure we were going to have twins in the family,' Agnes said, shaking her head. 'Not often I'm wrong.'

Chapter Thirty-Five

It was clear within days of little Arthur being taken home that he was a happy, contented baby. Perhaps his impatience to enter the world had been because he knew what awaited him: limitless amounts of love and cuddles – smiling, cooing faces, soft voices singing lullabies and giant hands stroking his warm cheeks. Like all babies, he cried when he was startled, hungry or tired, but he was always quickly placated. He wasn't, though, overly keen on sleep. Joe joked it was hardly surprising – *who would want to sleep with all that fuss being foisted on him?*

Lucille and Hope thought little Arthur – or Artie, as they had renamed him – was the best thing ever to come into their lives. Their toys were cast aside in favour of their new playmate, and although Artie couldn't do an awful lot to start with, he still moved when prodded and poked, and made funny expressions and noises. Best of all, he didn't scream and cry all the time like some of the babies that came to Aggie's nursery.

Agnes lost count of the number of times she told Polly how fortunate she was to have such a happy newborn. He was a healthy, well child, a diagnosis confirmed by Dr Billingham, who popped in every now and again. He didn't have to, but Polly was glad he did, and told him so.

The only time Artie's little face was guaranteed to crumple up in upset and anger was whenever Polly tried to give him the bottle instead of the breast. He cried and cried until he was once again nuzzled up against the soft mounds of his mammy's boobs. As a result, Polly had to renege on her promise to return to work within weeks of giving birth.

'I'm so sorry,' she said to Helen when she took Artie back to the place of his birth a month after his dramatic entrance into the world. 'I feel like I've gone back on my word.'

'Don't be daft,' said Helen as she walked around her office, 'this little one needs his mother at home more than we need you here.' She looked down at baby Artie as she swayed him gently. 'Isn't that right, little one? Your god-mother thinks Mummy should give you her undivided attention until at least the end of the year.'

She looked up to see Polly's reaction.

'That's what Ma says,' Polly admitted.

'Good, we're all agreed,' Helen said, handing Arthur back. 'He's heavy, isn't he?'

Polly laughed. 'Tell me about it. I'll probably come back to work with stronger arms than when I left.'

'Tommy all right?' Helen asked as they made their way out of her office to introduce Artie to the admin workers.

'Yes, he's writing lots—' Polly stopped herself. 'Or I should say, he's making *me* write lots, telling him every lit-tle detail about his son.'

'Let's hope he gets home soon,' Helen said as they walked into the open-plan office, where they were imme-diately hit by a chorus of oohs and aahs.

As the weeks passed by and the trees started to relin-quish their leaves, Polly would often look at the miracle she had grown inside her and believe that anything was possible. Every night she would sit in the chair that Art-ie's great-grandfather had commandeered during his time living with the Elliots, and just like the old man, Polly would listen to the news on the BBC Home Service. There was jubilation the length and breadth of the country when reports of Italy's capitulation came across the airwaves, and later when Allied forces reached Naples. Rome would come next, and from there Berlin. At least this was what was hoped. At home, Sunderland had not seen a single air raid since May – which was also true for most of the country. Hitler's firepower was needed elsewhere.

Hearing the sounds of the riveters' fusillades under the dull northern sky day after day, week after week, you could almost hear the collective will of the shipyard workers – men and women – knowing that what they were building was a vital weapon if the war was to be won. Every rivet driven felt like a punch against the enemy. A victorious punch.

Rosie held off taking on another welder, believing the women needed to feel free to talk about their secrets. If another woman joined their squad, they would have to watch their tongues. Now, more than ever, she felt they needed to be able to talk whenever they wanted to. Her squad had always been close, but after everyone's secrets had been revealed, they had become more protective of each other.

Every Monday morning, following their dutiful Sunday trips to see their respective families, the squad would ask Angie and Dorothy how it had gone. Hannah had done some research into the laws governing bigamy and the possible jail sentences should someone be found guilty, but had decided not to tell Dorothy. Sometimes ignorance was bliss.

She often wished the bliss of ignorance for herself, but it was not to be. Her aunty Rina had told her that they had to face up to the reality of what was happening in Europe – and ensure that as many people as possible knew about it. When Hannah heard that the commander of the SS, Heinrich Himmler, had ordered the Romani people to be put 'on the same level as Jews' and placed in concentration camps, she told the women, as well as Basil and those she worked with in the drawing office – just as she did when news filtered through that the Nazis had liquidated the Janowska concentration camp in western Ukraine, murdering thousands of Jews after a failed uprising.

Knowing the truth about Jack's long absence, the women tried not to hold it against Helen that she had been the one to tell her mother about Gloria's affair with Jack, but Dorothy and Angie in particular found it hard. Gloria reminded them of how Helen had changed since that time, how she had clobbered Vinnie with a shovel when he had been beating her half to death, and how she had risked her life to save Hope's – but there was still an underlying resentment.

Gloria tried not to show how much she missed Jack, but now the truth was out, it was hard. She started to phone Jack more regularly, always with Hope, but a part of her wondered if it only made her miss him even more.

Love continued to blossom for Dorothy and Toby, and although their chances to be together were infrequent and brief, it made for a more intense affair. Like so many other couples, they spent more time thinking and talking about each other than actually being together. The women enjoyed teasing Dorothy and there was regular banter about the not too distant sound of wedding bells, followed by Gloria's stern warning and finger-wagging that Dorothy should do everything in the right order – marriage first, children second. Her comments were, naturally, accompanied by Dorothy's outrage and theatrics.

Angie and Quentin also only managed to see each other a few times after their 'date that wasn't a date' at the Palatine, but they now spoke regularly on the phone. Dorothy joked that Angie's 'lover boy' must have a sixth sense as he always seemed to call whenever they were at Mrs Kwiatkowski's. Angie gave Dorothy the evil eye, saying that 'her *friend* Quentin' was probably just using his nous, rather than any extra sense he might possess, and was phoning when he knew there was a good chance they'd be there – after work.

The march towards winter saw Mr Havelock fall ill with chronic bronchitis. Refusing to go to hospital, he was given round-the-clock nursing at home. As he made a slow recovery, he had time to stew over various aspects of his life. Top of his list was the Ashbrooke Gentlemen's Club. His time convalescing did nothing to assuage his fury at being refused membership, or his determination to find out more and make whoever was responsible pay.

Pearl, in the meantime, was also continuing her quest to find out more – helped by Bill. Every fortnight, she would slip into Agnes's faded blue dress, put her hair into a bun and spend more time putting on make-up so that it looked natural than she normally did plastering it on. She was still nervous each time she approached the entrance to the asylum, but she knew it would be worth it. It felt as though every visit was bringing her a step closer to the truth.

Henrietta seemed to be getting more coherent and, thankfully, was keeping the visits a secret. She appeared to enjoy the whole subterfuge – just as Pearl appeared to enjoy her time with Bill and their luncheons in the Railway Inn, not that she would admit it.

In contrast, Bel's unhappiness and resentment seemed to be growing steadily, like an infection left untreated. It was made still worse when Polly told her about the women's secrets and how Miriam was using them to keep Jack in Scotland.

'Like father, like daughter,' Bel said, outraged. 'Nasty, wicked ... manipulating people. Using the misfortune of others to get what they want.'

Hearing about Martha's, Dorothy's and Angie's mothers had shocked Bel, but she was also infuriated that her friends, too, would be in the firing line if their mams' secrets were ever trumpeted about by Miriam.

'But you know what really makes my blood boil,' Bel said, 'is that it's Hope that's really suffering! She's the one who is being made to grow up without a father. There's plenty of children having to grow up without their dads thanks to this war, but Hope having to suffer Jack's absence because Miriam doesn't want to face up to the fact her marriage has ended – or rather that she doesn't want anyone to know ...' Bel's voice trailed off and she shook her head in disbelief.

Polly thought that it was so like her sister-in-law to think of the child in the middle of the maelstrom above all else.

She was relieved, though, that after the birth of little Artie, she and Bel had regained some of the closeness she felt they had lost.

'I'm so sorry,' Bel told her one evening when they had been up late chatting on their own. 'I just found it really hard when you were pregnant. I couldn't help it,' she confessed.

The two hugged.

'I really wouldn't know what I'd do without you,' Polly told her, 'you're *my best friend in the whole wide world.*'

Bel laughed. It had been their saying when they were young.

Agnes was also massively relieved to see that Bel's pain at not falling pregnant had not worsened with her grandson's arrival, which instead seemed to have given her daughter-in-law comfort – a gentle balm for an invisible wound.

Work kept Bel busy, and she continued to go to launches with Helen, regardless of whether Mr Havelock and Miriam would be there. They had a clear run for a while due to Mr Havelock's illness, during which time Bel lay awake at night and prayed that his lungs would pack in, or fill with fluid and choke him to death. She knew it was wrong, but she didn't care. And so she continued to say her prayers.

She admitted to Helen how she felt and was surprised when she laughed it off. That was what she liked about Helen. She was pretty unshockable. It helped enormously, of course, that Helen hated her grandfather and her mother almost as much as Bel did – but not quite.

They talked about the hold Miriam had over Gloria and Jack – and bonded over their outrage that Hope was being so cruelly separated from a loving and caring father.

Bel noticed that Helen never spoke much about Dr Parker. Occasionally, she would say something, or he'd come into the conversation, and she saw the grief at a lost love in Helen's deep green eyes. He still occasionally popped in to see her at work if he was over the north side of the Wear, and they still spoke very occasionally on the phone – *when* he remembered to call her back – but it was clear he was now serious about Dr Eris.

Of course, Helen was not short of admirers. Matthew was now a regular figure in her life, although Bel was unsure whether that was because of work, or because he orchestrated it. Either way, Helen didn't seem to mind.

When autumn started to creep into winter before its designated time, no one seemed to care too much, or complain. As long as there were no more bombs being dropped from the night skies, the townsfolk were happy to endure whatever Mother Nature wanted to chuck at them.

And as they edged towards December, with the bombing of Berlin and the British Eighth Army's advance into Italy, as well as the Soviet forces' advance on the Eastern Front, it seemed that victory could be just around the corner.

Chapter Thirty-Six

The Havelock Residence, Glen Path, Sunderland

Friday 3 December

'Come in!' Mr Havelock barked.

Eddy opened the door to the office and took one step into what he and Agatha called the 'inner sanctum'.

'Your visitor has arrived,' Eddy announced, putting his hands behind his back and standing ramrod straight. There was no slouching in the Havelock residency.

'Well, show him in!' Another bark. The master of the house was not in a good humour today.

Eddy disappeared for a minute before opening the door wide.

'Mr Robert Thurley,' he announced, moving aside to allow the ex-detective-cum-private-eye to enter the room.

'Please, call me Bob,' he said, glancing at Eddy and then ahead at Mr Havelock.

Eddy saw the thunderous look on his master's face and made a hasty retreat. Whoever this Bob was, he was glad he wasn't standing in his shoes at this moment. He hurried down to the kitchen; he reckoned he'd just have time for a cuppa and a piece of rhubarb pie the cook had baked.

'Did you use the tradesmen's entrance round the back?' Mr Havelock demanded. He remained seated behind his desk.

'Yes, yes, I most certainly did, sir,' Bob said, taking a few steps further into the office, stopping by the chair in front of Mr Havelock's huge oak desk.

'For God's sake, man, sit down!' Mr Havelock waved his hand impatiently at the chair. 'I don't want you hovering over me for the duration.'

Bob lowered his considerable bulk onto the seat, adjusting his tie as he did so, something he did when he was unsure of himself.

'I hope you've got some good news for me.' Mr Havelock poured himself a whisky but didn't offer the same to his guest, who would have very much appreciated one. A large one.

'It might well be construed as good news,' Bob said, pulling out a large, grubby-looking handkerchief and wiping his forehead. 'It's certainly *news*.'

'Good. Good.' Mr Havelock stared at Bob and waited. 'Well, come on, then. Spit it out.'

'Sorry. Yes. Of course.' Bob fidgeted about in his jacket pocket and pulled out his notepad. He flipped it open.

'First off, it would appear the Ashbrooke Gentlemen's Club is owned by a Mr George Macalister. Former captain in the Ninth Battalion of the Durham Light Infantry. Awarded the Distinguished Service Order for "gallant and distinguished services".'

Mr Havelock raised his eyebrows and took a sip of his whisky. He had presumed the club was owned by the Frenchwoman Eddy had spoken to on the phone; she'd certainly given that impression.

'Any financial improprieties?' His aim was to get the place shut down.

'No, not that I could see. It all seems above board.'

'Damn!' Mr Havelock took a mouthful of whisky. He'd wanted – *expected* – to find some kind of dodgy dealings.

'It would also seem that the club is very popular.' Bob looked up at Mr Havelock. 'Although whether it is so popular that it really is unable to take any more members, I think is doubtful.'

'Facts. I just want facts!' Mr Havelock snapped. His patience was wearing thin.

Bob cleared his throat. He was looking forward to having a nice frothy pint of bitter followed by a double whisky chaser when he was out of this mausoleum.

'The place is legit. And is managed by a very attractive coloured woman, who goes by the name of ...' he turned over a page '... Maisie Smith. It is doubtful that this is her real name. She hails from London, but this is where it gets interesting.' He looked up at Mr Havelock. 'Maisie Smith came up north to find her real mother, who gave her up at birth. Left her down south in the big smoke at some unmarried women's home which had the baby adopted out.'

Mr Havelock shifted forward in his chair. Now it was starting to get interesting.

'Maisie succeeded in tracking down her birth mother here in the east end.' Again, a flip of the notebook. 'A Miss Pearl Hardwick.'

Bob looked up to see if the name meant anything to Mr Havelock, but his face appeared impassive, so he continued.

'At the same time as being reunited with her mother, Maisie also discovered she had a half-sister.' Another pause while Bob consulted his notes.

'Mrs Isabelle Elliot.'

Bob looked up and saw a flicker of recognition on the old man's face.

He waited. Thought the old man might volunteer some information.

He was wrong.

'Anything else?' Mr Havelock barked.

'No, not really,' Bob said.

'Well, *is* there or *isn't* there?' *His appetite had been whetted; he wanted to know more.*

Bob shook his head. 'No, sir.'

Mr Havelock pulled out the top drawer and took out a little tin box. He put it on the desk and opened it. He took out a number of banknotes, licked his finger and thumb and counted them out. He slapped them on the table.

'As agreed.'

Bob stood up, realising their meeting was over. *Thank God.* Time for that drink.

Mr Havelock placed a bony hand on top of the money just as Bob was about to pick it up. He stared up at the ex-policeman.

'I want you to find out *everything* you can on the three women you've just named. *Everything.* No stone left unturned. You hear me?'

Bob nodded.

'If you do,' Mr Havelock removed his hand, 'there's plenty more where that came from. *A lot more.*'

Bob's heart leapt for joy for the first time since he'd stepped into this godforsaken place. Mr Havelock might be a cantankerous old man, but he was a rich cantankerous old man and he had money to spare. Quite a rarity these days. This could be a good little earner for him.

Mr Havelock turned and pulled a bell to summon Eddy.

The meeting might well be over, he thought, but the investigation was only just beginning.

His instincts told him there was something else going on here – and his instincts were rarely wrong.

Chapter Thirty-Seven

Saturday 4 December

'What's Charlie up to today?' Gloria asked. They were all sitting around their usual table in the canteen. 'She's not in the office, so I'm guessing she's either working at the café or with Georgina – or Lily?'

Rosie laughed. 'That just about sums up Charlie's whereabouts during a weekend.'

'So, which one is it?' Angie asked.

'Bet you she's shopping with Lily,' Dorothy said.

'She is indeed,' Rosie said. 'Charlie had some kind of hockey tournament called a round robin. She was going to go home, get herself cleaned up and then the pair of them were heading into town.'

'Does Lily *walk* into town?' Martha asked. The idea of Lily shuffling her way into town in one of her tight dresses, high heels and tall hairdos seemed improbable.

'Goodness, no,' Rosie said. 'Lily? Walk anywhere? Not in a million years.'

'George?' asked Hannah, taking a bite of her sandwich.

'Correct. Any excuse to get his MG out for a spin,' Rosie said, reaching over and topping up her tea. She glanced out of the window and saw a rag swirl past. The wind was getting up, but at least it would stave off the rain.

'So, Lily's definitely not going to get married on New Year's Eve?' Dorothy asked. She and Angie had been massively disappointed when Rosie had told them the news.

'Definitely,' Rosie said. 'She says there's been too much happening for her to spend the time on organising the *wedding of the decade*.'

Hannah chuckled. 'Too much time spent with Charlie more likely.'

'Too many early mornings,' Bel chipped in. 'Maisie says it gets to nine o'clock on an evening and then all Lily does is yawn until they shoo her off to bed.'

'George doesn't mind the wedding being cancelled?' Martha asked.

'The word they're using,' Rosie said, deadpan, 'is *postponed*. But no, you know George – he's so laid-back.' Rosie had often wondered if George's need to put a legal stamp on his union with Lily was to safeguard her. Not that he'd ever admit that to Lily, who would be outraged at the mere suggestion that she needed safeguarding. But, if that was the case, Rosie understood. If anything happened to George, Lily would inherit whatever he had, which was quite substantial.

As the women started chatting about what they had planned for their Saturday night, Rosie found her mind drifting off. Any talk of weddings always made her think of her own nuptials. Peter had proposed to her just before he'd gone off to be a hero behind enemy lines. A hero in all senses, in that the odds on him returning were not favourable. Like George, Peter knew that if he married Rosie and anything happened to him, everything he owned, including the house, would be hers.

Thinking of her brave husband made her stomach lurch, and it had been doing so more and more of late. The summer before last, she had received an envelope full of petals – pansies, the same as her wedding bouquet. Not long after that, Peter had surprised her, turning up out of the blue for an overnight stay. Every minute of their time together was still imprinted on her mind. Then, last Christmas Eve, Toby had brought her a letter – but since then, nothing. Not a whisper.

Rosie looked at Hannah, who was listening avidly to Dorothy as she held court, describing what she and Angie were going to wear for the Ritz that evening. If Hannah could be strong in the face of what she knew was happening in the concentration camp where her mother and father were being held, then so could she.

The women all started laughing at something outrageous Dorothy had said about Toby before she told them, holding her hands together in prayer, that there was a chance he might be able to make it back for Christmas Day.

Rosie felt an immediate swell of nerves.

With Toby there was always the possibility of news about Peter. Dorothy, thank goodness, understood and would always put Rosie out of her misery when she saw her after Toby's visit. Each time, Dorothy shook her head as soon as she saw Rosie in the yard, and each time Rosie never knew whether to laugh or cry. Laugh with relief or cry because it meant she had to continue living in limbo, not knowing whether Peter was alive. Or not. She would never say the 'd' word – not even in her head.

Chapter Thirty-Eight

Monday 6 December

'Ah, Georgina,' Helen said, switching on her electric fire. 'Come in, come in.' She shrugged off her coat. 'Doxford's have just launched *Empire Earl*. I feel frozen to the bone.' She rubbed her arms, looked through the glass, caught Marie-Anne's attention and mimed drinking a cup of tea.

Georgina sat down, clasping her hands and resting them on her lap.

'You do know I'm not doing any more –' she dropped her voice '– private-investigation work?'

'Yes, yes, I know. I just need you to do some research for me. Nothing underhand. It's all perfectly legit. To be honest, it's something I could probably do myself, but I simply don't have the time.'

Georgina relaxed. She wondered if Helen knew that her grandfather had contacted her father a while ago and asked him to do a job. Something told her that it might be beneficial for Helen to know this, but she couldn't disclose that information. It would be unethical, even if Pickering & Sons was no longer officially a Private Investigations firm.

Helen waved Marie-Anne in with the tea tray. 'Can you shut the door on your way out?' She got up and poured two cups.

'So, tell me, Georgina, how's your new job going? I keep seeing photographs with your name in the *Echo*.'

'It's going well,' Georgina said, taking her tea and smiling her thanks. 'Or I should say, as well as I could hope. They're using my photos – and giving me a picture credit.' She wanted to add that unfortunately the pay was poor, very poor, but didn't. It was why she was sitting there now.

'I know it's hard getting a lot of images past the censors these days,' Helen said. 'Can't let Jerry know too much.'

'Or get in the way of government propaganda,' Georgina added, raising a cynical eyebrow.

Helen laughed. Georgina might look the epitome of conservatism with her old-fashioned dress sense, but she was a radical at heart and unafraid to show it. She took a sip of her tea and grabbled in her bag for her cigarettes. The mention of censorship made her wonder again about what it was that Georgina had held back about Rosie when she had done her mother's dirty work for her. One day she'd find out.

'I'm surprised you're not writing articles as well as taking photos,' she said.

'Funny you should mention that, but I *have* started to. Some of my stories have been published, but they've not put my name on them.'

'Really?' Helen showed her surprise. 'What kind of stories?'

'Mainly court reports, inquests, council meetings – that sort of thing. And sometimes people tell me things and I follow up on them and see if what they've told me will make a story.'

'It all sounds very interesting,' Helen said. 'Very interesting.' *And also, perhaps, very useful. It could never hurt, having an ally on the local paper.*

'Unfortunately,' Helen said, 'the research I need doing is going to be quite boring in comparison to all your journalistic work – and will probably entail you having to pore over a load of dusty old law books.'

Georgina bent over and pulled out her notebook. She didn't care, as long as it paid well.

When she had written down exactly what Helen wanted to know, Georgina got up to leave.

'I'm sorry to have to ask you this,' Georgina said, feeling embarrassed, 'but I'd just like to reiterate that the work I did for you previously – and even more so, the work I did for your mother – remains between the two of us?'

'Of course, that goes without saying,' Helen reassured her, instinctively glancing down at the locked drawer where she kept the report Georgina had compiled for her; a report she had been wondering for a while now if she should give to Bel.

Helen watched Georgina leave the office, stopping to have a word with Bel and Marie-Anne.

It looked as though they all had their secrets, even the likes of Georgina.

Gloria had told her that Georgina had started to go out occasionally with the women from work and that they all thought the world of her. The last thing Georgina would want was for them to know that she had been the one to unearth all their secrets – and that she'd given those secrets over to Helen's mother, whose motivations, it must have been obvious to Georgina, were not for the greater good.

She wondered how Rosie and her squad – and Bel – would react if they knew.

Or perhaps it was more a case of *when* they knew, for they'd surely find out one day. Secrets could be buried, but it was inevitable that they would be dug up. It was always just a matter of time. And when they were, she wondered how forgiving the women would be.

Since the women welders had found out that she had been the one to tell her mother about her father's affair with Gloria, there had been a change in the air. Nothing obvious, just a cooling towards her. She knew Gloria would have tried to convince them that it was a long time ago, and that she would not do the same now – but she knew that the day she'd spilled the beans to her mother, she had triggered a domino effect.

She was now having to suffer the consequences of her actions – no matter how long ago they might have happened.

Chapter Thirty-Nine

The Grand, Bridge Street, Sunderland

Friday 10 December

'So, it looks like we're *not* going to have you home for Christmas – *again*.' Mrs Parker punctuated her reprimand by stabbing a piece of meat with her fork and popping it into her mouth.

Dr Parker looked at his mother. It was as though the less he saw of her, the stronger his loathing for her became when he did have to spend time in her company.

'There is a war on, Mother,' he said, his eyes flickering across to his father, who seemed to have become even more browbeaten since he'd last seen them.

'I think what John means,' Dr Eris said, moving her hand under the table and finding Dr Parker's clenched fist and squeezing it, 'is that he's needed here. Your son is one of the best surgeons in the county, probably one of the best in the country, and—'

'And so he should be,' Mrs Parker interrupted. 'He's had the best education anyone could want.'

Dr Eris forced herself to take a deep breath. *God, this woman was abominable.*

'I agree with Claire,' Dr Parker senior finally spoke up. 'John's needed here. You know the state some of our lads are coming home in.'

'Thank you, Edward,' Mrs Parker again interrupted. 'As we're all eating, I don't think we need reminding of the horrors of war.'

'Everything to your satisfaction?' The waiter had suddenly appeared.

Dr Parker senior threw his wife a warning look as she opened her mouth to speak.

'Yes, yes, very satisfactory,' he said, beating her to it. 'More than satisfactory.'

The waiter left before Mrs Parker had time to speak.

The sommelier appeared immediately afterwards and topped up everyone's wine glasses. Dr Parker would have preferred a pub meal at the Albion, but his mother had insisted on dining at the finest restaurant the town had to offer. It had been a toss-up between the Palatine and the Grand. Dr Parker had chosen the latter, but he wondered if that had been such a good idea as he kept thinking about the last time he'd been there – with Helen, at Polly and Tommy's wedding. *Was that really nearly a year ago?*

'So, there's absolutely no way you both can't come for Christmas?' Mrs Parker asked. She wasn't giving up. The thought of it just being her and Edward was depressing to say the least. 'I'll be doing a goose?'

'A goose sounds wonderfully tempting,' Dr Eris said, 'but, like John says, he's needed here. Or rather, at the Ryhope. The hospital's understaffed as it is. And we're starting to get quite a few repatriated prisoners of war.'

Dr Parker had to stop himself from reminding his mother that they wouldn't even be having this conversation if he, like many of the country's medics, had been working in makeshift tents just a few hundred yards from the front line.

'I'm guessing that because the Ryhope is a military emergency hospital, you've taken in some of our poor prisoners of war repatriated since Italy capitulated?' Dr Parker senior asked.

Dr Eris noticed the slight shake in the older man's hand and didn't need to ask why he didn't practise any more.

'We've taken in a few,' Dr Parker said.

'And do *you* also have to work, Claire?' Mrs Parker asked. She was determined to get the conversation back to Christmas. If the girl wasn't working, she might be able to persuade John that he couldn't possibly leave his sweetheart on her own.

'I do,' Dr Eris said. On hearing that John was working over Christmas, she had orchestrated it with the head of department so that she would work too.

'Even though you're just a psychologist,' Mrs Parker said. 'Sorry, I don't mean *just*. How awfully rude of me. What I meant was ...' Suddenly, she was at a loss for words.

'Don't worry.' Dr Eris stepped in to stop any more awkwardness. 'I know what you mean. My work is more gradual – long-term healing – whereas John is often needed right here, right now. If he's not immediately available, it can be the difference between life and death.'

Mrs Parker forced a smile, nodded and sipped her wine. 'Exactly, my dear.'

As the waiter came to clear their plates, Dr Parker caught sight of two women walking across the lounge to the bar. One of the women was blonde, slim and moneyed, the other dark, a little on the plump side, and also moneyed. Very much so. Both looked tipsy. They were greeted by two Admiralty. His heart did a slight turn. It was Miriam. And her friend Amelia. He hoped she didn't see him. That was all he needed.

As Claire asked his father about his work before retirement, Dr Parker's thoughts couldn't help but stray to Helen. He wondered how she was getting on with her mother after everything that had come to light. *God, he missed her.*

As she sipped her wine, he looked at his own mother, chipping in every now and again with some scathing, smart-alec comment.

His gaze returned to Miriam. He'd often said to Helen that their mothers were similar. Seeing them in such close proximity to each other, he realised just how alike they really were.

As they left the restaurant to catch a taxi back to Ryhope, Dr Parker stopped at the bottom of the steps and took Dr Eris in his arms. He kissed her.

'Thank you for tonight,' he said.

Dr Eris kissed him by way of reply.

This evening could not have gone better if she'd planned it herself. She had been expecting to have to juggle mother and son, ingratiating herself with the mother whilst at the same time staying in the son's favour. But it had not gone at all as anticipated and any balls she'd expected to have to keep in the air had been taken from her. Thank heavens for narcissistic mothers.

The fact that John's mother had been quite rude had gone in her favour. It had endeared her more to John. She had seen it in his eyes. The way he was protective of her in the face of his mother's bitchiness. And the cherry on the cake was that Dr Parker senior obviously thought the world of her. When he had been talking about his life as a surgeon in the 'good old bad old days', he'd quietly slipped in a comment that left Claire in no doubt that he would be more than happy to see his son married to such a 'fine, intelligent young woman'. She hoped Mrs Parker hadn't heard him otherwise the poor chap would be getting an earbashing all the way home.

*

Dr Parker took hold of Dr Eris's hand and squeezed it as they sat in the back of the taxi.

She'd managed his mother brilliantly – and stopped him losing his own temper into the bargain. His mother had always exasperated him, but whereas before he had been able to keep relatively calm, since the start of the war he'd found it increasingly difficult to keep a civil tongue when in her company. Having Claire there had kept the evening on an even keel. And what's more, she had his mother down to a T. You'd have had to be blind to see that the two women did not like each other, not one bit. And that suited him down to the ground.

He wondered for a split second how Helen would have reacted to meeting his mother; it would probably have been *him* calming *her* down. He doubted they would have made it through the meal without fireworks.

But he pushed his thoughts of Helen back. Far back. It was about Claire now. He had made his decision on the afternoon he had delivered Polly's baby. He turned his head and kissed Dr Eris on her neck.

She put her hand on his leg; her touch was gentle.

As they turned into the long driveway that led to the asylum, he wondered whether it was time to take their courtship a step further.

Chapter Forty

'Ma's on about me organising Artie's christening,' Polly said, pulling a face, '"before he's in short pants".'

Bel looked at Polly sitting in the frayed armchair, feeding Artie.

'I heard her,' Bel said. 'Something about "Artie'll grow up to be a little heathen if he doesn't get some holy water spilled on his head sometime soon."'

Polly laughed. 'I reminded her that Artie is only fourteen weeks old – not that she paid a blind bit of notice ... Anyway, where're you off to?' she asked, as Bel pulled on her winter coat, scarf, woollen hat and gloves. 'The Antarctic, by the looks of it.'

'Might as well be, judging by the weather out there,' Bel said, nodding her head over to the window that was rattling with the force of the wind and rain. 'Vanity will have to be sacrificed for the sake of being warm and dry – or relatively so.'

'Where yer off to, Isabelle?'

They both looked to see Pearl standing in the hallway, unlit fag in one hand, umbrella in the other.

'I'm going to the library to get some books out for Lucille. The school has got them in a frenzy about Christmas *already* and LuLu wants books on Santa Claus, Rudolph the reindeer, St Nicholas and the baby Jesus – in that order.' Bel got her gas mask and handbag. 'Maisie's meeting me there, and we're going for a cuppa and a chat somewhere nearby.'

Pearl was already making her way to the door. 'Tell her to pop in 'n see me in the pub when she's done – get a proper drink.' Pearl cackled. 'I've not seen her for ages.'

Bel looked at Polly and mouthed 'One week.'

'I will, Ma, but don't be too downcast if she's not got the time.'

Bel heard the door shut.

She walked over and kissed Artie on the forehead.

'He smells divine,' she said, closing her eyes for the briefest of moments.

Then she kissed Polly on the head, something she never normally did.

'Love you both so much.'

She hurried out of the kitchen before the tears that had started to prick her eyes showed.

When Agnes came back from Beryl's with Lucille in tow, she found Polly and Artie fast asleep. She was glad of the quiet. It had already been a long day, and it wasn't even teatime. Beryl had just got notice that her husband was a POW. The poor woman had been overcome with relief that he wasn't dead. *How expectations had dropped.* Audrey and Iris hadn't been about, which meant they'd been able to have a good chinwag. The GPO had the girls working all hours in the run-up to Christmas; the festive season meant more post and the continuing need for conscription meant a dwindling workforce.

Coming into the kitchen, Agnes took one look at her daughter and grandson and gently removed Artie from his mammy's arms and put him in his crib in the front bedroom. She let Polly sleep. She would reprimand her when she woke about coddling the little boy too much. It worried her that baby Arthur had come into this world without the presence of his daddy, although her worries were assuaged a little by Joe's love for the child and the time he spent with Artie. He might not have his daddy presently, but his uncle was a fair substitute – and hopefully just a temporary one.

For the baby's sake, as well as Polly's.

When Polly woke up, hearing her ma in the scullery and realising she had put the baby in his cot, she went to check on him. Walking into the front bedroom, she saw that Artie was just starting to stir.

'Right, time for a little trip out,' she said, hauling him out of his crib.

She looked at the clock. If she got a move on, she'd catch the Reverend Winsey before he had his tea.

It was time to set a date. And she knew exactly what day she wanted her son to be baptised.

A perfect day for so many different reasons.

Maisie hurried up the stone steps of the Hendon Carnegie branch library on the corner of Toward Road. She had walked past the distinctive single-storey building with its porthole windows and Edwardian baroque architecture countless times, but this was the first time she had ventured inside.

Shaking out her umbrella, which had nearly got blown inside out, she walked through the main door and into the foyer, where she was immediately hit by the smell of polished oak and noticed a very beautiful, intricately carved wooden counter. Seeing the back of Bel's blonde hair, she automatically shouted out her name.

'*Shh!*' The librarian managed to make the sound even louder than Maisie's greeting; the young woman's glare was equally ferocious.

'Sorry,' Maisie whispered, waving over at Bel, who had turned around. She had an armful of books. Maisie pointed behind her to the foyer, showing she'd wait for her there.

A few minutes later, Bel joined her. Her shopping bag was weighed down with the maximum number of books she had been allowed to take out with her library card as well as Agnes's and Lucille's.

'I think that lot will keep you going until well into the New Year,' Maisie joked. She was not a great reader herself, although she had become quite obsessed with anything written by F. Scott Fitzgerald and had vowed to go to America one day.

'I can't believe there are only two weeks to go,' Bel said. 'Although going by the level of Lucille's excitement, you'd think it was two days.'

'Come on.' Maisie pulled her into the calm of the little café just a few hundred yards down from the library. It wasn't quite up to her standards, but the weather today was awful.

'Any port in a storm, eh?' she said, opening the door.

Within a few minutes, they were as warm as toast and sipping hot tea. After chatting about Lucille and her continuing love of school, and then about Polly and the baby, Maisie tentatively edged the conversation towards the subject of Charles Havelock. It was, after all, her real reason for leaving the comfort of Lily's on such a wretched day.

'So, how are you feeling, you know, about *everything*?' Maisie gave her a look.

'By *everything*, do you mean not falling pregnant?' Bel dropped her voice; she didn't want the elderly couple sitting at the next table to hear. 'Or *the other*?'

'Both,' Maisie said, putting her teacup back on its saucer.

Bel let out a long sigh.

'Well, there's nothing I can do about not falling. Can't force it to happen, can I?'

Bel's words were tinged with anger and Maisie wondered if Lucille starting school was making matters worse. The gaping hole where another baby should have been was being stretched wider by Lucille growing up and becoming more independent.

'And *the other*?' Maisie asked.

Bel groaned. 'I can't seem to let it go. Can't let the sleeping dog lie. I keep poking it.'

Maisie looked at her sister. *Their ma had been right.*

'You know Ma never let me play near Backhouse Park?' Bel said.

Maisie shook her head.

Bel let out a short, sharp burst of mirthless laughter. 'Not that Ma knew where I was most of the time, but I did what she said and never went near there.'

'I can guess why she didn't want you there,' Maisie said.

'And you'd guess right,' Bel said, her voice low and deadly serious. 'Ma knew that man was poisonous … that whoever came within spitting distance of him was at risk of being defiled by him in some way. At least Ma did one good thing for me – she kept me away from him – kept me away from his toxicity.'

Which is exactly why Ma wants you to steer well clear of him now.

'Thank God he never had anything to do with my upbringing.' Bel almost spat the words. 'Look at Miriam – what a horrible woman. Look what she's doing to poor Hope, banishing Jack over the border. Blackmailing him and Gloria.' Bel had told Maisie what Miriam had done. 'And then there's his wife, Henrietta – in the local nuthouse.' Bel knew that Pearl would have told Maisie about her former employer. There was nothing her ma kept from her favoured child.

'Look at what he's got away with – *his entire life*,' Bel ranted quietly, leaning forwards so others could not hear.

Maisie listened to her sister and for the first time she saw their mother in her and it shocked her.

'And what do you want to do about it?' Maisie asked.

'I don't know,' Bel said, sitting back, exhausted by her own vitriol. 'I've thought about humiliating him publicly – you know, telling the world what he did to Ma and how I'm the product. But I know he'd only deny it and then it'd be me and Ma who would be the humiliated ones.' She took a deep breath. 'I've thought about telling the world he's a liar and that his wife's not dead but locked up in a madhouse, but he'd still wriggle his way out of that, wouldn't he? He'd probably have people feeling sorry for him. Make it seem like he was protecting his wife.'

Bel's eyes narrowed.

'I'd like to see him suffer a long and painful death,' she said, 'but unfortunately I've not got it in me to make that a reality.'

Thank God, thought Maisie.

When they said their goodbyes outside the café, Maisie told Bel that she'd better go and see their 'auld ma', as ordered.

As Maisie gave Bel a hug, she wanted to say something that might make a difference, but she knew there was nothing meaningful she *could* say. She'd suffered herself at the hands of men – men not dissimilar to Mr Havelock. She had dealt with them in her own way. Bel, however, had to find *her* way – and sooner rather than later, before her feelings became all-consuming.

*

When Bel said goodbye to her sister, she had lied about wanting to do a shop along Villette Road. Instead, she hauled her bag of books to the top of the street, turned right onto Ryhope Road and walked along to the main entrance of Backhouse Park. As though in defiance of her ma's long-ago words of warning, she strode through the park, daring the evil spirits she had imagined living there as a child to come and get her.

Striding along, her bag of library books banging against her legs, she thought of Kate. Poor Kate. She had suffered terribly at the hands of the nuns simply because she'd had the misfortune to be orphaned as a child. It had been the same with Charlotte and Rosie. They too had suffered because they had lost their mam and dad. Rosie at the hands of her sick uncle. Charlotte because she had been deprived of any kind of parental love or care.

And then there was her own ma.

All of them had been preyed upon by animals – men and women who did what they did because they could. Because there was no one to stop them. Because they could get away with it. So much hurt and heartbreak – so much pain caused by those who victimised the vulnerable. She felt the return of the anger that always seemed to be there, waiting in the wings, ready to hurry onto the main stage whenever it was given the chance.

She had always thought good overcame evil, but lately she had realised that good and evil were equally potent. And with that knowledge had come a feeling of responsibility that she must stop the continuum of evil so that others would not be contaminated. How she could do that, though, she was still trying to work out.

Bel felt the fire of vengeance burning furiously deep inside her. And she knew nothing but retribution would quench the flames.

When she came out the other side of the park on Ash-brooke Road, she walked around the corner and along Glen Path.

Reaching the place where her mother had first told her the truth about the man who had fathered her, she stopped and stared at the huge detached red-brick house. There was a van at the front, and she watched as two young lads in brown overcoats hauled a massive Christmas tree out of the back.

Starting early with the Christmas decorations, Bel thought bitterly. She inspected the lush green tree and thought how Joe would be lucky to find one half the size, and luckier still for it not to have shed most of its needles before he even got it into the house.

In her mind's eye, she could see herself walking up to the large front door and banging on it loudly – demanding that the man who lived there come and face the result of his past depravity.

But she didn't. Instead, she walked away. She would be back. She had made herself a promise. And she was not going to break it.

When Maisie jumped off the tram and hurried across the road to the Tatham, she thought that if she was Bel, she would get her vengeance by taking the bastard to the cleaners. She'd make him pay by hitting him where it hurt the most – in the pocket.

As she walked into the main lounge area, she waved over to Pearl, who grabbed two glasses and poured good measures from the expensive bottle of brandy Maisie had asked her to keep behind the bar as she couldn't abide what she called the 'cheap cooking brandy' they served in most pubs.

Pearl grabbed her fags and took the drinks over to the table in the corner where Maisie was settling herself. She didn't need to tell Bill she was having a break – Maisie was here and when Maisie turned up, everything and everyone got dropped like a bag of hammers.

'So, what's the verdict?' Pearl asked, putting the large bulbous brandy glasses down on the table and lighting up a cigarette.

'Not good,' Maisie said, gravely. 'Not good at all.'

Chapter Forty-One

Monday 13 December

'It's Polly and Artie!' Dorothy sprang up out of her chair at the sight of Polly bumping the door to the canteen open with her back and dragging the grey Silver Cross that used to be Gloria's through the doorway. One of the workers sitting at the table nearest to the entrance jumped up and kept the door open, which wasn't as easy as it looked. The wind had been blowing in from the North Sea all night and had not run out of steam.

By the time Polly reached the women's table, they had made room for her.

Hannah was first up to greet Artie.

'Can I?' she asked, nodding down at the baby.

'Please do,' Polly said, taking off her headscarf and shrugging off her coat.

'Well, this is a surprise,' Rosie said.

'You going stir-crazy at home?' Gloria laughed. Polly had confessed to her on numerous occasions when she had come to drop Hope off that much as she loved her baby boy, her mind and body missed work.

'Make that past tense, Glor – *gone* crazy,' Polly chuckled as she sat down.

'Well, yer look good for a crazy person,' Angie said, getting up to fetch a clean cup and saucer for their former workmate.

'You and the bab all right, pet?'

It was Muriel. She had brought them over a fresh pot of tea.

'We're good, thanks, Muriel. Apart from being nearly blown away by these winds.' She nodded over to her baby boy. 'Say hello to Artie.'

Muriel wiped her hands on her pinny and took the baby off Hannah. 'Eee, he's a bonny lad. Just like his dad.' She pulled a funny face at Artie. 'And his ma, of course.'

'You got some news?' Martha asked. There had to be a reason for Polly battling through the winds that had been sweeping and swirling their way through the town and into the shipyards. It was not the most enticing day to have a trip across the Wear – especially with a baby.

'I *have*,' Polly said. 'Much to Ma's relief, I've finally set a day for Artie's christening.'

'Yeah!' Dorothy clapped her hands.

'When?' Hannah asked, taking Artie back off Muriel, who couldn't ignore the growing queue at the counter.

Polly reached over and poured herself a cup of tea.

'Christmas Eve!'

Her words were followed by an instantaneous outpouring of excitement and joy.

'That's brilliant!' Angie said.

'Just brilliant,' Dorothy agreed. 'And can we bring our beaux?'

'Of course you can,' Polly said.

'Quentin's not a "beau"!' Angie snapped.

Everyone looked at her.

'Well, he's not, is he?' She looked at them all, her face like thunder.

Nobody said anything.

Dorothy raised both eyebrows, but not so Angie could see.

'Christmas Eve is such a wonderful day to baptise a baby.' Hannah quickly changed the subject as she sat down and continued to gently rock Artie in her arms.

'And so apt,' Olly said.

'What? Because Jesus was born the next day?' Martha asked, glancing over at Angie, who still looked angry.

'I suppose so. It signifies the start of a new life, doesn't it?' Olly looked around the table.

'Is it also because you and Tommy got married on Christmas Day?' Rosie asked.

Polly nodded. 'I just thought it would be lovely to have Artie christened around the time we got married. It might sound stupid—'

'Doesn't sound stupid,' Angie butted in. 'Sounds dead romantic.'

Polly smiled at Angie. Every time she'd been with her old squad of late, Angie had sniped at Dorothy and it was usually to do with Quentin.

'And the vicar was all right about having it on Christmas Eve?' Rosie asked. She knew Lily and George had bribed the reverend with a large donation for the repairs to the roof so that he would marry Polly and Tommy on Christmas Day.

'He did grumble a little, but I took Artie with me, which helped enormously.'

'Good ploy,' Gloria said, who was sitting next to Hannah. 'Who could refuse this happy chappie anything.' She tickled his stomach and he grabbed her finger with surprising strength.

'Do you think you'll all be able to get the day off?' Polly asked, looking at Rosie.

'I'm sure we can work something out with Helen,' Rosie replied. 'Is the service morning or afternoon?'

'Afternoon,' Polly said. 'Two o'clock.'

'Perfect,' said Rosie. 'We can do a half-day. Finish at midday. That'll give us enough time to go home and get ready. I'll sort it with Helen.'

'I'm guessing Helen's coming?' Dorothy said sullenly.

'As she's one of Artie's godparents, yes, she'll be coming, Dor.' Polly glanced across at Gloria. They'd chatted about the lingering ill feeling towards Helen.

'So, what's everyone got planned for Christmas Day?' Gloria asked. She looked around the table.

'Just the usual,' Martha said.

'Same here,' said Polly, thinking it would also be her first wedding anniversary and a year since she had last seen Tommy.

'Me and Ange were trying to work out how we could avoid having to spend Christmas Day with our *lovely* families, weren't we, Ange?'

'Aye, 'cos last year we had the perfect excuse, didn't we?'

Everyone looked at Polly, remembering the magical wedding day.

'Aunty Rina and Vera had an idea,' Hannah piped up, dragging her attention away from Artie, who was doing a good job of hypnotising her.

'Which was?' Dorothy asked hopefully.

'They wondered whether we should all have our Christmas Day meal together at the café.'

'That's a brilliant idea!' Angie said.

'Salvation!' Dorothy raised her eyes to the heavens.

'They thought we could pool our resources – coupons, money,' Olly said. 'Then they would buy and cook the food.'

'What a good idea!' Rosie said. She laughed. 'Anything to get out of doing a roast dinner.'

'And Charlotte will be kept busy all day into the bargain,' Gloria said.

'Exactly,' Rosie said. 'You read my thoughts.'

The rest of the lunch hour was spent writing a list of everyone who would be going. Rosie said she would ask Lily and George, who she was sure would come as she couldn't imagine Lily and Charlie being parted on such an important day. When Bel joined the women, she said she'd ask Maisie, but thought that her sister and Vivian were going to the Grand this year, and she doubted her ma would come if the pub got a licence as Bill would need her. Joe, she said, would want to ask the Major, and would that be all right? To which they said they'd be disappointed if he didn't come. Everyone loved the Major. Polly, especially, thought the world of him as he had given Tommy his flat for the week leading up to their wedding. Martha reckoned her mam and dad would be keen, and that her mam would want to contribute by baking some mince pies. Angie rubbed her hands in glee. They all agreed to invite Georgina and her father.

'Eee,' Dorothy said, nudging Angie, pleased that she'd cheered up a little. 'It's beginning to feel like Christmas, isn't it?'

Chapter Forty-Two

'I hear Polly asked you to tell Dr Parker about the christening,' Gloria said tentatively.

Gloria and Helen were making their way to the GPO with Hope, who was in her pushchair. The weather was now so bitterly cold that Gloria's calls to Jack were being made from the relative warmth of the telephone booths in the main post office in Norfolk Street.

'She did,' Helen said.

'How do you feel about him being Artie's godfather?'

Helen thought for a moment.

'Tough question,' Helen said. 'I suppose I should have realised Polly would ask him. I mean, he not only saved Artie's life when she nearly miscarried, but he also delivered him.'

Gloria looked at Helen. *The girl was still in love. She knew that feeling. Loving someone you couldn't have.*

'It's going to be a bit awkward, isn't it?' Gloria said. 'Especially if he brings that doctor friend of his.'

Helen laughed. 'That *doctor friend* is his girlfriend, Gloria. Probably his fiancée by now. She'll likely turn up with a great big diamond on her ring finger.'

'You don't want to invite anyone?' Gloria didn't mention any names; she didn't have to.

Helen burst out laughing. 'Oh, Gloria, I do love you. I'm guessing you're talking about Matthew?'

'I might be,' she smiled.

Helen didn't answer and Gloria didn't push. Instead, she asked, 'Do you want to come to Vera's for your Christmas dinner?'

'God, I think my mother would have me hanged, drawn and quartered if I dared to miss the dinner at Grandfather's.'

'I thought your mother usually had a big do on Christmas Day?' Gloria asked.

'She does, but since Dad's gone – or rather, since she got rid of Dad – she's not been too keen to entertain what she calls a load of boring old has-beens at home.' She waited for a man walking ahead of them to open the door. 'Thank you,' she muttered as she bumped the pushchair over the threshold.

'In reality,' Helen continued as they looked for a free booth, 'it's because she can't bear to see a lot of happy, or outwardly happy, couples around her dinner table and would prefer to get it done at Grandfather's before hurrying off to the Grand to whoop it up with Amelia. She's just keeping her fingers crossed that Amelia's husband doesn't suddenly get leave. As is Amelia, of course.'

Gloria shook her head. Her own situation couldn't be more different. She'd give anything for Jack to be home for Christmas. Anything.

When Jack hung up, he felt a deep dark depression settling in. He knew he shouldn't feel so down. The war was going well. The fact that they were conscripting men to work in the mines rather than sending them off to the front line spoke volumes. The Clyde and all the other shipyards in the country were churning out ships unhindered, thanks to the fact there had been so few air raids for the best part of the year. But none of that stopped his terrible feeling of homesickness. He'd fought it for so long, but after Gloria had told him about Artie's christening, it had overwhelmed him. He'd have loved to have seen Tommy's little boy – Arthur's great-grandson. Gloria had said he was the spit of them both. And the thought of having Christmas dinner at Vera's, with everyone there ... it sounded such a perfect way of celebrating the day.

Jack imagined walking down High Street East with Gloria, his daughter holding his hand, or perhaps giving her a piggyback ride, hearing her giggle. Then getting home, giving Hope her Christmas present and watching her unwrap it ... reading her a bedtime story, before going to Gloria, putting his arms around her, kissing her – lying in bed together without a care in the world, because nothing else mattered other than them all being together as a family.

This was going to be the second Christmas in a row that he hadn't been able to spend with his little girl and the woman he loved.

Damn Miriam! Damn, damn, damn her!

'I. Am. Not. Quentin's. Girlfriend!' Angie shouted, punctuating each word. Her face was bright red. 'Why can't yer get it through that thick head of yers!' She glared at Dor, turned on her heel and stomped out of the flat.

Dorothy had made the fatal mistake of teasing Angie one too many times while they'd been clearing up after a fish and chip supper with their neighbour.

Dorothy and Mrs Kwiatkowski stood motionless, listening to Angie thud her way up the two flights of stairs to the flat. They both jumped, hearing the door slam shut.

'Oh dear,' Mrs Kwiatkowski said.

'Oh dear, indeed,' Dor said, looking at the old woman.

'Wish me luck,' she said, before walking out the front door and up the stairs to face the music.

*

'Angie …' Dorothy tried her hardest to make her voice sound placatory. 'I'm sorry, I didn't mean to upset you.' She walked down the short hallway and into the kitchen, but Angie wasn't there. She stood and listened. She could hear what sounded like crying.

It couldn't be Angie, could it?

She didn't think she'd ever seen or heard Angie crying in the three years they'd been best buddies.

She crept to the door of her bedroom.

'Angie …' She gently pushed the door open.

She stood shocked at the sight of her friend laying prostrate on her bed, her head buried in her pillow, sobbing her eyes out.

'Ah, Ange.' Dorothy hurried over and sat on the edge of the bed. She put a hand on her friend's shoulder. 'What's wrong? Don't cry.'

Angie shrugged off Dorothy's hand and continued to muffle her sorrow into the folds of her pillow.

Dorothy waited. Partly because she didn't know what else to do. And partly because she sensed her friend just needed to cry her tears out.

Finally, Angie stopped and turned over.

'Yer just dinnit understand, do yer?'

'I don't,' Dorothy admitted. 'Although I do think this has something to do with me being a bit of a blabbermouth and going on about you and Quentin.'

'That's exactly it! *Me and Quentin.*' Angie sat up and dried her eyes on the cuff of her overalls. 'There is no *me and Quentin*. There can never be any *me and Quentin*.'

Dorothy looked at her friend and saw that the sorrow had been buried and the anger was back.

'But that's what I don't understand,' Dorothy said. 'Why can't there be any *you and Quentin*?'

'God, Dor, sometimes yer can be as thick as two short planks,' Angie spluttered.

Dorothy continued to look puzzled.

'Because, Dor,' Angie said, riled, 'people like Quentin don't court people like me. It's that simple. It's the way of the world. We're worlds apart. He's rich. I'm poor. He's posh. I'm not. He's practically aristocracy.' She laughed bitterly. 'God, I can hardly even say the word ... And I'm working class.'

'So?' Dor said.

'So!' Angie said, exasperated. 'People like Quentin don't marry or even court girls like me.' Another bitter laugh. 'They might want to have their way with them, but then they'll cast them aside 'n marry who Mummy 'n Daddy want them to marry. That's the way it is. Yer knar that!'

Dorothy was quiet. A part of her agreed with her friend – the other didn't.

'OK,' Dorothy said, getting ready to argue the point rationally. 'I agree with you that this is the case for many people. Perhaps even most.' She straightened her back and looked her friend in the eye. 'But I honestly don't think this is the case for Quentin. He's different. I've seen the way he is with you – and the way you are with him ... We're not living in the Dark Ages any more, Angie. Times are changing. People are changing. This war's changed us all in some way or another.' She laughed and picked at her overall. 'Look at us two sat here wearing these manky, dirty work clothes.'

Angie smiled. Dorothy took that as encouragement.

'I think you should both give it a go.' She thought for a moment. 'Or perhaps even talk to Quentin about how he feels.'

'Yeah, right, Dor,' said Angie. 'Next time I see him just drop it into the conversation – "Oh, by the way, Quentin, would yer consider gannin out with someone like me?"'

Dorothy conceded the point. 'All right ... But I just don't think you should let the fact he's from a rich, well-to-do-family stop you from being with him, if you both want to be with each other.'

'Dor, it's simple. I won't let myself fall in love with Quentin 'cos I know it can't go anywhere.'

It was on the tip of Dorothy's tongue to say, *It's too late, you have fallen in love with him*, but she didn't. For once she managed to hold back.

'Anyway,' Angie said, getting up and walking into the kitchen to make herself a cup of tea. 'This is all yer fault.' She reached into the cupboard for the biscuit tin.

Dorothy followed her and sat down at the kitchen table.

'How do you work that one out?' she asked, taking the tin off her friend and prising open the top.

'Because if you hadn't forced me to ask Quentin to Polly 'n Tommy's wedding – *because yer wanted to cop off with Toby* – I wouldn't be where I am now.'

After they'd had their tea and demolished most of the contents of the biscuit tin, Angie went to bed. Crying, she surmised, sapped all your energy.

When Dorothy heard Angie's gentle snoring, she crept down the hallway, put the door on the latch and padded downstairs to see Mrs Kwiatkowski.

She needed to talk to the old woman.

If there was one thing in life worth fighting for – it was love.

Angie might have given up on it, but she hadn't.

Chapter Forty-Three

Wednesday 15 December

Pearl and Bill looked out of the carriage window. The snow that had fallen gently but consistently overnight had turned the green fields and rolling countryside a pure white.

'It's pretty, isn't it?' Bill said as they sat shoulder to shoulder. They had the carriage to themselves. The weather had kept people at home today.

'Aye, as long as it dinnit stop us gerrin' to the asylum,' Pearl said, her eyes squinting against the brightness of the snow, made all the more brilliant by a clear sky and bright sun.

'It won't lay long,' Bill said, looking up at the sunny sky. It really was a perfect winter's day.

He glanced at Pearl.

'Looked like Ronald was on one last night?'

'Aye, he was that,' Pearl agreed.

'Looked like he'd got himself a new best mate,' Bill said.

'What? That baldy bloke with the big gut?' Pearl said.

'That's the one,' Bill said. 'Think they went back to Ronald's to down some of his black-market whisky.'

'They didn't hang around much after last orders,' Pearl mused.

'Yer didn't fancy joining them, then?' Bill asked, trying to sound as casual as possible and not as though he was desperately trying to work out if Pearl had feelings for that weasel of a man. 'I heard the baldy man with the big gut asking yer to join them for a "good sup" 'n game of poker.'

'Couldn't be bothered,' Pearl said. 'Plus, I needed my wits about me fer today.'

What she didn't tell Bill was that she wouldn't have gone back to Ronald's regardless. The fat bloke had given her the willies, but more than anything, she'd promised herself after her last blowout with Ronald that it'd be her last. It had been seven months now and she'd stuck to her word.

They sat in silence for a little while, both in their own worlds, thinking their own thoughts.

When the train started to slow down as it approached Ryhope station, Bill looked at Pearl.

'You seem nervous,' he said, 'well, more nervous than yer have done for a while.' It was true. After the first visit, Pearl had become much more relaxed about her trips to see Henrietta.

Pearl stopped herself biting back with some defensive comment.

'Aye, yer right, I do feel a bit jittery.'

'Because?'

She looked at Bill.

'I'm gonna ask her outright,' she said, grabbing her handbag and pulling out her cigarettes. 'I've decided. It's time.'

Bill's heart sank. He knew as soon as Pearl had what she wanted from Henrietta, that would be it. Their day trips to Ryhope would come to an end. Of course, he'd known the day would come, but he'd forced himself not to think about it. Had decided to just enjoy each outing they had together and not worry about the future. Now it looked as if the future had come. This might well be the last day out he had with Pearl, pretending to be her husband. He looked down at her left hand with his ex-wife's gold band on it and felt deflated.

*

When they reached the steps to the asylum, Pearl caught the sunlight glinting off the plaque at the side of the entrance. She took the last few drags on her cigarette, marched over and stubbed the fag end out on the polished brass. Bill heard her mumble something, but not what. Then again, he didn't need to. He could take a good guess.

After walking up the stone steps and through the main doors into the warmth, Pearl suddenly stopped dead in her tracks, squeezing Bill's hand and yanking him back. She pulled him over to the side of the foyer.

'Pretend yer talking to me,' she hissed.

Bill automatically looked round. He caught a glimpse of a smartly dressed blonde woman talking to another smartly dressed but younger woman.

'And dinnit look!' Pearl said, glaring at him, forcing him to keep his attention on her.

'Who's that?' Bill asked.

'It's his bloody daughter, Miriam,' Pearl said. She had moved slightly to the side so she could see past Bill. She was glad her fake husband was so tall and broad as he was doing a good job of blocking her from view.

'Who's she talking to?' Bill asked. He was staring at Pearl, whose eyes narrowed as she scrutinised the two women who stood chatting by the reception desk.

'One of the doctors ... well, I think she's a doctor here,' Pearl mumbled.

'Do yer think it could be Henrietta's doctor?' Bill asked, looking at Pearl's anxious face, her eyes fixed on the women behind him.

'Could be ... It would make sense,' Pearl said.

'So, my great-aunty's doing well by the looks of it,' Miriam said. Relegating her mother to the role of a more distant relative still felt odd, despite the fact she had been doing so for years. 'I've certainly noticed a huge difference in her.' Miriam eyed Dr Eris. She was a handsome woman. Very self-assured. She could see why she'd been able to bag Helen's doctor. 'Although, of course, she's still pretty delusional – still insisting I'm her daughter. Poor thing. I suppose that's what sometimes happens when you've been a spinster your whole life. You fabricate a family.'

'That could be the case,' Dr Eris said. 'But I wouldn't go as far as to say she's delusional. More the case that she's told herself a lie for so long, she now believes it to be the truth.'

'Isn't that what delusional is?' Miriam snapped. She much preferred her mother's old doctor. He would always agree with whatever she said.

'I'd like to see if she maintains this level of lucidity through to the New Year,' Dr Eris continued. 'If she does, she might even be well enough for an afternoon outside the asylum. Supervised, of course.'

Miriam had to stop herself laughing out loud. *That was never going to happen.*

'Well, let's not get ahead of ourselves, my dear. You've been my great-aunty's doctor for a relatively short time. Remember, I've been visiting her here for many, *many* years.'

'And that's the point.' Dr Eris wasn't going to back down. 'I believe Miss Girling has become institutionalised. That's why I think the next step will be to introduce her to the outside world. Gradually, of course.'

'We'll see,' Miriam said. *She'd have to chat with her father. It looked like he'd have to get her dear mama another doctor.*

'Let's have a chat when you're in next,' Dr Eris said. 'If you ring beforehand, we can have a proper talk privately in my consultation room.'

*

'Damn!'

Pearl suddenly bobbed back so that she was standing squarely in front of Bill. Seeing Miriam walking in their direction, she whispered, 'Pretend I'm upset,' before flinging herself at Bill and burying her head in his chest.

Bill put his arms around Pearl and held her close. 'There, there, it'll be all right,' he said, doing as Pearl had asked while he watched Miriam carry on walking past them and out of the front entrance.

He continued to hold Pearl. He was in heaven.

'She gone?' Pearl's muffled voice rose up from his chest.

Bill waited a beat, revelling in the feel of having the woman he was besotted with for one more moment.

'Yes, she's gone,' he said, reluctantly relinquishing his hold.

'Hi, Henrietta.'

Pearl hurried into the room. She was feeling uneasy after nearly bumping into Miriam. She wanted this done with as soon as possible. No hanging around. With any luck she could leave this forlorn place today and never come back.

'Ahh, Pearl, how lovely to see you.' Henrietta was sitting at a little round table she'd had put in her room. 'My Little Match Girl, forever faithful.' She gestured for Pearl to sit down on the spare chair opposite her.

Not for much longer, Pearl couldn't help thinking.

'Do you want a glass of water?' Henrietta had a jug on the table, next to a pile of books.

'Aye, go on,' Pearl said. 'My mouth does feel a bit dry.'

Henrietta got up and fetched two clean tumblers from a little cupboard above her sink.

'Henrietta, I've got something I want to ask yer,' Pearl said as Henrietta carefully poured out two glasses.

'Oh dearie me, that sounds rather ominous,' Henrietta said, sitting down. 'Let me guess ...' She put a finger to her temple, as though thinking. 'It's to do with the past? I know how much you like to talk about the past.'

Pearl saw something in Henrietta's eye that she hadn't seen before. It was as though she knew. Knew everything.

'Aye, it is, Henrietta,' Pearl said. 'It *is* about the past.'

She took a deep breath.

'I want to knar the truth about something. If I ask yer a question, will yer promise to tell me the truth?'

Henrietta let out a tinkle of laughter.

'The truth, the whole truth and nothing but the truth.'

Pearl forced a smile.

'Exactly.'

Bill was sitting outside on the bench, looking out over the snow-covered lawn. There were only the faintest indentations from where a bird had landed, otherwise the blanket of white was unspoilt. He had grown to like this place. It was not the dark, frightening madhouse people believed it to be. Seeing it through the seasons, first summer, then autumn, and now winter, he thought nothing could be further from the truth. It was quite beautiful. And very tranquil. And as he sat and waited for Pearl, enjoying the peace, his mind wandered to the future – to a future that he hoped could be.

'*Bill!*'

He looked round and saw Pearl coming out of the entrance, scrabbling around in her bag for her cigarettes.

She glanced over at the plaque for one last time. *No wonder. No bloody wonder.*

Bill hurried over.

'So? How did it go?' he asked, hoping she'd tell him she'd not been successful and that they'd have to come back.

316

'It went well,' she said, grabbing his hand automatically. *'Very well.'*

Bill's heart sank as they crunched up the gravelled pathway, still partially covered in snow.

'Sounds like we need to celebrate, then, with a drink and a nice bit of nosh?' he suggested. *Might as well. If Pearl had got what she'd wanted, there'd be no more days out as a pretend married couple.*

But then again …

Bill's thoughts moved again to the future he had just been imagining.

And with that thought, his spirits lifted and he glanced at Pearl and smiled.

Chapter Forty-Four

Monday 20 December

Helen looked up from her ledger to see Marie-Anne bossing around one of the new girls, telling her where she
wanted a length of rather tatty tinsel to go. She'd found a
box of old Christmas decorations in one of the cupboards
and had asked permission to put them up. How could
Helen refuse? Scrooge would have had nothing on her if
she'd said no.

She looked over at Bel, who was typing away. Or rather
bashing away. Her face looked as grim as the weather outside. Sleet and rain were presently lashing down against
the window.

Just as Helen was bending down to get her cigarettes out
of her handbag, the phone rang.

'Miss Crawford speaking,' she said distractedly.

'Helen! It's John here. So glad to have caught you!'

Helen's heart missed a beat. *Stop it! She wished her body
would wise up.*

'John! Lovely to hear you. How's things?'

'Good. Good. You?'

'Yes, all good. The usual frenzy before Christmas.'

There was an awkward silence.

'I'm glad I've managed to catch you. We seem to keep
missing each other,' Dr Parker said. He would have liked
to add that she never rang him back these days, but
didn't.

Helen was thinking just the same thing. 'Let me guess,' she said. 'You're ringing about the christening.'

'I am,' John said. 'I just wondered if you could pass on the message to Polly – let her know that I'm definitely coming, barring any kind of emergency.'

'And Claire?' Helen couldn't help crossing her fingers that Dr Eris couldn't make it. She scolded herself again. It shouldn't matter. *They were just friends.*

'Yes, yes, Claire wouldn't miss it for the world.'

I bet you she wouldn't.

'She's really looking forward to meeting everyone.'

'Dear me, John, you'll be telling us we'll all need to buy ourselves hats soon!' The words were out before Helen could rein them back in.

Dr Parker forced out an unconvincing laugh. 'I think it's a bit early for that.'

It was on the tip of Dr Parker's tongue to ask if Helen would be bringing Matthew, but he didn't trust himself with how it might come out.

'So, you keeping all right?' he asked instead.

'Yes, yes, nothing much new to report,' she said.

'I saw your mother the other night,' he said. 'She seemed in good form.'

'What? In the Grand?' Helen let out a burst of hollow laughter. 'Or need I ask. Where else would my dear mama be.' She paused. 'What were you doing at the Grand?'

'Oh, I was there with Claire ...' He hesitated. 'And my mother and father.'

'Really?' Helen couldn't hide her incredulity. 'My goodness, John, I think I *am* going to be shopping for a hat sometime soon. *Meeting the parents?*'

Dr Parker laughed a little nervously. 'More of an early Christmas get-together.' *Why was he making less of it?* 'You know, what with working over Christmas.'

'I'm sure that was the reason,' Helen said. She surprised herself at how jokey and light-hearted she sounded about it all when nothing could be further from the truth.

'*Dr Parker!*'

Helen heard someone shouting for him in the background.

'Always in demand,' she laughed. 'Get yourself off. I'll tell Polly you're coming – and Claire, too, of course.'

'Yes, thanks, Helen. See you there.'

After she'd hung up, Helen sparked up a cigarette. *God, Claire was well and truly getting her claws in. Not that John seemed to mind. Not one bit.*

If Polly hadn't asked her to be a godmother, she might have made an excuse and cried off.

She puffed on her cigarette and thought.

And thought.

Crushing the butt into the ashtray, she picked up the phone.

'Good afternoon, Matthew Royce speaking!'

'Matthew … Helen here.'

'Helen! You've just cheered up my day and as always sent my pulse racing!'

Helen sighed. Matthew loved playing the thwarted lover. Everything to him was a game.

'How's your schedule looking on Friday? Christmas Eve?' Helen asked.

Matthew didn't miss a beat.

'As of now it is clear. I am free for your ladyship.'

'Well,' Helen said stonily, 'I need an escort for a christening.'

'Little Artie's?' Over the past few months Matthew had slowly got to know Helen and the people in her life.

'That's the one,' Helen said, rotating her cigarette packet.

'I'd be more than happy to oblige,' Matthew said.

'Good,' Helen said. 'St Ignatius Church. No later than two.'

'At your service, my dear.'

Helen could hear in his voice that he was smiling and she hung up.

The klaxon had just signalled the lunch break.

'Can I have a word?'

Helen looked up to see Bel standing in the doorway.

'Of course, come in.'

'I just wanted to check it was all right if I got off an hour early on Thursday – it's Lucille's nativity.'

'Of course, *the nativity*. Did you manage to get her angel costume sorted?' Helen smiled. Bel had told her about Lucille's growing excitement about Christmas, and about being in the school's nativity.

'It's nearly there – thanks to an old sheet from Agnes, and Kate donating scraps from a couple of white dresses she's been making ... I was also going to ask if I could take the morning off on Christmas Eve? I don't want you to feel I'm taking advantage.'

Helen waved her worries away. 'Of course not, don't be daft. Are you needed to get everything ready for the christening?'

'No, no,' Bel said. 'Agnes is happily working herself into a frenzy on that front.'

Helen chuckled. 'I guess she's over the moon about having another grandchild.' As soon as the words were out of her mouth, she could have slapped herself. 'God, I'm sorry, that was so insensitive of me, Bel. I wasn't thinking.'

This time it was Bel who waved Helen's concerns away. 'Don't worry. Besides it's true. I just wish I could oblige.'

Helen looked at Bel and saw her despair.

'I really don't know what to say, Bel. I don't want to say *don't worry, it'll happen*, because I think it's insulting. Who am I to make such assumptions? I have no idea if it'll happen or not.' She stopped. 'Oh dear, I don't think that's what you want to hear either.'

Bel smiled sadly. 'There is no right thing to say. I just have to toughen up and accept that there's nothing I can do about it – be thankful for what I've got and not mope about what I don't have.'

Helen thought that was easier said than done, but didn't say so.

'So, if Agnes is in command of the christening ...?' Helen asked.

'Santa Claus,' Bel declared, 'is coming to town. And if I don't take Lucille, well, quite simply, there'll be another war on.'

Helen laughed.

'Don't you sometimes wish to be that age again – when everything was so simple? No worries.' She wanted to add 'no heartache', but didn't.

Bel manufactured a smile, not wanting to say that despite all her present difficulties she would never want to be that age again. When she had been Lucille's age her life had been neither simple nor without worries.

'Yeah!' Dorothy shouted over on seeing Polly bustle into the canteen. Bel was behind her.

'Where's Artie?' Angie demanded when she was within shouting distance.

'He's with his nana,' Polly said, reaching their table and sitting down. Bel went to get them a cup of tea.

'You all sorted for the christening?' Gloria asked. She thought about how Hope's christening had been a rushed affair as she had tried her hardest to arrange it without Vinnie knowing.

'Yes,' Polly said, 'just about. Not that I've had that much to do as Ma has taken charge. Honestly, she missed her vocation as a drill sergeant.'

Everyone chuckled. There was no arguing with Agnes when she had her mind set on something.

'And there's no way Tommy can get leave?' Martha asked.

'Not a cat in hell's chance,' Polly said. 'But I didn't expect for one minute he'd be able to.' She looked up at Bel walking over with two cups of tea.

'Thanks to my very persuasive sister in law here,' she smiled at Bel as she took her tea and made room for her, 'Mr Clement is going to take a couple of photographs so that I can send them to Tommy.'

'So, what brings you in today?' Gloria asked. 'I know where I'd be on a day like this.'

'Sorting out my start date,' Polly said, taking a sip of her tea.

'Yeah!' Dorothy shoved Angie. 'See, I told you she'd come back.'

Polly looked at Angie and thought she didn't seem quite herself.

'So, when *are* you coming back?' Hannah asked.

'In the New Year. Once I've got Artie onto the bottle.' Polly groaned. 'Which I'm finding easier said than done.'

'And is Tommy all right about you coming back to work?' Rosie asked, finishing off her shepherd's pie.

'Not really,' Polly said.

'And yer ma?' Gloria asked.

'Not really.'

'Looks like you've got resistance?' Hannah said.

'Most definitely,' Polly said, 'but they can't stop me.'

'Just off to the lav,' Angie said, getting up and hurrying off.

Polly waited until she was out of earshot.

'Is Angie all right?'

She looked at Dorothy and then at the rest of the women.

'Not really,' Dorothy said. She exhaled theatrically. 'To cut a long and very dramatic story short, as we all suspected, Ange is in love with Quentin. And we're also sure Quentin is in love with Angie.'

'Well, we're not *totally* sure,' Hannah said.

'Yeah, and we don't want Angie to get hurt,' Martha chipped in.

'Regardless,' Dorothy continued, 'I've told Mrs Kwiatkowski, who's known Quentin for ages, to find out – and to make sure Quentin's not going to lead our Ange up the garden path, use her and then fling her aside.'

'Not that Angie would let Quentin use her,' Gloria butted in.

'Precisely,' Dorothy said. 'And that's where it all gets a bit complicated.'

She gave Polly a quick résumé of what had happened last Monday.

Looking up, she saw Angie coming back into the canteen. *God, she'd never known anyone get themselves to the loo and back as fast.*

'So, basically,' she said, starting to speak as quickly as possible, 'Ange seems adamant that it could never work out with Quentin. In her words, "people like Quentin dinnit marry or even court girls like me."'

Dorothy had run out of breath by the time Angie arrived back at the table.

'What yer all gassing about?' she asked.

'Toby,' Dorothy said, quick as a flash. 'And how his jaw's gonna hit the ground when he sees me in the dress I've got for the christening.'

Angie's eyes went to the ceiling.

'Yer ever heard of modesty, Dor?'

*

As everyone piled out of the canteen, Polly asked Hannah how her aunty Rina and Vera were managing. Hannah laughed. 'Aunty Rina says Vera is grumbling like mad and loving every minute of it. And Vera says Aunty Rina is grumbling like mad and loving every minute of it. So, all's well.'

Polly chuckled. She didn't ask if Hannah had received any news about her parents as she knew either Bel or Gloria would have told her straight away.

Feeling someone tap her shoulder, she turned around.

It was Rosie.

'Don't forget Charlie's available for any chores that might need doing – whether for the christening or –' she looked from Polly to Hannah '– Christmas dinner ... In fact, for my sake, if you could find something for her to do, it would be much appreciated and would be accepted in lieu of a Christmas present.'

Polly and Hannah both laughed.

'I'm just going over to tell Ralph and the rest of his crew about the christening.' Polly looked around and grabbed Martha. 'Do you mind telling Jimmy and his lot? Tell them I really don't expect them to come, but I wanted everyone who came to the wedding to know they are welcome.'

Martha nodded. 'Will do.'

As they were hit by a blast of wind and rain, they all went off in their separate directions.

Polly heard Angie's voice shout after her.

'If I were yer, I'd not come back to work until the spring!'

Chapter Forty-Five

Tuesday 21 December

'Darling, come and have a look at our Christmas tree!'

Helen had just walked through the front door and was tapping the fresh snow off her shoes. Driving on the road this evening had been a challenge. The dropping temperature had turned the roads into an ice rink, and then, just as she'd driven across the Wearmouth Bridge, she'd hit a snow flurry and barely been able to see through the windscreen. She put her handbag and gas mask down on the hallway floor. Walking into the living room, she was glad to see the fire was going.

'Doesn't it look wonderful?' Her mother gestured towards the tree, spilling some of her gin and tonic as she did so.

'It does, Mother. You've done well to get one at all – never mind one that's so gorgeous.'

'Well, the suppliers owed me one after last year's debacle.' She eyed her daughter.

'Just shows you,' Helen said, knowing that her mother would have found out the truth about her missing tree, 'every cloud has a silver lining.'

'Helen, you are a woman after my own heart. When you want something, you just go out and get it. Sod the consequences,' Miriam said, a smile playing on her lips. She knew Helen hated it when she reminded her of just how alike they really were.

Helen bit back a reply.

'You been on the razz tonight, Mum?' she asked, going over to the drinks cabinet.

'I wish!' Miriam said, walking over to inspect the tree up close. 'I've been in all evening, organising the decorations for the Christmas tree.'

Helen's heart went out to the poor unfortunate souls who had been tasked with decorating the tree under her mother's command.

'Well, they've done an excellent job,' Helen said, pouring herself a drink. 'Do you want a top-up?'

'You've read my mind,' Miriam said, turning and walking over to give Helen her glass. 'Easy on the tonic.'

'You not going to the Grand tonight?' Helen poured a good slosh of gin and a dribble of tonic and handed it to her mother.

'I'm having a night off.'

'And Amelia? You two also having a night off from each other?'

'Harvey's back in town,' Miriam said, taking a sip of her drink. 'He's been given a day's leave so they're celebrating Christmas early.'

'So, Amelia's going to be on her own on Christmas Day?'

'Hardly, my dear, she's having dinner at the Grand with some friends.'

By friends, Helen interpreted, she guessed her mother meant whichever Admiralty was flavour of the month.

'Which is where I'll be going as soon as we've all done our duty and had our Christmas dinner at your grand-father's,' Miriam added, walking over to the fire and giving it a prod.

Helen felt her heart lift. If her mother was bailing early, then that meant she could too. She was dreading having Christmas at the Havelock residence. She had barely stepped foot in the place since she had found out about her grandfather.

'I know this might sound a strange question, Mother,' Helen sat down on the sofa, 'but do you actually *like* Grandfather?'

Miriam turned round and scrutinised her daughter. 'That's a very odd question to ask.' She sat in the armchair and took another sip of her drink.

'Well, do you?' Helen asked again.

'Of course I do, darling, he's my father, isn't he?'

'I suppose I was just thinking about when he was younger. When *you* were younger.'

Miriam looked at her daughter.

'Darling, life was different for families then. Children were seen and not heard, or better still, not even seen. Which was most definitely the case for Margaret and me. Dear Mama had had enough of us both by the time we were twelve and thirteen and packed us off to boarding school. Then, when we'd served our time there, we were packed off to finishing school.'

Miriam loved to sound like the victim, but truth be told, she'd never liked being at home, had quite enjoyed boarding school and had absolutely loved the finishing school in Switzerland.

'It must have been hard for you all when Grandmama died.'

Miriam's head snapped up to look at her daughter.

'What do you mean?'

'Just that,' Helen said, surprised by her mother's reaction. 'Grandfather losing his wife. You and Aunty Margaret losing your mother – so unexpectedly.'

'Mmm.' Miriam took a sip of her gin and looked back into the fire.

'The funny thing is,' Helen continued, 'I can't remember for the life of me what Grandmother died of. Someone asked me the other day and I felt bad that I didn't know.'

'Who asked you?' Miriam's attention was back on her daughter.

'Oh, just someone at one of the launches, I forget who,' Helen lied.

Miriam took a sip of her drink.

'Mother caught some vile disease when she was abroad on holiday in India – she died out there.'

'How tragic,' Helen said. She wondered if she had died knowing what her husband had done. To Pearl. And possibly to other young girls.

'Anyway, enough of all that.' Miriam waved her hand as though shooing away the ghosts of times past. 'I forgot to tell you I saw Dr Parker in the Grand the other night. He was with his new girlfriend and, by the looks of it, his parents. He's the spit of his father. I was going to say hello, introduce myself and Amelia, but we ended up being swept off to dinner at the Palatine before I had the chance.' Which was a lie. On seeing that Dr Parker was with Dr Eris, she couldn't get out of the place quickly enough. Luckily, the woman hadn't spotted her.

'Yes, he said he saw you too,' Helen said. There it was again. That feeling of physical pain on imagining John and Claire having a cosy 'meeting the family' meal. *Bet you John's parents fell for her hook, line and sinker.*

'So, where did you go galivanting off to this evening? You're not usually in this late,' Miriam said.

'Mother, you wouldn't know what time I'm usually in as you're usually out.'

Miriam chuckled. 'Well, you've got to make the most of life while you're here, haven't you?'

Helen cringed. She had thought the same thing this evening when she'd agreed to go to dinner with Matthew.

'I've just been out with a few friends,' Helen said.

There was no way she'd give her mother the satisfaction of knowing the truth. She'd be on the phone straight away to Mr Royce senior, organising their own 'meeting of the parents'.

Chapter Forty-Six

Hudson Road School, Hendon, Sunderland

Thursday 23 December

'There's no room in the inn,' Lucille said, a convincing frown on her forehead as she glowered at Mary and Joseph.

Bel blinked back the tears as she proudly watched her little girl, standing arms akimbo, a cushion stuffed under a borrowed woollen jumper, acting her little heart out. The temperatures might be below zero outside, but inside the school hall it was warm and stuffy. Lucille's cheeks were flushed red, which complemented her innkeeper's look.

Lucille had forsaken her role of angel as the real innkeeper had become ill at the last moment and Lucille had been the only one not to cry when the teacher told her flock of little cherubs that one of them was going to have to ditch their wings to become the baddy who tells Jesus's mam and dad they can't have a room.

Bel and Joe were sitting in the second row from the front. Joe had a firm hold of his wife's hand. Giving her a quick sideways glance, he could see the tears starting to glisten in her eyes. He knew those tears were not just because this was her daughter's first nativity, but because it might be the last 'first nativity' she got to go to.

Joe looked behind him to see that his ma was not doing such a good job of holding back her own tears and was unashamedly letting them run down her face. Pearl was next to her and was decidedly dry-eyed. He wondered if this was *her* first nativity; he couldn't imagine Pearl ever being present at Bel's. Polly was standing at the back of the hall with baby Artie, who had started to get tetchy at the beginning of the performance when the shepherds, tea towels on their heads, had shuffled onto the stage.

An hour later, everyone was making their way out of the school building and buttoning up their coats as they faced the icy-cold weather outside. Joe said his goodbyes and went straight off to be with his unit, while Pearl hurried off to the Tatham.

Within half an hour of stepping over the threshold to the Elliot household, Polly had put Artie down and then ended up falling fast asleep herself.

Not long afterwards, seeing how shattered Lucille was after her stage debut, Bel had had little resistance in getting her daughter to bed.

'Mammy ...' Lucille could barely keep her eyes open '... was there *really* no room in the inn, or was the man just being mean?'

Bel smiled down at her daughter. 'I don't know, sweetheart. Why don't we have a chat about it tomorrow?' She leant down and kissed the top of her head. 'Sweet dreams.'

By the time Bel was drawing the door ajar, Lucille was asleep.

Walking into the kitchen, Bel was glad that there was just Agnes sitting at the table, a fresh pot of tea in the middle of it.

'Do you think the innkeeper really didn't have any room?' Bel asked. 'Or he just didn't want the hassle of having a pregnant woman under his roof?'

Agnes laughed and poured their tea.

332

'Well, it wouldn't surprise me. Especially as they clearly had no money and weren't married into the bargain.'

Now it was Bel's turn to laugh.

'Things haven't changed much, have they?'

Bel eased herself into the chair. She was tired; she had been on her feet all day. She knew what Mary and Joseph had felt like, although she would have given anything to have been in Mary's condition.

'I kept thinking all during the nativity about how *you* took *me* in,' Bel said, looking at Agnes. 'I had nowhere to go, was locked out, Ma was God knows where, with God knows who – but you didn't turn me away, did you?'

'I think it would have taken a hard-hearted woman to have done that,' Agnes said.

'Of which there are many,' Bel countered.

They were quiet for a moment while they drank their tea.

'But it must have been hard work,' Bel said, putting her teacup on its saucer and sitting back in her chair. 'You had me to look after when you already had Pol and the twins to bring up – and let's face it, the twins were a handful.'

Agnes smiled, thinking of her sons as young boys.

'I didn't really think about what it must have been like for you until I became a mother myself – and I've just got the one ...' Bel's voice wavered.

Agnes reached over and took hold of her hand.

Bel swallowed back the tears. 'I'm all right, really, Agnes ... I wish I could just be happy with my lot.'

'It's a difficult time of year,' Agnes said. 'Baby Jesus this and Baby Jesus that ...'

Bel laughed sadly. 'I know. And all LuLu wants for Christmas is a baby brother or sister. I thought little Artie might keep her happy, but it's as though now he's arrived on the scene, it's spurred her on in her determination to have a brother or sister all to herself.'

There were tears in both women's eyes.

'Life can be a funny one,' Agnes said. 'Takes us places we hadn't expected or planned. But remember,' she squeezed Bel's hand before letting it go and getting up from the table, 'the unexpected doesn't have to be bad. It can bring surprises. Good surprises.'

Bel watched as Agnes bent over to get the single malt from the cupboard and poured a drop into both their cups.

Bel took a sip and swallowed, grimacing a little as she felt the burn of the whisky.

'What I was going to say, before I nearly started to blubber,' Bel said with a slight laugh, 'is that you took me in when you already had your hands full. You were on your own, widowed, no family, no money, three children, and then I tipped up like Little Orphan Annie and you waved me in, clothed me, fed, looked after me—' Bel swallowed more tears that were threatening to silence her.

'But most of all,' she said, 'you loved me.'

'Of course I did,' Agnes said, looking at Bel. 'How could I not? You were a totally lovable child. Who grew into a totally lovable young woman.'

Bel took another sip. Her mind was back in the past, remembering how Agnes had divided the few clothes Polly had to accommodate the little stray she had taken in. As Polly and Bel had only one dress each, it meant that every night when they'd got ready for bed, Agnes would wash both dresses, wring them out and hang them by the range so that they were dry the next day.

'I used to wonder why you were always stooped over the poss tub.' Bel smiled at Agnes. 'It was only when one of the girls in the class – that awful girl ... can't remember her name – but it was only when she started taking the mick because Polly and I wore the same clothes every day that I realised why.'

'I think that was Polly's fault.' Agnes's smile grew wider as she recalled her daughter as a child. 'She was such a tomboy. Forever getting into scrapes and ending up looking like she'd spent the day down the pit. You, on the other hand, would always keep yer dress in pristine condition. Hardly a mark on it. I only washed yer dress as well in case yer thought I was giving Pol preferential treatment.'

Bel looked at Agnes. Tears started to prick her eyes. 'I'm so glad you did, though. I loved waking up and climbing into my clean clothes, still warm from the range. I can still smell the washing powder you used.' She looked at Agnes. 'You had that big box of Lux you kept right at the back of the scullery in the corner.'

Agnes whooped with laughter. 'That was from my friend Val. She worked at the Luxdon launderette down Smyrna Place. She used to – how should I say it – *acquire* the odd box every now and again. She'd take half out for herself and give me the other half still in the box.'

'Well, if I ever meet this Val, I'll have to thank her. The smell was heavenly. I used to feel like a princess every day I walked to school with Pol. Smelling so nice and feeling so clean.'

Agnes took a slurp of her tea and chuckled.

'Unlike Pol, who would have gone without a wash for weeks on end if I'd have let her.'

'I know,' Bel laughed. 'It was like you were subjecting her to some kind of torture.'

The women smiled and sipped their tea, both enjoying their own memories.

'You know, Agnes,' Bel said, 'I don't think I've ever really thanked you for taking me in. God knows what would have happened to me if you hadn't.'

Agnes dismissed Bel's words with a shake of the head.

'There's a part of me that still feels guilty,' Bel admitted. 'For putting on you so. Not that I think I would have given you much of a choice if you *had* shut the door on me. I think if you had chucked me out, I'd have just sat on your doorstep and begged to be let back in.'

Agnes sat back on her chair and looked at Bel.

'There's something I've never told yer. Something I should probably have told yer before now,' she said, putting her cup and saucer down on the table. 'That day Pol brought yer back here, it wasn't a chore. I didn't have to wrestle with my conscience before reluctantly taking yer in. Far from it. I was glad.'

Bel looked surprised.

'You see,' Agnes said, 'if Harry had made it back from the war, I'd definitely have had more children. I know I would have certainly kept going until I'd had another girl.

'I'd been thinking that day,' Agnes continued. 'Had been thinking for a good while, to be honest, that Polly needed another sibling. Yer see, Pol absolutely doted on her two brothers, which mightn't have been too much of a problem – if they hadn't have been twins. Teddy and Joe loved Pol to bits, don't get me wrong, but they were each other's world. They were more like one than two separate beings.'

Bel nodded her understanding. She had thought more than a few times that it had been inevitable she would fall in love with Joe after Teddy was killed. It was like their souls were the same.

'And then,' Agnes continued, 'all of a sudden, there yer were, looking like a little chimney sweep, eyes red raw and puffy because yer'd been crying so much, and it was as though, in a strange way, I'd got my wish.'

Bel was sitting stock-still, taking in every word Agnes was saying. This was the first time they'd ever talked properly about the past and how it was that she had become a part of the family.

'I could see,' Agnes said, her eyes staring at the range as though it were a porthole to the past, 'that Polly was lonely, but also that she was trying to be like them so she could be a part of their gang. But she was hankering after the impossible. She was becoming more and more boyish and maybe because of that she wasn't making any friends at school.'

Agnes brought her attention back to Bel.

'So, yer see, it's me that should be thanking you. Because when yer turned up looking like a little street urchin from a Dickens novel, it might have looked to the outside world that Agnes Elliot had a heart of gold and had taken the poor Hardwick child in, but in reality I needed yer as much as you needed me.'

Agnes looked at Bel and could see tears welling in her eyes.

'We *all* needed yer. I did. Pol did. The boys did. Yer might have felt that I was doing all the giving, but I wasn't. Anything I gave I got back in bucket loads.'

A solitary tear trickled down Agnes's face and she wiped it away.

Bel had given up wiping her own away. Her face was wet now, and she didn't care.

'You know, Agnes,' she said, her vision blurred, 'I think that is the nicest thing anyone has ever said to me.'

Chapter Forty-Seven

'Come in come in!' barked Mr Havelock.

'Ah, Bob, good to see you, old chap! Come in! Sit down!'

Bob looked at Charles and thought he seemed in very good spirits – certainly in a better mood than last time he'd been there.

He parked himself on the chair in front of the large oak desk and got out his notebook.

The old man was going to be in an even better mood when he heard what he had found out about the three women he was so interested in. It had ended up being quite an enjoyable job – drinking until the early hours and playing cards. It hadn't even mattered that the tart behind the bar wouldn't play ball; the bloke he'd milked for information had been easy prey. And the information he'd siphoned from him that night had fuelled his investigation, which had, in turn, taken him down some very interesting avenues and led to some very interesting discoveries.

Yes, he was definitely going to be in Mr Charles Havelock's good books by the time he left today.

He might even wangle a Christmas bonus out of the old man – the ammunition he was about to provide him with certainly deserved one.

Chapter Forty-Eight

Joplings, High Street West, Sunderland

Christmas Eve

Bel was surprised to see that Santa had a real beard. She knew this because of the yellowing of the whiskers around his mouth; his belly was also real, as the buttons on his red Father Christmas outfit were so strained they looked ready to ping off.

Lucille had tight hold of her mammy's hand. They had been waiting in the queue for a long time to see Santa Claus and she had been able to inspect him from tip to toe. He was exactly what she'd expected. Just like in the pictures in the books from the library.

'Ho! Ho! Ho!' Santa Claus slapped both hands down on his knees and leant forward to look at the next child waiting in the never-ending queue. It was eleven o'clock and he was gasping for a cuppa.

'And who do we have here?' he asked, his tone rhythmic. He had 'jolly' down to perfection. He stuck out a big, gnarly hand.

'Lucille,' she replied, tentatively taking hold of his hand.

'Lucille!' the old man said. 'Now isn't that the bonniest of names?' He looked from the little girl up to the woman who was obviously her mother. They were both blonde. Both had the same heart-shaped faces. Both stunners.

'And has Lucille been a good girl this year?' Father Christmas creased his brow at the bright-eyed little girl and her mam, who, he thought, looked a bit jaded – then again what mother didn't these days. Especially the day before Christmas. They were all going to have some explaining to do in the morning as to why Santa hadn't been able to bring their children what they wanted.

Santa slapped his leg. 'Come on, take a pew and tell Mr Claus what you want.' He gently lifted Lucille up and perched her on his leg so that her feet were dangling just short of the ground.

'Now, whisper in my ear what it is you want from Santa this year.' He turned the side of his head towards Lucille's angelic face.

Lifting her hand and cupping it to Santa's ear, Lucille whispered her Christmas wish.

Bel couldn't hear what Lucille said, but she saw that whatever it was it had made Santa smile. She caught his eye and gave him a quizzical look.

Santa laughed.

'This little girl says she wants a baby sister or brother – preferably both,' he said, raising his eyebrows at Bel, then looking back down at Lucille. 'And is your daddy at home?'

Lucille shook her head slowly from side to side. 'No, he's buried in a place called *Af-ri-ca*.' She took her time over the pronunciation. Her mammy had shown her on a map where it was.

The smile left Santa's face and he looked up at Bel.

'But I have another daddy,' Lucille suddenly piped up, gazing up into Santa's milky blue eyes.

'Ah!' Santa said, the beginnings of a smile returning.

'They were brothers.' Lucille had decided she liked Santa and he wasn't as frightening as she had first thought.

'Twins,' she added.

The old man worked hard not to show his surprise, or judgement.

'Well then,' Santa said, 'I'm sure you'll get what you want, Lucille.'

Bel felt her anger resurface. She had been trying to keep it weighed down – it was Christmas after all, time to be happy and carefree, not moody and resentful.

'Sometimes, *Santa*,' Bel said, glowering at the old man, 'sometimes we don't always get what we want, do we?'

Santa gave Bel an apologetic look. He understood. *Who would want to bring any more children into this world at this time?*

Lucille looked from her mammy to Santa.

'But *Baby Jesus* was given as a gift at Christmas!' she said adamantly.

Realising he had to back-pedal and fast, Santa looked at the little girl on his lap and asked, 'Tell me, Lucille, what else do you want?'

'Don't want anything else!' Lucille declared, hopping off Santa's knee.

She looked up at Father Christmas and gave him a wide smile.

'That's all I want, thank you.'

When Lucille burst through the front door, she ran down the hallway and into the kitchen, where she found Artie in his Moses basket in front of the range. The dogs were in their own basket but were keeping an eye on the baby. Lucille dropped down next to her cousin and smothered him in kisses. She then started telling him all about Santa Claus. Artie gurgled and reached up to the smiley face beaming down at him.

'How was it?' Polly asked. She was putting out a plate of sandwiches next to the pot of tea on the kitchen table, being careful not to move the central display: a candle surrounded by holly and tinsel. Lucille had made it at school, along with the paper chains that were hanging around the mirror above the mantelpiece.

Bel looked at Polly and then at her daughter.

'Lucille told Santa,' she said quietly, 'that she wants a brother or a sister, ideally one of each.' Her face was sombre. As if it wasn't bad enough that she was desperate for another child, her daughter was too.

Polly grimaced. They had all pooled together to get Lucille some toys as well as some chocolate – a rarity these days. Polly hoped the bar of Cadbury's they had managed to acquire, and the toys – both the ones bought and the ones made by Joe – would take Lucille's mind off her growing demands for Mammy to have another baby.

'You all prepared for the christening?' Bel asked.

'More or less,' Polly said, pouring their tea. 'I just need to pop Artie into his gown before we leave.'

'And how're you feeling?' Bel knew that her own need for a child equalled Polly's need for Tommy to come back home.

'I'm all right,' she said, fishing a letter out of the pinny she was wearing over her best dress. 'A letter came this morning.'

'Perfectly timed,' Bel said.

Polly gave it to her.

'It's to Artie,' she said, 'telling him how much he would love to have been here, but that he will be thinking about him all day.'

Bel supped her tea and read the letter.

She wiped tears from her eyes.

God, if she wasn't feeling like snapping people's heads off, she was trying to stop herself sobbing her eyes out.

Chapter Forty-Nine

Driving past St Ignatius Church, Helen saw there was already a crowd outside, chatting, smoking, jigging from one foot to the other and clapping their hands to keep warm. She'd had to drive slowly because of black ice. She was keeping her fingers crossed that it didn't snow; she really disliked driving in bad weather, although by the looks of the dark, expectant clouds, she didn't think crossing anything would have much effect. The skies were ready to dump their load. The weather forecasters, for once, looked as though they were going to be right. They were in for a white Christmas.

Helen had left work the moment the klaxon sounded out. She had handed the reins over to Marie-Anne, who had been more than happy to exchange the christening for being head honcho for the afternoon. Helen had nipped home, where she had managed to avoid seeing her mother, who'd been too busy bossing about Mrs Westley, the cook, to notice her daughter's presence in the house.

Miriam had decided to throw a Christmas Eve party, which meant Mrs Westley had to somehow concoct a peacetime feast out of wartime rations. Helen had congratulated herself for her stealth as she couldn't face the venom that would have come out of her mother's mouth if she'd found out Helen was to be a godmother to Polly and Tommy's baby. She didn't need reminding that she had once – not that long ago – tried to split them up.

Parking around the corner from the church, she got out of her beloved sports car – and rejoiced, not for the first time, in the independence of being able to drive. Why hadn't she learnt sooner? Once she'd grabbed her handbag and gas mask, she slammed the door shut. Getting out her lipstick and compact, she added a fresh layer of Victory Red before adjusting her long wool coat, pulling the belt tight to show off her figure. It was out of force of habit, but she also wanted to look as stunning as possible – more stunning than Dr Eris, at any rate. Walking in her high heels like a model in a fashion show, she turned the corner and as she sashayed her way towards the crowd, conversations stopped as those attending the christening could not help but stare at the Hollywood beauty heading towards them.

'*Helen!*'

Matthew stepped forward to greet her, giving her a kiss on both cheeks.

'You look ravishing, as always.'

'Thank you, Matthew.' Helen smiled and then looked behind him to see Dr Parker and Dr Eris. She took a deep breath. Normally, she would have given John a kiss on both cheeks, but she stopped herself. It wasn't appropriate now that he was with Claire – and even less so when she was standing right next to him and had a tight hold of his hand.

'Hi, Claire, it's lovely you've both made it.' Helen sounded the epitome of politeness. An outsider would never have guessed that she meant anything else. 'How are you? I haven't seen you for ages.' She paused. 'Last time we spoke was outside the asylum, the day after that awful air raid.'

'That's right,' Dr Eris said, as though thinking hard to remember the occasion. 'Gosh, was it really that long ago?'

'It was – May,' said Helen. She couldn't help but look down at Claire's left hand. She felt a wave of relief at seeing it devoid of any kind of jewellery. Still, she had a feeling it wouldn't be long before there was some, certainly if Claire had her way.

Helen looked up to see John's brown eyes on her. They held each other's gaze for a split second before he looked away. It was fleeting glance, but it threw Helen.

'Shall we go in?' Helen looked down at her watch. It was five minutes to two. People had already started to put out cigarettes and stub out cigars before meandering into the church.

Walking into the nave, Helen saw that a few Christmas decorations had been put up, and on either side of the altar there were two displays of white and red chrysanthemums, which had been quite artfully mixed with branches of holly and other green foliage. The church looked pretty, but not half as spectacular as it had at Polly and Tommy's wedding. Thanks to her and John's gift of two very grandiose floral displays, as well as the beautifully decorated Christmas tree her Mother had unknowingly gifted, the place had looked spectacular.

Looking towards the altar, she saw Polly holding baby Artie. She could just see his ivory christening gown showing through the thick shawl he was wrapped up in. Thank goodness he wasn't crying. There was nothing worse than church acoustics for a squalling baby. She smiled as she walked up the aisle. Next to Polly was Agnes, looking very much the proud grandmother, and then Dr Billingham. Why Polly had to ask him to be Artie's godfather, she had no idea. She had hoped never to set eyes on the man again after her miscarriage, but it looked like he would be around to haunt her for a good while yet. Strange that he and Polly got on so well.

Just as she reached everyone, the Reverend Winsey suddenly appeared behind them and they all turned and moved aside.

'Everyone set?' he asked.

'Yes, yes,' Polly said, looking down at Artie, who seemed quite happy with all the attention he had been getting and was smiling up at her.

The vicar put his arm out to show it was time for everyone to take their seats and stop chattering around the font.

Helen looked to the left and saw that Bel and Joe were already seated. Major Black was in his wheelchair, with Lucille standing next to him. She was gripping the armrest with both hands, her head heavy on his shoulder. She already looked bored. The Major and Joe were both in their regimental uniforms. Helen knew that Polly had asked Joe to be a godfather, but he had declined, saying it would be hypocritical.

Bel, as always, looked very classy and very pretty in a little black dress Helen had not seen her in before. She was also wearing quite an unusual fascinator, which Helen guessed had been made by Kate – headwear was becoming another one of her signatures.

Looking towards the back of the church, she saw Dorothy and Angie hurrying in at the last minute. Honestly, they looked as though they were just about to hit the town, not attend a church service. Goodness knew what they looked like when they had their weekly jaunts to the Ritz.

'Thank God for that,' Angie said; her breathing was heavy from having to half walk, half jog from the flat to the church.

'Made it in time – just,' Dorothy said, relieved.

'We wouldn't have been dashing if yer hadn't got me to change my dress at the last minute.' Angie tugged a little self-consciously at the red dress Dorothy had convinced her to wear.

'It's Christmas Eve!' Dorothy gasped. 'If you can't get done up to the nines at Christmas, when can you?'

Angie was just about to walk up the aisle to sit near the front when Dorothy pulled her back.

'Let's stay here,' she said, stepping into one of the ornately carved wooden pews and sitting down.

'Why?' Angie asked, surprised her friend didn't want to be as near to the action as possible.

'I want to be able to chat without anyone huffing and puffing at us, like they did at Polly's wedding,' Dorothy explained.

Angie looked towards the front of the church. The vicar was gesturing that Polly and her clan should take their seats.

'All right,' Angie conceded. 'Good job I've got good eyesight. Do yer not wanna sit by the aisle?'

Dorothy shook her head and patted the hard wooden seat next to her.

'No, I don't,' she said.

Angie stared at her friend. She always insisted on sitting at the end.

'Come on, Ange, park it – they're about to start.'

Dr Parker, Dr Eris and Matthew settled in the pew behind the Elliots.

'Drink at the Tatham afterwards?' As soon as the words were out of Dr Parker's mouth, he regretted them. *Was he a glutton for punishment? Watching Helen getting all cosy and lovey-dovey with her new man.* Or was it because he just wanted to see Helen? Because he missed her?

'Well, I can certainly ask Helen,' Matthew said. He glanced at Dr Eris and could see a distinct lack of enthusiasm on her face. 'But knowing Helen, she'll want to go back to the yard before the end of the shift, especially with everyone having Christmas Day off.' He certainly hoped so. He didn't want Dr Parker realising he'd made a huge mistake and chosen the wrong woman.

Dr Parker moved along the pew to allow Helen to take her seat next to him. As godparents they had to be near the aisle, ready for when they were needed.

'*We are gathered here today* ...' Reverend Winsey's voice boomed out, along with a stream of icy breath. The roof might have been mended but the church was just as cold as it always was.

Dr Eris leant into Dr Parker and took his hand. She would have to think of some excuse not to go for a drink, or at least to keep it short and sweet. She did not want John spending any more time with that woman than he absolutely had to. And as much as Matthew was making a good show of acting as if he was with Helen, she wasn't so sure. As a psychologist, and a good one at that, she had become pretty astute at reading people's body language – and her guess was that Helen and Matthew were not an item, much as Matthew clearly wanted them to be.

'Would the godparents come out and join us, please?' The vicar held out his arms in a welcoming gesture.

There was a shuffling of feet. Helen and Dr Parker stood up and walked towards the font. From the right, Bel and Dr Billingham appeared.

'Two doctors as godparents,' Lily whispered to Charlotte, who was wedged between her and George. 'Little Artie's definitely going to have the best medical care a child could hope for.'

Charlotte heard Lily but was keeping her eyes firmly on the main stage – Polly was wearing a lovely burnt-orange dress and a vibrant green shawl. Her hair was piled high, with just a few curls dangling down, framing her face. She put her hand to her own thick brown hair and resolved that it would be her style for the Christmas Day celebrations tomorrow at Vera's café.

'And with Helen as one of the godmothers,' Lily continued, muttering more to herself than to anyone in particular, 'the little lad will want for nothing either.' She felt an elbow dig her in her ribs and turned to see Rosie glaring at her.

Lily looked behind to see Martha and her parents watching proceedings as though they were at the flicks. Next to them were Hannah and Olly. They were holding hands and would have looked the epitome of a carefree young couple were it not for the dark bags under Hannah's eyes. With her parents in one of Hitler's notorious concentration camps, it was hardly surprising. In the pew in front was Gloria. Hope was perched on her knee. She was growing up at a rapid rate. *Was it really two years since she had sat in this very church and watched Hope undergo the same ritual?* Kate was next to them and was doing a good job of keeping Hope entertained. Lily knew Kate had been desperate to make a christening gown for Artie, but Agnes had put her foot down and insisted he be baptised in the family heirloom. From what Lily could see, it was looking a little raggedy. She'd got the impression Polly would have quite liked a new one, but she had the sense to realise when to go against her ma and when not to. Next to Kate was Rosie's friend from way back, a skinny little scamp of a girl called Georgina, and further along were Vera and Rina.

None of them looked like they'd heard her, or if they had, they were pretending not to have.

Lily forced her attention back to the proceedings. The vicar was telling baby Artie that Christ was claiming him as his own and that he was to receive the sign of the cross. There were a few coughs and the odd sneeze, but other than that the vicar had an attentive audience. Lily braced herself for an ear-splitting scream as the vicar dipped his hand into the font and made the watery outline of a cross on Artie's brow. There was a shriek rather than a scream as Artie reached up to the vicar with his pudgy little hands. He obviously thought this some kind of game.

Dr Eris watched Helen as she smiled. There was no denying the woman was too glamorous for words. *This was pure purgatory. And afterwards they were going to have to endure drinks with her and her doting spaniel, Matthew.*

It had to be said, though, that Matthew was a very good-looking spaniel, and of good pedigree according to what she'd picked up. The Royces were a well-known shipbuilding family – and very obviously moneyed. Matthew, wearing what looked to be a Savile Row suit, had managed to drop it into the conversation that he was Eton-educated and, thanks to his father's ill health, had clambered up the ladder at a rate of knots and was running the Pickersgill's shipyard.

Why, it had to be asked, wasn't Helen waltzing him down the aisle? He might be a widower, but he was still a great catch.

But of course she knew why. Helen wanted *John*, not *Matthew*.

Well, she damn well couldn't have him. She'd missed the boat. And Claire was going to make sure it didn't sail back into port.

Polly looked down at Artie as she held him over the font and the vicar sprinkled holy water onto his forehead. Artie's little expression was one of pure joy. He turned slightly in her arms, looking for the water. Her baby boy, she was sure, would have been happy to have been in the font splashing around. *So like his father*, thought Polly. *Happiest* when he's immersed in water. His great-granddad too. Polly suddenly had an image of the old man smiling down at them. He, too, had lived a good part of his life submerged in the waters of the Wear. She'd lay money on her son following in their footsteps.

'I baptise you in the name of the Father, and of the Son, and of the Holy Spirit. Amen.'

The congregation automatically repeated, 'Amen.'

Polly conjured up an image of Tommy, which wasn't hard, as every time she looked at Artie she saw the man she loved.

Look what we created.

See how happy he is.

See how healthy he is.

See how loved he is.

Suddenly Polly felt tears sting her eyes.

Now all he needs is his da.

So, just you make sure you come back to us, Tommy Watts.

Come back to us.

And soon.

Just as Polly was thinking of the man she loved, so too was Gloria.

The christening was making her relive the drama of Hope's christening, a little over two years ago, when Jack had burst through the church doors, dripping wet, with Arthur behind him, and had seen his daughter for the first time.

Gloria kissed Hope's mop of black hair. So like her dad's. And so like her sister's. She looked at Helen as she walked back to her place with Dr Parker. She took hold of Hope's little hand and waved at her. Helen smiled and waved back as she sat down again. Gloria hoped she was holding up. She looked perfectly fine, but that was Helen, she hid her torment well – of losing both her own baby and the man she loved.

And, of course, Helen missed her father dreadfully.

As did she.

As would Hope, if she knew who her father was.

'And now for the reading from the Gospel According to Luke, chapter two.'

Reverend Winsey looked up at his attentive audience. There was row upon row of red noses and the prayers had been speckled with a good trumpeting of nose-blowing.

'And Joseph also went up from Galilee, out of the city of Nazareth, into Judaea, unto the city of David, which is called Bethlehem; (because he was of the house and lineage of David:) to be taxed with Mary his espoused wife, being great with child.'

Bel looked at Lucille, who had been remarkably well behaved. Perhaps because she was now no longer the baby of the household.

'And so it was, that, while they were there, the days were accomplished that she should be delivered. And she brought forth her firstborn son, and wrapped him in swaddling clothes, and laid him in a manger; because there was no room for them in the inn.'

Lucille's head snapped round to her mammy at the mention of the inn.

Bel smiled as her daughter pointed to her chest proudly.

As Bel listened to the story of the nativity, she sighed. There was no escaping babies. They were everywhere she turned. Everywhere she looked she saw either expectant mothers or babies in prams. And now, with the onslaught of Christmas and the incessant chatter and references to the Baby Jesus, she felt as though she was having a huge tub of salt rubbed into a wound that felt increasingly raw with each passing day.

All she wanted was to be a mother to a brood of children. It was what she'd always wanted. To create the family she'd never had. But even that had been denied her.

It seemed like just about any woman who wanted to was able to get pregnant – as well as a good load of those who didn't.

Bel laughed bitterly to herself as the vicar ended the reading.

Even Mary had managed to get pregnant – and she was a bloody virgin!

'Thanks be to God ...'

Just as the vicar was finishing the service, those at the back of the church heard the click of the latch on the main door, followed by a gust of freezing cold air.

Angie and Dorothy automatically turned around.

'It's Quentin!' Angie spoke out of the corner of her mouth in a half whisper.

Dorothy didn't say anything, just watched as Quentin had a quick look around before finding the person he was looking for.

Then his face lit up.

Angie and Dorothy were staring at him as he walked quietly across the flagstones to where they were sitting.

Angie's face showed surprise and the beginnings of a smile.

Dorothy's showed absolutely no surprise, and she was beaming like the Cheshire Cat. She was pleased to see that Quentin had done his best to look as dapper and as handsome as possible. He had on a smart black suit with a starched white shirt and a silver-grey tie. A scarf was hanging around his neck, and his strawberry-blond hair, which was almost identical in colour to Angie's, had been Brylcreemed back. Dorothy thought he looked a little like Fred Astaire.

And just as with Fred and Ginger, Quentin only had eyes for Angie. And she for him.

Reaching his hand out as he approached her, he cocked his head back towards the door and mouthed, 'Come on.'

Angie hesitated, turning to look at Dorothy, who hissed in her ear, 'Go!'

Grabbing her bag and gas mask from the floor, Angie slid out of the pew.

She looked back at Dorothy, who was waving them both off as though this was their maiden voyage, which in a way it was.

'What are you doing here?' Angie asked as soon as they were out the main doors. As she spoke, she stopped still in her tracks and gasped. It must have snowed from the moment they'd all gone into the church and stopped just before she and Quentin had stepped outside. It was a winter wonderland. The grey urban landscape was now crystal white.

'Wow! It's beautiful!' Angie said, taken aback.

'Isn't it just!' Quentin said, not once taking his eyes off Angie. *How could he have?* She looked amazing.

Angie looked down at Quentin's hand, which was still holding her own.

'You can let go of my hand now,' she said.

'Perhaps I don't want to.'

As Quentin looked at her, a few snowflakes that were still floating in the crisp, icy air landed amidst the small smattering of freckles on her face.

Angie opened her mouth, but nothing came out. She allowed him to keep hold of her hand.

'Come on, I've booked a table at the Palatine. It's my Christmas present to you. An early one because, unfortunately,

I've only got a twenty-four-hour pass and have to leave early tomorrow morning – very early.'

Angie felt a shiver of nervous excitement as they walked down Suffolk Street.

'You cold?' Quentin stopped, took off his scarf and tied it loosely around Angie's neck like an oversized tie.

'What's going on, Quentin?' Angie said.

'Everything's going on,' he laughed. 'Now come on, let's get this tram. I don't know about you, but I'm starving.'

Chapter Fifty

The Tatham Arms, Tatham Street, Sunderland

Mr Clement and Georgina were sitting with their cameras on the table, deep in conversation. Georgina had been shadowing Mr Clement as he had taken the photos of the christening. Knowing they were being done for Tommy's benefit, and with a small amount of rationed film to use, Mr Clement had taken one of Polly and Artie, and one with family and friends next to the font. He had warned Georgina that not all babies were as willing to pose for the camera as Artie.

'Looks like Mr Clement has found a protégé,' Rosie said to Polly as they each took a cup of tea from the tray on the bar. The pub had been turned into a tea room for a few hours to celebrate Artie's christening.

'Oh, I almost forgot.' Rosie opened her handbag and pulled out a white envelope with *Artie Watts* in swirling handwriting on the front. Lily had asked her to give it to Polly, along with their apologies for having to leave so quickly after the service. Rosie didn't have to explain that Christmas Eve was always a busy time, and that Maisie and Vivian hadn't made it to the church as they were holding the fort.

'It's from Lily and George.'

Polly looked at the envelope and knew that it contained money.

'Honestly,' she said. 'Please tell them that they shouldn't have. As if they haven't given us enough already.'

'I will, but it'll fall on deaf ears,' Rosie said. They both supped their tea and looked around at the mix of guests.

'Oh, there's Dr Billingham,' Polly said, putting her tea down. 'I best introduce him to everyone.'

'And I better save Charlie,' Rosie said, nodding over at Mr and Mrs Jenkins. Charlotte was shuffling about from one foot to the other, something she did when she was bored.

'Helen ...' Dr Parker managed to squeeze through a group of lively locals. 'I just wanted to wish you a Happy Christmas before we headed off.'

'Ah, that's nice,' Helen said as Gloria quickly turned away and started talking to Dorothy.

She leant in and gave John a kiss on the cheek. Sensing that someone was watching her, she turned slightly; out of the corner of her eye she could see Claire watching their every move.

Dr Parker returned an equally chaste peck on the cheek.

There was a moment's awkwardness.

'You look like something's on your mind,' Helen said, thinking he seemed ill at ease; it wasn't surprising, considering he had eagle-eye watching his every move.

'Yes, actually, there is,' John said, loosening his tie, which all of a sudden felt tight. 'I know we haven't seen much of each other lately,' he continued.

Helen batted away his apology. 'You've got work – and a girlfriend.'

'I know,' he agreed, 'but I want you to know ...'

Looking into Helen's emerald eyes never failed to mesmerise him.

'Yes ...' Helen cajoled.

Suddenly there was a roar of laughter from the revellers behind and someone knocked into her, causing her to almost fall into John's arms.

'Sorry,' she said, stepping back.

John laughed. 'Looks like everyone's getting into the Christmas spirit.'

'What were you saying?' Helen could feel herself flush at having been so close to him, even if it had just been for a matter of seconds.

'Well, lately I've been thinking,' he said, 'thinking how close we have become these past few years.'

Helen smiled and nodded. Her mind flashed back to when she'd first met John at a charity do she'd attended at the museum, and how she had gone to him for help when she had found out she was pregnant. How much water had gone under the bridge since then.

As if reading her thoughts, John touched her arm briefly.

'We've been there for each other,' he said, his face earnest.

Helen let out a short burst of laughter.

'Well, I think it's been more a case of you being there for me, John,' she said, thinking of how he had supported her when she was pregnant – and saved her life when she had miscarried.

John knew what was going through Helen's mind.

'You've been there for me too,' he said, wanting to add that she had been the light in his life these past few years. When his work at the hospital became so dark he felt it was going to overwhelm him, it was Helen who had brought him light and laughter. And love.

'But now you have Claire,' said Helen. She glanced over to see that Matthew was chatting to Dr Eris; she no longer had her beady eye on them.

It was on the tip of John's tongue to say, 'And you have Matthew,' but he didn't. This was not about Claire or Matthew but about his relationship with Helen.

'Regardless of that,' John said, 'I still want us to continue to see each other – to be friends.' He paused. 'I might be sounding a little sentimental here,' he looked at Helen, who was looking back at him, her green eyes encouraging him to go on, 'but I think it would be a great shame if we lost the friendship we have – I think we've got something special.'

Helen smiled.

'I totally agree with you.' Her smile widened. 'I'm glad I'm not losing you.'

John laughed, out of relief and because he felt happy. He really didn't think he could imagine a life without Helen in it. Even if it was just as a friend.

If John had read Helen's mind at that moment, he would have realised she felt exactly the same. And if he had, there was no way he would have left the pub with Claire.

But John was not a mind-reader.

And so they wished each other a Happy Christmas and parted as friends.

Over the next hour, everyone chatted, drank tea and ate sandwiches, and little Artie was passed around like a parcel and didn't seem to mind one bit. Gradually, the guests left and were replaced by the pub regulars, who didn't object to their local being invaded as Bill had told them they could finish off what was left of the sandwiches.

As Dr Billingham had the entire day off and wasn't on call, he'd swapped his tea for brandy and was in good spirits. When he said his goodbyes, he thanked Polly for making him Artie's godfather – something, he said, he hoped she wouldn't regret when he began trying to persuade the little boy that a life in medicine was the one to have.

Polly laughed, telling him that was fine by her.

'And one day, hopefully, I'll meet Mary,' she said, giving him a farewell hug. 'You're welcome to bring her to the house to meet Artie any time.'

Polly saw what she thought was sadness cross his face as he wished her a Happy Christmas and made his way a little unsteadily out of the pub.

Dorothy had been in high spirits, which was not unusual, but what was surprising was that she had left earlier than she'd have done normally, so determined was she not to miss the return of the 'lovebirds' – or rather, a couple she hoped had become lovebirds since leaving the church.

Vera and Aunty Rina were not far behind as they were set on making tomorrow's Christmas dinner the best ever – or at least the best to be had during a war and with an ever-increasing list of rationed goods. Everyone had enjoyed a good chuckle on hearing that Aunty Rina had recently been introduced to Albert and, on learning about his allotment, had offered him a place at the table if he allowed her to raid his vegetable patch. Albert had, of course, agreed, but warned Rina that in December there was not much to raid – apart from sprouts and potatoes, which Rina said was exactly what she wanted.

Helen had been disappointed that John hadn't stayed longer, but after their brief chat, Claire had dragged him back off to Ryhope.

Matthew, on the other hand, wanted to stay until Helen was ready to leave, but she told him she had a personal matter to sort out and that he'd fulfilled his duties, thank you very much, and now she wanted shot of him. He hadn't taken offence and, after shaking just about everyone's hand in the pub and telling Polly he wished her and her handsome baby a very merry first Christmas together, had left a generous christening gift behind the bar, telling Bill that it was to toast the baby's health. Helen knew it was a lot by the way Pearl's eyes had come out on stalks.

Watching him leave, Helen realised that, much as she had fought against it, she liked Matthew, although much as she hated to admit it – and despite the conversation she'd just had – her heart was still very much with John.

Making her way through the tea drinkers, now being infiltrated by a growing swell of regulars and workers who had finished early for Christmas, she reached Bel.

'Sorry, can I borrow you for a minute?' Helen looked at Bel and then quickly at Agnes, who was holding Artie.

'Of course you can,' Bel said, putting down her cup of tea and following Helen. 'You going back to work?' she asked as they walked out of the main lounge bar and into the hallway.

'I am,' Helen said, 'I wouldn't dare leave it all to Harold. God knows what we'd come back to on Boxing Day.'

Bel laughed. Harold was more a hindrance than a help these days. She watched as Helen started scrabbling around in her handbag.

'I really hope I'm doing the right thing,' Helen said, her face serious as she found what she was looking for and pulled out a brown envelope.

Bel saw it had the words *Private and Confidential* on the front, then her name, *Mrs Isabelle Elliot*.

'It looks official,' Bel said. She felt apprehensive.

'It is … and it isn't,' Helen said. 'I hope you're not going to hate me for this, but I thought it might be something you'd want. It's been locked away in my drawer at work for the past seven months. I've been dithering ever since I put it there as to whether or not to give it to you. Whether you would want it. Whether it was right.'

It was true, Helen had thought long and hard about what she was now doing with the report. She had argued the case for and against giving it to Bel, wishing more than anything that John had been there to help with the decision, playing devil's advocate, as he was wont to do.

'Either way, I decided I didn't want it near me any longer. So I thought I'd give it to you as a gift of sorts – or perhaps it would be better described as a poisoned chalice … I don't know. It's up to you to decide what you want to do with it. Keep it, use it, burn it – do whatever you wish with it.'

Bel looked at Helen, her face showing her confusion.

The door to the lounge opened and Maud, one of the old ladies who owned the sweet shop a few doors down, shuffled past.

'What I mean,' Helen said, 'is that it's something that I think you *will* want. I feel like we've got to know each other since – well, since I realised we are …' she looked round and dropped her voice '… related.'

Bel nodded. She would say that they'd become friends. She certainly felt more like a friend to Helen than her aunty.

'Here you are,' Helen said, putting the envelope in Bel's hands. 'Please accept my apologies for employing someone to find out the truth for me, but as I've already told you, I just had to know. Curiosity killed the cat and all that.' Helen let go of Georgina's report, which had been neatly folded in two and put into a sealed envelope. 'Do what you want with it.' She paused. 'And know that whatever you do with it, it's all right by me.'

Helen forced a smile, then turned and hurried down the tiled hallway and out of the front door.

As she stepped carefully through the snow, dodging the local children who were running around, chucking snowballs at each other, she took a deep breath.

She just hoped to God she had done the right thing.

Bel turned and walked to the toilet, passing Maud on the way and pasting a smile appropriate for a Christmas christening on her face. As soon as she got through the door to the Ladies and saw no one else was there, she dropped the smile, walked into the cubicle and locked the door.

Putting the toilet lid down, she tore open the envelope and started to read the two sheets of neatly typed notes.

''Ere, Maud.' Pearl waved the old woman over to the bar. 'Did yer see Isabelle when yer went to the lav?'

Maud looked puzzled for a moment before she realised that Isabelle was, in fact, Bel. No one else ever called her by her full name.

'Yes, I did,' the old woman said. She tried to keep her dealings with Bel's ma down to a minimum. Waste of space. Next to no morals. And common as muck.

'Well, what was she deeing out there?' Pearl had seen Bel leave with Helen and had been watching the lounge door like a hawk, but neither of them had returned.

'She was talking to Miss Crawford, one of the godparents,' Maud said.

Pearl felt herself bristle. If Helen had been a girl from down the street, it would have been 'Helen', not 'Miss Crawford'.

'And then,' Maud continued, 'when I was coming out of the lavatories, Bel was going in.'

'What? On her own?'

Maud nodded.

Pearl took off the pinny she had been wearing to make the tea and sandwiches and stuffed it under the counter before lifting the hatch and coming through to the other side of the bar. She caught Bill's eye for a second before weaving her way across the lounge and out of the door. Turning left, she headed down the hallway and into the Ladies.

'Isabelle!' she shouted out, even though there was no need. There were only three cubicles.

'Ma!' Bel's voice could be heard from behind the only door that was shut.

'What yer deeing in here?' Pearl demanded.

Bel unlatched the door and walked out.

'I would have thought that was obvious,' Bel snapped.

Pearl saw the toilet lid was still down and Bel hadn't pulled the flush.

'Isabelle, if there's one thing I know for certain about yer – yer never use a public lavvy, *never*.' She scrutinised her daughter. 'The number of times yer used to have the screaming heebie-jeebies when yer were a bairn if I even dared suggest you use a loo for the great unwashed. I used to think yer had a cast-iron bladder, yer could hold it for so long until we got home.'

Pearl watched her daughter wash her hands, even though there was clearly no need, and it was then she saw the envelope that had been stuffed in Bel's handbag.

'So, what's gannin on?' she demanded. 'Yer thick as thieves with that Havelock girl 'n now yer squirrelled away – in the lav of all places – with what looks like a letter of some sort.' Pearl nodded down at Bel's handbag.

Bel turned to face her mother, drying her hands on paper towels and chucking them in the bin. She pulled the envelope out of her bag.

'Here,' she said, giving her ma the report. 'Some bedtime reading.'

And with that she walked out of the Ladies and back to the Christmas christening cheer.

There was no way Pearl was waiting for bedtime to read what her daughter had just handed her – and which, it didn't take a genius to work out, Helen had given to Bel.

Walking back through the lounge bar and ducking under the hatch, Pearl shouted over to Bill, 'Am just gannin for a break.' Bill nodded. He knew something was up.

Pearl poured herself a whisky and went through to the back room. Grabbing an ashtray, she lit a cigarette and took out the two sheets of paper that had been folded into the envelope. It wasn't a letter, as she had expected, but a document of sorts. A typed report. And it only took her a few seconds to know what it was about.

Her. And Isabelle. And her daughter's father.

As she started to read, she felt the pull of the past. A past she had tried most of her life to blot out, to run away from – to forget. Now, here it was – right in front of her – typed out in black and white. And whoever had done it, had done a thorough job.

Pearl's eyes widened.

Her employment at the Havelock residence had been confirmed by the housekeeper, Agatha, and the butler, Eddy, who had relayed how she'd started work as a scullery maid in September 1913. Even though there had not been a vacancy, the lady of the house, Mrs Catherine Henrietta Havelock, had employed Pearl 'due to her resemblance to the Hans Christian Andersen character "The Little Match Girl".'

Pearl, a 'young and pretty fifteen-year-old girl', had worked hard and 'seemed to be happy in her employ' until the following Easter, when she was asked to work 'upstairs' to cover for a young girl who had to take time off due to a dying relative.

Only the cook had tried to protect her, telling her to 'keep clear of the master'. When she'd asked why, the cook said he could get 'a bit nasty' when he'd had a few. Pearl had taken that to mean he had a temper on him, which hadn't perturbed her. Her own da had been free with his hands; she knew how to get out of the way and avoid a good hiding.

365

Pearl thought about the young girl called 'little Annie'.

She hadn't realised until later that there was no dying aunt to whom little Annie had had to go and pay her last respects. The chambermaid, who looked much younger than seventeen, had obviously found herself prey to Charles's perverted sexual needs when he had visited the previous Christmas. Had she been the only person in the house not to realise that?

The report stated that Pearl had left the Havelock residence in the middle of the night following 'a going-away party for the master', a chief negotiator for one of the big shipping companies.

Pearl's hand automatically went to her throat, as it always did when she thought of that night.

She had thought she was dreaming that there was something around her neck, stopping her from moving, from shouting out, from breathing. Her panic had intensified as she'd gulped desperately for air. And then she had woken, expecting to be free from what had fast been turning into a nightmare, only to then realise that the night terror was real. She was suffocating. A hand was around her neck and was squeezing it with increasing pressure. Her face was squashed into the pillow. She was choking. She managed to lift her head a fraction and gasp for air, her eyes frantically trying to see who was behind her. She caught sight of a strand of blond hair – then the flash of a man's profile. It was the master – and he was pressing his whole weight on top of her. He was stronger, much stronger than she would have imagined a man of his stature could be. And he was strangling her and then releasing his grip, allowing her a few precious seconds to suck in air. And then she felt an awful pain – the searing violation of her person. She screamed but her desperate pleas for help were silenced as he pushed her head down into the pillow to muffle her cries. She tried desperately to free herself, but it was hopeless. The hand around her neck squeezed her more tightly, until her vision clouded over and darkness prevailed. Only then did the pain stop.

Pearl took a deep breath, forced herself to concentrate on the report, but it was hard. Images of that night pushed through.

When she had come round, a part of her thought it had been a dream, until she saw herself in her little mirror – the bright red marks around her neck that were already starting to bruise. In the flicker of candlelight, she had lifted her nightie and seen the blood and marks down below.

Pearl took a drag on her cigarette. Her hand had started to shake. The report stated that she had not taken her maid's uniform with her, which Eddy and Agatha had said had struck them as unusual; the maid's outfit, 'a smart navy blue dress with white collar and cuffs, along with a starched white apron and cap, were hers to keep, to take by right'. But Pearl had left them, which was 'unusual for a young girl with barely two pennies to rub together'.

It had taken her ten minutes to clean herself up, put on her clothes and stuff what few belongings she had into her big cloth bag. She'd left the maid's outfit that Henrietta had made such a show of giving her. She did not want to take anything from this place. Not one single reminder. And then she'd left. But that night, as she stole out of the tradesmen's entrance, quietly tip-toeing down the gravel path by the side of the house, her heart in her mouth, her head thumping, petrified that the master would come and drag her back in, she was not to know that she had, in fact, left with something from that godforsaken house – and that 'something' would be a constant reminder of the horror, the violence and the injustice of what had happened to her that night.

Pearl took a mouthful of whisky and read on. Eddy and Agatha had been asked if they knew why Pearl had left so suddenly. The pair had replied they'd no idea.

'Pfft!' Pearl spat out loud.

Taking another sip of whisky, she continued to read.

The report stated that nine months after Pearl had done her midnight bunk, Isabelle had been born. Eddy and Agatha admitted that Pearl had not had a sweetheart, or any friends who were male. As far as they knew 'she never even left the house and seemed content to simply work and live on the premises'.

Pearl puffed on her cigarette. *How true.* She had only ever gone out the back, into the gardens or to the vegetable patch; very occasionally, she had popped into the stables to stroke the horses.

'In conclusion,' the last paragraph read, 'in light of all the evidence above, and due to the striking similarities in looks between Mr Charles Havelock and Mrs Isabelle Elliot, it would seem highly likely that they are father and daughter.'

Pearl stubbed out her cigarette. She was sure she was not the first, nor the last, to have been left with a permanent reminder of the violence that man had enjoyed inflicting. She thought of the maid before her.

Pearl sat back.

She'd always known Isabelle was courting trouble when she'd started work at Thompson's. The Havelock girl must have seen the inherited resemblance and gone rooting around in her family's murky past. Got someone professional to look into it. Got a report on it all. *And got more than she reckoned for, that's for sure.*

But why had she given the report to Isabelle? That didn't make sense. Pearl thought she'd have pushed the skeletons back into the cupboard, not got them out on parade.

If all this came out in the open, the Havelock girl would be responsible for hanging her grandfather out to dry.

Pearl finished off her whisky, put the report back in the envelope and pushed it into her skirt pocket.

The time was coming.

As she'd always known it would.

Chapter Fifty-One

'So,' Quentin said once they'd had their starters, 'we are agreed. That just because something is posh, it doesn't make it right?'

'We are,' said Angie, looking at Quentin and thinking that he looked very posh in his suit and tie but very right indeed.

'And that there's nothing to say that the way you talk is wrong, and the way I talk is right.'

'That neither is right or wrong. That's just how we are. Different,' Angie said, taking a sip of her wine.

'Exactly,' said Quentin.

After chatting and chuckling their way through the main course and listening to a very beautiful rendition of 'Silent Night' by carol singers from the local amateur dramatics group, they both agreed to skip dessert. After Quentin had paid the bill and given the waiter a generous tip, the pair made their way from the restaurant, through the main foyer and out into the eve of Christmas.

Again, Quentin took hold of Angie's hand. This time she pulled away.

'I can't, Quentin,' she said simply, her face suddenly serious. 'I'd love to, but I can't.'

They both waited for a tram to pass and Quentin looked at the woman with whom he was completely and utterly in love.

'I'm not going to ask you why you can't because I know,' Quentin said.

Angie looked at him.

'What do you mean, you *know*?'

'I know you think you can't because I'm posh and you're not – and that I'll just cast you aside like some used rag and then walk down the aisle with someone my "mummy and daddy" think is suitable.' Quentin grimaced just thinking about any girl his parents would have him marry.

'Bloody Dor 'n her big gob!' Angie said.

'Actually,' Quentin said, 'for once it wasn't Dorothy.'

Angie looked askance at Quentin.

'Not Mrs Kwiatkowski?'

Quentin nodded. Not only had Mrs Kwiatkowski told him, she had also given him the Spanish Inquisition as to whether or not his intentions towards Angie were honourable.

They turned right up Foyle Street. Quentin slowed down and took Angie's hand.

He took heart from the fact that this time she didn't pull away.

They both stopped.

'I want to be with you, Angie. Court you, date you, whatever you want to call it. I just want to be with you.'

Angie was staring at Quentin. 'I want to believe you, Quentin, I really, really want to.'

'Then do,' he said, his voice imploring. 'I want to be with you. And if you also wanted to be with me, then my expectations would be for us to get married. To have a family.'

Angie had gone pale.

'Oh, God! Now ... I'm scaring you ... I've barely even held your hand and I'm talking about marriage.'

He looked at Angie and saw it in her eyes.

Saw that she felt the same.

He bent his head and kissed her.

Gently at first, and then with a passion he had been forced to hold back for so long.

And she kissed him back with an ardour that she, too, had been forced to hold back for so very long.

Watching Angie and Quentin stop and then kiss, Dorothy sucked in air and grabbed Mrs Kwiatkowski's arm.

'Oh. My. God. How romantic is that?' she said, not taking her eyes off her friend and the man she could now officially call Angie's 'beau'.

'Don't look, it's rude,' Mrs Kwiatkowski said, freeing herself of Dorothy's grip and stepping away from the window.

They had both been peeking through the blackout curtains in Mrs Kwiatkowski's living room. They were in complete darkness, out of fear that a glimpse of light would make it through any small gaps while they spied on the two lovebirds. They had been standing there for a quarter of an hour, afraid they would miss them coming home, and had only just been able to make the pair out in the darkness as other Christmas revellers hurried past them.

Dorothy sighed and reluctantly relinquished her viewing point as Quentin and Angie began to stroll, their arms wrapped around each other, towards the flat.

'You know, Mrs Kwiatkowski,' Dorothy looked at the dark outline of her neighbour as she felt her way across the room towards the light switch, 'I don't think we could have hoped for a better result.'

Mrs Kwiatkowski switched on the light. She was smiling.

'For once, Dorothy, I agree with you.'

Chapter Fifty-Two

Brookside Gardens

'It's a shame Tommy couldn't be there today, isn't it?' Charlotte asked. She was standing in front of the fire. Rosie was behind her, trying to recreate the 'updo' that her sister's idol had been wearing at the christening.

'Well, that's war for you,' Rosie said.

'She must miss him, mustn't she?' Charlotte said, taking a sidelong glance into the mirror above the mantelpiece. Her sister was doing a surprisingly good job.

'Yes, I think she misses him an awful lot,' Rosie said, taking a hairpin from the mantelpiece and pushing it carefully into the French knot. 'Not that she'll let it show.'

'Like you,' Charlotte said, pushing a strand of hair out of her eyes and looking at the photograph of Peter on the mantelpiece.

Rosie didn't say anything. For some reason today had been hard for her. Throughout the whole ceremony she'd kept thinking about Peter; kept seeing a vision of him smiling as he walked towards her, his mac flapping open as it always did, his grey-blue eyes sparkling as he brushed back his greying hair. If someone had asked her about the christening, she doubted she'd have been able to tell them much.

'You must really miss Peter,' Charlotte persevered.

Rosie patted her handiwork and turned Charlotte round by the shoulders so she could see herself in the mirror.

'I do miss him,' she said. 'Now, what do you think of my skills as a coiffeur?'

Charlotte looked at herself, turning her head to one side and then the other. Rosie picked up the hand mirror from the coffee table and positioned it so that her sister could see what it looked like from behind.

'That's brilliant,' Charlotte said. 'Nearly as good as Vivian.'

Rosie smiled. 'Let's hope I can recreate it tomorrow.'

'Thanks, Rosie.' Charlotte looked at her sister. 'If I make us a hot chocolate, will you tell me about Peter?' she asked tentatively.

'Why do you want to know about Peter?' Rosie asked.

'I don't know – I'm curious, I guess.'

Rosie looked at her little sister who was no longer little. She had shot up and was now the same height as her. She had turned fifteen in the summer, and looking at her with her grown-up hairstyle, she was clearly becoming a young woman.

'All right,' Rosie acquiesced. 'You make yourself a hot chocolate – I'll have a cup of tea – and I'll do you a swap. I'll tell you what you want to know about Peter if you tell me about the group of boys that hang around the school when the bell goes.'

Charlotte coloured. 'Nothing much to tell.'

They headed into the kitchen.

Rosie sat down at the little kitchen table as Charlotte poured a cup of milk into the saucepan and lit the hob.

'So, tell me everything – from the start,' Charlotte said, filling the kettle.

Rosie pulled her dressing gown around her and sat back in her chair.

'It's rather long and complicated,' she said.

Charlotte's face lit up.

'All the better. A Christmas Eve story,' she said, getting the tray ready and putting out a plate of biscuits. 'A Christmas Eve *love* story.'

One with a happy ending, Rosie prayed.

As Charlotte finished making the drinks, Rosie told her sister a little of Peter's background – how he was a widower whose wife had died of cancer some years previously.

'So, he's not got any children?' Charlotte asked. It had never occurred to her to enquire before.

Rosie shook her head.

Moving into the sitting room, they settled down on the settee with their hot drinks and biscuits and Rosie started to tell Charlotte a sanitised version of her rather tumultuous relationship, skimming over their initial meeting when Peter had come to tell her about their uncle's death – this story was about love, not hate.

'A few months later we bumped into each other,' Rosie said. 'I'd just got off the ferry and was on my way home – Peter was working with the Dock Police just a little further along the quayside.' The chemistry between them had been undeniable – not that Rosie told her sister that.

'After that we started to meet up for a cup of tea at Vera's. Got to know each other,' Rosie said.

Charlotte knew a little about their café courtship, thanks to Vera.

'So ...' Charlotte paused, unsure how to phrase her next question. 'It must have been difficult for you to tell Peter about everything – especially Lily's – with him working for the police and everything ...?'

Rosie took a biscuit and bit into it, giving herself time to think.

'It was difficult when he first found out, and we didn't see each other for a while.'

'Really? Why?' Charlotte said.

'We just needed time to think,' Rosie said. 'But, in the end, we realised we loved each other and wanted to be together – regardless.'

'So how was it you got back together?' Charlotte asked.

Rosie suddenly laughed, realising why Peter was on her mind so much today.

'Funnily enough,' she said, 'he was waiting for me after I'd been to a christening. Hope's christening.'

'So, you made up?' Charlotte asked.

Rosie felt the rush of love and excitement she'd had on seeing Peter waiting for her outside the flat – how they had kissed and, later, made love.

'We did,' she said.

As Rosie continued to answer Charlotte's questions, she realised she was enjoying talking about Peter. It seemed to bring back the happiness of that time. One of the happiest in her life. She rarely talked about Peter, perhaps because she thought about him so much. But chatting about him to her sister seemed to bring him closer. Brought the three of them closer, closer to the dream she had always had – of being a family.

A dream that would come true – *if* he made it back.

She just had to hope and keep on hoping.

'I can't wait until I fall madly in love,' Charlotte sighed on hearing how her sister had rushed to the station to catch a train to Guildford to see Peter one last time before he left for the war.

'Well, there's plenty of time for that,' Rosie said. 'And I haven't forgotten about the boys at school –' she looked at the clock and saw it was nearly midnight '– who I will grill you about tomorrow.'

She put both their empty cups and the crumb-strewn plate on the tray and picked it up.

'Come on, let's get ourselves to bed, otherwise Santa won't come.'

Charlotte laughed.

'Doesn't matter, I've got everything I want anyway,' she said.

Rosie felt a lump in her throat.

With those few words her little sister had just given her the best Christmas present she could ever have wished for, apart from good news about Peter.

*

Bel lay awake in bed with Joe snoring gently next to her. He'd been out like a light the moment his head hit the pillow. It had been a busy day. He'd been out with the Home Guard, then helped with the christening and afterwards had gone into town to get the tree, which he had insisted on loading into and then unloading from the delivery truck. She wished he wasn't so stubborn when it came to his leg. He tried to behave as though there was nothing wrong with it and suffered the consequences afterwards. He'd said goodnight to an excited Lucille and had crashed out himself not long afterwards. Pain was exhausting.

Thinking about their rather scabby tree, with its even scabbier decorations, Bel thought about the lush green one that had been delivered to the Havelock house, which led her to think of all the privileges Charles Havelock had enjoyed his whole life. She'd wager he had never known the constant gnaw of hunger, or the feel of a brutal northern winter biting into your very bones. That he had always been given the best medical care; any slight twinge looked at, cared for, paid for.

She thought about all the people she knew.

All the hardships they'd had to endure.

She thought about Kate and the miserable life she'd had. About Rosie and her constant fight to keep her sister safe. And Agnes, bringing up her children while grieving for her husband. Her mind wandered to Hannah, worried sick about her parents. And to the women welders and all their secrets that came with a price. And then she thought of the power Miriam had wielded over them all for almost two years.

And at the heart of it was poor little Hope – an innocent in all of it.

Suffering the punishment of others by being forced to grow up without her father.

Bel thought about the report Helen had given her. She thought about its damning contents. Contents that could possibly be incriminating – or which at the very least had the potential to ruin Mr Charles Havelock and his lily-white reputation.

And the more she thought about the report – her gift from Helen – the more she knew what she had to do.

Chapter Fifty-Three

Christmas Day

Pearl, along with most of the town's children, had lain awake most of the night – only she had no interest in snatching a glimpse of Santa. Her mind was churning over and over. Isabelle had been ready to pop for a few weeks, and now that the Havelock girl had given her that damned report, it wouldn't be long before the geyser blew. Not long at all.

As soon as she heard Lucille's excited cries that Santa had been, Pearl got up and made herself ready. She sat at her dresser and put on her make-up. She felt like one of those tribal Indians putting on war paint. Today, she sensed, was going to be a Christmas to remember for all the wrong reasons.

'Nana! Nana!' Lucille shouted out on seeing Pearl walk through into the kitchen-cum-living-room. The two dogs were in an equal state of excitement and were wrestling with a growing mound of newspaper that had been used as wrapping paper. Agnes was in the scullery, and Bel and Joe were sitting at the kitchen table drinking tea, having watched their daughter open her presents with glee. They both had smiles on their faces.

Lucille held a plastic doll up to her grandma as though it were a trophy she had just won.

'That's a grand dolly,' Pearl said. 'Better than a bag of coal, eh?' She turned her attention to Bel. 'Can I have a word?' She nodded towards the yard. 'Out back.'

Bel's smile dropped. 'And *Merry Christmas* to you too, Ma.'

Joe got up and kissed Pearl on the cheek. 'Merry Christmas, Pearl.' He'd warmed a little towards his mother-in-law of late. She was making an effort. Bill was clearly a good influence on her.

'Thanks, Joe, yer a good 'un.' She pulled a face and cocked her head at her daughter. 'Too good for this 'un.'

Bel shook her head. 'Come on then,' she said, grabbing her cardigan. 'I'm guessing you've got your fags?'

Pearl held them up.

'Happy Christmas, Agnes,' she said, opening the back door. 'Bet yer glad yer not having to fanny on feeding us lot today?'

'My second year!' Agnes laughed, wiping her hands on her pinny. 'Think I could get used to this being-cooked-for malarkey.' Last year they had all been at the Grand, enjoying a wedding breakfast that had made them momentarily forget they were at war.

Pearl stepped out into the yard and was startled by the brightness of the snow. It had been snowing on and off since yesterday afternoon and was now a few inches thick. She lit a cigarette while Bel followed her out, pulling her cardigan around her and folding her arms.

'Is it about the report I gave you?' Bel asked.

Pearl had given Bel the report back after reading it, but they hadn't had a chance to talk about it. By the time Pearl had finished her shift last night, Bel and Joe had already gone to bed.

'Aye, in a roundabout way,' Pearl said, blowing smoke up into the sky. It was just starting to get light.

'Yer knar, when I had Maisie 'n gave her up, I thought I'd done the right thing,' she said, before taking another drag. 'But now I'm older, I dinnit think it was. I think it would have been better if I'd kept her, knowing what I know now.'

Bel wondered what Pearl did know. Maisie had always been vague about her upbringing.

'When you came along ...' Pearl flicked ash into the virgin snow '... I couldn't do it again – give another bairn up. So, I kept yer.'

She looked at Bel.

'But now I think I should have given yer up.'

Bel stared at her mother.

'Do you?' Bel was surprised.

'I dee, Isabelle. Let's face it, yer life couldn't have been much worse than it was with yer auld ma. I walked out of that house after what he did 'n my life just went to pot.' Pearl took another long drag. They both stood in silence for a moment. 'Yer saving grace was her indoors.' Pearl turned her head towards the house.

Bel stood there, oblivious to the cold and wet that had started to creep through her shoes from the carpet of snow. She had hated her ma for most of her life. It was only recently that she'd let go of the anger, or rather, had transferred it to the person it should always have been aimed at – Charles Havelock.

'I mightn't have been much cop as a mam,' Pearl said, 'but I know yer, Isabelle. Knar exactly what's going on in that head of yers sometimes.'

Bel was still staring at her ma.

'So, I want yer to promise me something, Isabelle,' said Pearl. 'What's that, Ma?'

'I want yer to tell me if yer gonna dee owt,' Pearl said simply. She didn't need to go into any more detail. Her daughter knew exactly what she meant.

Bel was quiet. Her mother had never made her promise anything in her life. Not even as a child.

She nodded.

'I want yer to say it,' Pearl demanded.

Bel stared at Pearl. She had never heard her ma sound so serious.

'I promise,' she said.

There was a moment's silence.

Pearl chucked her cigarette butt into the snow.

'Now, let's gan inside before we both turn blue.'

*

Kate, Charlotte, and Rosie were standing by the front door at Lily's. They all had large wicker baskets in their hands. They were well wrapped up with hats, scarves and gloves. Charlotte's and Rosie's cheeks were already red after the walk from Brookside Gardens to West Lawn. It was a beautiful winter's day – there was snow underfoot and the sun was high in the sky, although it was still bitterly cold.

Stepping out onto the front step, Charlotte took one last look at the tall Christmas tree, which had been beautifully decorated, at the end of the hallway. Lily really did have style.

'Everyone ready?' Kate asked.

Rosie and Charlotte nodded.

'Be careful, *mes chères*,' Lily called out, bustling down the stairs. She was still in her dressing gown, having enjoyed the most wonderful lie-in.

Kate frowned at Lily. 'Why do we have to be careful? Being homeless doesn't make you any more dangerous than the next person.'

'You know what I mean, Kate,' Lily said, giving her a hug, and then Charlotte. 'And Merry Christmas!' She sang the words. 'Or as they say in France ...' She looked at Charlotte.

'Joyeux Noël!' they both chorused.

'Hold your horses!'

It was George making his way down the stairs with the help of his walking stick. He, too, was still in his dressing gown.

'Just a few coins,' he said, pulling out a leather pouch from the pocket of his green paisley robe. He gave it to Kate.

'They just need some frankincense and myrrh now,' Lily quipped under her breath.

As Kate, Rosie and Charlotte made their way down the pathway to the little wooden front gate, Maisie and Vivian appeared in the doorway.

'Merry Christmas!' they shouted out. They too had contributed to the contents of the baskets; it had been a trade-off for not going out with Kate and her two helpers.

*

While Kate, Rosie and Charlotte walked into town and around the places Kate knew well, where those with no home and no money sought shelter, Polly was sitting on her bed, looking down at Artie in his crib. He was wide awake and had just been given a couple of toys from Santa that he was only moderately interested in. He was looking up at his mammy, who was holding something in her hands that was making a slight crinkling sound as she straightened it out on her lap.

'"Dear Polly and Artie,"' Polly began, looking again at Artie, pleased to see she had his attention.

'This is from Daddy,' she explained.

Artie gurgled by way of reply.

Polly looked out of the window and up at the blue sky. She had to squint as the sun was out. The weather was almost identical to Christmas Day last year. The day she and Tommy had married.

She looked back down at the letter.

'"Merry Christmas!"' Polly made a happy face at Artie, which he returned. '"Or as they say here in Gibraltar: *Feliz Navidad!*"'

Polly looked at Artie.

'Oh, *there now*, Daddy's learning Spanish. He can teach you when he comes back.'

If he comes back.

'"It's as hot here as I know it will be cold back home. How I wish I was frozen stiff with the two people I love more than anything else in the world. But because I can't be, I want you both to know that I will be thinking of you every minute of today. And that I love you both so very much. With all my love, Tommy/Daddy."'

Polly wiped a solitary tear from her eye, just catching it before it dropped onto the letter. She would not cry. She had resolved that today was going to be a happy one. She had much to celebrate, not only the letter from Tommy, which reassured her he was alive and well, but today was their first wedding anniversary – and their baby boy's first Christmas.

*

Helen had tried to enjoy a lie-in – it was Christmas after all – but couldn't. Her body clock was set. It wasn't going to budge, so she gave up on sleep and wandered downstairs to make herself a cup of tea and a piece of toast. At least the house was quiet, and her mother was still sleeping off what she guessed would be a hangover from hell. She'd snuck in when the party was just getting into the swing last night and had successfully avoided having to be in any way a part of it. It was bad enough having to see John and Claire joined at the hip for most of the day, without then being subjected to an evening of her mother's friends' inane chatter.

Padding into the kitchen, she was surprised to see it so clean and tidy. Poor Mrs Westley must have been up all hours getting the place back to normal.

Helen put the kettle on.

Today was going to be hard work. A laborious Christmas dinner with her mother and grandfather. The irony of having to spend Christmas Day with the two people she disliked more than anyone else she knew – and those two people being her family – did not escape her.

She thought of John.

How she would have loved to have popped to Ryhope to see him after he'd finished his shift. Now that she had her own transport, she could have just nipped there after her mother had made her excuses and swanned off to the Grand.

She could have done – were it not for Claire.

She and John might have cemented their friendship, but there were still boundaries to abide by.

*

Dr Parker had been up early and was on the ward for rounds at eight o'clock sharp. He was glad. He'd not slept brilliantly after yesterday's christening.

If he was honest, he'd wanted to stay a little longer at the pub, but Claire had said, politely of course, that she'd had enough.

He understood that a smoky, working-class pub in the east end was not Claire's idea of a fun Christmas Eve on a rare day off, so he'd suggested they nip into the Palatine for a drink and to listen to some carolling before they jumped on a bus back to Ryhope. It had been incredibly festive, and he'd tried to stir up that carefree joyousness you were meant to have at this time of year, but he'd failed. Not that he'd let it show.

He'd been surprised to see Angie and Quentin in the restaurant. They'd looked so happy, gazing at each other in a way that made it glaringly obvious they were hopelessly in love. It had made him doubt his feelings for Claire, which was stupid. Angie and Quentin were younger. They were different people.

As he unhooked one of his patient's charts from the bottom of his bed, he forced a smile and wished him the obligatory 'Merry Christmas'. Not that this young man would think there was much to be merry about. He'd just had an amputation from the knee after gangrene had set in. He'd been lucky it hadn't spread; not that the young lad nodding back off into a morphine-induced sleep would see it that way.

Dr Parker moved on to the next bed.

At least he was in good company here in not having the greatest of desires to celebrate Christmas. *How could he partake in the frivolity of the festive season when there were hundreds of other doctors and surgeons – never mind thousands of nurses – on the front line, putting their lives at risk to save others?*

He hadn't told Claire, but he had put in another request to be sent to whichever battlefield needed him the most.

He had decided to keep on appealing their refusals to let him go until he wore them down.

That was *his* Christmas wish.

*

'I'll see yer all later in the pub!' Pearl popped her head into the kitchen. Joe was playing a game of dominoes with Lucille, Polly was feeding Artie, and Bel was helping Agnes clear up the breakfast dishes in the scullery.

'It's a bit early to be opening up,' Bel said, drying her hands and looking at the clock on the mantelpiece.

'Lots to do,' Pearl said, 'it being Christmas 'n all.'

'We'll bring back two plates yer can warm up later,' Agnes said.

'Aye, ta, Agnes, that'll be nice.'

'So, you're going to be working behind the bar all day?' Bel asked.

'No rest for the wicked,' Pearl said. 'Besides, we're one of the few pubs to get a licence, so we're expecting to be full to bursting.'

'Nana, Nana!' Lucille had pushed herself onto her feet and was offering her grandmother one of her pear drops.

'Ah, no thanks, pet, yer auld nana's sweet enough.' She patted her on the head. 'See yer all later then.'

She turned and left, coughing her way down the hallway and out of the front door.

When she saw that the snow was still thick and looked as though it had no intention of melting despite the sunny skies, she cursed. Pulling her coat around her, she trudged down Tatham Street, going in the opposite direction to the pub.

Fifteen minutes later she reached her destination – a small terraced cottage off Villette Road. She hadn't expected to be knocking on their door so soon, but after the Havelock girl's 'present' to Isabelle last night, she'd known she had to act fast.

It had surprised her that the couple hadn't moved. They'd stayed put these past thirty-odd years, which had made it easier for Pearl to track them down.

It wasn't until she was sitting in their front lounge, bare of any kind of Christmas decoration, that they explained how if they moved away it would be as though they were leaving their daughter behind. And they couldn't – wouldn't – do that.

As Pearl drank her tea, she could see they were counting the days until they could leave for good and join the daughter they missed so much.

After stepping back out into the snow-covered streets, Pearl carried on up Villette Road, turning right onto Ryhope Road. Some revellers high on Christmas spirit pulled over in a car and asked her if she wanted a lift. Normally, she would have jumped in, but she couldn't stand the sight of their happy faces, not after the conversation she'd just had. She needed to acclimatise herself and so she waved them on. After twenty minutes of scrunching through fresh snow, though, she wished she'd accepted their offer and put up with their smiley faces.

Turning left into West Lawn, she arrived, finally, at her second port of call.

*

'Here you are.' Rosie handed a blanket to yet another beggar. She hadn't realised there were quite so many homeless people in the town.

'Ta, pet,' said the old man, who didn't look as though he'd had a wash since Christmas last. If then.

Rosie watched as Charlotte gave him some food and Kate crouched down and put some money in his hand. She stayed talking to him for a little while. Rosie caught the odd word. She was telling him where he could find shelter – it was the nearest Salvation Army hostel. The old man nodded and gave her a toothless smile, but it was clear he had no intention of leaving his spot under the railway arches.

Rosie looked at Charlotte. Her little sister's face was full of concern. This was certainly a Christmas she would remember.

*

When Lily opened the front door to find Pearl standing on the step, her first thought was that she wished she'd told Maisie to tell her to use the back entrance. Ushering her in, she did a quick check, but thankfully there wasn't anyone else about. She was glad Pearl had come, though. After her phone call to Maisie last night from the pub, they'd heard that Pearl feared a Christmas Day surprise that was in no way a good one. Not for any of them.

Chapter Fifty-Four

By the time everyone was settled in Vera's café, the windows were steamed up and the air was warm and full of chatter. Charlotte, Hannah and Olly had arranged the tables so that they made one long rectangle down the length of the cafeteria. Kate had commented that it reminded her of the famous oil painting of *The Last Supper* by Leonardo da Vinci.

While Kate had put her finishing touches to the table decorations, Charlotte had disappeared into the kitchen to make the gravy, which was becoming her forte having mastered the skill during her time working with Muriel in the canteen at Thompson's. Having spent the morning with the town's down-and-outs, Charlotte was feeling grateful. There was nothing like the misfortune of others to make you count your blessings.

Rosie, on the other hand, had been left a little down following their morning's trudge through the snow to areas of the town she had no wish to revisit, for she had kept seeing Peter's face in all the poor souls to whom she had handed blankets. The same questions kept looping round and round in her head. *Had Peter's true identity been revealed? Was he languishing in some prisoner-of-war camp?*

Or worse still, had *he* had his last supper?

She tried to join in the Christmas spirit, but found it hard.

Gloria was also trying her best to join in the festivities, for her little girl's sake if no one else's. Watching her now, with her short, bobbed jet-black hair, she was the spit of her dad. In some ways it was a huge comfort that Hope was the image of the man she loved, the man she craved to be with; in other ways, it caused her tremendous heartache.

After everyone had settled in their seats, Vera started to serve up. Rina and Charlotte brought out the plates while Agnes took hot tea to those who enjoyed a cuppa with their meal and Lily offered the other revellers a choice of wine or port.

George had brought a bottle of single malt, which he held up to see who wanted to partake. The only nods and raised glass tumblers came from those sitting nearest to him – Major Black and Joe.

Mr Pickering was sitting next to his daughter, Georgina, who was sitting next to her new mentor, Mr Clement. Next to him were his wife and three children. As they all looked down at their steaming plates piled high with food, they agreed it had been a great idea for everyone to pool their resources and rations as there was no way they could have individually replicated what was now making their mouths water. Georgina and Mrs Clement agreed wholeheartedly, admitting that their skills in the kitchen were somewhat lacking.

Mr Clement and Mr Pickering exchanged looks and didn't argue the point.

As Charlotte and Rina put the last plates down in front of Albert, Beryl, Iris and Audrey, Vera followed, carrying three plates, one balanced on her forearm in true silver-service style.

Charlotte sat down next to Lily, her face lighting up when she saw that she'd poured her half a glass of wine. Looking nervously over at Rosie, who was sitting opposite, she was glad to see she seemed a million miles away. She took a large gulp before her sister had time to return to planet Earth and stop her.

Seeing that the two cooks were now settled in their places, and that both women were reaching for their glasses of port, Lily stood up with her wine glass in her hand.

Bel checked her handbag was still by her feet. Its contents were weighing heavily on her mind. If she were competing with Rosie and Gloria for the ability to put on a happy face when feeling anything but, Bel would win first prize hands down. As she laughed and joked with Polly and divided her attention between Artie and Hope, no one would have guessed the myriad of thoughts that kept racing around in her head. Watching Hope toddling around the room, occasionally screaming with excitement, made her think of Helen. There was no denying that the two were related. She knew Helen had been a real daddy's girl. Hope would be, too, if she ever got to spend any time with her father.

Helen had told Bel that as a rule the family didn't tend to sit down to their Christmas dinner until two o'clock and then it was a long-drawn-out affair, with aperitifs, as well as a starter. Thinking of Mr Havelock lording it in his huge house, eating canapés and admiring his huge, wonderfully decorated Christmas tree, Bel felt the familiar surge of anger. Vera had managed to get hold of what could only be described as a midget fir tree. An ancient midget fir tree at that. It wasn't even green any more. Most of the needles had dropped off and the few measly decorations were hanging off skinny brown branches that looked more like twigs.

'A toast!'

Bel looked up to see Lily, looking spectacular as always in a green velvet dress.

'To a very Merry Christmas,' Lily declared. *'Bon appétit!'*

They all raised their glasses and teacups.

'Merry Christmas!'

Angie was watching everyone at the table as they tucked in. She put food in her mouth and chewed but didn't taste a morsel. She was floating on a cloud. It was as though she was untouchable. As though the serenity she felt was impenetrable.

So, this was what it felt like to be in love.

After that first kiss, they had stayed with each other until the moment Quentin's car had arrived at the front door to pick him up.

Angie yawned, forgetting to put her hand over her mouth.

Dorothy nudged her.

'Wakey, wakey, lovebird!'

Angie smiled at Dorothy, not minding the rather robust shove – or being called a 'lovebird'.

Dorothy looked at Gloria and rolled her eyes. They all knew, of course, that Angie and Quentin had finally got it together. Dorothy had exclaimed more than once this afternoon, '*At last!* It's only taken them an entire year!'

Angie hadn't minded. She didn't feel like she would ever mind anything ever again.

'*My Christmas wish is for you never to change,*' he'd said.

Angie knew she would never forget those words, spoken as they'd sat, their arms wrapped around each other, on Quentin's settee. Angie, of course, had laughed loudly, and Quentin had looked at her and said with serious eyes, 'I mean that. You're perfect the way you are – and I love you for precisely the person you are now.'

They had shared the happiest, saddest goodbye, Angie standing at the top of the stone steps to the flat, Quentin's cardigan wrapped around her, his slippers on her feet.

Quentin had gone to get in the car, had stopped and turned, and then ran back up the steps to kiss her for about the hundredth time that night, before promising he would be back as soon as he could. And she had watched as the car had pulled away, wheels spinning a little in the icy snow, waiting until the red lights disappeared around the corner.

Only then did she realise that it had been on these steps that they had first met.

And with that came another realisation – it had been there that she had first fallen in love with Quentin.

And it had taken her all this time to realise it.

Toby jumped off the train and hurried out of the station, keeping his fingers crossed there'd still be a few taxis about, even though it was Christmas Day. He'd got delayed in Scotland, but thankfully the trains had all been running on time. No air raids to cause disruption due to an agreement that today there would be no German bombers clouding their skies, just as Berlin would have a respite from a week of raids by the Allies.

Walking out of the main entrance and into daylight, he stopped dead – he'd never thought of this part of town as particularly pretty, but today it was like a scene from a Christmas card. Brilliant white snow lay everywhere; even the bomb site where the town's department store had once stood looked almost picturesque.

Seeing a lone taxi idling by the side of the road, he hurried over and jumped in.

'The salubrious establishment known as Vera's on High Street East, old chap!'

The driver forced a smile, hoping the posh accent meant a generous tip.

*

'Toby!' Dorothy's screech managed to sound out above the noise of loud chatter filling the café.

Everyone turned to look as Toby stamped snow off his boots. He looked at his audience and gave them a salute, then took off his cap. Dorothy thought he looked the handsomest man on the planet in his smart army uniform. Clambering out of her seat, she straightened her figure-hugging dress and tottered over to greet him. Toby's smile was as wide as his embrace. Scooping her up in his arms, he lifted her so that her toes were only just able to touch the linoleum flooring and gave her a big smacker on the lips.

'Give me a moment,' he whispered in her ear. 'I've just got to have a quick word with Rosie.'

Rosie watched as Toby came into the café. Her heart was pounding. *Had he heard anything?* Dorothy had been unsure if he was going to be able to make it today. During their Christmas dinner, Rosie wasn't sure who had been looking at the door the most – her or Dorothy.

Something told her that if he made it here today, he'd have news. Perhaps because last Christmas he'd come armed with a letter.

God, she hated this!

Wanting – not wanting Toby to turn up. Wanting – not wanting to hear something. Nothing was better than something, as nothing meant nothing – but something might mean news that he was dead.

Dead.

There, she'd said the word in her head.

Dead. Dead. Dead.

Accept it – Peter might be dead.

Rosie watched Toby take Dorothy in his arms and kiss her and then whisper something in her ear. And then her heart started thumping, felt like it was going to explode in her chest. He was looking around the café. *He was looking for her.*

He saw her.

He didn't smile.

It was bad news.

He was walking towards her. She wanted to stand up and scream at him to go away.

She didn't want to know.

And then, as he got nearer to her, she saw the beginnings of a smile.

He wouldn't smile if he had bad news. *Would he?*

Rosie stood up, would have walked towards him if her legs had not become lead weights. 'Peter?' She heard her voice. It sounded strangled. Hoarse.

Toby took both her hands. *'Peter's fine. We've just had news. He's OK.'*

Rosie stared at Toby.

Everything had gone quiet.

'He's fine,' Toby repeated, putting his arms around her and giving her a hug.

'Peter's alive?' Rosie spoke into the coarse green material of his army uniform.

'Yes, he's alive,' Toby said.

And then he felt her body relax and judder as she sobbed and sobbed. He held her while she cried – and then cried some more.

When she finally pulled away, she realised everyone was silent. And everyone was staring at her. She saw Charlotte standing next to Lily, then George walking over to her and instructing her to sit back down. The Major wheeled his chair over to Toby, cocked his head over to the table at George's bottle of whisky.

Vera suddenly appeared at her side with a large brandy, muttering that she thought she also needed one herself.

And slowly everyone started to half laugh, half cry.

Peter was alive. Their joy was not so much for Peter, even though those who knew him liked him, but for Rosie. The woman they all loved and who they were desperate to see have a happy ending.

The war was still raging, and there were still no certainties, but Peter was alive. And their friend's heart remained intact. For now, at least.

'A toast!' Toby declared, his large whisky raised in the air.

'To Peter!'

Rosie looked up at Toby and smiled. The tears still trickling steadily down her face.

'To Peter!'

All their voices were strong and determined.

As they gathered to listen to the King's speech, Mr and Mrs Clement came over to say hello to Polly and baby Artie.

'He's gorgeous,' said Mrs Clement. 'Can I?' she asked, putting her arms out.

'Willingly,' Polly laughed, handing over Artie, who smiled at Mrs Clement and immediately made a grab for her perfectly styled victory rolls. She didn't seem to care. She kissed his chubby little hand, causing him to forsake her hair for the thick sparkling necklace she was wearing.

'It was good to see Dr Billingham yesterday,' Mr Clement said, lighting up a thick cigar that looked the same as the ones the Prime Minister smoked.

'Oh, I didn't realise you know each other?' Polly was surprised.

'Yes, Richard and I go way back,' Mr Clement said. 'Makes me feel old just thinking about it,' he laughed, and started puffing away, creating a cloud of smoke.

Mrs Clement coughed and walked over to chat to Agnes, taking Artie, who seemed happy to remain in her charge.

'Very sad, though –' Mr Clement blew out smoke and coughed '– about his daughter.'

Polly looked puzzled. 'Who? Mary?'

Mr Clement nodded and coughed again. He was not a regular smoker.

'Poor girl. So young. So pretty. So much going for her.'

'What? You don't mean she's dead?' Polly suddenly felt nauseous. She was staring at Mr Clement, trying to read his face.

'Yes,' Mr Clement said. 'Got caught in the Blitz.'

Polly felt as though her stomach was doing a very slow somersault.

'What? Recently?'

Surely Dr Billingham would have mentioned it? She would have known.

'No, no,' Mr Clement said, 'she was caught in one of the first raids.'

He thought for a moment.

'Yes, must be about three and half years ago now. Summer of 1940. She was in the East End, walking home after a late shift.'

'Oh God.' Polly had gone white. 'That's terrible. How awful.'

'Yes, Richard took it badly – not surprisingly.' He cast an eye over at his three girls, who were thankfully still too young for any kind of war work. 'No one saw him for a while. I don't think anyone knew where he was. Then he just seemed to reappear. Started back at the hospital as if nothing had ever happened.'

Mr Clement looked down at his cigar as though wondering whether to risk another puff.

'Never mentions her ... Mary ... God rest her soul.'

Polly felt the tears coming.

She looked up to see Rina clapping her hands.

Vera was fiddling with the wireless.

'Looks like it's time for the King,' Mr Clement said.

Needing to feel her own child in her arms, Polly relieved Mrs Clement of Artie as the voice coming out of the radio solemnly announced to the nation, 'His Majesty King George the Sixth.'

The slightly hesitant words of the King floated over Polly's head.

She didn't hear his words of hope, nor his talk about the nation's spirit and the 'bright vision of the future'.

All she could think of was Dr Billingham.

Her heart felt like it was breaking for him, and as it did, tears dripped down her face and onto her baby boy, who smiled up at his mammy and tried to catch the salty raindrops that were wetting his warm cheeks.

Tears were also dripping unchecked down Rosie's face as she listened to the King talk of 'the fighting spirit of France reborn'.

She didn't care that others could see she was crying. She had dropped her defences and she was happy to let them stay down for a while, letting all the emotions she'd held back pour out of her as she listened to the words of the country's monarch.

Listening to him, she believed every word he spoke of hope and victory.

For Peter was alive.

He was alive.

As the national anthem sounded out, Bel tugged Joe's sleeve and told him she was going.

Joe bent down and kissed her. His face was stern. He asked her if she was sure and was there anything he could say to make her change her mind. Bel shook her head.

She nodded over to Lucille, who was standing next to the Major, her chin up, back straight, her little chest puffed out. The Major also had his chest puffed out and his shoulders back as he turned slightly and gave the little patriot by his side a wink.

Bel kissed Joe once more, then grabbed her handbag and gas mask and slipped away, disappearing out of the door and into the fading light of what would turn out to be a Christmas Day she would never forget.

Chapter Fifty-Five

'See yer back in an hour. Dinnit be late,' Pearl shouted after Geraldine as she left the pub.

Geraldine purposely ignored Pearl. She took her instructions from Bill – he was the boss, the licensee, not Pearl, much as she'd like to think she was.

They both heard the door crash shut.

Pearl finished off polishing the last few glasses.

'We've got some sandwiches I saved from yesterday out the back if you want?' Pearl said.

'Drink first?' Bill replied.

'Do yer even need to ask?' Pearl laughed, grabbing her packet of cigarettes from under the counter.

Bill poured them each a large whisky and the pair nestled themselves on two bar stools.

Bill raised his glass.

'Merry Christmas!'

'Aye, Merry Christmas!' She grabbed her drink, chinked glasses and took a large sip.

'What a year, eh?' Bill mused.

'Aye,' Pearl agreed, 'and it's not over with yet. Least I won't be dragging yer over to Ryhope any more, eh?' she went on. 'Seeing as I finally got what I needed from Henrietta.' Pearl let out a short burst of laughter. 'Eee, it only took us nigh on five months.'

'Not that I minded being dragged there,' Bill said. *Talk about an understatement.* 'I quite enjoyed our day trips. The

401

scenic train journeys. The pub lunches … Makes a change from being stuck here day in, day out.'

'I knar,' Pearl agreed. 'Take out dropping in at the asylum 'n they would have been grand.'

'I suppose we could—' Bill started to say when Pearl suddenly jumped off her stool.

'I keep forgetting …' she said, ducking behind the bar and grabbing her handbag. She came back out, repositioned herself on her stool and began scrabbling around in her bag.

Bill watched her.

'There it is!' she said, giving a big sigh of relief. 'Thought fer a moment I might've lost it. Eee, my heart's going nineteen to the dozen.' She put her hand on her bony chest to prove her point. With her other hand, she held up Bill's ex-wife's wedding ring.

'If yer've gor any sense,' Pearl said, her thumb and forefinger pinching the gold band, 'yer'll flog this 'n get yerself a bit of dosh.'

Bill looked at the ring before taking it from Pearl.

Pearl took a sip of her drink and a puff on her cigarette and watched as Bill got off his stool and lowered himself to the floor so that he was on one knee.

'Have yer dropped it, yer clumsy clot?' Pearl was scouring the floor, looking for a glint of gold.

'I've not lost anything, Pearl,' he said, looking up at her.

It was only then that Pearl saw he was holding the ring in his right hand. His left was on his knee, keeping him steady.

'Wot yer deeing, yer daft beggar? Yer been at the Christmas spirit or summat?' Pearl was trying to sound jovial, but in truth she was shocked.

'Not yet,' Bill said with a laugh, 'but I fully intend to later.'

'Come on, ger up!' Pearl laughed nervously.

'I was wondering,' Bill said, not making any attempt to move, 'if you would like to wear this for real?' He held the ring up to Pearl, his eyes searching her face, desperate to see something, anything other than an outright rejection.

'What yer talking about, yer daft ha'p'orth?' Pearl said.

'I'm asking you to be my wife. For real. Not for pretend,' Bill said.

Pearl stared at Bill.

She opened her mouth, but nothing came out.

Pearl reached down to take the hand that was holding the ring and helped Bill to his feet. In all the time he had known Pearl, Bill had never seen her so serious. So tongue-tied.

'What's wrong?' he asked.

'Nowt's wrong,' Pearl said.

Bill put his arms around her, pulled her off the stool and held her close.

'I love you, Pearl Hardwick,' he whispered into her ear. 'And I want you to be my wife.'

Pearl looked up at Bill.

She opened her mouth to give him her answer.

'*Ma!*'

They both heard Bel's voice before they saw her.

They immediately jumped apart like two teenagers caught canoodling.

Bel banged through the lounge door.

'Ma?' Bel looked at her mother and then at Bill. They both looked guilty.

'You all right?' she asked.

'Course I am,' Pearl said.

'How much has she had to drink?' Bel asked Bill.

'Just that.' Bill nodded to the whisky that had barely been touched.

'Good,' Bel said.

She looked at Pearl.

'I'm keeping my promise,' she said simply.

Pearl didn't say anything, just grabbed her handbag and then her winter coat.

She looked at Bill.

'I'll give yer my answer when I get back.'

And with that she turned and followed her daughter out of the pub and into the street.

'Need I ask where we're gannin?' Pearl asked as they walked down Tatham Street. It was now almost deserted. It was getting dark. Everyone was inside, in front of roaring fires, enjoying the rest of their Christmas Day.

Bel didn't answer. Her ma knew full well where they were going.

'That all sounded very cryptic,' Bel said as they crunched through snow, hitting the pavement as they walked under the railway track. '"I'll give yer my answer when I get back"?'

'None of yer business,' Pearl said as they turned right into Salem Street.

They trudged through grey-white snow that was now turning to slush.

'So, come on,' Pearl demanded. 'What's the plan?'

Bel took a deep, nervous breath and checked her watch. She was hoping she had timed this right.

As they turned left onto Toward Road and made their way to the place Pearl had done her hardest to avoid since she'd left there all those years ago, Bel told her ma her intentions.

Pearl listened.

If she was surprised at anything her daughter said, she didn't show it.

When they finally reached the long stretch of road known as The Cedars their feet were numb. Neither of them cared. Both were concentrating on what was to come.

The overhanging trees that lined the wide residential road might have been bare of leaves, but their snow-laden branches still acted as a partial canopy, which had kept the pavement clear. Bel stepped up her pace now they were unhindered by icy slush. If she slowed down, she might chicken out, change her mind.

And she had to do this.

Had to.

Pearl struggled to keep up. This was the second time she'd been over this way today, and after being on her feet most of the afternoon, she was tired. She forced her legs to move more quickly. She could rest when all of this was over – hopefully for good. Hopefully, after today, she could leave this godforsaken place behind. For bloody ever.

By the time they turned right into Glen Path, they felt the beginning of sleet on their faces and then the odd hailstone.

Bel put her hand over her face to stop the sting of ice on flesh.

Was this a sign she should turn back?

Well, if it was, it was too late.

She looked at her ma as they reached the driveway of the Havelock residence.

Pearl had her handbag on her head to try and protect herself from the hailstones now spitting down fast and furious.

She felt her stomach turn as they both stepped onto the gravelled driveway and walked up to the front door.

Chapter Fifty-Six

Can I help you?' Eddy looked down at the two women who were now covered in identical cloaks of speckled white.

Pearl stared up at him, as she had done that night all those years ago. The man had barely changed. He was the same, just older.

'We've come to see Mr Charles Havelock,' Bel said in her best King's English. She was trying hard to keep the nervousness out of her voice, just as George VI had tried his hardest to hide his speech impediment when he addressed the Commonwealth.

'Well, I very much doubt he will be seeing uninvited guests today,' Eddy said, scrutinising the two women. 'It being *Christmas Day*, after all.'

Bel stopped herself snapping back that they were well aware of what day it was. It was *because* it was Christmas Day that they were here.

Eddy gave the two women another sweeping look, from the shabby leather boots they were wearing to their worn winter coats. There was something about the older woman, though, that seemed vaguely familiar. He left the door ajar and disappeared.

Pearl looked at her ma, who had gone as white as a sheet. She wondered if it had been such a good idea to bring her. Pearl had been hardly able to bear looking at the place the last time they were there and then they'd been across the road – not about to walk into the house she had avoided like the plague her entire life.

They both heard Helen's voice before they saw her.

'Well, didn't they say who they are, Eddy?' There was the clip-clop of heels on the tiled hallway as she approached the partially closed front door. 'What? You just left them out there – in the middle of a snowstorm?'

Hearing the impatience and put-down in Helen's tone made Pearl feel the first smatterings of sympathy towards the Havelock girl.

The large oak door swung open. Helen was standing there in the same dress she had worn for the christening.

'Oh my goodness!' she said as soon as she saw who it was. 'Come in, come in, before you both freeze to death.' She gave Eddy a look like the summons, stood aside and waved them both in.

Bel forced a smile, took a deep breath and stepped into the warmth.

Pearl followed. For a moment she was the Little Match Girl – fifteen years old, about to drop with exhaustion and desperate for a job and a roof over her head. She forced herself back into the present. She had to stay with it, be strong. This was important. Probably one of the most important things she had done in her life. And for once, she wasn't going to mess it up, like she did most things.

'My, my, who do we have here?' Miriam was leaning against the open doorway of the dining room where they had just finished the final course of their Christmas meal. As Miriam had started drinking earlier than normal, she was already a few sheets to the wind.

'Come in and get warm.' Helen ushered Bel and Pearl past her mother, who managed to look down her nose at them despite being the same height.

Bel looked at Miriam as she walked past her, smelled the gin. It still felt odd that she was her sister. Strangely enough, she reminded her more of her ma.

Bel and Pearl's white cloaks started to fade as they entered the warmth of the large dining room where the fire was blazing. Pearl scanned the room; it hadn't changed, not one bit.

'Eddy!' Helen commanded. 'Take their coats and put them somewhere to dry.'

Pearl chalked up another brownie point for the Havelock girl.

She shook off her coat and handed it to Eddy. She wondered if he recognised her. Unlikely. She had changed a lot since then.

Bel put down her handbag and gas mask and turned her back to Eddy, forcing him to help her out of her damp woollen coat. She had seen the rich women do the same when she'd been at the Grand. Eddy obliged. He had no choice. They were the guests. He the servant.

Free of her coat, Helen saw that Bel was also wearing the black dress she'd had on yesterday. She looked stunning. Regal almost.

Pearl looked at her daughter and felt a swell of pride.

Miriam a surge of pure envy.

There were now two beautiful young women in the room – one a dead ringer for Betty Grable, the other a Vivien Leigh lookalike.

'Well, well, well, who do we have here?' Mr Havelock's voice boomed from the far end of the long dining-room table. He had been taking in every detail of his two impromptu guests. At last some excitement on this dreary, uneventful Christmas Day spent with a daughter who was a lush and a granddaughter who was barely able to disguise her dislike of him.

'Forgive me if I don't stand to greet you,' he said, glancing down at his legs, 'but I'm not quite as mobile as I used to be.'

408

Bel knew this to be a lie. His legs had moved perfectly well at all the launches she'd seen him at.

His eyes narrowed as he studied mother and daughter.

For a moment, Pearl was snapped back into the past, standing with all the other servants, part of Henrietta's 'cavalry', being inspected by the master as though they were cattle.

'I think you know who your guests are, Grandfather,' Helen butted in, stepping forward so that her hands were resting on the back of a dining chair. 'This is Mrs Isabelle Elliot, whom you have met a few times at various launches.' She then turned her attention to Pearl. 'And this is her mother, Miss Pearl Hardwick.'

Bel returned Mr Havelock's penetrating stare. A smile was playing on his thin lips. She saw for the first time a glimpse of the cruelty he thrived on.

Did he know?

No, he couldn't.

Could he?

'Of course, of course,' Mr Havelock said, reaching for his cigar, which was lying on the side of a large cut-crystal ashtray. 'Like my legs, the old memory isn't quite what it was.'

Another lie. Did anything truthful ever come out of the man's mouth?

Bel caught Miriam snickering as she walked over to her seat at the table and sat down.

'Would our guests like a drink?' Mr Havelock asked, the epitome of geniality.

Eddy looked at the pretty blonde and then at her washed-out-looking mother. *He knew her. He was sure of it.*

'No, thank you, Eddy,' Bel said.

Eddy thought her tone was familiar – as though she knew him, or at least knew of him.

'Ma, would you like anything to drink? I'm sure *Eddy* here will be pleased to oblige, or perhaps Agatha can make you a hot drink?'

Eddy looked at Bel. *She does. She knows me and she knows Agatha too.*

And then it clicked. *The young woman who'd quizzed them about one of the maids.* He looked at Pearl. This worn-out wreck of a woman was Henrietta's Little Match Girl.

Pearl looked at Eddy and saw the recognition in his eyes.

'I'll have another G and T, Eddy,' Miriam chirped up. 'Looks like I'm staying a little longer. The day's suddenly got interesting.'

Bel glanced at Miriam and then at the huge Christmas tree in the corner and she felt the cohorts of anger marching forward.

'As I'm sure you're aware,' Bel said, looking from Miriam to Mr Havelock, 'this isn't a social call.'

She picked up her handbag from the floor and placed it on the table.

'I've come here to tell you ...' Bel looked her father in the eye.

Just then Eddy came back with Miriam's gin and tonic balanced on a silver tray. He placed it in front of the woman he'd known since she was a child. Not that this endeared her to him any more.

'That'll be all, Eddy.' Mr Havelock gave him his orders.

Eddy did as he was told. Walking out of the room with the tray under his arm, he left the door ajar just enough so that he and Agatha could eavesdrop.

'I'm sorry, Mrs Elliot,' Mr Havelock said, the sneering smile back again. 'What was it you were about to say?'

Bel took a breath, but again was interrupted.

410

'Sorry, my dear,' he said, 'I've a terrible habit of interrupting people. My granddaughter's always reprimanding me for it, aren't you?'

He narrowed his eyes at Helen, who was still standing, her manicured red nails gripping the top of the chair. The look he gave her was wholly without mirth.

'You do, Grandfather,' she said, returning the look.

A smile slid across Mr Havelock's face. 'I also like to guess what people are going to say –' he looked back at Bel '– and I would bet my net worth, which is substantial, that you are going to inform me that I am your father.' She'd always reminded him of someone, from first seeing her at the old diver's funeral, but it was only recently that he'd realised the person she reminded him of was himself.

Bel glowered back at him. *Damn it! This was meant to be her surprise. Her Christmas present.* She felt the anger breaking through the surface.

'Well,' Bel said, trying to keep her voice steady, 'if you were a betting man you would keep your net worth, Mr Havelock, for I *am* your daughter – much as it pains me greatly to have to admit it.'

Mr Havelock let out a bitter laugh.

'Well, it would seem you have the Havelocks' acid tongue. Either that or you have been spending too much time with my darling granddaughter.'

He again turned his attention to Helen, who, in turn, threw Bel a concerned look.

'Oh, dear me. Not again,' Miriam butted in, faking a yawn. 'Not another impostor trying to bleed us dry of our hard-earned cash.'

Mr Havelock looked at his daughter, who was now beginning to slur her words; *she* had never done a *day's* work, never mind a *hard* day's work, in her life.

411

Bel dug inside her handbag and pulled out the two-page report that Helen had given her in the hallway of the Tatham after Artie's christening.

'I have here evidence that proves I'm not an *impostor*.' She threw Miriam a scathing look. *Was the woman blind?* Apart from the age gap, they looked identical. Same nose, lips, complexion and hair.

'Apart from the fact that we look so alike ...' Bel spoke directly to Mr Havelock '... I have in my possession a report that I believe would likely stand up in a court of law as evidence that you did father me. Coupled with the result of a blood test to show blood type, I think you might find that it would be ruled that I am not some charlatan, but, as I've said once before, *unfortunately* your daughter.' Bel could feel her body start to tremble. A combination of nerves and anger.

She walked over to the man who had sired her and spread the two sheets of evidence in front of him.

'And,' she hissed, 'I will make it perfectly plain that my mother was in no way a willing participant in my conception. I will tell the judge and jury and anyone else who will listen that you are a rapist. A sick and perverted old man who likes nothing more than violating young girls – and when I say "young", I mean *young*.' Bel swung her head to look at her mother, who was now sitting in a chair that was positioned across from Miriam.

'How old were you again, Ma?' Bel didn't wait for an answer. Her poor mother looked as white as the snow falling outside.

'*Fifteen years old*,' Bel said.

She looked at Miriam and then back at Mr Havelock.

'And if my knowledge of the law serves me right, the age of consent in our country is sixteen.' Her visit to the library had been well worth it.

Mr Havelock looked at the woman he knew was his. *How dare she speak to him like this?* His eyes blazed with pure fury. For a moment Bel thought he would strike her. She fought the impulse to take a step back.

'Get out! Get out!' Miriam demanded. 'How dare you and your slut of a mother come in here, spouting such poison.'

Bel saw her ma start to get out of her chair; knew she wanted nothing more than to rip this vile woman to shreds. She threw her a warning look and Pearl forced herself to remain seated.

'Eddy!' Mr Havelock looked over everyone's heads at the partially closed door, behind which he knew his man-servant and housekeeper would be listening to every word.

In a beat, Eddy reappeared. He still had the silver tray under his arm.

'Be a good chap and go into my office and bring me my chequebook.' Mr Havelock was desperately trying to claw back his couldn't-care-less demeanour, but the little bitch had rankled him.

Eddy nodded, his face deathly serious. He turned and left the room.

Suddenly, Agatha arrived in his place. 'Excuse me, sir, do you want me to call the police?'

'For God's sake, Agatha.' Helen turned around to look at the housekeeper. 'Do you see any need to call the police? Is anyone being attacked or hurt in any way?'

Everyone looked at Mr Havelock's granddaughter. She had just shown whose side she was on. There wasn't a person in the room who wasn't taken aback. Mr Havelock, Miriam, Eddy and Agatha had never thought that Helen would go against her own flesh and blood.

Neither had Pearl. Bel was the least surprised. She threw Helen a look that spoke her gratitude. Agatha straightened her back and pursed her lips but remained standing where she was. Eddy hurried back in with the chequebook and pen and walked the length of the table to where the master was sitting.

Bel looked at Eddy and then turned to stare at Agatha. 'You two,' she said, her voice strong, 'you knew what was going on, but you turned a blind eye. You did nothing.'

Agatha stuck her nose up in the air. Eddy inspected his shiny black butler's shoes.

Mr Havelock seemed indifferent to Bel's words.

'Right,' he said, pulling the top off his pen. He was now all business. 'How much do you want?' He looked up at Bel but ignored Pearl, whose eyes he felt upon him for the first time. 'I will also, of course, have to get you to sign a legal disclaimer.'

It was now obvious to them all that this was not the first time someone had come knocking at Mr Havelock's door, accusing him of paternity, and been sent packing with a pay-off.

'Oh, Mr Havelock,' Bel said, bitterness and vitriol dripping from her voice, 'I don't want your money. Far, far from it.'

Mr Havelock cocked his head and appraised Bel.

'So, what do you want, Mrs Elliot?'

Bel took a step back. She needed to get a little distance between herself and this monster whose blood she shared.

'I thought you liked to guess what people are just about to say?' Bel forced herself to look at her father. It sickened her to see just how similar they looked.

Only then did it hit her – like a bolt from the blue – and she realised why her ma had struggled to love her.

She had been a constant reminder of the man who had raped her and ruined her life.

414

Bel made herself concentrate. All of a sudden, she just wanted this done. She wanted to leave this place and never come back. Just like her ma had done all those years ago.

'Justice,' Bel spat out. 'What I really want is *justice*.'

She looked at Helen, whose attention was flicking between Bel and Mr Havelock.

'I want justice for what you did to my ma – and God knows how many other young girls. I'd like you strung up. I want the whole world to know exactly what you are.'

Bel glanced at Miriam, who now looked a little lost. Or was that the effect of the gin?

'But,' she added, 'I'm not stupid enough to think that what I want is possible.'

'This is getting interesting,' Mr Havelock said, closing his chequebook and putting down his pen.

Bel clenched her fists.

He smiled. 'Please, do carry on.'

Bel took a deep breath. She glanced at Miriam again. This concerned her, after all.

'In exchange for my silence, I want Jack to be able to return home. To be with the woman he loves, but more than anything to be a father to his little girl, Hope.'

There, she had said it. Now she really did just want to get this done and go.

'You cannot be serious!' Miriam banged her glass down on the table, her mouth taut. 'My husband,' she spat the words out, 'is not going anywhere, my dear. He's staying exactly where he is – over the border and as far away from this place as possible.' She let out a slightly hysterical laugh. *How had the spotlight suddenly turned on her?* 'He's certainly not going to set up home back here with his mistress and his bastard.'

Out of the corner of her eye, Bel saw Helen turn and glare at Miriam. She could tell this was the second skinning alive Miriam had just dodged. Her luck was going to run out if she wasn't careful.

Helen looked at Bel and her respect for her grew tenfold. She had always liked her as a person and as a friend, but what she had just done had taken her aback.

Bel could have taken her grandfather to court – she mightn't have won, but she would have had the satisfaction of seeing his name dragged through the mire and being tarnished for ever, and there was always the threat that more of her grandfather's victims might come out of the woodwork. But instead, Bel had sacrificed her burning need for vengeance to help Hope – to give a little girl her daddy back.

It was exactly what Helen had wanted to do with the report – she had said as much to John all those months ago. If *she* had done it, though, it would have been for personal gain. Hope was her sister, and bringing Jack home would give Helen her father back too. But Bel wasn't getting anything out of this. It was incredibly unselfish. True kindness.

Helen quickly turned to leave but bumped into Eddy and Agatha, who hadn't had a chance to move out of the way.

'If I were you two, I'd start packing my bags. You're both named in that report,' she hissed, before slipping out of the room and walking across the hallway and into her grandfather's office.

Shutting the door, she hurried over to his desk and picked up the receiver of his shiny black Bakelite phone.

'Well, that's a very honourable ask,' Mr Havelock said to Bel. 'A very apt sentiment for this time of year.'

He took a sip of his whisky. He was back in control and loving it. It was time for him to play his trump card, now that he'd seen his opponent's hand.

416

'Relinquishing your need for revenge – and a substantial amount of money, I have to add – for the happiness of my son-in-law's illegitimate daughter.'

He gave a sickly smile.

'But it's not really about the child called Hope, is it? This is about you. You see yourself in Hope. A young girl with no father to speak of.'

He lit his cigar and puffed.

'It must have been hard, growing up a bastard. Children can be so cruel, can't they?'

For the first time he looked at Pearl.

'Unless your mother here spun some yarn about your father being a war hero. I do believe that was quite a common story from the mouths of young mothers back then who found themselves in the family way with no man about the house.'

'She would never have given you that honour,' Bel spat back. 'She told me you were dead. And how I wish to God that had really been the case. Hopefully, I'll get my wish one day soon.'

Mr Havelock laughed.

'Oh, sorry to disappoint, my dear, but the Havelocks are known for their longevity. I certainly don't intend to shuffle off this mortal coil any time soon.'

He sighed.

'Well, much as I would love to sit here and banter –' he looked up at the clock '– time is getting on, so I'll keep it brief and to the point. You, my dear,' he said to Bel as though she were a schoolchild, 'will leave here with no more and no less than what you arrived with, because, you see, I have been doing my own research, just as you did.'

He pushed the two sheets of paper away from him as Helen came back into the room.

'And as a result, I know *all* about you, your crippled husband, the daughter you had with your first husband – and I know all about the woman who's been like a second mother to you. And, of course, I know all about your *ma*.' He looked at Pearl.

Every word he spoke felt like a threat.

'And so it will come as no surprise that I know you also have another half-sister, another bastard – and *coloured* at that, although I have to say, a very beautiful, very exotic-looking woman – who calls herself Maisie Smith.' He raised his eyebrows to show his scepticism. 'I know that Maisie was formally adopted as a baby and that she has led a very unconventional life.'

Bel was feeling more uncomfortable by the second.

'Unconventional and – many would say – immoral.' He looked around the room. He was enjoying the attention. 'I do hope I'm not telling you anything you don't know?' he asked with false sincerity. He looked at Bel.

Her heart sank. If he knew what she thought he knew, then he had the upper hand.

'You see, I found out – much to my surprise and quite by mistake, I have to add – that Maisie not only runs the Ashbrooke Gentlemen's Club, which is apparently so popular it can deny membership to my good self, she also works next door. And that might look from the outside to be a normal residential home – albeit a very grandiose one – but it is in point of fact an upmarket whorehouse ... a house of ill repute ... a bordello, brothel, call it what you may.' He paused, enjoying the look of defeat on Bel's face.

'So, you see –' he made a point of looking at his watch as though he was late for another appointment '– if you say or do anything which in any way threatens me or my family, I will take what I know to the authorities, who I'm sure will be round there at the speed of light. And it wouldn't be because they want what's on offer, tempting though that might be.'

He chuckled.

'And obviously it goes without saying that all of the secrets of the women who work at Thompson's will be unveiled to the outside world.'

He paused.

'And that I will, of course, also take great pleasure in finding ways of ruining not only *your* life, Mrs Isabelle Elliot, but also the lives of all those you hold dear.'

Mr Havelock surveyed the room and was heartened by all the shocked faces.

Pearl took a deep breath. It was time. She stood, straightening herself up to her full five feet. Everyone looked at her. Since walking into the house, she had not uttered a single word.

'Like yer just said, time's gerrin' on,' she began, 'so I'll not fanny around 'n use ten words when one'll dee.' Her focus was on Charles. She battered back the image of his face that night. 'Yer've raped God knars how many young girls – like yer did me – girls who had nothing 'n no one. Yer hurt those yer knew damn well couldn't fight back. Yer took what wasn't yers 'n yer ruined lives.'

Her eyes were boring into him. 'Remember Gracie? ... Nah, course not, they must've all merged into one. Well, yer mightn't be able to remember her, but her mam 'n dad remember you – remember how their girl came to this house to work, all happy as Larry 'cos she'd got a job as a chambermaid, thought she might even end up a lady's maid fer the mistress if she worked hard. But she left, didn't she? Shortly before I got took on.'

419

She stopped. 'But I'm getting ahead of myself here.' She looked around. It seemed that everyone had turned to statues and it was only her and Charles in the room.

'Yer did the same to Gracie as yer did to me, and like me, Gracie ended up with yer bastard growing in her belly. Aye – yer've gorra son 'n all.'

She took a deep breath. 'Her mam 'n dad weren't sure whether their Gracie did what she did 'cos of what yer did to her, or 'cos she had to give the bab up 'n it broke her heart, but a few months after she gave up the poor little mite, Gracie's mam came back one day from the shops 'n found her hanging from the bannister. Poor woman went grey overnight. She said she'd be happy for the truth to come out. Yer see, sometimes things happen to a person 'n they don't care any more. About anything.'

The room was so quiet you could hear a pin drop. 'But I'm digressing,' she said. 'We were talking about my girl Maisie, weren't we?' Pearl kept her focus on Charles.

'She told me yer'd wanted to join the club – that she turned yer down – said the thought of having yer there, knowing what yer did to me 'n other young girls, made her feel sick. She knew, though, that yer'd try 'n get yer own back –'cos that's what people like yer are like. She knew there was a good chance yer'd find out about Lily's place when yer started poking yer nose around, 'n that yer'd probably try 'n use it as some kind of leverage.'

She surveyed the room. 'Well, I saw her this morning 'n she said to tell yer that if yer want to grass them all up, that's fine by them, most of them would ger off with a slap on the wrists 'n some sort of paltry fine, but if yer did gan ahead 'n dob them all in it, then Lily's little black book, which isn't so little by all accounts, will also find its way into the hands of the police. And that every one of those businessmen, judges, lawyers 'n high-up coppers in that little black book will know that it's yer fault that their names are being chalked up on some blackboard in police headquarters – that it's yer fault they're being pulled in for solicitation, *yer fault* they're the laughing stock of the upper crust, *yer fault* their wives sent them packing.

'So,' Pearl said, looking at her watch, 'yer give Isabelle ... yer give *my daughter* – and I say *my* daughter 'cos she's not yers, never was 'n never will be – yer'll give her what she wants 'n we'll call it quits.'

She looked at the old man.

'Forgive me if we dinnit shake on it. We'll just take each other's word for it. Agreed?'

Mr Havelock looked at the woman he remembered well as a fifteen-year-old. She was wrong to say they all merged into one. He remembered them all.

'*Agreed?*' It was Helen.

Mr Havelock looked at the Judas in the family. 'Agreed.' He said the word through clenched teeth, glowering at Pearl. The bitch might have got the better of him today, but there was always tomorrow. He would not be defeated. Not by the likes of her.

Pearl turned as though to walk away but stopped suddenly in her tracks.

'*Bloody Nora,*' she said, smacking her hand on her forehead, 'I'd forget my head if it was loose.'

She looked at Mr Havelock. She dropped the faux joviality. Her face was now deathly serious. 'I nearly forgot to tell yer that Henrietta says to wish yer a Merry Christmas.'

Mr Havelock stared at Pearl.

She saw for the first time a glimmer of fear in his eyes, making every sickening second of being back in this house worth it. She looked away and towards the other end of the room. 'Eddy! Me 'n Isabelle will have our coats now, thank yer very much.'

Mr Havelock made to get out of his chair.

'What do you mean, *Henrietta says Merry Christmas*?' He glanced nervously over at Miriam, who returned an equally worried look.

Pearl laughed. 'Honestly, sometimes yer educated folk can be really thick.' She laboured over each word. 'Henrietta. Says. Merry. Christmas.'

Eddy had come back into the room with both coats.

Pearl copied her daughter from earlier and stood with her back to Eddy while he helped her into her still-damp coat. He had purposely not put it on the radiator to dry.

'Well,' Mr Havelock said, still not sure if Pearl was bluffing and hoping to God she was, 'I didn't know the dead spoke. Unless you've been to some sort of seance.' He forced a laugh.

'I think yer well knar that yer wife is alive – and very well, actually. Yer daughter will confirm that, won't yer, Miriam? Yer ma's making much more sense lately. Very coherent. Henrietta was telling me all about her new doctor. Some skinny woman with a strange surname.' She pretended to think for a moment, enjoying the looks of growing horror on both their faces. 'Eris ... that's the one. Dr Eris.'

'What – you mean Grandma's alive?' Helen was gobsmacked. She looked at her mother and then at her grandfather. *And what was this about her being looked after by Dr Eris?*

'Not that anyone knows who Henrietta is,' Pearl said. 'I think yer'll find yer grandda made her into a "Miss" and gave her the name "Girling".'

Pearl looked at Bel and gave her the briefest of smiles.

'I knar what yer all thinking. How did I find out that Henrietta was not just alive, but holed up in the local loony bin? Well, a little bit like the *master* here,' Pearl said the word in a tone that could only be described as contemptuous, 'it was completely by chance. Some might say it was divine intervention; I think it was probably just coincidence. But whatever it was, me 'n Henrietta were reunited. Fancy that, eh?'

She looked at Eddy and Agatha standing in the open doorway. Agatha's chin was practically touching the floor.

'And once we'd been reacquainted ...' she paused '... the mistress showed herself as having a good memory. Very good indeed. Recognised me straight away, she did.' She paused again. 'You see, I'd always wondered – did Henrietta knar what was going on under this roof?'

Pearl's attention was back on Mr Havelock. 'Over the years, I've wondered if perhaps she was as sick in the head as yer are 'n if she was gerrin' the maids fer yer – to keep yer happy. I even wondered if she did it so that yer wouldn't start on yer own daughters, 'cos let's face it, we all looked like them, didn't we?'

Pearl looked at Miriam. She had gone a ghostly shade of grey.

'But Henrietta didn't knar, did she? Not fer a good while – she's the kind of person doesn't like to think anything bad, lives with her head up in the clouds most of the time, or in some book. It might have taken the mistress a bit longer than it would've done most, but she eventually worked it out ... Ahh, the irony of it all. Henrietta was gerrin' maids that looked like her two girls 'cos she missed them – missed her two daughters, what with them always being away at some posh school. But, dear, dear, when she realised she'd been bringing yer prey on a silver platter, she was not pleased – not pleased at all.'

Pearl was staring at Mr Havelock. Now she had forced herself to face him, she couldn't take her eyes off him.

'She found out what yer were deeing, told yer she knew, said she was gonna blow the whistle on yer – yer must have got quite a shock. Talk about the worm turning.'

Pearl looked round at her audience – all speechless.

'So, what did yer dee? Yer banged her up so she wouldn't spill the beans on yer, didn't yer?'

Her eyes fell on Miriam.

'Yer da got yer ma locked up, pet, which, let's face it, was easily enough done. She was naturally short of a slice or two, but she was no madwoman. She'd never have hurt a fly. But yer father here –' she nodded in disgust at the head of the table '– greased the necessary palms. Gor her taken away. And, it gans without saying, no one would believe the word of a madwoman over that of Mr Charles Havelock. Especially when he was dangling a large cheque in front of them like a big fat juicy carrot, with more on the horizon if they played ball.'

'Did you, Father?' Miriam's voice was uncannily low. 'Did you get Mother locked up?'

'Well, yer'll be able to ask her for yerself now, pet,' Pearl butted in. 'She's singing like a bird, although at the moment she's just singing to me and one other person who shall remain nameless. Of course, I can always ask her to keep it to herself for the time being. We've become quite the chums, me 'n Henrietta.'

Pearl buttoned up her coat. The show was just about over.

Bel took the cue and stood up. Her mother had played her winning hand – *and what a hand it was*.

'So, we'll just see how things pan out, eh?' Pearl said.

She looked at Mr Havelock and then Miriam, before addressing Helen.

'I'm really looking forward to meeting yer da, pet. Sounds like a lovely man. I'll let him settle in first, though.

He's got so much catching up to dee with little Hope, bless her.'

She gave Mr Havelock one last look before turning and walking out of the dining room with her daughter by her side.

Chapter Fifty-Seven

As they turned right out of the driveway and started along Glen Path, neither woman spoke for a short while. Bel looked up at the black skeleton arms of the trees lining the road, their ghoulishness redeemed by the glistening frost and the patches of fresh snow that seemed to illuminate the darkness.

They walked on through the snow. It was sparkling white. A fresh layer had covered the icy grey slush they had trudged through on the way there.

'Why didn't you tell me about Henrietta?' Bel said eventually. There were so many questions she wanted to ask, so many things she wanted to say to her ma, she hardly knew where to start.

'I *did* tell yer about Henrietta,' Pearl said.

'Just that time you'd wandered into her room by mistake,' Bel said, glancing at her ma. 'You didn't say you'd been there to visit her – and frequently, by the sounds of it.' Suddenly the penny dropped. 'Of course, your days out with Bill!' She stared at Pearl. 'There was us all thinking you two were going out on dates.'

Bel laughed. She felt high. Drunk on all that had taken place.

'I should have guessed,' she said as they walked on. 'Borrowing Agnes's dress! Eee, Ma, you can be a bit of a dark horse, can't you?'

Bel was walking fast and Pearl was struggling to keep up. It was as though every ounce of energy had been sapped from her. All she wanted was to be sitting in the Tatham with a large whisky in front of her. She'd definitely earned one.

As they turned left and started walking along The Cedars, they both jumped when they heard a car hoot its horn behind them.

It was Helen in her green sports car.

She pulled over, leant across to the passenger door and opened it.

'Hop in, you two, this is your sleigh ride back home!' She too was feeling intoxicated, even though she'd not had a drop to drink.

Pearl jumped in first, not caring that she'd be shoulder to shoulder with the Havelock girl. Bel squeezed in after and pulled the door shut.

As they slowly made their way along the wide, tree-lined street, then across Ryhope Road and down Villette Road, Pearl's eye caught a flash of red. It was a robin redbreast and it had settled on the wooden gate to the Barley Mow Park – opposite the street where Gracie's mam and dad lived.

For the first time, Pearl smiled.

When they turned into Tatham Street, they were surprised to see everyone outside the pub rather than inside in the warmth.

As they got nearer, they saw why – the Salvation Army brass band was blasting out 'Good King Wenceslas' and everyone was singing along.

> *Good King Wenceslas looked out*
> *On the Feast of Stephen,*
> *When the snow lay round about*
> *Deep and crisp and even.*

Brightly shone the moon that night,
Though the frost was cruel
When a poor man came in sight,
Gath'ring winter fuel.

As they climbed out of the car, they heard the trumpets and cornets and surprisingly in-tune vocals.

'Hither, page, and stand by me,
If thou know'st it, telling,
Yonder peasant, who is he?
Where and what his dwelling?'
'Sire, he lives a good league hence,
Underneath the mountain,
Right against the forest fence,
By Saint Agnes' fountain.'

As the three women crunched through the fresh snow, dodging an energetic snowball fight, they saw that their family and friends were in the crowd.

'Bring me flesh, and bring me wine,
Bring me pine logs hither,
Thou and I will see him dine,
When we bear them thither.'
Page and monarch, forth they went,
Forth they went together,
Through the rude wind's wild lament
And the bitter weather.

Polly was standing with Artie, who was so well wrapped up against the cold he looked as if he was in a cocoon. Next to her were Agnes and Beryl, arms linked, and behind them were Iris and Audrey, who were singing their hearts out and smiling at the two Home Guard lads on either side of them.

> *'Sire, the night is darker now,*
> *And the wind blows stronger,*
> *Fails my heart, I know not how;*
> *I can go no longer.'*
> *'Mark my footsteps, my good page,*
> *Tread thou in them boldly,*
> *Thou shalt find the winter's rage*
> *Freeze thy blood less coldly.'*

Toby was standing behind Dorothy, his arms wrapped around her, keeping her warm. Angie was linking arms with Kate, who was standing next to Alfie. Mr Perkins had his arm around Mrs Perkins, and Hannah and Olly were holding gloved hands next to them.

> *In his master's steps he trod,*
> *Where the snow lay dinted;*
> *Heat was in the very sod*
> *Which the Saint had printed.*

Rosie was standing behind Charlotte and had her hands on her shoulders; both looked happy, very happy. Martha was towering at the back, not wanting to spoil everyone's view of the smartly decked Christian soldiers who were filling the street with the sound of Christmas.

Gloria was next to her holding a tired-looking Hope, her legs wrapped round her mammy like a monkey. As soon as she spotted her big sister, her little face lit up. Helen hurried over, a little unsteady in her high heels.

Therefore, Christian men, be sure,
Wealth or rank possessing,
Ye who now will bless the poor
Shall yourselves find blessing.

Bel turned when she heard her daughter cry out 'Mammy!' and saw Lucille charging towards them. Bending down, she picked up her little girl, gave her a cuddle and put her back down.

'Nana!' Lucille looked up at her grandma.

Pearl ruffled her granddaughter's hair.

'All right, pet,' she said. 'Yer had a good Christmas Day?'

Lucille nodded.

'Eee, well, best get myself a drink before I die of thirst,' she said, turning to go to the pub.

Bel caught her arm.

'Thanks, Ma,' she said.

'Nowt to thank us fer, Isabelle.'

Bel smiled as she watched her ma make a beeline for the Tatham.

Chapter Fifty-Eight

As soon as Helen had left in her car, Miriam had demanded that the chauffeur, who was meant to be having a day off, drive her to the Grand – drive her anywhere, as long as it was away from the house.

Looking out of the window as they drove down Ryhope Road, she recalled the day her father had told her he had been forced to commit their mother. It had been a shock, but she had not questioned his actions. Why would she? The lie he'd constructed about her mother dying abroad had made sense. They were saving her good name – the family's good name.

Had her mother really tried to do the right thing and been punished for it?

As they drove into the town centre, she thought of Eddy and Agatha. *Had they known?* The looks on their faces suggested they had. *No, no, no, no, she did not want to think about all of this.* But she had to – how could she not? Had a part of her known all along what her father was really like? Was that why she and Margaret had always orchestrated invites to friends' houses over the holidays, so that they spent as little time as possible at home when their father was there?

God, she wished Margaret lived nearer. She was the only person she would be able to confide in.

As the car pulled up on Bridge Street, Miriam was already planning a trip to her sister's in the New Year – if not before. Tomorrow even. She needed to get away. Run away.

Her father was a rapist.

A monster who had imprisoned their mother.

And now, to top it all, she would have to face the ridicule of Jack coming back.

The humiliation when the gossipmongers got wind.

The hurt he would bring with him.

Miriam stepped out of the car and walked up the steps to the Grand.

She needed a drink.

Chapter Fifty-Nine

After the Salvation Army had moved on, everyone piled back into the warmth of the pub.

Bel, her mind whirring with so many thoughts and feelings, found a seat in a relatively quiet corner and told Joe all that had happened.

Joe, of course, was just relieved that Bel was all right. Knowing her intentions, he'd been worried sick from the moment she'd left Vera's. They had talked about it beforehand. Bel had told him that she believed her failure to fall pregnant was perpetuating her need for vengeance, but she'd realised that even if she satiated her need for retribution, she'd still be left with a feeling of emptiness. Hatred and vehemence had blinded her – and once they had been pushed aside, she had been able to see more clearly. More rationally.

And with that new perspective, she had decided to use what she had to do good.

Joe wondered how long it would take Jack to get back home once he got wind of what had happened and realised he was now a free man.

All the women knew something was up, though not what, when Bel had snuck off as the King's speech was starting. Joe had said she needed to sort out a family matter. They knew not to probe further. When they'd seen Helen, Bel and Pearl arrive at the pub together, they knew whatever it was, it must have been serious – but also that whatever had happened had gone in their favour as they all looked happy.

Tired but happy.

Pearl told Bill what had occurred over a large whisky, all the while puffing away on a cigarette.

The more he heard, the more he realised that Pearl had always known how dangerous Charles Havelock was, that she had been right in worrying about the safety of her daughter should he ever find out about her, or should Bel ever tell him that she was his illegitimate child. A child who had proved the man he really was.

Pearl had been the unexpected heroine of the hour, not that she would ever admit it. But she had been. She had found out the truth about Henrietta and in doing so had saved her Isabelle, as well as those her daughter loved and cared for.

Pearl was Mr Havelock's ghost of Christmas past – and she'd brought Henrietta with her.

Bill wondered what would happen to Henrietta. And whether Pearl would keep on seeing her. She might have to if she wanted to keep the upper hand. That, however, was a subject for another day.

Tonight, he only wanted to know the answer to one question.

One very important question.

Helen sat with Hope on her lap and chatted to Gloria, but not about what had taken place at her grandfather's. Instead, they talked about Jack, and, of course, about Bobby and Gordon, who had sent their mam a Christmas card. The King's speech, Gloria said, had made her feel hopeful that she might see them soon, although she had laughed a little bitterly when she'd added that her sons would probably see their baby sister before Jack did.

What a Christmas Day.

Helen would never have thought she could muster a positive thought about Bel's ma, but she had done something tonight that had shocked them all.

She was glad it was now all out in the open – glad that she had seen for herself the real Charles Havelock, even if it had not been a pretty sight.

It hadn't surprised her to hear that there had clearly been other victims like Pearl, although her heart bled for the poor girl called Gracie – and for Gracie's parents, still suffering.

She'd been totally bowled over by the revelation that Bel's sister Maisie was a *call girl* – and the eccentric Lily a *madam*. But then again, now that she knew, it seemed almost obvious. It was what she had learnt about her grandmother that had truly shocked her.

Her grandmother was alive. The poor woman had been locked up in an asylum most of her life. *How could anyone do that to another person?* To someone you had married, who had borne your children? She wouldn't say *someone you loved*, because she doubted her grandfather was capable of loving anyone but himself.

When Helen went to the bar, she saw it was the same barmaid who had served her last New Year's Eve, which automatically made her think of John. *God, how she had wanted to kiss him that night when she'd gone outside to wave him off.* She reprimanded herself. *She really had to accept that she couldn't have him.*

Turning around, she got a shock to see Rosie, Polly, Dorothy, Angie, Martha and Hannah standing there.

'We haven't had a chance to wish yer Merry Christmas,' Angie said, looking at Helen and smiling. She and Dorothy had decided to 'let bygones be bygones', urged on by the rest of the women.

'A toast!' Dorothy declared.

They all raised their drinks.

'Merry Christmas and a Happy New Year!' they all chorused.

Helen joined in the salutations. She knew she had been forgiven and the frostiness towards her had thawed. They all chinked glasses.

She mightn't have John, but she had her friends.

That was one Christmas wish that had been granted.

Chapter Sixty

Helen looked at her watch. It had gone nine.

'I reckon this little girl's ready for her bed,' she said.

'Yes, yer right,' Gloria said. 'I've been putting it off.'

'Because you're having to go back to a cold, empty flat?' Helen guessed. 'On Christmas night?'

Gloria laughed. 'Don't rub it in!' She stood up and put on her coat. 'I don't know – I must be getting soft in my old age.'

'Come on then,' Helen coaxed, gently lifting Hope, who stirred from her slumber and wrapped her legs around her big sister. The three squeezed themselves through the throng.

When they reached the hallway, Helen handed Hope over.

'You don't fancy coming back for a while?' Gloria asked.

'No, I think I'll stay for a bit longer,' she said. She could see Gloria was disappointed.

'Yer could have a hot chocolate 'n tell me what *really* happened today? Yer won't have to worry about anyone eavesdropping.'

Helen laughed. 'I'll come round and tell you everything tomorrow, OK?'

Gloria stepped out into the snow. Tatham Street was quiet, but the snow meant there was no need for her little electric torch.

'See you tomorrow, then.' Gloria smiled and started the short walk back to her flat.

'Bye!' Helen said, before hurrying straight back into the pub. Squashing her way through the increasingly raucous revellers, she grabbed her coat, handbag and gas mask and retraced her route back to the lounge door, down the hallway and out the front.

She could just about make out Gloria, carrying Hope on her hip, traipsing her way down Tatham Street.

She followed them both, again wishing she had worn more sensible footwear. As soon as they had turned left into Borough Road, Helen quickened her pace. She reached the corner just in time to see them crossing the road.

As soon as they reached the other side, Helen took a sharp intake of breath as she spotted the dark outline of a man. He was wearing a coat as well as a trilby and was carrying a duffel bag over his shoulder. He appeared to be looking for someone.

Turning around, he spotted Gloria and Hope.

Helen watched as Gloria slowed down and came to a dead stop.

Only then did Helen hear her father's voice as he called out to the woman he loved – and the daughter he had not set eyes on for almost two years.

'Gloria!'

His voice sounded out loud and clear.

He dumped his bag in the snow and strode towards mother and child.

'Hope!'

Helen could hear the joy in her father's voice.

As he reached them, he folded them both in an embrace.

Helen stayed exactly where she was, her eyes glued to the family reunion.

'Jack! Oh, Jack!'

She heard Gloria's shocked, muffled voice.

'I can't believe it! Yer here! Yer here!'

Jack stepped back and took Hope from her. He kissed her on the head and then held her high in the air.

'My beautiful little girl!'

Helen remembered how he used to do the same to her when she was small.

And as he held Hope high and spun her round in the air, Helen heard her tired but excited little voice cry out.

'Daddy! Daddy!'

With tears trickling down her face, Helen laughed and cried all the way back to her car.

Jumping into the driver's seat, she turned on the ignition and rubbed her hands together to get warm. Putting the car into first gear, she slowly pulled away. The snow had stopped, so her visibility was good. She slowly went through the gears and after making her way out of town, she was soon driving along the coastal road.

The twenty-minute drive seemed to pass in a blur of thoughts and emotions.

Arriving at her destination, she pushed open the car door and stepped out onto snow-covered gravel. Hurrying up the front steps, she pulled open the heavy front doors and walked across the tiled foyer to the main reception desk.

She was glad to see someone was there, in spite of it being Christmas Day.

Genevieve looked up from her book.

'Can I help you, dear?' She vaguely recognised the dark-haired young woman but couldn't quite place her.

'Yes,' Helen smiled. 'I've come to see someone I haven't seen in quite a while.'

'Well, it must be someone very special for you to come out here on a Christmas night,' the elderly receptionist chuckled.

'It is,' Helen said. 'She's been here a long time. A very long time. Her name's Henrietta.'

'Ah, *Miss Girling*,' the old woman said, pushing herself out of her seat. 'Come with me, dear, I'll take you to her. This place can be like a maze.'

Chapter Sixty-One

When Bel, Joe, Agnes and a very sleepy Lucille got back to the house, they looked in on Polly and Artie. They were both fast asleep. Polly in her bed, still holding Tommy's letter; Artie curled up in his cot like a little dormouse in a nest of blankets, his thumb pressed up against his little button mouth.

Walking back into the kitchen, Agnes poured herself a cup of tea that Bel had made and then declared she was 'bushed' and was off to bed.

Before she left, she gave Bel a look that demanded honesty. 'Are yer all right?' She knew something had happened today but not what.

'I am ... I really am,' Bel reassured.

'Good,' Agnes said, turning and making her way up the stairs to her room. Whatever had happened, it would seem that it had brought Bel some peace of mind.

Hearing the bedroom door shut, Joe took his wife's face in his hands and kissed her.

'Merry Christmas,' he said. 'You know how much I love you, don't you?'

Bel nodded. 'And I you,' she said, kissing him back.

Joe hobbled over to the cabinet and poured himself a small whisky. 'Here's to you, Arthur, wherever you may be.' It was now exactly a year since the old man had left them all to go and join his Flo.

Bel allowed Joe to put a little tipple in her tea and they chatted until it was half ten.

'You go up,' Bel said, getting up and giving Joe a kiss. 'I'm going to nip across and see Ma. I won't be long.'

Joe gave her a questioning look.

'I just want to check up on her. Make sure she's not overdone it with the whisky.'

'She didn't look too bad when we left,' Joe said, 'so fingers crossed.' They both knew, though, that Pearl had a habit of hitting it hard just before last orders, and that Ronald was always there, propping up the bar, telling Pearl there was a bottle back at his with her name on it.

'Don't fall asleep, though,' Bel said. 'I want to ask you something when I get back.'

Joe gave her another puzzled look.

Bel pulled her coat back on and slipped out the front door. Stepping out into the street, she breathed in the ice-cold air and stood for a moment. It was so still and quiet. The calm after the storm.

She looked up into the clear night sky. As she sought out the stars and the crescent-shaped moon, she felt finally at rest. All the anger and resentment that had been part of her for so long had left her – at last. Love and understanding had taken their place.

Taking another deep breath, she walked across the road to the Tatham. She just hoped her ma wasn't too far gone. But if she was, she'd bring her home and put her to bed. It was the least she could do for her after today.

She opened the main door and stepped into the passageway.

She'd never been here when it was so quiet. She wondered briefly if Bill had forgotten to lock up. She found herself tiptoeing towards the lounge door; for some reason it felt as though she shouldn't be there.

Tentatively, she opened the door and popped her head through the gap. What she saw shocked her and brought a smile to her face at the same time.

442

Quietly pulling the door to, she tiptoed back down the hallway and out of the front door. Still smiling, she walked back over the road and into the warmth of the house.

Now it was her time to ask the person she loved an important question.

She felt a ripple of nerves.

She hoped desperately that, like Bill, the answer she'd get might be yes.

'Get yerself away, Geraldine. We'll finish off here.' Bill smiled at his barmaid. They'd all worked their socks off tonight; the festive spirit, though, had made people generous and Geraldine had probably equalled her wages in tips.

'Thanks, Bill,' she said, grabbing her coat. She automatically switched off the main light, leaving just the lights behind the bar on.

'See you tomorrow!' she shouted out, ignoring Pearl.

'Yer too soft with that girl,' Pearl grumbled. Her comments, though, were only for show. She was glad Bill had sent the girl packing. She just wanted to sit and have a drink in peace and quiet. No more verbal sparring.

'Here you are,' Bill said, reading her mind. He put his best bottle of Scotch on the bar and poured a measure in his two best whisky glasses, which he kept for personal use. Coming round the other side of the bar, he sat down on the stool next to Pearl and raised his glass.

'Merry Christmas.'

'Aye, I'll second that,' Pearl said, chinking his glass and taking a mouthful of whisky. This was only her second drink of the night. She was going to enjoy every drop.

'So,' Bill said, 'quite a day, eh?'

'Yer can say that again.'

Bill looked at Pearl.

'You went to war with the great Mr Havelock and won – that's some feat,' he said, taking a sip of his drink.

Pearl gave a throaty laugh. 'Yer helped me get there,' she said. 'Henrietta was my ace.' She looked at Bill. 'All those trips to Ryhope paid off. Teamwork, eh?'

'Definitely,' Bill said. 'Teamwork.'

They were both quiet for a moment. Enjoying the stillness.

'Of course, you do know I'm not letting you go tonight until you give me an answer,' Bill said, his eyes not once leaving her.

Pearl gave him a questioning look.

'Answer?'

Bill smiled.

'Yes, an answer to the question I asked you earlier on, before you ran off to divide and conquer.'

Pearl suppressed a smile.

'Yer knar what my memory's like, Bill. I think yer gonna have to remind me.'

A huge smile spread across Bill's face as he clambered off his stool and eased himself down onto one knee.

He pulled out the gold band from his waistcoat pocket and held it between finger and thumb.

'Pearl Hardwick, will you do me the honour of becoming my wife?'

Pearl slid off the stool.

'Aye, William David Lawson, I will do yer the honour of becoming yer wife.'

As Bill got back to his feet, they both felt a slight breeze and looked towards the door. Geraldine mustn't have shut it properly.

'Come here,' Bill said, putting his arms around his future wife and stooping to kiss her.

'There's just one condition, though,' Pearl said, poker-faced.

'And what would that be?' Bill asked.

'I want a new ring. It's bad luck to have yer ex's.'

Bill barked with laughter.

Chapter Sixty-Two

When Bel came into the bedroom, Joe pushed himself up so that he was sitting up straight.

'I've been lying here, racking my brains as to what you might want to ask me,' he said as Bel got changed for bed, 'but I can't think what it might be.'

Bel wrapped a shawl around her thick cotton nightie and sat on the edge of the bed.

'And by the look on your face, it's something serious,' he said, a nervous smile playing on his lips.

Bel took a deep breath.

'Well, I guess it *is* serious … And I totally understand if you don't want to.'

'Now you've got me worried.' Joe's face showed the verity of his words.

Bel moved around so that she was facing her husband.

'There's nothing to worry about,' she reassured. 'It's nothing awful, but I do need you to be honest – and not just say yes to please me.' She paused, feeling the return of butterflies in her stomach. 'And I won't be disappointed if you say you need time to think about it.'

'Now I really *am* worried,' Joe said, his eyes fixed on his wife.

'The thing is, as you well know …' Bel smiled sadly '… I've been thinking a lot about getting pregnant – or rather, about *not* getting pregnant. And perhaps because I've been thinking about babies and families, and because of everything that's been going on, I've been thinking

446

about my own childhood, how Agnes took me in, basically brought me up, became a mother to me – did what my own ma was never able to do.'

Joe nodded.

'And I've been thinking with everything that's been happening how different my life would have been had your ma not taken me in.' Bel sighed. Tears were glistening in her eyes. Joe leant over and touched her face. She took his hand and held it for a moment before letting it go.

'I knew a little bit about Kate's life before Lily took her in, but I hadn't realised just how awful it was.'

Joe furrowed his brow.

'Oh, Joe, I could cry now just thinking about it.'

'The nuns?' Joe asked. He'd caught whispers of what went on behind the closed doors of Nazareth House and knew Kate had gone there after her mam died.

Bel nodded.

'They made her life a living hell,' Bel said. 'They beat her, abused her, treated her like a dog. Worse.'

'Is that why she ended up on the streets?'

'Yes, can you imagine that? Feeling safer on the streets than in what's meant to be your home.'

Joe was listening, rapt.

'And I kept thinking about when I was young, how I could easily have ended up being taken away by the welfare and dumped somewhere like that – would have, if it wasn't for Agnes.'

Joe nodded. He remembered a number of times when his ma had given some cock-and-bull story to some officious-looking person who'd come knocking on their door.

'That was the only time I saw my mam lie outright,' Joe said with a sad laugh.

'When Teddy died, I accepted that it would just be me and Lucille – and then you came back and threw my world into even greater chaos.'

Joe smiled.

'But more than anything, falling in love with you also reignited my dream of having more children – of having a family. A big family. You know all I've ever really wanted is to be a mum.'

'I know,' Joe said, leaning over and kissing her softly on the lips. 'I remember saying to you we could have a whole football team if that's what you wanted.'

'And I remember saying you might rue the words.' Bel let out a soft, sad laugh.

They were quiet for a moment.

'You know, your ma always wanted more children,' Bel said, 'would have had more if your da had made it back from the war.'

Joe looked surprised. 'Really?'

'She only told me the other day. She said when I came along it was like she'd got her wish.'

'That's nice. Ma's not one for sentimentality,' Joe said.

Bel laughed.

'You know,' she said, becoming serious again, 'I think I knew as soon as I didn't fall straight away that something was up. Everyone kept saying, "Oh, it'll happen. Don't worry." But something inside of me just knew. Knew that for some reason I wasn't going to be getting that football team I wanted. I tried to tell myself to be happy with you and Lucille – which I am. You know I love you both to pieces?'

Joe took her hand and squeezed it.

'I know you do – as does Lucille.'

Bel gave a sad smile.

448

'And I know I should be so grateful for what I've got,' she continued. 'I'm so lucky in so many ways ... But I still can't stop myself wanting to be a mum again. And feeling desperately sad that I can't be a mother to more children. Not just Lucille.'

Joe looked at Bel. 'But if it's not happening, we can't make it ...'

'I know, I know,' Bel said, sitting up straight. The butterflies had started up again. She fixed her gaze on Joe. 'I know I can't make nature do something she clearly doesn't want to do – but there is another option.'

Joe looked puzzled.

'I could *still* be a mother,' Bel said. 'In a way – like Agnes. She didn't give birth to me, but she was a mother to me.'

Comprehension started to show on Joe's face.

He eyed Bel. 'I think I might know what you want to ask me.'

'Do you?' Bel looked questioningly.

Joe nodded.

'And what is it you think I want to ask you?' She had her fingers crossed behind her back.

'You're thinking that there are so many children out there who need a mother – and a father – and you think we would be able to give them a good home. A loving home. I think yer thinking that you want to do the same for a child like Agnes did for you.' He paused. 'I think you're going to ask me if I'd be up for adopting.'

He looked at Bel. 'Would I be right?'

Bel took a deep breath and nodded. 'Yes,' she said, 'you would. So,' she looked at Joe, 'if I asked you – what would your answer be?'

Joe kept his face deadpan. 'If you come over here,' he put his arm out, 'I'll tell you.'

Bel moved over and cuddled up.

Joe kissed her head and neck before whispering in her ear: 'I'd love to. I think it's a wonderful idea.'

Bel pulled away in excitement and sat up. 'You would? You really would? No hesitation? Honestly?'

'Honestly,' Joe said. 'Without hesitation ... I actually can't believe we haven't thought about it before now.'

'Oh Joe, neither can I!' She kissed him and kissed him again. 'I've been thinking that myself. It's like the answer's been there right in front of me and I couldn't see it.' Bel snuggled back into Joe's arms.

'Well, now we've had the blinkers removed,' Joe said, 'I think we shouldn't waste any more time.'

'Really?' Bel said.

'Really,' Joe repeated.

'You busy tomorrow?' he asked.

'No,' Bel said, a wide smile spreading across her face. 'I'm free the whole day. How about you?'

'Free the whole day ... Fancy a trip down to the Town Moor?'

Bel squeezed his arm. It was where the town's main orphanage had been built in the middle of the last century.

'Oh, Joe, I'm so excited! You really want to go there tomorrow? You don't want time to think about it?'

'I don't ... Do you?'

'Definitely not,' Bel said, snuggling up.

They were quiet for a moment.

'Oh, Joe, I don't think I'm going to be able to sleep.'

Joe chuckled.

'Me neither,' he said, bending so that he could see Bel's face. 'Of course, there's absolutely no reason why we shouldn't still keep on trying naturally as well, is there?'

'Oh, no, of course not,' Bel said, glancing up at Joe and giving him a very serious look.

Joe laughed and pulled her close.

Bel kissed him.

'Joe Elliot, I love you so much.'

'And you, Mrs Elliot – you have no idea just how much I love you.'

'Oh, I do,' Bel said, kissing her husband on the lips, then on his neck. 'I do.'

Epilogue

Sunderland Boys Orphanage, Town Moor, Sunderland

Boxing Day

'I hope you don't mind us coming today. We weren't sure ...' Bel's voice was full of uncertainty, although what she and Joe had come here to do today, they could not be more certain of.

'No, no, please, come in, we are always open.' The head of the orphanage ushered them in from the cold and closed the door.

'Did you know today is St Stephen's Day?' the old woman asked. 'Some call it the Feast of St Stephen.'

Bel and Joe shook their heads.

'St Stephen was the first Christian martyr. So, this is in fact a saint's day, the second day of Christmas,' she said, swishing past them. 'Follow me. We'll go to my office. It's nice and warm there and we can talk in private.'

Bel and Joe followed the matron, who walked surprisingly quickly for her age and her size, down the long hallway and into a large office that could only be described as chaotic. There were books everywhere, files and documents spread out across her mahogany desk, and, as promised, a roaring fire.

She bustled over and gave it a hearty prod.

'Please, sit down, make yourselves comfortable.' She gestured towards two leather armchairs in front of her desk.

Joe waited for Bel to unbutton her coat and sit down before he eased himself into the chair with the aid of his stick.

'It's Mr and Mrs Elliot, isn't it?'

'It is.' Joe pushed himself back up and offered his hand to the matron, who returned a firm handshake.

Seeing the couple's surprise that she knew who they were, she explained.

'I know your mother, Joseph.'

Bel looked at her husband. She didn't think she had *ever* heard anyone call him by his proper Christian name.

The matron turned her attention to Bel and took her hand in her own.

'And you, my dear, are Isabelle Elliot. Formerly Isabelle Hardwick.'

For the first time Bel didn't recoil at being called Isabelle. Nor did she feel ashamed of being a Hardwick.

'I know of both families quite well,' she said, clasping her hands together and placing them on top of her desk. 'When you barely venture outside the east end and you get to be my age, there's not many families you don't know.'

Bel was glad to see there was no judgement in her words or tone.

'I would say how can I help you? But I think I can guess.'

Bel smiled. Joe took hold of her hand and squeezed it.

The old woman pulled out a file from under a mound of papers on her desk and opened it. She took out an official-looking form and handed it to Joe. Then she yanked at her top drawer, retrieved two pens and handed them to the couple she had no doubt would make wonderful parents.

She should know. She had seen them grow up. Knew that Isabelle had not had the easiest of upbringings and had been widowed and married within a year. She'd heard the gossip doing the rounds at the time.

'Cup of tea?' she asked, getting up and going over to a pot by the fire.

'No thank you,' Bel said. Joe shook his head. He handed the form to his wife to fill in. She was, after all, a secretary with a certificate in shorthand and typing to her name.

By the time the matron had finished her tea, and some leftover Christmas cake, Bel and Joe were signing the bottom of the form and handing it back to her.

'So, what happens now?' Bel asked.

As though in answer to her question they heard an ear-splitting cry. It was shortly followed by another cry, equally ear-splitting.

Bel started to get up out of her chair. It was her instinctive reaction on hearing a baby cry.

'Would you like to see our two new admissions?' the matron said. 'Although you might need some earplugs. They've been crying their little hearts out since they were brought to us.'

Bel and Joe followed the old woman out of the office.

'They came to us in the early hours,' she informed them, shuffling down the corridor, 'and they've already sent a couple of the nurses doolally.'

Walking into the nursery, Bel spotted two nurses both trying desperately to shush and calm their tiny charges.

'Do you mind?' Bel asked as she reached the first nurse.

'Not at all,' the young girl said, the relief on her face showing that she meant every word.

The matron and Joe watched as Bel swayed the crying newborn in her arms, whispering love into the little girl's ear. After a few minutes the crying started to splutter to a stop, and as one baby stopped sobbing so did the other.

The nurse with the second baby looked at Joe and held the baby out. Joe hobbled forward and took the baby in his arms, breathing a sigh of relief that it did not start crying again.

Now that she could hear herself speak, the matron told the nurses to go and get themselves a cup of tea.

'The mother died in childbirth,' she told Bel and Joe. 'She might have survived if she'd managed to get herself to hospital, but it was too late,' she said sadly.

'And the father?' Joe asked.

'Like your brother, Edward –' again the matron threw Bel by using Teddy's full name '– he died out in North Africa. Although not on land, but at sea. Which is why they've been brought here.'

Bel looked at the baby Joe was holding. A boy.

'So, they're twins?' Bel asked.

'They are indeed,' the matron said. 'But unfortunately, as one is a girl, we're going to have to split them up.'

Bel and Joe knew that the orphanage had been built for the sons of lost seamen, with the aim of training the boys they took in to become seamen themselves.

'No room at the inn for the little girl, I'm afraid,' the old woman said. 'Her gender dictates.'

'Well, there's room enough in our house for them both, isn't there?' Bel glanced up at Joe, who nodded and smiled his agreement.

The matron eyed the young couple. *For once it would seem He'd listened to her and she'd been granted her Christmas wish.*

Bel looked at Joe; her eyes were bright and brimming with tears.

'Looks like Agnes was right after all,' she said.

455

Welcome to

Penny Street

where your favourite authors and stories live.

Meet casts of characters you'll never forget,
create memories you'll treasure forever,
and discover places that will stay with
you long after the last page.

Turn the page to step into the home of

Nancy Revell

and discover more about

The Shipyard Girls...

Dear Reader,

Like most of us, I've made many, many wishes during my lifetime – some of those have been granted, others haven't. There were a few of those wishes which felt so important to me that I wondered how I'd get through life if they didn't become a reality. I was pretty sure I would wither up and die. But I didn't. What I discovered after a while was that I mightn't have got what I'd wished for – but I'd instead been gifted the unexpected, which, as time went on I realised was just as exciting – and definitely worth living for. I hope, dear reader, that you *do* get what you wish for in life, but if not, then I hope you don't feel that it's the end of the world, but rather the beginning of something different. Something which will make you equally as happy, if not more.

For now, though, I wish you all good health and lots of happiness, and, of course, a wonderful Christmas!

With Love,

Nancy x

HISTORICAL NOTES

Here's a real-life photograph of Mary, Princess Royal and Countess of Harewood, controller commandant of the ATS (Auxiliary Territorial Service), at the launch of *Greenwich*, which is featured in this latest instalment of The Shipyard Girls series. It was printed in the *Newcastle Journal* in July 1943.

The caption reads: 'The Princess Royal arriving at the north-east shipyard yesterday to launch the merchant vessel Greenwich, the first tramp steamer to be christened by a member of the Royal family.'

READ ON FOR AN EXCLUSIVE
EXTRACT FROM MY NEW NOVEL

The Shipyard Girls
on the Home Front

Nancy Revell

COMING FEBRUARY 2021
PRE-ORDER YOUR COPY NOW

Christmas Day, 1943

The Tatham Arms, Tatham Street,
Sunderland, County Durham

The initial rush of euphoria and instantaneous joy Gloria felt upon seeing Jack and being reunited with the man she loved – the man she had loved from the innocent age of sixteen – was quickly pushed aside by fear and panic.

Gloria blinked to clear her vision, which had become blurred by the sudden onset of tears at watching Jack be reunited with his daughter. Hope's shrieks of joy and excitement were filling the air, breaking the silence of this unforgettable Christmas night.

'What are yer doing here, Jack?' Gloria asked, furtively looking up and down the street. The rapture in her face was gone; anxiety was now at the fore. 'Yer shouldn't be here. What if someone sees you?' Images of her workmates – Dorothy, Angie and Martha – flashed in front of her eyes. Their families' secrets unveiled. Dorothy's mum's bigamy, Angie's mam's infidelity, and Martha's birth mother a child murderer. Their lives – and the lives of those around them – ruined in one fell swoop.

'Don't worry,' Jack was quick to reassure her as he lowered a giggling Hope back down, 'it's all right. Everything's been sorted.'

Gloria looked around. *Thank God there was no one about.* She looked across at The Burton House pub on the other side of the road, suddenly terrified that someone might come out and clock them. Clock Jack. With Hope in his arms. Outside her flat. Then shoot across to the other side of the Wear and sell them out to Miriam.

'Let's get inside!' She hurried to the top of the steps to her flat and had a quick scan of the street, feeling another wave of relief that there was still no one about, before clomping down to her front door. Jamming the key into the lock, she looked over her shoulder to check that Jack and Hope were right behind her.

Pushing open the door, she flicked on the light and ushered Jack inside. He ducked slightly, at the same time kissing the top of his daughter's head.

As soon as they were over the threshold, Gloria pushed the door closed and dropped the latch. Only then did she allow herself a sigh of relief. They were safe. Away from prying eyes.

'What on earth possessed yer to come back?' Gloria said, taking off her coat and automatically going over to the electric gas fire and switching it on. She turned to see Jack gently putting Hope down; he was smiling as he ruffled her mop of raven hair.

'Jack, this is taking a bit of a chance,' Gloria said, walking towards the man she still couldn't quite believe was here.

He put his hand out and pulled her close, kissing her gently at first and then with more passion.

'It's safe,' he said, pulling away briefly. 'I wouldn't have taken the risk otherwise. Trust me.' He cupped her face in his hands and kissed her again, savouring the feel of her lips on his own. Her mouth tasted of sweet berries. Port. Her favourite tipple.

Gloria gave up trying to question him, believing him, knowing he would never put others in danger to satiate his own selfish needs. She kissed him back, the feel of his lips reassuring her that this was real. That he really was here.

'Daddy!'

They both looked down to see Hope staring up at them, her hand grasping Jack's trouser leg as she started to tug it.

'Come here, my gorgeous little girl—' Jack let go of Gloria and reached down. 'My, my, someone's grown up since I saw her last.' He picked Hope up again and kissed her little button nose, causing her to scrunch up her eyes and giggle. 'Two years. Two whole years.'

Gloria heard sadness and a shred of bitterness.

'*Daddy*,' Hope said again, as though practising a new word. A word she had only ever spoken into the receiver of a black Bakelite phone.

'Aye … *Daddy*.' Jack suddenly felt his throat constrict with emotion.

Hope's face creased into a smile and she touched his face with one hand.

Gloria felt the tears welling up.

'I'll tell yer what—' Jack looked at Gloria and then back at his daughter '—why don't I read yer a bedtime story, eh?'

Gloria looked at Hope and pulled a happy face, mouthing the word 'story'.

'*Story!*' Hope clapped her hands together.

A wide smile spread across Jack's face and he took a step towards Gloria, to the woman he had never stopped loving since they had been childhood sweethearts – since Miriam had forced them apart for the first time when they were still young – and kissed her again. Nothing, he vowed silently, would ever part them again. Nothing.

'I don't think I've ever felt this happy in my entire life,' he said, his eyes glistening with the sting of tears.

'Nor me,' Gloria said, as she kissed him back.

Gloria watched as Jack read Hope her favourite bedtime story, Beatrix Potter's 'The Tale of Two Bad Mice.' It had become her favourite after they'd been forced to spend the last air raid with a rather frantic mouse scurrying around in Mr Brown's Anderson Shelter.

Looking at Jack, Gloria saw the physical changes the past two years had brought – his hair was now more grey than black and his face looked tired and weather-beaten, but physically he seemed strong, certainly more muscular than when she had seen him last on that awful day when Miriam's blackmail had led to his banishment and they'd been forced to say a rushed farewell in the porch of St Peter's Church.

Gloria looked at Hope. Her dark lashes were lowering as she tried desperately to stay awake. Jack's voice was soft as he relayed the mice's tales of mischief in the doll's house, knowing that the lilting rhythm of words would soon send his daughter into a deep slumber.

Sensing her eyes on him, Jack glanced back at Gloria and winked before turning another page of the hardbacked book. Gloria noticed how full of life he seemed. There was not a trace of the confusion he had been left with after coming out of a coma weeks after nearly drowning on his way back from America. After he'd come round, he'd lost his memory, as well his physical strength – looking at him now, it was clear he had regained both. He was the Jack of old. And if Jack said it was all right that he was here, then she believed him.

Hearing the familiar sound of her daughter's gentle snoring, Gloria stood up, careful not to make a sound. Jack followed, putting the story book down on the stool by Hope's cot and tiptoeing out of the room.

As soon as they were out in the hallway, Jack pulled her close and they kissed – this time for longer, and without interruption.

'God, I've missed you,' Jack murmured.

'Please – tell me yer here to stay? For good?' she asked, her voice barely a whisper.

'I'm here to stay,' Jack reassured her. 'For good.'

Gloria kissed him again, curious to know more, but not wanting to talk. They had spoken on the phone so much since Jack's exile, she suddenly felt tired of words. She only wanted the feel of his mouth on hers and his body pressed against her own.

Sensing her passion, Jack looked at Gloria. 'I've waited two years for this moment,' he said, his breathing becoming heavy. 'I don't want to wait another minute.'

'Me neither,' Gloria said.

And with that she took his hand and led him into the bedroom.